SEE YOU SOON

GRIM REAPER

A DARK MILITARY ROMANCE
BOOK ONE

LEXIE AXELSON

Cover Designer: Jaqueline Kropmanns

Scene Break Design: Etheric Tales

Proofreading: Rebekah May-Humphries, Aleena Martinez

❀ Created with Vellum

See You Soon

Operator Grim Reaper

A Dark Military Romance

Important Note

TRIGGER AND CONTENT WARNINGS TO KNOW

Dear Readers,

Please keep in mind this is a Dark Romance. This book is intended for readers 18+. This story contains triggering topics and situations such as rough, explicit sexual situations, graphic violence, graphic murder, graphic language, PTSD, mentions of suicide, mentions of rape, domestic abuse, addiction, autassassinophilia, sadomasochism, anal, near-death situations, religious trauma, kidnapping, acrophobia, and aerophobia.

Your mental health matters.

This book ends on a cliffhanger.

To all the hurt souls that think they're not capable of love and change,
you are.

And to my dark romance besties that love a man in a uniform,
Welcome to the whore-zone
It's call of booty time

PLAYLIST

Take My Breath Away : Berlin
Take My Breath Away : EZI
Cardigan : Taylor Swift
Cruel Summer : Taylor Swift
Drinkin' Problem : Midland
Must Be The Whiskey : Cody Jinks
Dark Paradise : Lana Del Rey
Shades Of Cool : Lana Del Rey
Simple Man : Lynrd Skynrd
Do I Wanna Know? : Arctic Monkeys
Chop Suey : System Of A Down
Rayando El Sol : Mana

Acknowledgments

To My Supportive Husband,
Because of you, I know what love at first sight is.

CHAPTER 1

ARI

"**M**y baby is dead! Not my baby, please! Not my baby! Ay Dios Mio! Mi hijo! Oh my God, my son!" My mother's aching voice screamed over and over again, the voice of a mother who had just been told her firstborn child was dead. My brother, a Navy SEAL, dead at age 30. It was a memory I would never be able to shake. The look on her face, as if the blood had been drained leaving a pale reflection, the terror and agony in her voice, was terrifying and would traumatize me for the rest of my life. The sound was so terrifying I wanted so badly to cover my ears with my hands to drown her out. She was in pain, and I instantly feared for her health. To see my mother who never cries, always so positive, just completely break into a billion pieces as I held her while also trying to process the news myself.

My older brother was dead.

Every time I step into his untouched bedroom at our house, like right now, my mind goes back to that day. I open the door to his room as if expecting to see him on his bed practicing new music and the memories catch up to me, flashing me back to that day when two uniformed men knocked on our door.

I don't know how but, at that moment, seeing my mom

completely fall apart, killed me, but it also changed me. I had to fake my strength at that moment to be strong for my mother. I so badly wanted to fall apart as well but I am the only person left to take care of her, to be strong for her when she can't for herself. I silently hold her in my arms, brushing her peppered black and gray hair with the palm of my hand. She continued to wail and make incomprehensible sounds in my chest.

I decided the best thing I could do at that moment was to pray to her. The rosary. My mom had raised us to be religious and to go to God for everything, and live our lives by His commandments. Deep down inside, I had some different views when it came to Catholicism, but never expressed my views to her, avoiding her disappointment.

Gunshot wound to the chest. Gunshot wound to the right leg. Gunshot wound to the neck. The cause of death was blood loss. Paul bled out before he could make it back to the hospital. I cringed trying my hardest to snap out of the horrid memory that haunts me. As I stared at him in his casket, dressed in his uniform, laying there dead, I had the overwhelming urge to shake him. Shake him awake because they did so well covering his wounds he just looked like he was sleeping. I wanted to punch him in the shoulder like I always did and tell him to stop faking. Stop joking around because this wasn't fucking funny. I so badly wanted to but all I could do was cry until I felt sick and drained. The only positive thing I could think of was that his death only ensured I made the right choice in becoming a nurse.

I initially wanted to be a pediatric nurse, but after my brother's death, I knew I needed to be a trauma nurse.

Sometimes, Paul's military friends come by the house whenever they're not working or have the time and they'll check on us to see how we're doing. I never pay them any mind as it still hurts to see them able to come home in one piece with a beating heart, but my brother would never again. I was jealous, angry and I knew it was dark but why did it have to be my brother?

Why?

One of his friends named Kane, would always try and make conversation with me. Always doing little things here and there like doing chores around the house or small talk with my mother... to make up for Paul's loss and I despised it. There's nothing no one could do to make this loss hurt any less. My best friend would never return. He was supposed to walk me down the aisle when I got married. My video gaming partner. *My protector.* The man of the house.

My brother was a good simple man. He had the purest heart. The only downfalls of his character were his stubbornness and black-and-white mentality. But he always made sure my mother and I were always taken care of financially when he entered the military. His morals were a big part of his character, leading to him always putting others before himself.

It hurts so much and it feels wrong to go on without him. I witnessed my mom almost die from a heart attack when she received the news. I wanted to die too but we both have to find a way to go through this grief without harming ourselves. I must find a way to go on, and if I have to fake my strength... I will. If I have to push through and place my own needs last, then that's what I'll do.

Paul would not allow my mom to torture herself with grief every day but how do you tell a mother to move on? I wouldn't dare.

Still, I haven't let myself scream since that day when that's all I want to do. I'm trying so hard not to implode, break, or shatter my beliefs in Catholicism.

I snap out of my thoughts when my phone buzzes. Still staring at my brother's room, a Sublime tapestry over his headboard. Bookshelves on one side of the wall. His Gaming PC is on another side. A soccer ball sits in the corner along with his guitar. Everything is clean and organized. My mother takes it upon herself to clean his room every weekend as if he was still here to inhabit it.

She would even grab a pile of clothes from his closet and wash it, fold it, then put it back as she used to do all the time for him when he was home.

When he was alive.

She still can't let him go but it's to be expected, he was only buried two months ago. I guess it's therapeutic for her, so I never say a word.

I finally grab a hold of my cell phone to find a text from Meredith letting me know she's outside my house waiting for me. She's been one of my closest friends since high school.

I've passed all my exams and licenses to practice as a registered nurse and I just signed my first contract to start practicing. I haven't told anyone yet, but I'm going to sooner or later. I won't stress about that tonight, as this night was about celebration.

Country Music plays loud through my ears and chest and the air smells like cigarettes and alcohol. My kind of place after a stressful week of impactful decisions. A Friday night out with my best friend is just the perfect way to start the celebration that she's completely unaware of. We're in one of the most popular country bars in the city and we have our cowboy boots on, ready to dance the night away.

"How does it feel to finally say, you're a Registered Nurse?" Meredith shouts over the music while cheering her beer to mine. Our beers collide loud and we both chug a bit of it down.

"My God, it doesn't even feel real yet. It's surreal." I exclaim with pure joy. I'm smiling ear to ear while my long black hair jumps up and down as we dance.

Meredith and I did everything together since High School. We've been best friends ever since we sat down next to each other at lunch one day during our freshman year. As scared, lost, fourteen-year-old strangers, we looked at each other hesitantly before we sat down at an empty table. We hit it off instantly. After bonding over our favorite tv-shows, we became closer than ever.

"I need to get another drink; I'll be right back." I practically yell into Meredith's ear making sure she can hear me. She nods, acknowledging me.

The bar is packed. Full of heartbroken, single, and even married people just looking to let loose tonight. I quickly reach the bartender and ask for a strawberry daiquiri. The bartender immediately asks me for my identification.

He probably thinks I look sixteen. I don't blame him, my short 5'1 height doesn't help, and the youthful skin genes I get from my mom. I pull out my ID and the bartender nods as he confirms I'm of legal drinking age.

I'm twenty-two years old and still, get asked if I want a kid's menu when I go to restaurants. I sit down on a bar stool as I wait for my drink. "Wagon Wheel" begins to play and I can't help but move my body to the beat of the song. An enormous western neon cattle skull is placed in the middle of the wall across from me. I'm so busy thinking about the big decision I recently made, *secretly,* last weekend that I don't notice a man sitting next to me, staring. I haven't told anyone just yet, but this big decision is so important to me that I didn't want anyone's opinions or judgments to deter me from my happiness.

"Didn't figure you were a daiquiri type of girl." His deep voice says as he takes a sip of his beer. He's wearing a black hat with dark blonde waves peeking through, with a black shirt. I see half-sleeve tattoos on his very well-defined biceps. I swallow nervously, biting my lip trying hard to unglue my eyes from him. I take a deep breath and regain some confidence to respond.

"Oh yeah... what did you figure then?" I taunt, my eyebrow raising with curiosity, keeping the conversation going. His body intrigues me, enticing me to talk more.

He turns away from me and now he doesn't bother to make

eye contact with me. Instead, he stares at the television on the wall in the corner of the bar. A football game is playing across the screen with black subtitles running across the lower screen.

"Sangria." He finally turns to me, no smile, completely serious. His bright blue eyes stare into my soul, emotionless.

I'm so intimidated by his look of no expression; I blush and look down at my hands. He looks straight into my brown eyes and I can't bear the attention.

"Wow... you're good... those are my favorite." I giggle looking down at my boots. Sangrias are my favorite. But tonight, I wanted something a little different.

Finally, the bartender gets me a daiquiri and I thank him, handing him my debit card in exchange.

"Wait, Gabe, put it on my tab." The man next to me intervenes and puts his hand gently on my hand and card. It sends an electrocution of desire through me, and I don't want to move.

"Oh, you don't have to do that. I—"

"I want to." He says, smoothly with a small smile.

I give him a smile in return.

Who is this man? And why am I so attracted to him already?

"Didn't figure you were a shiner type of guy." I tease, trying to make small talk. I can't just walk away now, not after he bought me a drink. At least that's the excuse I'm telling myself so I can stay longer talking to him. There's this aroma around him sucking me in.

He smirks.

"Shoot," He dares.

I squint at him, trying to figure him out. I always felt like I had this superpower. To be able to read people's emotions and figure them out. I'm almost never wrong.

"You're a whiskey kind of guy. But tonight is different," tapping my nails on the counter of the bar before continuing.

"It wasn't such a bad day today at work, you're in the military, and you're just trying to drink to get the edge off without getting too hammered. Am I close?" I ask, quirking a brow, with a giddy smile.

"Hmm. Jack Daniels." He hums. He looks at me and I can feel the connection between us. He admires me, but he quickly catches himself as a small pause between us goes silent. We were both smiling at each other, and he quickly changed glances to the game playing on the TV.

"Hey, what's taking you so long?" Meredith pops up right behind me, out of breath, stealing the moment between the man and me away.

"Sorry, I—" I look at the man, then back to Meredith, then back to him. I don't know his name. Yet, it doesn't matter because he seems already uninterested. He's already disconnected himself from the conversation and it stings.

"Let's go dance!" Meredith pulls me away by my arm strongly, knocking me off my balance. Miraculously, keeping the daiquiri in my hand from spilling over. She keeps pulling me until we get to the dance floor. Another song starts to play and we're slowly moving our bodies to the song.

"Who was that guy? He's hella hot," Meredith asks, moving her eyebrows up and down. I laugh and roll my eyes.

"Doesn't matter. He's in the military and you already know my deal." Shrugging her off, I drink more of my strawberry daiquiri. The troubled past of my recent relationship with my ex-boyfriend has me steer clear of anyone associated with the military. The man was responsible for the scars I carry from the physical and mental abuse that I endured.

"Oh my gosh, get over that dumb ass. Not all guys are like Shane." Meredith mutters in disgust. She hates Shane, my ex-boyfriend. As did everyone. As did I.

"Yeah well, I'm not in the mood to entertain anyone right now. Plus, I don't think the guy is interested."

"Did he buy you that drink?"

"Yes but—"

"He's interested."

"But —"

"Shut up Ari. You need to loosen up, finally sleep with some-one, have fun, military or not, because guess what, he's coming back to you in three, two..." Meredith was no longer looking at me but rather looking at someone behind me. My eyes widen and butterflies start heavily, thrashing around inside of me. Meredith starts to walk away, disappearing into the crowd as I feel a tap on my shoulder. I bite my lip and turn around, slowly.

Unsurprisingly, I turn around to the same man at the bar but now he's towering over me. He's tall, my guess is over six feet easily and a nervous smile spreads across my face.

Now that he's standing in front of me, his muscles are on full display, his frame was massive and I can tell he keeps up with his physical fitness. He's intimidating and it's hard for me to look him in the eyes without the hot warmth in my cheeks burning. My heart's pounding from the immediate attraction. His straight white teeth with sharp incisors are pulled into an irresistible smile and I can't help but notice his dark blonde facial hair is grown out over his jawline. It's sexy.

"Danny."

He reaches his hand out for mine to shake and I'm hesitant to take it. This feels like a bigger moment than it is. Like I can already see our ending before it begins. Grabbing his rough textured hand in my small one, he squeezes me gently.

"Ari."

CHAPTER 2

ARI

Danny still has my hand in his, shaking it. He smiles and I laugh as we shake hands awkwardly longer than usual. *He knows what he's doing.*

"Did you want to dance?" I ask. His hand is still shaking mine.

"No." He stops shaking my hand and instead leads me toward an empty table away from the dance floor. I follow him, with my hand holding his. My eyebrows raise at his curt reply.

No? I guess he's not the dancing type. Neither am I.

"I want to get to know you more and can't really do that on the dance floor while the music is blasting really loud." He pulls out a chair in front of me and I sit down.

"That's fair... what would you like to know?"

"What's a girl like you doing in a bar like this?" Danny sits down in front of me.

"Well, I just graduated nursing school. I'm stressed. Happy. Relieved. I don't go out often at all but tonight was special, to say the least."

"Huh." Danny studies me before continuing. "Well, congratulations."

"And what about you, this doesn't really seem like your type of scene, *marine*." I gesture towards the building.

"Sailor, actually."

Oh, Navy.

I nod, the conversation sinking into me while I admire the mystery of Danny.

Did I really want to get more involved in this conversation?

The more I talk to Danny, the more intrigued I was, and I really had my walls up from my past relationship with a marine. Military is military, it's all the same to me.

"What's *a girl like me* then, what did you mean by that?" I ask, referring to his first question.

He pauses, and he squints at me.

"Broken."

His tone is serious, his gaze trying to figure me out. His smile gets replaced by his beer. He takes a sip but he's still staring straight at me. For the first time since we met, I was a bit speechless. I didn't know what to say.

How did this stranger know what I'm truly feeling inside?

There was a pause between us. Moments were going by in silence as Danny waits for me to respond.

I can feel my throat tightening up and I want to cry. I let out a short laugh as my eyes water. I blink the tears away, hoping he won't notice. I look at the dancing crowd behind Danny, trying to look for Meredith as a sense of distraction.

I want to reply but I physically can't. Not when I'm still grieving my brother's death. Not when I'm buzzed with alcohol and getting choked up for a lot of reasons, around a stranger. A stranger that read me like a book. A stranger that had the most beautiful shade of blue eyes I had ever seen.

Saved by the bell, Danny's phone starts to ring and he reaches into his pocket and pulls it out quickly. He looks at the Caller ID and a heavy sigh escapes him as he reads it.

"Fuck." He mutters, stressed out.

"Oh... everything okay?" I ask. I was glad something inter-rupted us so I wouldn't have to say that I was still damaged by an abusive ex-boyfriend. Or stressed out from an impactful decision I had made last week that I had yet to tell anyone.

"Work." He sighs again, looking down at his phone, typing.

"It was nice meeting you, but I've got to go... I'll see you soon." Danny stands up, looks at me from his phone, with a small smile, and walks away. I stare at Danny's back as he walks out of the exit to the bar. With every step he takes, my heart sinks lower.

His last sentence raises questions and doubts.

See you soon?

I truly appreciated these short moments I just shared with a stranger, knowing I wouldn't see him again.

I was disappointed. For the first time in a while, I felt alive. A flicker of thrill and undeniable steam radiates inside of me.

Danny noticed me.

Truly noticed me. Someone I connected with so fast just by a glance at first sight. So cliche, but I was intrigued and enchanted by this man I had just met.

"Dude, this hangover is killing me. Why did I drink so much last night?" I ask Meredith while opening a bottled water and taking Tylenol. Nausea and vomiting were taking over me like a virus.

"We're dumb sometimes." Meredith groans over the phone. I'm in my bedroom the morning after. It's nine in the morning and I had woken up with a headache from hell. I called Meredith on the phone as soon as I woke up to check if she was dying just like me. Turns out she was suffering too but not as badly as me.

I get that familiar feeling of something coming up and I started throwing up in the toilet again. I forget to mute myself on my phone and Meredith's hearing everything but it's too late to fix it.

"Oh God, you're not pregnant right?" Meredith's tone is laced with disgust.

I flush the toilet and clean myself up before responding sarcastically.

"Oh yes, a twenty-two-year-old that hasn't had a dick inside of her, makes sense." I retort.

"You never know. Go to your gynecologist recently? Maybe they pulled a Jane The Virgin on you."

Suddenly my phone buzzes. I check it and a text appears from an unknown number.

Unknown:

Hello Ari, this is Danny.

Wait, what? Like Danny? Like Danny the Sailor, I met last night and mysteriously had to leave mid-conversation?

"Wait, what the fu—. I don't remember giving my number out. Meredith! Danny, the hot stranger guy, just texted me. Was I that drunk I didn't remember a detai—" I rant, freaking out, nervously. Meredith cuts me off.

"Oh yeah about that... I kind of like... gave him your number as he was walking out of the bar to his truck last night." Meredith giggles over the phone.

My eyes widened in embarrassment.

"Meredith! You didn't! And you failed to tell me?" I scold.

"What? I stepped out to smoke, and I saw that he was leaving. Then I'm *guessing* he remembered you were with me and asked me for your number, so I gladly played Cupid and gave it to him. It's fine. You're welcome!" Meredith's condescending tone irritates me.

"I don't know what to say... you know this isn't exactly my year..." This past year has been the most tragic for me. A break-up from a toxic boyfriend, my brother dying, and stepping into a role of responsibility for my mother and myself.

"Baby Girl. Not every guy's like Shane, stop it."

Of course, Meredith immediately only thinks of the guy that

has stained my romantic life but he was a blip in my worries compared to the death of my only other sibling.

I bite my lip and text him back,

Hi Danny.

"It's your fault if I get hurt again." I sigh in defeat.

"You'll be thanking me at your future wedding, actually." Meredith chuckles.

"Woah, chill out. Plus, I can't be thinking or getting distracted by anything or anyone right now. I'm leaving overseas to Iraq soon and I need to stay focused." I again, rant on with no filter. I quickly cover my mouth, realizing what I had just revealed.

Squinting my eyes, disappointment reveling in my stomach.

I hadn't told anyone yet that I signed a contract for the U.S. Army as a contracted civilian nurse. I did this to honor my brother, who succumbed to his wounds from a mission he was on. Nobody knew, not even my mother who I would eventually have to tell. I don't think she's ready to hear that her remaining child just signed up for the military as a nurse. I don't know how she's going to react. Whether it would be a bad reaction or a good one.

"Wait, hold up. Rewind! You're leaving where?" Meredith yells in shock.

CHAPTER 3

ARI

I t's early morning, just shy of six a.m. I stare at my reflection in the mirror while I adjust my pink cross necklace across my neck just below my collarbones, making sure it's not backward. Showered, hair straightened, and natural makeup applied, I was ready for church. Ever since my brother passed away, I made sure to accompany my mother every Sunday at her request. I dreaded every morning I had to join her with my damaged faith hovering over my mind.

I was lying to her when I said my faith hadn't been altered. It had faded after the death of my brother. I was angry and questioning my entire life, because… why would God take away a soul like my brothers? In such a horrific and unexpected way to top it off. I feel like I'm playing pretend with myself every day now. I was pretending to still be the, *everything happens for a reason*, optimistic, and unbroken woman I was raised to be.

Truth is, I was struggling every single day to live a life where my brother no longer existed in it. I was no longer that girl, but I was going to try like hell to be.

If that's what it takes to make my mother feel like she hasn't lost us both… then I'd keep pretending.

I walk over to my box full of printed Polaroid photos from my brother. It was placed safely, on one of the top bookshelves in the corner of my room. Paul would print one photo of us, each time he had to leave for anything pertaining to the military. It started the day before he shipped off to Boot Camp and ended on his last deployment. I always had at least one photograph on hand, keeping it close because it made me feel safe.

The only man in the house was gone.

My father abandoned our family when I was a child. I can barely remember what he looks like. The memories were fuzzy and faded. His face was a shadow every time I tried to picture him in my head. My mother kept photos of my father and us as children together. She offered many times if I wanted to look at them and know the person who helped give us life... but I refused to be reminded of what he looked like. I'd prefer he stayed a shadow implanted in my brain.

If he could abandon my mom to start a new life without us, he wasn't worth remembering or stressing over. However, my mom is stuck in her ways and religion. She never moved on from her ex-husband because she thought it was a sin. Paul always took on the role of the man of the family.

The protector. The responsible one. Always the one in charge. While I took on the role of the little sister that persistently tested his patience.

I was having one of the bad moments where I replayed every single conversation we had together. From the bad ones that originated from fighting to the good ones that were rooted in sibling banter. Second-guessing every single choice of words we exchanged. Regretting words, I had said and things I hadn't said. Regretting every action that affected him in a bad way.

I'm staring at my little wooden box that contains all of the photos he's given me. There were about ten inside. I tip-toe and reach for it. Finally, after struggling to hook it with one of my fingernails, I succeeded. Letting out a breath I was holding, I open it. Scanning for my favorite picture and I stop when I see it. All the photos on it have a funny message or something simple. I took the one I favored and put it in my purse. I would be taking this to Iraq as a symbol of Paul's protection and love.

I'm scrolling through my phone when I get an email alert that grabs my attention. I scramble to open it when I see it's from a Book Event that all of my favorite authors were attending. It was a massive, extraordinary event where popular authors would meet all of their readers and the book community they had built. My heart sank when my eyes scrolled over the information. It was only an update, and we were still on the waitlist to receive tickets.

I was still on the waitlist. Paul had attempted to get us both tickets to go to the event that was to be held a year from now. He was confident we wouldn't be on the waitlist long and that we were going to attend. It was perfect timing since I would already be back from my first rotation as a nurse. It was to be held in North Carolina and it was so close to where I lived, just a few hours away.

Paul had already pre-paid them, sending the money to my account. It was placed into my savings account collecting dust with false hope. I throw my phone on the floor with such force, I thought I had broken it but the carpet flooring softens the blow. Anger and grief burned into my eyes, tears threatening to make their way out. I turn around and bury my face into my pillow, sobbing because the reality that one of my brothers' last hopeful thoughts, wouldn't come true.

"Don't worry baby sis, you think so negatively. You'll get those books signed by your favorite author while I watch. You're going to be ugly crying and I'll make sure to take videos and never let you forget it."

Paul's voice is in my head as I remember the conversation we had when we found out the Book Event was sold out.

Just another reminder that kills me softly.

I sip my iced coffee and it feels cool on my tongue. Wiping the cold foam off my lips, I take a deep breath in. My mom and I were at our local coffee shop. I thought the caffeine would help me find the courage to tell my mother what I signed up for. My nude-colored painted nails, tapping the table. I look up at my mother, my eyes stick on the bags under her eyes. She works part-time but the hours were draining on her body. She was a care-taker for a wealthy doctor's mother.

"Ma... how are you feeling... right now, at this moment?" I try to half-smile through my anxiety, biting my lip. I wanted to get an idea of what mood she was in.

"I'm okay, tired but I'm okay. Proud of your recent accomplishments mija." She places her hand on mine, giving me a small squeeze. She was referring to my new title as an official nurse.

"Ok good, because I'm about to tell you something and I don't know how you're going to take it."

She widens her eyes with fear beaming at me.

"You're pregnant." Her veiny hands cover her mouth.

"Ma! No! God!" I say, yelling in whispers, looking around to see if anyone heard her accusation.

"You're still a virgin, right?"

"Mom, that's not important," I whisper embarrassed.

"Mija... look, your first time shouldn't be with just any guy, it should be with someone you mar—"

"Mom, I'm going to Iraq as a trauma nurse for the Army and I'll be there for six months." I blurt it out, watching my mom closely. Praying she wouldn't start to yell at me in the midst of a busy coffee shop.

She doesn't move. I can tell her body is tense. She was digesting the news. Her eyes hadn't moved from mine, and it felt like an eternity of silence from her. She hugs her gray-blue knit sweater tighter around her, crossing her arms.

Then she starts crying, silently sobbing.

Oh my gosh. What have I done?

"Mom, I'm sorry I... just think this is something I have to do." Holding her hand across the table, comforting her.

"Mija... these are tears of joy. Paul would be so proud. Your brother was my world. Don't get me wrong you are too, you guys are *both* my world. And he would be so proud of his baby sister, following in his footsteps in helping our country, like this."

Well, I wasn't expecting that.

The rain starts to pour down hard outside, and I can see the lightning in the sky through the windows of the coffee shop. It was already seven at night, the sky was overshadowed with dark clouds everywhere. I shudder as the loud thunder causes vibrations through the walls.

I smile back at my mom. I'm speechless. My emotions take over and I start to tear up. I couldn't imagine how my mother was feeling having lost a child and now she was losing me, but not in the same way.

"I'm happy you understand my decision, Mom. I just feel like I can help people like Paul. Help sailors or even soldiers who are injured and hopefully save their lives." I choke up while I grab my coffee. I take another gulp, hoping it stops me from crying more.

"I understand mija. Go do what you have to do, I'm proud of you and I'm always here for you. Just… promise to call me every day." My mom smiles.

My mom and I started to gather our things. She grabs the umbrella she carried with her to prepare for the rain. A category 2 hurricane is headed straight towards the Carolinas, and we decided to stock up on groceries and grab a coffee on the way home.

We walk towards the exit, and we stop right in front of the doors so my mom can open her umbrella to prepare for the rain.

Suddenly, the door opens, and my heart skips a beat. I'm feeling nervous and my stomach is filled with butterflies. I feel as though I'm frozen in time.

Danny.

"Ari." Danny greets me just as surprised as I am. He's easily the most beautiful man in this world.

I fall apart at the way he says my name.

Danny and I both stand there, not moving, locking eyes. I had ghosted Danny. I was never good at texting even more so with a stranger. I felt like I was in an embarrassing dream where you're caught with your butt crack showing. My mom notices the awkward engagement and makes an obvious, cliche clearing her throat noise.

"Umm, sorry Mom. This is Danny. Danny, this is my mom."

Gesturing towards Danny, he looks towards my mom, giving her a warm smile. He reaches out to her, shaking her hand. I can tell my mom is taken aback by Danny and his presence. She looks starstruck as if she's meeting her celebrity crush in person, blushing at Danny as he shakes her hand. I'm laughing hard internally at my mom's interaction.

"Danny is?" My mom is smiling at me, lifting one eyebrow at me.

"Umm..." I start not knowing how to finish my sentence. I don't know what to say. I had just met the man.

"We're friends." Danny chimes in for me.

Oh?

"Oh my gosh, really? Your friends with Ari?" My mom gushes, excited. I roll my eyes with a small smile.

Yes, Mom, I have friends, it's not that hard to believe.

My mom still lives in a harsh mentality that I can't be friends with the opposite sex without it being more than that.

"Well, ma'am we just met," Danny answers. That same deep voice makes my cheeks burn. I'm so attracted to his voice, it's so captivating.

"Oh really, where?" My mom asks, looking at me suspiciously. I panic. I don't want her to know the details of how we met. My mom's very strict and conservative. She's against drinking alcohol, smoking cigarettes, parties, tattoos, etc. All my life, she's tried to the best of her abilities to inflict those views onto me.

"Alright Mom, I think it's time for us to go. The groceries are in the car and the storm is about to roll in, we need to prepare for the hurricane." I begin to usher my mom out of the coffee shop, walking past Danny. My mom makes it out through the doors first but my hand is on the doorknob, about to close it. The sound of rain is instantly louder as I walk outside.

"Ari."

I turn my head back to Danny. I never texted him back after our short exchange of text messages. I didn't want this to go anywhere if it was.

"Yes?"

"I'm leaving on deployment soon. I was supposed to leave today but the hurricane delayed our departure so I'm leaving right after the weather is right again. I want to take you on a date. And since you're not answering any of my texts, I guess I'll just have to corner you until I get the answer I want." He smirks.

I hesitate to answer.

Lord, how badly I just want to scream yes at him.

But I was damaged. Damaged by my ex-boyfriend and the recent grief that drowns me every day. I didn't know if starting a possible relationship or even a friendship, was the right move for me.

"I—"

"Of course, she can go on that date. She's free! Mija, I can drive myself home, you go with him. Okay?" My mother quickly cuts in and I'm in shock at her persistence.

A minute ago, she was questioning my virtue and now she's pushing me to go with a man she doesn't know very well.

"Mom, but—"

"Okay see you later, love you mija." She quickly turns around and leaves, forcing me to stay with Danny. I'm glaring at my mom's back as I watch her retreat to her car.

She betrayed me.

She jogs away holding the umbrella over her head.

I guess I could run after her but I can't deny wanting to get to know Danny more. I can't deny the attraction I feel towards him. I bite my lip, turning around to him, forcing a smile.

"So... you go to Chrome Beans?" I ask, referring to the coffee shop we're standing in front of. I've been going to Chrome Beans since I was a high school student. This is a place for me to escape sometimes. Coffee and a good book always seemed like a vacation from reality. My friends and I shared a lot of memories here. We would meet here and have study dates for big exams.

"Yeah, I'm glad I decided to get some coffee."

I blush. We're still standing in front of the coffee shop's doors, underneath a roof that's blocking the rain. My heart's pounding, incredulously.

How did this guy I just met make me feel this way?

Danny's all-black hoodie hugs his figure so well. He makes black my new favorite color.

"Are we having a coffee date, or would you like to eat something?" He flirts. He arches a brow, waiting for my response. He's confident. I don't know how but just the way he moves; it does something to me.

I smile at him, thinking about his question. The same thrill of feeling alive returns when he says the word, *date*. His blue eyes are full of anticipation as he awaits my response. Thunder again hits the area making me jump up, stunned by its volume. The wind starts to pick up, growing stronger as it blows by us, causing my long hair to fly everywhere.

Danny sees me shutter and puts his arm over my shoulder and pulls me closer to him, protecting me from the harsh wind. His touch feels electric.

"I think I would like to eat," I respond to him after clearing my throat. I look up at him and I regret it because it sends a sensation in between my legs I hadn't felt in a long time. He nods.

At this moment, I feel like we're in our own little world. A sweet world, full of tension between us. It was a really nice, short-lived moment.

"Ari-cakes?"

A familiar voice asks behind us, ruining the bubble we're in. A voice I was afraid of. A voice that had broken my heart completely not too long ago. A voice that belongs to the person that made me swear off military men.

Shane.

CHAPTER 4

ARI

My heart sinks deep into the pit of my stomach. Hearing his voice brought back so many memories of abuse and heartache and here I was in between Danny and Shane. Both looking at me with confusion. Their expressions read, *who is this guy*. They both size each other up and I grow uncomfortable. I turn around to face Shane. He looks the same except his brown hair is longer. Seeing his face makes me go cold and scared. The Shane I knew from months ago, was a very jealous man and I can tell seeing Danny with me, bothers him. He starts chewing his gum aggressively the longer he stares, smirking at me and Danny.

"Oh Shane, hi..." I mutter. The feelings I had when I was with Shane come back but it's nothing romantic. It's fear. Like getting seen with Danny was wrong and I felt like I was cheating on him. It was like getting caught red-handed with the other man.

I had to mentally remind myself, I was single, and that relationship was long gone. I was finally out of his toxic grasp.

"How have you been Ari-cakes?" I cringe when he calls me by the nickname he gave me, *Ari-cakes*. He hasn't called me that since we were together.

"Fine. Great." My tone is icy.

I didn't dare try to continue the conversation. The interaction between the three of us quickly fills with awkward silence and Danny drops his arm that he had around me.

Unsurprisingly, I'm upset and craving his arm to be thrown over me again. It felt natural. It made me feel safe.

"I'm glad to hear… you still get Chrome beans?" Shane asks, flashing me a quick smile trying to give me the impression he still knows me. But he doesn't. He will never know me again. He will never get the pleasure of *hitting me again* or his sick attempts to drag me into the depths of his abuse.

"I think we should get going." Danny intervenes. Danny looks like he's watching Shane, intently. He furrows his brow at him as he gets closer to me. Shane's shorter and leaner than Danny.

It was like he read my mind or body language. I didn't want to talk to Shane anymore. I'd rather get as far away as possible from him. It took everything I had in me to get over him. He cheated on me and broke me down emotionally, *and* physically. Standing in front of him right now, made me feel like the old trauma I healed from was reopening.

Funny enough, he was the one who ended things with me. He cheated on me for the third time and left me for another woman who could give him things I couldn't. Every time he cheated; I would forgive him. I was so weak, I loved him no matter how much he hurt me. Then finally, when he was no longer interested in the woman he left me for, he came crawling back but I rejected his every attempt at reconciliation. I blocked him. I blocked his number and on social media. And I never heard from him again.

That is until now.

I cried for weeks over him. We were together for a few years.

When he joined the military, he became toxic in our relationship, and completely changed.

Of course, when you first begin a relationship there's a lovey-dovey phase but then he revealed who he truly was.

For me, that wasn't long after he became a marine.

"I think that's a good idea," I reply softly, looking away from Shane and rather into Danny's blue eyes.

"I'll see you around then." Shane gives me a wicked smile and enters the coffee shop. I let out a relieving sigh.

"Ari-cakes, eh?" Danny asks me, humor in his voice.

"Let's just go please," I beg.

Danny leads me to the parking lot and we're both walking fast in silence, as the rain falls. I follow him until we got to a pickup truck. He opens the passenger door for me, and I climb in.

Danny closes my door quickly and jogs over to his side, attempting to avoid getting completely soaked by the rain.

"Where would you like to eat?" He asks as he closes his door behind him.

"I'm not sure... the weather's getting bad." I'm still shaken up by running into Shane, my voice comes out like a whisper and Danny notices how uncomfortable I'm feeling.

"Hey I can take you home, it's ok —"

"No." I immediately respond, cutting him off. I look up at him and give him a reassuring smile.

Seeing Shane threw me off. My heart stopped for a couple of seconds out of fear. I finally escaped him but when I saw him at Chrome Beans it reminded me of all the feelings I would get when I was with him. It shook me to my core. Still, I wasn't going to allow him to ruin the possibilities with other men.

"How about we grab takeout? And we can have dinner and a movie at my place?"

Dinner and a movie at his place sound like a dream after the whole year I've had so far. Experiencing domestic abuse followed by my brother's passing was the hardest thing I've ever had to go through. I didn't just lose my brother; I lost my best friend. We were so close.

"I'd like that."

"This is it," Danny announces, casually.

We pull into his property, driving through a front gate. After picking up Brooklyn-style pizza, I took a glance at his property. A beautiful two-story home on acres of land. It was gorgeous. It had a front porch and a wrap-around fence.

"Wow, Danny, your place is nice."

I grew up in a small three-bedroom house in an over-populated neighborhood. So, this house looks like paradise to me. It was so spacious and modernized.

"Thank you."

I should be scared, but I feel completely warm inside next to Danny. He has been such a gentleman to me since we met. I hadn't been on a date since Shane and I broke up months ago. I *wasn't* breaking my *no military-men* rule yet.

With the pizza box in his hand, Danny gets out and walks to my side of the truck, and helps me out of the passenger seat.

"Short girl problems." I laugh as his hand holds mine. With every slightest touch he gives me, butterflies flutter harshly inside of me. As I get closer to him, his strong cologne scent catches me. His scent was marvelous, it was radiating woodsy and rebellious.

Even though I just met Danny, it feels like a breath of fresh air out of the darkness. I feel safe with him, something I never felt with Shane.

When we reach his porch, he grabs his keys and unlocks the front door so quickly like he probably had a thousand times.

The first thing I see when he reaches over to his right, switching a light on, was a very rich spacious wood cabin-themed home. It was absolutely mesmerizing, I felt like I was in a very expensive lodge in the mountains.

"Wow..." I look up to the ceiling and noticed every single detail of his house was well thought out and designed.

Danny looks amused at my astonishment. We reach the living room, and he turns on his electric fireplace followed by a large tv screen that was mounted on the wall above it. This was a date night I hadn't imagined going on anytime soon. Simple yet amazing. I was never attracted to men who thought flaunting fancy things would impress me.

"Would you like some red wine?" Danny asks me after putting the pizza down on his living room coffee table. He makes his way into the kitchen area where a large island is in the center of his kitchen, with a bar area in the corner. Lots of wine, liquor bottles, and beer were on display like a collection. He must be a heavy drinker.

"Yes please." I politely reply. I walk over to the couch and get comfortable, sitting on a soft cushion. I really hope he's not expecting anything more from me than just a date of getting to know each other.

Danny returns with a wine glass and a drink for himself. He turns on the weather channel after he places my wine glass down, the glass making a collision noise as he sits next to me. I grab the glass of red wine and take a sip. My taste buds jump in excitement as the red wine rolls down my throat. I look over and Danny's watching me with a glass of whiskey. He's so handsome, his strong jawline covered in a short beard, and those blue ocean eyes I could stare into forever.

"I thought military men couldn't have beards," I say with eyebrows raised curiously. It was one of the first things I noticed about Danny. Before Paul became a Navy SEAL, he always had his facial hair clean-shaven and well-kept.

"Yeah, we typically can't. I'm getting deployed though so I get the okay."

"That explains it."

"Who was that at the coffee shop? Is that why you're so sad?" Danny asks as he grabs his whiskey, drinking almost all of it.

"Umm... it's a long story," I reply, drinking more of my wine.

I want to get more relaxed with the strong tension going on between us. I highly doubt Danny would be interested in hearing a story about a toxic ex-boyfriend and losing my brother. If he's like the military men I envision them all to be, he's probably just looking for a one-night stand before he deploys.

I put my wine glass down, sighing. Thinking negatively about myself always gets the best of me. A guy like him surely couldn't be interested in me like that.

The rain starts to really pour down heavily outside with strong winds making the house creak. Loud howling through the cracks of the windows. The sound of water splashing down on the porch outside is soothing. I can see lightning hit over and over again amongst the dark clouds, through the large glass windows that showcased his acres of land.

"I've got time."

I start to bounce my leg up and down, anxiously. I get anxious every time I talk about Shane. Danny seems genuinely interested and curious enough about my life, and it felt good. This man I just met who's totally hot, and such a gentleman. But… I felt like there was a whole side of him he wasn't sharing with me. I just didn't know if that side was *good or bad*.

"The guy that called me *Ari Cakes*," I roll my eyes, "was actually my most recent ex-boyfriend. His name is Shane. He's actually in the Marines. He's your cliche tool bag. He cheated on me several times. And every single damn time, I would forgive him like a dumb ass. Things even got so bad he started putting his hands on me."

I look up at Danny, studying his expression. His body grows tense and he's stiff.

"Finally, after the last affair he had, he ended things and I didn't take him back. He begged but I stood strong. It took everything I had in me not to give in. My brother, who's no longer here with me, helped me get past my abusive relationship at the time."

Then I could feel the sting in my throat. I choke up and I fight so hard against the tears that were starting to fill my eyes. Here I was opening up to a stranger during a hurricane watch in his house.

What could go wrong?

"If I were your brother, I would've kicked his ass," Danny says firmly, grabbing a hold of his empty glass. He stands up and starts towards the kitchen and fills it up with more whiskey.

"Oh, trust me, Paul, my brother, he almost did. Shane showed up at the house one night, begging me to get back with him and Paul put everything on the line for his baby sister and almost got into a physical fight with him. I got in the middle and separated them before it could escalate further. I lied and told Shane I had called the cops so he fled."

The memories of that specific night come back flooding into my mind like a movie, as I explain it to Danny.

Paul and Shane stood in front of each other getting into each other's faces meanwhile Shane calls Paul every name in the book, tempting him to make the first punch. Paul towered over Shane, laughing at his lame attempts to act tough.

Paul didn't say one word back to him. He just smirked and let out small laughs at his attempts to get under his skin. This only made Shane rage even more. Paul kept his composure, smiling wickedly, and I didn't know how.

My heart pounded in my chest; I cried out of intense fear because I feared for Paul's career if he engaged in a physical fight with Shane. I was on the porch looking at them, hopeless, begging them both to stop. They were on the front yard grass, and I could see our neighbors turning on their lights to investigate Shane's shouting.

"I just want to talk to your whore of a sister!" Shane shouts.

"You won't ever get that privilege again, Mitchell, as long as I'm around you'll never lay a finger on her again," Paul said it so calmly and I didn't understand how.

"She likes my fingers, Paul. Tell him Ari Cakes. Tell him about all the

times I made you come on them." Shane said with disdain. He's sick. I can't believe he just shared that.

I watched Paul uncross his arms from his chest and they turned into fists. He was about to give in to Shane. He was going to risk his career but I wouldn't let him. He raised his fist but I had to do something. I wasn't going to watch my brother end his career.

"Stop it! Shane! Get the hell out of here! I called the police already, they're close!"

Neighbor's dogs started barking, attracting more attention to the situation. So, I lied and said I called the police. Shane finally stopped and he stared straight at me when I intervened, over Paul's shoulder. I locked into his eyes, and they were of hurt and hatred. He pointed his finger at me, and I winced. Soon after, he got into his car and drove away. Paul watched him the entire time as I wept.

That was the last time I saw him, until today.

I told Danny in detail about the things Shane would do to me. The times he slapped me so hard in the face he would make me bleed. The times, when I caught him in lies so he would try to manipulate me and get his way out of them. He would accuse me of being crazy or explain that it was *my fault* he cheated on me. The times when he was overly jealous if I talked to another guy, he would call me a whore, a slut, and then sexually assault me after.

I never let him put his dick in me though. My virginity still haunting me. But Danny didn't need to know that part.

After Shane showed me his true colors, I knew if I gave myself fully to him, I would keep running back to him.

I look up at Danny. He's clenching his jaw, taking in everything I just told him. His body stiffened and I can tell the stories were only making him upset. The way he's looking at me, it shockingly makes me feel like the safest I've ever felt with a man. What felt like the longest minute in time, Danny's deep voice finally says, "You didn't deserve any of that. That's not love. I sure as hell don't know what love is but I know it's not that. No man should ever put their hands on a woman. That's a pathetic weak piece of shit."

I look up at him, aching to embrace him as the words roll out of his tongue.

"Paul died two months ago. I still refuse to believe it. It doesn't feel real."

"How'd he pass? I'm sorry if I'm asking for too much."

"No, it's fine. He was a Navy SEAL. He died on a deployment."

Danny stills. He squints his eyes, studying me.

"Although I don't know the details, just the autopsy report."

I decide to change the subject before things grew more uncomfortable. I wanted to know what his interests were. I wanted us to get to know each other without talking about heavy topics. So, we talked about almost everything we liked and eventually went back to the subject of my brother Paul. As I'm opening up about him, I can see Danny's behavior change as if a light bulb turned on over his head. Suddenly, Danny blurts out.

"I'm sorry about your brother but his name... Are you talking about Paul *Alvarez*?" Danny asks me, in shock.

"Yes."

"Ari, I... I knew him. We were friends, best fucking friends. We met years back on my first deployment. We were on different teams but we worked closely together. We did that a lot, actually. We've been friends for years. Yet... I never knew about you... Of course, no details were ever spoken about you. Paul was very private about his family life. All I knew was he had a younger sister and a mom waiting for him at home."

Holy shit, he knew him? Small world.

Danny looks at me to see if I was going to break. With a glance like that, it was like he was asking me for permission to go on. I nod, biting my lip, a tear escaping my right eye. I quickly wipe it away with my hand. Crap. I didn't want to cry in front of Danny like this. But anytime there was an opportunity to talk about my amazing big brother, I took it. The pain was still fresh, and I didn't know when it would ever get better.

"It's okay, go on, please." I urge.

Danny reaches into his pocket, grabs his leather wallet, and pulls out a picture of him and Paul together with a bunch of other guys. A group photo of them on deployment is what it seemed like. All of them with their beards grown out, extremely sun tanned, and dirty, while holding rifles. Danny and Paul were smiling in the left corner as if laughing at their own inside joke. Even in a current situation like a dangerous deployment, Paul always seemed to find light in dark times, this photo shows proof of that. It was the first time I saw Paul with his lame attempt at growing a beard and I couldn't help but giggle.

"Wait, are you *Rider*?" I ask. It all comes full circle. My brother would tell me about his over the phone while he was deployed and Rider was one guy who he consistently brought up. He shared stories about pranks they would pull on the other guys they worked with.

"Yeah. My full name is Daniel Rider."

I put my hand over my mouth.

"Can I take a picture of that please; he looks so happy in it."

"Of course."

"Wait, why haven't I met you before? Why didn't I see you at the funeral?" I ask bothersome.

Why wouldn't he attend his funeral if they were good friends? Why is this my first time meeting him?

Danny lets out a sigh. He looks down at his glass of whiskey, his hands tightening around it showing white knuckles. Then he looks back at me, ashamed. Small wrinkles appear on the edges of his eyes as he glares, sadly.

"I did. I was there for the burial. In the back, I was over-looking it all. I watched them put him into the ground. I apologize for not privately sharing my condolences with you and your mother, but it was really hard for me. My team showed up to the burial though."

As soon as he says it, it occurs to me that he's a special operator too. His head hangs down in defeat. He closes his eyes tight, rubbing the back of his neck with his hand.

My eyes widen.

"Team?" I ask quietly.

He nods.

Holy crap.

"Oh? Are you a Navy SEAL?"

CHAPTER 5

ARI

"It's something I don't tell anyone on the first date." He sighs.

Oh.

He's a SEAL just like Paul?

My heart skips a beat. I can feel my cheeks getting hot and I'm blushing. I let my hair fall over my cheeks as I turn away from him so he can't see my face. I've never felt this way with any guy ever. No one has made me feel so alive before and we barely know each other. This was a first for me.

"So why the Navy?" I ask softly. I wanted to continue the conversation and break from my awkwardness. I truly wanted to know more about Danny. He was one of my brother's closest friends. I didn't think I could like him even more in such a short amount of time, but this changed everything. The fact he was associated with my brother made me more comfortable around him. It made me feel like he was no longer a stranger.

"Well, my father was a SEAL, so it was up to me to carry on the family tradition." I watched his jaw clench at the words, *family tradition*. Something about the way he said it made me feel like there was animosity towards his family.

"I also just want to be a part of the best team in the world and kill bad guys. Simple. As. That."

"How many deployments have you already done?" I ask curious. Danny looks at me, his face hardens, and he stares into my soul again.

"Seven."

I look back at him and I can tell there was more to his words. There was pain underneath the stone-cold emotionless face he was using as a mask. I so badly wanted to reach out and grab ahold of his hand and give him a gentle squeeze... but, I held myself back.

"How long were these deployments?"

"They all varied. The longest was a year. They can go from three months to a year, just depends"

Geez.

"And how long are you leaving for, this time around?" I was hoping he would say a few weeks only. Wishful thinking. I just met such an amazing guy and he was leaving already. This night was probably our last together unless we kept in touch somehow.

"I don't know," Danny says. He stands up and walks back to the kitchen and pours a large amount of whiskey back into his glass. The thunder outside keeps getting louder and more consistent. Lightning flashed through the windows, lighting up the house with blue rays of light. The temperature in the house feels like it's dropping even more due to the strong cold winds. Either way, I can't help but notice Danny keeps the inside of his house cold; I was freezing.

I decide to follow him over to the kitchen, hoping every stride would warm me up. I sit down on a bar stool at the kitchen island that's between us. The island was a beautiful rustic wooden color.

"Do you drink a lot? Often?"

Danny smirks. I can feel myself getting hot. Even his smirk was so damn gorgeous.

"Is every weekend considered a lot?" Danny chuckles.

"Umm, maybe?" I wasn't a drinker. I only drank on special occasions. So every weekend did seem like a lot to me. But I don't blame him for drinking often. His job seems like it's a stressful one to have. I can only imagine all the trauma he's already been through with all of the deployments and losing a close friend on one of them... *my brother.*

"How old are you?"

"Thirty-three."

Why am I so attracted to that?

"You?"

"Twenty-two."

"So why did you choose nursing as a career?"

That's an easy question.

"Because I want to help people. I want to help people that can't help themselves. I want to save people that can't save themselves..." I swallow the lump in my throat. "Like Paul." My voice comes out dry and hoarse.

Danny looks at me and his eyes soften. He glances at the windows outside watching the trees sway like they're about to snap.

"Paul was an amazing big brother. We were supposed to go to the upcoming Bloomings Author Event, together."

Danny turns again toward me and I can tell it makes him uncomfortable when I bring up Paul.

"The weather's getting even worst," Danny mutters after taking another drink of his whiskey. He changes the subject and I don't blame him. The hurricane was about to roll in and I didn't want to leave. My heart drops and my smile fades. I didn't want to go home just yet but I knew it was getting dangerous outside. I just didn't know how I would be getting home since Danny drove me here.

"Yeah, it is."

An awkward silence fills the room. Thunder was the only sound filling the silence every second. I look up at Danny and he's staring at me. I blush. I can't handle the way this man looks at me.

"How could you read me so well at El Devine? How could you tell that I'm... *broken?*" He turns towards me, giving me his full attention. His Adam's apple bobs down as he swallows more of his drink.

"You wear your heart on your sleeve."

"That obvious huh?" *How embarrassing.* I need to learn how to control my face.

"Don't be ashamed of that. That's what makes you, *you.* Not many people do that anymore in this fucked up world. It's rare and I think that's my favorite thing about you so far. You're rare."

I'm stunned. He looks at me with such intensity, unfaltering seriousness and I'm breaking. The chemistry between us is undying. It keeps getting stronger the longer I'm close to him. I'm holding my breath and my heart pounds. I can't believe he makes me feel this way. Light starts to flicker and the tension rises in between us as he walks closer to me.

"So... ever kill anyone?" I softly chuckle, awkwardly. Way to break the ice, Ari.

As soon as the question left my lips, I wanted to slap my forehead. What a stupid question. What a terrible joke. I shake my head, aggressively looking away from him, gritting my teeth.

Danny sighs.

"Not today." He grins before continuing.

"Ari, didn't Paul tell you to never ask those questions? Tsk, tsk, tsk."

"I'm sorry. Stupid question..." I look down at my phone, opening my Uber app. I'm desperate to get away from him after revealing my horrible social skills. I'm mortified I need to go home.

Forget that I need to relocate to a different state.

What is wrong with me?

"I should go, I'll find a ride home on the Uber app. The

storm's rolling in and I don't want to keep you from preparing for your deployment," I say, faking the hardest smile I could throw on. I stand up walking towards the entryway to his front door, every step is fast and desperate.

Stupid question. Way to embarrass myself. I haven't been on a date in a long time. I'm extremely rusty on my flirting and apparently social skills.

I'm halfway to his front door when his hand catches mine, spinning me around into him slowly. My face meets his chest, and I look up at him nervously.

My heart is beating so hard I wonder if he can hear it. His touch always sends electrifying heat into me. I look back at his hand, his skin rough on my palm.

"Don't go." He looks down at me, his other hand still holding onto his whiskey.

"My flight got canceled, remember? I won't be leaving tomorrow after all, at least until the hurricane clears. And I highly doubt any Ubers will be accepting any requests given the weather..."

The smell of his cologne traps me in a frozen state since our bodies were almost touching. It's such a unique sexy smell and I want to smother myself into his shirt.

"So..." I swallow, anxiously. "What are you implying?" It came out almost a whisper.

I knew what he was implying. He wants me to stay the night. I never did one-night stands, that was never my thing. I wasn't that type of girl, not that there's nothing wrong with it. I just wasn't comfortable doing that... yet why was I hoping that I would be underneath him naked tonight? The thought of us both naked sends me into a mess of emotions. I feel ashamed of my lust. I felt shame for thinking such an intimate thought and a large part of me didn't care.

I bite my lip, looking up at Danny. Danny's jaw clenches as he looks at my lips. I can feel the tension between us and it excites me.

"I think you should stay the night because of the hurricane, I guess we didn't really think this through..." he lets go of my hand and massages the back of his neck.

Thunder erupts and the lights begin to flicker on and off.

"Yeah, I think so too..." I breathe. Our bodies were almost touching.

Our eyes lock into each other and I feel him leaning in more towards me, closing the distance, slowly.

I can't handle it. I can't handle the fire that's blazing in between my thighs, and I want to run. I'm so shy and I hate myself for it.

"How tall are you by the way?" I blurt out, stopping him from getting closer. Danny's face softens.

"6'6."

I look at him, really looked at him and I can see a scar peeking out of the sleeve of his shirt. I lift my hand to it, touching it.

"Oh... is this a scar? How'd you get this?" I ask, intrigued. Danny looks down at my hand trailing his scar. That's when I see a glimpse of the scar's length. It didn't end there; it looks like it keeps going but I can't see where.

"On one of the deployments... with Paul actually." Danny laughs as he watches my hand on his tricep.

"Can I see how far it goes?" I ask curiosity gnawing at me. Danny shrugs, drinking more of his whiskey, then placing his glass down on a nearby table. I was confused, all he had to do was lift his slee —

Oh...

I was not expecting Danny to slip his shirt off over his head. The shirt brushes over his dark, sandy blonde hair. I was now facing his very well-toned, tattooed back. The scar went from his shoulder blade all the way down to the back of his tricep, like someone had slashed him with a knife, diagonally. He has a massive realistic-looking tattoo of a Grim Reaper engraved in flames all over his back. Whoever the tattoo artist was did a perfect job well done. It looks so detailed like a photograph. Finally, I get a full view of his half sleeve. There are angels with wings and demons wrapped into each other tattooed beautifully on his arm.

I walk closer to him, eyeing his sun-kissed tan skin. I looked at him for permission with my eyes before I touched the scar, again.

"May I?"

Danny nods.

I touch the scar following it up to his right shoulder. The scar feels soft underneath my fingertips.

"How'd you get it?" I ask. I can't imagine being wounded like this. The pain, the stories, and the injuries he carries due to these deployments. I wanted to know them all. I start to feel myself going sad knowing he had suffered through pain. Every piece of evidence on his body looks like he's been through hell.

"I don't want to dampen tonight with those stories… so I won't share, for your sake." He says putting his shirt back on. My heart sinks a little, I shouldn't pry like this, but I respect his decision.

"Oh... okay I get it." I half-smile.

"It's just I don't think it would do any good sharing it but maybe one day soon." He says as he starts to walk away from me. My heart jumps a little with giddy at the thought of us continuing to hang out.

Danny reaches out for my hand and I grab it. He leads me back into the living room. I sit down on the couch and cross my legs together as Danny grabs the TV remote and turns it on, flipping through the channels.

"I want an update on the weather."

"Good idea. I've got to check in with my mom. See how she's doing." I take my phone out of my pocket and send her a text.

Danny's still standing in front of me, watching the weather

channel and I'm internally freaking out. I'm going to spend the night with one of my brother's friends. It feels so wrong to be here. I feel like I'm pushing my boundaries for the first time in a long time and I'm secretly loving it. Either way, my mom must be so worried about me since I haven't returned home. I'm puzzled by the fact she hasn't been harassing me yet.

Mom, everything okay? I'm staying the night with him because of the hurricane. I should be back home tomorrow when the hurricane has already passed through.

I wonder how she's going to react to me telling her that I'm staying the night with a guy I barely know. I bite my lip, nervous. My mom replies two minutes later. I'm bouncing my knee up and down, awaiting her response.

MOM: Everything is good. That's the smartest thing to do right now. Stay with Danny until the hurricane passes. By the way, I recognized him. He's one of Paul's friends from the military. I knew he looked familiar.

Great. Am I the only one who didn't know Danny? My family has met him before me.

ME: Wait. How do you know him?

"Damn, the hurricane still hasn't weakened, but it will soon." Danny's voice interrupts my thoughts and I set my phone down. I looked back at him as he bends down to sit next to me. Then I was hit by his cologne scent again and I melted. His smell was so good.

MOM: Paul would send text me pictures when he was gone mija. Danny appeared in them sometimes.

I smile before turning my phone off.

"Oh wow. That's not good." I look at the news reporter across the TV screen. It was a man underneath an umbrella, near the beach of the Carolinas where the hurricane was approaching. Winds are picking up and rain falls hard onto the news reporter as he delivers information on what's happening on the beach. He's yelling at his microphone trying not to get drowned out by the noise of high winds and crashing rain. I found humor in watching the reporter struggle to stay in place as the strong winds kept pushing him over.

I can't hold it in any longer, so I start laughing. Maybe, it's the alcohol getting to me already.

"What's so funny?" Danny asks. I meet his gaze and he brightens with admiration. He's admiring me as half of his lips turn into a smile that causes me to paralyze by the overwhelming attention.

"I will never understand why news reporters put themselves in a dangerous situation like this just to *tell us* how dangerous it is to be outside, and that we should evacuate the area. It's just silly and hypocritical."

Danny laughs as he sits down close to me, "You're not wrong."

We both start to laugh hard and for the first time in a while, I look at Danny and all I feel is pure bliss since my brother's passing.

Danny and I look at each other as our laughter dies down. His gorgeous blue eyes stare into mine. His hand brushes over his beard as I feel that sweet moment full of tension again. Him having known Paul, makes me feel even more comfortable with him than I already was. To me, he wasn't a complete stranger after all. An uncomfortable feeling tugs below my stomach. I look down and I can feel myself blushing. My heart rate picks up and I start biting the inside of my lip, gently out of anxiety.

I look back at him and he's moved even closer to my face. He leans in more and so do I. His eyes are looking at my lips and I know what's coming. I close my eyes and he closes the gap between us with his lips. As soon as our lips touch, a storm of emotions rocks me. His kiss is so gentle, it's consuming me. Our lips brush each other softly and I swear I can see stars in the dark.

Then he changes the pace by speeding it up. It goes to an aggressive, hard, *I need you right now*, kiss. His tongue brushes against my lip waiting for me to return it with mine and I immediately react. Our tongues thrash against each other and he tastes so damn good. *Cigarettes and whiskey.* I'm in shock at how much I'm enjoying swallowing his taste. His right-hand cups the side of my head bringing me even closer to him and he's brushing his thumb back and forth on my cheek.

Then, he's rougher. He squeezes my hair tight, pulling it down so I'm now facing the ceiling and he starts biting on my neck, hard. It causes me pain but not enough for me to break away.

I'm scared. But... not of him. I'm scared that the pain arouses me, and I'm conflicted within myself. I close my eyes as his lips and teeth suck on my neck. Then, he trails kisses down my chest. Arousal creeps down into my bones, my clit throbbing for his touch. I could feel his facial hair poking into me and I'm enjoying it. I smile as he worships my body.

I didn't know this night was going to go this way at all and I was enjoying every second of it. His hand lets go of my face and goes for my shirt instead. My chest tightens and I don't know how to feel. His hand slowly begins to undress me by pulling my shirt up a bit. I've never felt more alive in my life. As soon as his hand touches the skin of my stomach the hairs on my skin stand up. My entire body erupts in goosebumps. He reaches for the clips of my bra and unhooks it with one hand. He lightly pushes my chest down and I obediently follow his lead. My hair falls to the side, a low moan slips away from my lips, and Danny hums. He lifts my shirt upwards just below my chin, not fully unclothing me. I react so fast, holding my forearms over my hard nipples.

Danny takes notice, his eyebrows raising.

"Ari, is this your first time?"

I freeze. *It's that obvious?*

His elbows rest on the couch, keeping his weight off me. He's on top of me, and I can feel his thick, solid bulge against the inside of my thighs through his jeans. I'm instantly nervous and my breathing quickens, my hands grow clammy and I feel like I'm in a fantasy. I've never felt so sure about this in my life, yet I was so nervous. The way Danny makes me feel so sure about the choices I make; I want to hold onto that feeling for eternity.

I bite my lip and nod.

"Yes."

His face is only about three inches away from mine. He doesn't respond. Instead, he looks at me. And I'm looking back at him, into his eyes, getting lost in a trance and it feels like we're the only two people left in this world. He lifts one of his hands, caressing my cheek, rubbing his thumb over it. I close my eyes and nestle into it, enjoying every fiber of his skin on mine.

"Don't hide your beauty away from me. You're so addicting."

His words loom over my head and my insecurities fade away, like my morals.

He then removes my forearms away from my breasts and I relax them to my sides. He's commanding my body with his hands, and I let him. I don't recognize myself anymore. Danny grabs my cross necklace and pushes it to the side. The cross getting lost in my hair that's sprawled out on the couch.

He begins to plant kisses around my right breast, and I suck in air as he takes my nipple into his mouth, sucking on it so hard I arch my back begging for more. His teeth bite hard on it, causing such an explosive reaction from me and I moan. My clit pulsating, begging to be touched. Thunder bellows outside as he moves to my other breast and puts it into his mouth again. I feel like I'm as light as a feather and I'm about to fly into a new world of sensuality.

He squeezes my other breast with his hand and then pinches my nipple with his fingers. One breast is being sucked and the other is pinched. Pain and pleasure weren't something I had ever imagined blending so well with each other, but Danny makes this combination I want to explore.

A moan escapes me and Danny trails his tongue all the way down to my stomach, going over my belly button. He begins to undress my bottoms and I began to pant. My chest jumps up and down with my heavy breathing and I feel my underwear soaking. He pulls my bottoms down leaving my pussy bare. He has his head in between my thighs, throwing them both over his shoulders, pulling my pussy closer to his mouth.

"Please," I beg.

Danny grins and doesn't waste any more time. His hands grip my thighs and my hands come alive going for his soft hair, getting lost in the strands. His tongue starts at my slit, up and down thrusting in a cycle of pure erotic euphoria. Teasing my clit every time he goes upwards. Leaving me yearning for more, then he's back down in my slit.

"I could drink you forever Ari, you taste so fucking heavenly." He says as I feel his tongue disappear from my slit and instead thrust inside of me and I lose it. His tongue is inside me and I'm enchanted. He's playing with my clit, circling it with his finger and my legs begin to tremble with pleasure radiating down into my feet. I can't handle this pleasure, it's too much. A low scream escapes me and I'm growing disappointed that it's not his cock.

He stops fucking me with his tongue and starts to play with my clit instead. His tongue makes me forget my own name with the way it's speaking to my clit and I'm boiling inside, arching my back and pushing his head closer to me until I'm riding his face.

It's all too much. Then he takes my clit into his mouth, he sucks on me and I cry out of nirvana, not caring who can hear me and I'm breaking, trembling, shattering into an explosion of happiness when my orgasm rips through me.

Danny feels my orgasm and he hums with satisfaction.

Suddenly, a loud vibration from his phone intrudes our enclosed world and Danny stops fucking me with his mouth and lets go of my clit. My head drops down onto the couch when I realize he's stopped, his attention elsewhere.

I didn't think I was the type of girl to have sex with a guy she barely knew but with Danny... I felt like I just might become one. I've never felt this way with any man. I've never connected with someone on so many levels. The age difference was intimidating, and it makes me feel like I was out of my element being with an older man. It felt dangerous, inviting, and tempting.

Both of us breathe hard as we stare at each other, a fire has been ignited between us and I didn't want it to get put out just yet. His thumb brushes over my lips, and I hear a low, deep frustrated growl coming from Danny's throat.

"Sorry about that, I always have to be on alert with my phone." Danny turns away from me as he pulls out his phone and I rest on my back to the couch, taking a deep breath in, trying to calm all of my awakened nerves.

I watch Danny as he looks at the screen of his phone and I can tell it wasn't good since his whole demeanor changed. His jaw clenches, his body stiffens, and he looks upset. My thoughts are scrambling and I'm wondering what could have appeared on his phone for it to kill the mood entirely.

"What's wrong?" I ask.

Danny locks his phone screen and turns to me with a reassuring smile.

"Nothing," a short pause fills the room.

"Work." He says putting his phone down on the coffee table. Would work really be texting him this late?

I don't know much about how his job works but what I did know, was that it sounded like a lie.

Lightning strikes close by as I see familiar blue rays flash through the windows again. Thunder follows and growls loudly and the whole house shakes.

"So—" I was about to ask if he had a condom before he interrupts me.

"We should go to sleep. I've got to finish up some stuff here and make sure everything's good to go before I leave for deployment. I'll sleep on the couch and you can take my bedroom." Danny says cutting me off. His voice was curt and cold. He adjusts himself farther away from me on the couch.

My heart drops.

What changed? Was that his girlfriend calling him and not *work*?

Oh. Gosh. He must have a girlfriend. He's absolutely gorgeous, why wouldn't he have one? I should have asked.

Wait.

If he had a girlfriend, why is he kissing me then?

A thousand questions were running through my head, and I need to slow myself down.

I begin to dress myself again pulling up my bottoms and relapsing my bra together.

I look at him, fully clothed again, confused and slightly hurt. Danny finally looks back at me after staring at his phone again. I can tell he knows how I'm feeling. I'm easy to read and it's one of my flaws I strongly despise.

"I'm sorry, I just have a lot on my mind." Danny says not looking at me.

"I get that. Trust me I do..."

I was leaving for Iraq very soon. I was extremely nervous and scared. Signing up to work at a hospital overseas to help out our military men like Paul, had me on edge. This night with Danny felt like such an amazing distraction from the stress of it all these past few months.

I felt like I just got rejected when things were going so right between us. My throat feels dry so I look down at the drink I left earlier and drank more, the cold liquid going down my throat. Danny turns to me and he's staring daggers at me the entire time.

"I would very much like to fuck you until the sun comes up." Danny's deep husky voice says with confidence. I was not expecting him to be so blunt, so much so...

I started to choke on my drink.

I place my drink down trying to recover from the oxygen that escaped me unexpectedly. Danny pats my back as I swallow the rest of my drink that got stuck in my throat and I regain my breathing. I look back at him, and he's smirking, devilishly.

I clear my throat.

"So, why don't you?" I tease, my voice low.

"I can't."

"Why not?"

"I respect you too much."

DISRESPECT ME.

Oh, Lord. Where the hell did that come from? The fact that I was so tempted to blurt that out… I'm in shock with myself. My personality and morals change when I'm around him as I'm starting to learn.

"I respect Paul. I respect your family. And I can't. The more I get to know you, I know you're going to want more... and I can't give you more, this was a mistake." He rambles. "I'm not a relationship guy. I don't date. I can't offer you anything more than sex. My job comes first and that's all I've ever known. I won't change that."

Danny turns away from me.

"Let's get some sleep, I'll show you to my room and I'll take you back home in the morning when the hurricane passes." Danny gets up from the couch and I feel like I did something wrong.

I take a few seconds to process everything on the couch, I stare at the TV still playing and I'm buried in confusion. I force myself up and catch up to him. He starts to go upstairs, his steps heavy ending with loud thuds, and I quietly follow as I process everything he just told me. The more I processed, the angrier I got.

I mean I wasn't expecting him to ask me to be in a relationship so soon, we just met for crying out loud. I didn't want that either. But we're adults. I knew this was a possibility of where this was going, but I didn't know that he would cut me off after he got what he wanted from me.

So why did he ask me to come here with him? Was he planning to just fuck me and not speak to me again?

He probably was.

I swallow, anger filling my core. This is why I swore off military men. They're all the fucking same. I thought he was different. I should have known better. I went from feeling like I knew Danny my entire life to feeling like he was just a beautiful stranger again.

Danny turns on the lights in his bedroom after he opened the door for me to enter. I look around and I can feel myself boiling. It was going to be his last night of fun before he left for deployment.

I was going to be his last night of fun.

Danny didn't enter the room. He just stands there in the hallway still, with one of his hands in his pockets.

"If you want to get more comfortable, my clothes are in those drawers over there, you can go through it and pick out whatever you want to sleep in."

I grab the doorknob and look at him.

I was tired of biting my tongue. Maybe it was the alcohol coating me with bravery but I can't hold my words back anymore.

"So, what was this? What was the point of this Danny? I was going to be your one-night stand before you leave on deployment?"

Danny looks at me, defensive.

"Ari, no, of course, no—"

I close the door on him, not giving him a chance to finish.

Chapter 6

DANNY

Ari slams the door on me before I can get another word in and explain myself. I feel horrible that I made her so upset. I feel horrible that she thinks I was going to just fuck her and then exit her life forever. But she had every right to be upset because *she was right. I was going to do just that.*

I stand at the door debating with myself if I should knock and explain why I can't take this any further. I sigh, frustrated. I feel defeated. I'm not good at these things. I raise my hand about to knock, then let my hand fall back to my side. There's nothing I can say or do at this point. I think it's best to give her some space. I don't want to bother her with these kinds of things even though I know I owe it to her.

But I don't care.

The selfish part of me prevails yet again and I don't care to explain myself. Was I wanting to have a one-night stand with her? Definitely, when I first met her at the bar. There's no denying how mesmerizing she is. Not only her beautiful smile and curves but she has this charm about her, taunting me... But now I realize, everything is different. I just found out she's Paul's sister... and how amazing of a person she is. I'll feel like a total asshole if I just fuck and ghost her.

I decide to head for a cold shower to get rid of the intense heat I was feeling from the moments we shared on the couch. Remembering the way her lips felt on mine... her taste so fucking captivating. I wanted to take her right there on my couch.

I walk towards the bathroom door, opening it. Running my hands through my hair, drowning in my thoughts.

I mean, I knew Paul had a sister, but I never knew what she looked like. I didn't even know her name. He was very protective over her and never showed me or any of the guys what she looked like. He wanted to avoid any commentary or curiosity about her life. He kept his family life extremely private. Whenever we were home simultaneously, we always hung out at my place or Kane's.

I couldn't just have sex with Ari. I can tell she's a sweet, kind soul and I'm not going to corrupt her with my demons, my baggage, and the stress of me leading her on. Especially since I'd be extremely busy these next few months and I wouldn't even be able to entertain the thought of keeping in touch with her.

The mission always comes first. My team. My country. My job. My duty as a Navy SEAL. That's why I only did one-night stands. Or friends-with-benefits type of shit. I didn't want any type of distractions that came from women. Anything that could risk me catching feelings, I avoided at all costs. That's why I wanted to keep it as simple as I could. Wine and dine, women, women that knew what I wanted clearly, revealing my boundaries and kinks, and then I would leave. Every woman that I had sex with, knew this about me, going in. No commitments and I'm not going to start now.

I walk over to the shower and turn it on. The shower head spills out cold water, hard. Purposefully to get rid of the blue balls Ari just gave me. I begin to undress, taking off my shirt first and I stare at my reflection a minute longer. Looking at the scar on my triceps and remembering Ari's fingertips trailing it.

When I kissed Ari, I knew it would be different with her. The way she kissed me, the way she smells, and the way she bites her lip when she gets anxious, sends me into a total mess. I respect her too much to take her right then and there on my couch. My phone ringing broke us apart ruining the moment, deterring my dangerous lust towards her.

The phone call was coming from one of the girls I had recently started sleeping with. After I broke away from Ari and read the caller ID, it was a dreadful reminder of the man I truly am. It was hard to face her again when I read Nora's name on my phone screen. So I stopped it right then and there. I was also getting questions from the team about our deployment.

Nora was calling me almost every day after we slept together, a few weeks ago. I told her, in a nice way, that I wanted to just be friends and I was going to be very busy and couldn't see her again any time soon. Which was half true. My career puts stress on my personal/social life when I'm home. Even when I wasn't working, *I was working.*

After hearing Ari's stories of her abusive ex-boyfriend, I can't help but feel like I need to protect her for the rest of her life. I knew it was something Paul would have wanted me to do. *It is something he wanted me to do.* As Paul comes into my head so does one memory where he only opened up about his sister and mother, *one time.* I jump into the shower as my mind leads me back to that night.

We were out on a mission, hiking toward our objective area in the middle of the night, overseas. The moon was the only light we had. We could barely see each other's faces. We had a lot of time to just bullshit and talk about anything. It was Paul and I along with his team and my team of guys, around ten of us. He explained how he looked forward to coming back home to his mother's cooking after the deployment was over and how he was so proud of his baby sister; she had just told him a few days earlier that she got into a great nursing program. He had the biggest smile on his face as he expressed his happiness for his sister. Paul was always finding joy in the darkest of things.

Then he stopped in his tracks and looked at me and our other friends who were listening to him talk. I could hear his voice in my ear like it was yesterday, vividly.

"Promise me something guys." Paul stopped in his tracks and so did we. The sound of dirt and rocks beneath our feet, made the crunching noises halt, as we all stared at Paul, waiting.

Paul's voice sounded serious, and I could tell he was fighting back his emotions, which was very unlike Paul, so I listened close.

Paul looked at me, then at Rooker, then at Kane.

"If anything happens to me, please look after my mother and sister. Make sure they're always good and safe. That's my job right now. I'm the only man in that house right now. My dad left us when we were young and they only have me to count on. Promise me, you'll look after them if I die." His leadership voice came out demanding as if he was ordering us.

"Yeah... sure man," Kane said with no hesitation.

"Of course," Rooker says at the same time as Kane.

All the members of his team agreed and nodded but I couldn't open my mouth. The conversation felt uncomfortable and ridiculous.

I didn't say anything at first. Maybe it was the selfishness in me stopping me from agreeing right away. I hesitated. When I make a promise, I'm a man of my word.

As an only child, I never had other siblings to look after or bond with. But Paul, Rooker and Kane were like my brothers. They were the closest thing to a sibling relationship I've had. I'd do anything for them.

"Grim?" Paul asks again.

I looked up at him and half smiled.

"First of all, nothing is going to happen to you, jackass," I say, laughing as I push Paul's shoulder away from me. I gritted my teeth as the words left my mouth knowing full well, there was always a possibility that one of us wouldn't come home. His rucksack jolts him back a little with the collision of my hand and he takes a step back to catch his balance. Then I continued.

"And second of all, of course, bro, we're all here for you... we're all here for each other."

In most of my memories from deployments, I tend to purposefully try and forget and only remember certain parts. Deployments are cruel to my mind and were the reason for the demons I had. Mostly, because of the Death that would follow. Deployments are the reason I drink almost every night. If something triggers my memory, they come back in flashbacks. The things I've been through are not easy on a human being but I can take it. Even if I can't, I always find a way to keep pushing through, no matter what. Quitting wasn't something that I ever did.

I never take long in the shower. I turn off the shower when I'm done, and I dry myself up quickly wrapping the towel around my torso. I glance at my phone that was near the sink, checking the time. It was already two in the morning. Fuck. I'm always in bed early and woke up early. I spent hours talking to Ari getting to know her and time went by so fast.

I found out her favorite comedy show is Parks and Recreation. Mine was The Office. We had a civil debate on which show was better. I still think The Office is better whereas Michael Scott is iconic. I now know she's a trauma nurse which was inspired by Paul. I know she loves horror movies whereas I only like to watch comedy or action/adventure. I know she played soccer in high school while I was the dork that loved art class. Drawing and painting are still one of my favorite things to do. I know her favorite color is green, and she likes to read, travel, and occasionally play PC games. She prefers cold, rainy weather whereas I prefer hot weather all year long.

Lights start to flicker again as the hurricane is almost done passing through our town. I check the weather through my phone and the worst should be gone by five in the morning. Of course, it would continue to rain throughout the week, but all the dangerous storms should have passed. Luckily, the hurricane was downgraded to a tropical storm.

I feel like I need to check on Ari before I go downstairs and sleep on the couch. I also have to grab my boxers and the rest of my clothes. I always sleep naked, but I have a special guest, so I decide to be appropriate and wear clothes.

I softly knock on the door and unsurprisingly, I get no answer. I gently and quietly open the door to my bedroom. The lights is off but the lamp on my nightstand is on. I see Ari curled up underneath my blankets, already sleeping. I smile. Even asleep, she looks so angelic and peaceful. I just met this girl and I already feel something burning within me whenever I get close to her.

I finally step into my bedroom and quietly get my clothes out of the dresser without waking her.

Success.

I'm closing the bedroom door when I see that she starts to move underneath the covers, groaning, sadly. She's muttering words I can't make out. Then I realize, she's dreaming. Whatever she's dreaming sounds like a nightmare.

"Paul, don't go," Ari mutters. Then she quiets down and stops moving drifting into a deeper sleep, quickly.

She's having a dream about Paul. My heart sinks. She's still grieving. I frown, finally closing the door to my bedroom and I make my way downstairs. Almost all of the lights in my house are turned off.

Spending time with me must've triggered her emotions about him. *Hell, she's triggered mine.*

I passed the worst parts of the grieving stage, and I almost feel healed. With the help of whiskey, cigarettes, and bar hopping. I wouldn't let myself completely feel the loss of Paul.

I'm determined to not ever feel the extent of losing my brothers if I want to keep my career and sanity. I have walls up to prevent myself from enduring the tragedies of death. I go to the kitchen and I head for my favorite pick of poison.

CHAPTER 7

ARI

Meredith is driving me back home from Danny's house. Emilia is in the backseat, texting back and forth with a wedding planner. I asked her to pick me up early in the morning before Danny woke up. I want to avoid him and an awkward goodbye. The worst part of the hurricane has passed so it was safer to drive out. The storm didn't do too much damage as anticipated which was good. That means Danny can get on his flight and I can get back to my normal life as it was before I met him.

"Damn, he lives all the way out here in the beautiful countryside?" Meredith exclaims while looking around at the acres of land on each side of the road. There were ranches all around this area.

"Please keep your eyes on the road. I don't feel like dying today." I roll my eyes at her.

"Okay, one rude. And two, it was one time, when are you going to let that go?" Meredith says, shaking her head while her attention comes back to the road. She's talking about the time when she swerved off the road, almost killing us, while staring at some shirtless guy jogging with his dog on the sidewalk.

"Umm... never. We all have the one friend that drives us

crazy... *and that's you.*" I say, swinging my face in her direction, dramatically. My eyes glared.

"I feel like I'm a survivor every time I get out of the car with you." I joke, teasing her.

"Ugh, I guess that's fair."

I nod while resting my head against the window.

"So, are you gonna tell me what happened? You're not going to give me the details on how a great mysterious Navy guy is keeping you safe and giving you shelter from the hurricane?" Meredith winks, moving her eyebrows up and down.

I sigh, annoyed.

"No."

"Why not?"

"Cause."

"Cause why?"

"Because... Meredith. We didn't have sex."

"What?" Meredith and Emilia shout baffled simultaneously, her voice high-pitched.

"Yeah, we didn't. And I really don't want to talk about it. All I will say is... or rather ask you is..." I bite my lip wondering if I should talk to her about this part of my life. We do tell each other basically everything so why not.

"Spit it out," Meredith says, tilting her head forward down.

"Do I come off as a romantic? Can you tell I fall under the category of a relationship type of girl... in the first impression?" I ask, unsure of wanting to know the answer.

"Hah. Definitely a relationship type of girl. You fall hard and easily. You are a fairytale, rainbows, and butterflies, always believing that there's good in every single person you meet, type of girl."

I look at her with my mouth dropped open. I didn't expect her to come back with that answer. Her comments are harsh.

"Geez, I think a simple yes would have sufficed." I shake my head. How long has she been holding onto that one?

"Look Ari… you don't know the man. We know how religious your family is. Your mother's always reminding you to *save yourself for marriage.*" Emilia throws imaginary air quotes.

"You're right… I'm not even sure how my mom pushed me to leave with him yesterday. She's usually so strict and judgmental so yesterday was a shock that she let me leave with him. I don't know him but I'm tired of being scared. It feels… different with Danny." I concede. "But I won't be seeing him anymore."

"Ok… bullet dodged, let's move on. I don't want to hear a story about how you *almost* lost your virginity. Let's start planning our next night out please."

Meredith rolls her eyes and raises the volume in her car. She's blasting Taylor Swift music. I'm a hopeless romantic but she's the one blasting, her catchy love songs. I look back at Emilia and she shrugs, shaking her head at Meredith's blunt behavior.

I look outside the window pondering about Danny. The weather is still windy and rainy, with dark gray clouds even though it's early in the morning and the sun should have been out. Humidity is higher than usual.

Meredith's words linger in my head.

"Hah. Definitely a relationship type of girl."

I bite my lip as I feel my body on fire. Fire out of rage and hurt. Why does everyone make me feel bad for wanting to believe that everyone is good? In a world full of pain and unforgiving people, I want to be a part of the good. I truly believe you can make a huge impact on someone's life just by smiling at them. But the constant criticism from my best friend *and then from Danny.* I feel belittled. I appreciate and respect Meredith's opinions but it doesn't mean that it doesn't hurt to hear it.

At this moment… something washes over and I decided to challenge myself. No longer am I going to feel belittled because I fall in love so fast? Maybe I won't be a *'relationship type of girl'* anymore. Maybe… I'm going to let myself indulge in my emotions more and speak my mind, loud and clear.

CHAPTER 8

DANNY

Ari left this morning, and it shockingly bothers the shit out of me. I've done this many times. A girl comes over, and we fuck. She leaves the next morning, or I do. But this wasn't like *many times.* I've never not finished what I've started with a woman but last night was different, nevertheless.

I woke up with a hangover from hell. After Ari went to bed, I finished half a bottle of Jack Daniels alone. I sat in the dark, as the hurricane passed through, by my lit fireplace, drinking in silence. Sitting on the couch where I made Ari come with my mouth. She was sleeping upstairs, and I was heavily tempted to wake her up with my cock several times. I left her begging for more and it took everything in me to not take her innocence last night.

I watched the flames burn through the wood as I continued to serve myself glass after glass and it still wasn't taking the edge off. The sound of thunder was the only thing keeping me company.

She's Paul's sister.

Fucking hell.

The morning brought clarity and I was losing myself again.

The alcohol will no longer blur the battles I'll endure for the rest of the day.

His death brought different types of demons over my head that I've never had. Call it survivor's guilt but it was more than that. *It felt more than that.* I was there when he fucking died in my arms.

I can't tell Ari this. I can't tell her the details about how he died without feeling like the devil. I'd rather not live to see how she would react to such a gruesome memory. The story behind his death is something that very few know about. Only the people there on that mission that killed Paul knew.

As a team, we always refrain from telling families the details about their loved one's death. There's a protocol to it all and we couldn't open our mouths about it. Not one single peep.

So, I drank. And drank more and more until I fucking couldn't feel my own pain anymore, racking out on my couch, thinking about Ari's sweet taste. She tastes so different from all the others. She is the forbidden fruit in my world and I'm the serpent in her ears, calling her name. I want to lure her into my world, but I would be a selfish asshole if I took her. Who am I kidding? I am a selfish asshole but the respect I have for Paul, draws the line.

It's ten in the morning when I finish brushing my teeth. Nora's already blowing up my phone and I'm getting irritated by her persistence. Yet, if she's willing to scratch this itch of desire, I won't say no. I decided to give in. Nora never minded the no strings attached nights we have together and that's the way I like it. She isn't the only woman I have this type of relationship with. There are others but lately, she's more eager. I give in to Nora and set up plans with her, texting her back.

But If I can't have Ari... no one will. I'm going to make sure of it in my own way. I had stopped myself from paying my respects to Paul's family for a reason. I couldn't look them in the eye without feeling like I had taken a part in destroying their lives. Still... I made a promise to Paul when he was alive.

And I had to keep it, better late than never... right?

It doesn't matter. I won't keep running away from the promise now, not after feeling this attraction I have for her.

I was already past the grieving stage, and I feel almost completely ridden from the looming guilt, and yet... when I found out Ari is his sister, all the healing comes to a halt.

I'm smoking on my front porch, scrolling through my phone since the work group chat is active with text messages going out. Everyone is hounding me for updates on the deployment since I'm the one everyone answers to. I'm the one in charge of my team so I have to give out orders and updates. The hurricane puts a delay in our departure and that disappointed everybody including me.

There's one thing that gives me a reason to live. A reason to wake up every day with a purpose, and that was my job. Kill or be killed is the anthem of every single deployment. The hurricane kept us home just a little longer and the boys are eager to get back to work. *So am I.* It's going to be another few days before we leave since we have to set up new traveling arrangements.

I refuse to let myself get distracted by this new feeling that erupts in my soul. And her name is Ari.

My gate alerts my phone that there's someone trying to get through on my land and I open it to see my mother's Range Rover requesting access through the cameras.

What's she doing here?

I grant her access and watch the single road that's in between the ever-green trees that block the view to my gate and the main road that leads into the city. While I wait for my mothers' vehicle to emerge, I can't help but wonder if she's brought my father.

We haven't spoken in years. Nothing more than greetings and farewells and there's a good valid reason for the animosity.

Finally, my mother's vehicle emerges and it's just her. No one is in the passenger seat and I'm immediately relieved. I don't have the energy to deal with my father. Just the sight of him makes my hands turn into fists.

My mother on the other hand is no different than my father but we carry our relationship on better terms. My parents are both cold and distant with me but my mother and I manage to keep in touch always.

The hangover's kicking my ass, but I won't show it. The Tylenol's starting to kick in and my headache is starting to subside.

My mother parks her car and she quickly walks towards me. She has her Tom Ford sunglasses on and is dressed in all expensive clothing. My mother's footing gives her a hard time as she walks across the yard to the porch. My parents are wealthy and yet I want nothing from them. Everything I have since I joined, I've earned from my career in the military.

"Daniel." My mother's heels stop short next to the chair next to mine as she greets me.

"Mother," I say, taking another puff of my cigarette, my eyes squinting, adjusting to the sun rays behind her.

She whips her short blonde hair back over her shoulder and takes off her sunglasses, studying me. Her blue eyes pierce through me and I give her a sarcastic smile.

"Are you not going to offer your mother one?" She says pointing to the cigarette and taking a seat. I pull another cigarette out of the pack and hand it to her. I pass her a lighter too, clenching my jaw.

We sit in silence, smoking, enjoying the cool air and gray skies.

"Daniel. When am I getting grandbabies? I'm not getting any younger. You aren't either Daniel, you're in your thirties. I'm entering my sixties you kn—"

I cut her off.

"I know, Mother. I know."

I'm cold and curt. I blow out smoke from my lungs in the

opposite direction of my mother. The smoke flows into the air, lingering. She's been pressuring me for grandkids recently and it's out of nowhere. She never pries into my personal life but lately, she's taken a particular interest in it, specifically *grandchildren.*

"I would love to see my grand babies running around in the mansion. I've already started to baby-proof parts of the house, all we need is the little ones to fill it. You're our only hope to carry the Rider name..."

"Mother, respectfully, I will not be bringing any *grand babies* into this fucked up world," I growl. I stand up aggressively throwing the cigarette to the floor, putting it out under my boot. I meant it. My military career completely changes the way I thought about procreating. My work schedule and the way my career takes the utmost priority over everything deters me from even entertaining the idea of becoming a father. It's not that I don't like kids, I just don't believe in bringing any of my own into this brutal world.

The evil that lives in this world is sickening. No one knows the extent of what I've seen besides my team and me. The stories, the horrid memories are engraved into my brain like poison. I work hard every single damn day to not let it get to me. And sometimes, it does.

Clearly, I self-medicate with my favorite addictions when I can.

Witnessing a terrorist group attack was one of the last straws for me. An evil terrorist group planted bombs and land mines on a children's playground killing and injuring babies, kids, and families. Having to carry out blown-up innocent kids from a seesaw was one of the hardest moments of my career. Holding a four-year-old on the brink of death is a haunting memory that I remember like it was yesterday. Nausea rushes into my vision as the memory hits me, and I swallow. These poor kids lost their lives from a simple routine fun day they look forward to.

I walk towards the fence I have wrapped around my porch leaning my forearms on it, sighing.

"Daniel, you haven't been the same since... since... It's been two months and I'm worried about you. Get help. Talk to someone if you won't talk to me anymore." My jaw clenches and I know what she's referring to.

"He was my best friend. No matter what I do..." I pause taking in a deep breath. The wind of the hurricane still lingers, and it feels good against my skin, watching it slither through the tall trees, making them sway across my land.

"It won't bring him back." I breathe. My mother is the only person that knows the details surrounding Paul's death. She's the only person I opened up to since it was required by my boss. I rejected the mandatory psychiatric therapy I was issued to take so, they made sure I was talking to someone about it.

"Daniel, it wasn't your fault son. And you know this. You know that. Stop torturing yourself because Paul wouldn't want this. He wouldn't want you blaming yourself for something that was out of your control."

She' doesn't get it but I won't talk about it any further. I've lost several brothers in the forces on deployments, but Paul's passing hits me harder because it was my fault. His blood spilled on my hands and just that memory alone, makes it difficult to move on.

I sigh, brushing my beard down with my hand. I need to let this guilt, fully go. I was better than I had ever been before. Two months have passed, and I've gone from constant insomnia, bar hopping, one-night stands, and drinking until I was numb to being able to sleep again without needing whiskey or random women. Last night was the first night in a while that I've divulged in my old ways because of *her*. Because of Ari. She brings a lot of emotions I've deserted and ran from and I hate her for it.

It's irrational for me to blame her for coming into my life and ripping open a healing wound. But I'm not a rational man. I need to stay away from her. I fucking hate the effect she has on me. It's detrimental to my journey of going back to my old ways before Paul passed. I like the way I am. I'm accustomed to the simplicity of my life.

Work, train, eat, drink, sleep, repeat. And Ari threatens that.

I need to stay away from her and yet... I don't want to.

And I hate that even more.

"You need to come visit us more often. Your father needs his hunting buddy again. Get him away from me for a couple of hours." She chuckles.

"You know I don't have time. And I'd rather spend my days off at home. Plus, I already do... *other* kinds of hunting." I smirk trying to hide the darkness looming in my voice. She knows I'm referring to my job. My mother's aware of what I experience but I spare her from all the gruesome, graphic details.

My mother sighs in defeat.

"Well, it's good to know your sick sense of humor is still intact."

CHAPTER 9

ARI

It's my last night of fun before I have to leave to start my job as a nurse. My travel fare is entirely paid for and a little barracks-esque room waits for me for the next six months. A few days have passed, and the town is recovering well after the impact of the hurricane. Luckily, the hurricane didn't cause too much damage in our area compared to the beach towns. Meredith has dragged us all out to the same bar on a Friday night, with our other friend Emilia and I'm not feeling up to it. Stress is overtaking my life. This is going to be my first time on a contract, and I just dove straight into the deep end of the pool choosing a military hospital in Iraq. I'm questioning myself repeatedly since then.

Why did I sign up to do this as my first experience on the job?

Then I remember, it's silly to question myself when my brothers' death is the reason for it all. I want to help men and women like him so I'm letting go of my doubt and giving it to God.

Give it to God and get wasted.

It's a short contract anyways. Only six months and then I'll return back to North Carolina. I haven't talked to Danny since his tongue was inside of me on his couch in the middle of a hurricane. He hasn't reached out and I imagine he's already across the world by now. It's been about a week since then.

Why would he reach out anyways?

He's in special operations. Men like him and my brother were literally always gone. It was like I blinked and then they weren't there anymore. My brother was never home. And if he was home it was only for a little while and then he was somewhere doing something and he couldn't tell us a thing about it. His job was so secretive, and it sucked because I would have loved to know his stories. Things that he had experienced in different countries. Now that he's dead, I don't think I'll ever get to hear them.

It's getting close to one in the morning and the girls and I are dancing the night away. I'm sweating, and I can feel my eyes getting tired. I'm definitely buzzed but I want to keep drinking.

Meredith and Emilia follow me toward the bar. The music is so loud I can barely hear myself think. Country pop music is blasting and I'm growing tired of the same songs. Emilia is the sober one out of us three and our designated driver. I had spent the entire day before, studying trauma, so I can be prepared for the first day on the job.

I'm worried about leaving my mom. This is going to be her first time without both of her children close to her… but I know she's going to be okay. She's returned to the church more routinely since my brother's passing and made new church friends. So, she has a close group of friends that can distract her from my absence.

"*Bitch*, stop being so sad, you're killing our vibe." Meredith snaps, waving over the bartender, Gabriel. She's trying to get his attention while my mouth hangs open. She has always been so blunt and has no filter.

Meredith has grown close to Gabriel due to her constant trips to El Devine over the past year.

"I'm sorry, I've just got a lot on my mind." I snap back at her, leaning on the counter of the bar. I'm so easy to read and I hate that about my face.

"I can't believe you're leaving so soon and suddenly," Emilia whines behind me as she pushes her light brown hair away from her sweaty forehead with the palm of her hand.

"I know... I'm excited though. Nervous... but excited. I've worked so hard for this moment and it's so close." I say whiffing air against my neck hoping it would ease the heat and cool me down. I'm wearing an all-black blouse and jeans with my cowboy boots on.

"Paul would be so proud of you!" Meredith shouts in my ear. The music is so loud she thinks screaming in my ear is going to help her. I palm my ears, glaring at her.

"I can hear you fine! No need to yell at me!" I shout back. Meredith breaks out in giggles and I know the alcohol has taken over her. She ignores my evil eyes, and I can tell something has captured her attention. She looks behind me, her eyes widening with a smile tugging at her pink lips.

"That's him." Meredith nods her head at Emilia, motioning behind me, down the counter.

"Just don't turn around," Meredith orders me. She leans in and continues to whisper in Emilia's ear covering her mouth to Emilia's head.

"What? Who?" I ask, looking at Meredith and then at Emilia.

"Oh my gosh you mean, Navy dude?" Emilia squeals, looking behind me, her pale cheeks blushing a rosy shade.

"Hush!" Meredith corrects her while nudging her into her ribs, with her elbow.

Shit… do they mean, who I think they mean?

My body stiffens. Panic ensues every nerve inside of me. I mouth to Meredith.

"Danny?"

Meredith nods and my heart skips a beat. I try to keep it cool and move my body slowly, turning behind me. I want to confirm it with my own eyes. I turn around slowly, rocking my head to the tune of the music, trying to be less conspicuous.

Sure enough there he is. No wonder it's so hot in here, the devil is sitting two chairs down.

There's one man in between us, an older man with gray hair who's paying no attention to his surroundings but only to his phone.

Danny's sitting down with a glass of what looks like whiskey in his hand. He's twirling the glass of alcohol in his hand, lost in thought and for the first time since seeing him last, *he's the one that looks sad this time*. Still, he looks gorgeous as ever dressed so simply. He's wearing a black sweatshirt, a baseball cap, and what looks like his dog tags under his shirt. Heat encapsulates me and rushes in between my legs. It should be a crime for Danny to look so undeniably handsome. Even his side profile causes me to lose my morals and it isn't fair.

Already turning my head, something catches my eye and I stop midway before I go back to shooting glares at Meredith. A beautiful perky blonde woman, wearing a very revealing dress that barely covers anything, sits next to Danny on the right side of him. Her beach-wavy hair jumps up and falls over her shoulders as she sits down, giving Danny a kiss on the cheek and stroking his arm, massaging him.

I knew it. He has a girlfriend. It explains why he got so weird after putting his mouth in between my legs.

I turn back around to face Meredith and Emilia. They both are analyzing what just happened and empathy is written all over their faces. They both frown and Emilia touches my shoulder, reassuring me.

"I'm fine. Honestly, it's whatever, I had a feeling something was up." I shrug. But it was a lie. It wasn't fine. This man had his teeth on my nipples just a few days ago and now he's sitting next to his girlfriend as it appears. He's a fucking slime bag. My body grows cold, the heat subsiding and vanishing as quickly as it appeared. All I wanted to do is go back to the dance floor and not let my last night with my friends go to waste.

Gabriel finally approaches us taking our requests for new drinks. Meredith orders more tequila shots and I had already taken about three sangrias before this, so I passed on ordering more drinks, settling for one of the shots.

"Alright, I gotcha ladies." Gabriel winks at Meredith.

"Gabe! I need another drink here for the lady." A deep voice roars over the music and I've come to know that voice all too well. Danny calls over to Gabriel and I watch him realize who Gabriel's talking to. At first, Danny looks shocked to see me but then his expression disappears in a flash, replaced with a wicked smirk.

Gabriel has his palms, supporting himself up with the counter, and looks over to Danny and the girl next to him.

"And what would the lady like?" Gabriel asks nonchalantly.

Danny then grins at me and that grin looks so new to me, there's something so sinful about his smile. He's never looked at me like that before and it takes me back, uncomfortably.

Was he drunk?

"A sangria." He calls over to Gabriel, his blue eyes never leaving mine and I know he did this to be spiteful.

I mouth the word, *asshole*, to him hoping he gets it through his mind I'm catching onto his antagonization. He knows that's my favorite type of drink and now he's ordering it for 'the lady'. His grin widens even more when he sees my eyes glare at him. He looks unashamed knowing I'm seeing him now with a different woman on his arm. Literally. The results prevail: he's another slimy military guy.

"You got it, Danny!" Gabe responds.

"Wait you know him personally?" Meredith asks Gabriel while tugging on his sleeve, stopping him from leaving.

"Yeah, that's Danny Rider. He's a good friend of mine. We served together. I'm out of the Navy now but we still keep in touch. There's not a thing I wouldn't do for the man. He saved my life multiple times in Afghanistan." Gabe says, his words rushing out of his mouth, hurrying to go get all of our drinks done. Gabriel whips around and starts on all the orders.

I turn towards Meredith and Emilia.

"Do you want to leave?" Emilia asks.

I hesitate. I just found out that Danny had a girlfriend this entire time and the proof was sitting two chairs down.

But most of all, why was he being so weird and rude towards me? I don't understand why he's trying to get under my skin.

Shouldn't he be apologetic and not trying to get under my skin like I did something to deserve it?

I'm sorry I ate you out on my couch while I'm taken by someone else. Would be a good start. All those lies he spewed about not being a relationship type of guy upsets me.

I would be lying if I said I didn't care and for some odd reason I did. I'm so fucking naive. I always fall in love quickly and believe every single man I meet is honest and won't hurt me. You would think I learned my lesson with Shane, but I'm a stupid girl. A stupid *'relationship' 'sheltered' girl.* I contemplate leaving and I would usually agree in this situation that it's best for me to go and just end the night on some ice cream and Parks and Recreation. But I'm trying to start over and become a new version of myself. A version of myself that stops letting others affect me so much.

"Fuck no," I reach out for the tequila shots next to me and grab one. Gabriel was fast with our order but now he's attending to Danny, both of them laughing about something I can't hear.

"Salud," I shout at Meredith and Emilia raising my glass in the air, then downing the burning liquid. Meredith and Emilia just stare at me bewildered but I don't care. I wince as it burns down my throat and I let out a sigh to catch my breath. I slam the glass down on the counter and I grab Emilia and Meredith by the hands, pulling them towards the dance floor.

"Are you sure you're, okay?" Meredith asks, studying me.

"I'm fine," I say, annoyed. Meredith and Emilia both look at each other and shrug before finally joining me and we start dancing the night away again. My vision's starting to blur and spin but I don't care. It feels good to finally let myself indulge in some drinks, let loose and get drunk with my girls and not cower away from a man that intimidates me with only his presence.

CHAPTER 10

DANNY

Another wave of guilt washes over me seeing Ari's face while Nora was all over my arm whispering sexual shit in my ear. It's officially the night before I leave on a deployment and I'm feeling eerie knowing Paul isn't going to be there and never will. We were attached to different SEAL teams. But for some odd reason, as luck would have it, we were almost always running into each other somehow while deployed. Unfortunately, that won't be happening anymore.

All I've been feeling these past couple of nights since Ari left was buried guilt and memories coming back up, I had of the night Paul passed. She brings all the anxiety and reminders of him. No matter what I did, I can't escape the faults I feel when it comes to Paul's last moments. If getting heavily hammered on whiskey helped ease the pain, then that's what I'm going to do. If Nora's willing to distract me from my horrible pain or to relieve some stress, then so be it.

Nora already knows it's never going to be anything more between us and so it's just easy. It's only sex with her. After fucking Nora a couple of nights since I've been back home from deployment, she knows I'll never commit to her, or anyone for that matter. She knows I'm not the type of man to romanticize her. Every woman I've shared intimacy with, knows I'm always busy and training, with no commitment in sight from me. But... With Ari, it's different. I can't bring myself to just fuck her. I already want more from her after I tasted how delicious she is, how sweet and pure her soul is. Her smell so intoxicating. Her perfume's so sweet, I just want her to surround me at all times. It's all I think about since she left my house, and I hate her for it. I hate *myself*.

I turn around still sitting at the bar, facing the dance floor now. My whiskey in hand, I search for Ari. She looks pissed and I can't blame her. Maybe if I antagonize her, she'll hate me as much as I hate her. Truth is, I don't fucking hate her. I hate how much I want more from her, and I can't touch her. I want to stay respectful in some sort of way since she's my dead best friend's sister.

I finally find her dancing in the middle of the dance floor, and she has a smile on her face as she laughs with her friends. Seeing the way her body moves and the way her jeans show off her perfect curves. My jeans get tighter and I clench my jaw, placing the glass of whiskey against my lips, taking a sip. She's so beautiful. I feel like I'm the luckiest man in the world just being in the same room as her.

What are the odds that we end up seeing each other again in this bar? *This is probably the last time I'll drink here.*

"Babe, why don't I relieve some of that stress, right here? Right now." Nora interrupts my thoughts, pushing her hand toward my groin, and massages over my jeans. I'm assuming she can tell how tensed up I am since I met her tonight at El Devine. I hardly make any conversation with her. She's doing all the talking and I like it like that, prefer it like that. I never am good at holding conversations but for some reason with Ari, I can't stop talking. She makes me feel like I can trust her. I look back at Nora's heavily caked-up face and hesitate. I don't want Nora. I want Ari's hand on me instead.

"Don't call me that," I mutter disgusted, licking my teeth. I hate being called any pet names.

I finish up my whiskey before setting it down on the bar counter. If I can't have Ari, I need some other way to release this tension and Nora's always ready to take care of my needs, lately. I met Nora a couple of weeks ago, in a bar of course and she understood the boundaries I have. I don't like nicknames, no kissing on the mouth, and no dates. Just sex.

"Let's go," I say, grabbing her manicured hands. I get up from my chair, trying my damn hardest to stop myself from stumbling. I went overboard tonight with Jack Daniels and I can't cut myself off, I'm feeling euphoric as the alcohol starts to alter my body and mind. I always turn to alcohol as an escape from my demons and lately, it's a new way of feeling like a new person. The evil that's inside of me has always been my normal.

I head for the exit of the bar, feeling relief I'm getting farther away from Ari. It takes all my strength not to just pull her off the dance floor, throw her over my shoulders and take her away to my house again and fuck her the way I've been imagining since I met her.

Suddenly, Nora pulls my arm hard stopping me in my tracks.

"I don't want to leave just yet babe. I meant it when I said *right here*." She starts to walk backwards, pulling me with her. A wicked smile's on her face and she bites her bottom lip, attempting to seduce me. I'm confused at first, but then I watch her guide me toward the restroom, which was unisex.

Oh well.

I smirk letting Nora pull me into the restroom that only has one stall in it. She had been texting me nonstop these past two weeks and I finally give in to blow off some steam. She locks the door and pulls down my pants and puts me in her mouth.

I feel like a piece of shit. Who am I kidding? I am a piece of shit. Because the whole time Nora has my cock in her mouth, sucking, I keep thinking of Ari. My hands go to grip Nora's hair, and I imagine Ari's mouth instead. Her sweet full soft lips and her black hair in my hands.

Hopefully, this keeps the edge off from taking Ari home tonight because I want to really show her just how much of an *asshole I really am.*

CHAPTER 11

ARI

It's nearing two in the morning now and I can't help but feel like I want the night to keep going, I want it to never end. Everything is just so simple right now in this moment, feeling the music blasting through my bones, with my closest friends. *Everything is simple.* I'm dancing right now in this bar for my enjoyment even though I can feel my bladder starting to bug me. I'm drinking way too much, and it's catching up to me.

The girls and I decide to sit at a table on the other side of the dance floor and catch our breaths after a couple of songs.

"Emilia! Have you guys picked a date yet for your wedding?" I ask while tying up my hair in a ponytail. Emilia is getting married to her college sweetheart, Harry. He graduated about a year ago and Emilia is just graduating this year. Both of them are computer science majors. He just landed a big job with a huge company, and he decided to propose soon after. He wanted to wait after he secured a well-paying job so he could gift her the wedding of her dreams.

"We did actually. Thank you for bringing that up. It's going to be a beach wedding, on one of the North Carolina beaches. And you guys are of course, my bridesmaids. What do you guys think of baby blue for the color of the bridesmaids' dresses?" She says, giddy.

"I think that's perfect. I love blue." Meredith exclaims, putting her palm on Emilia's playfully.

"Ok, but like... when is it?" I pry again.

"Sorry, it's going to be this fall. Autumn time. I love fall weddings; flowers are changing colors and scorching hot weather is leaving." Emilia says, getting excited.

"I'm so happ—"

Meredith cuts me off by tapping my hand frantically. She's looking behind me and my eyes widen. She's signaling that someone is behind me, and I don't even need to guess who it is. Emilia's smile turns into a frown as she sinks back down in her chair next to Meredith. What the fuck does Danny want?

I turn around rapidly, standing up at the same time, ready to finally blow off some steam. I'm drunk and feeling brave, I guess. My black hair whips around my face and I shout,

"What?"

To my surprise, it isn't Danny. It's *Shane*.

My heart sinks and my eyes widen with fear. Was he stalking me? First Chrome Beans and now this bar? My bravery subsides and I just feel uncomfortable now. Shane looks great but that's what enticed me in the first place, his good looks brought me in only to abuse me when I got close. He's wearing a striped button-up red shirt and jeans, his usual type of fashion hasn't changed.

"Is that any way to say hello to your first love?" Shane says as he puts his hand on his chest as if he's hurt by my tone. I scoff.

You were never my first love. The first guy to hit me, yes.

I ignore his lie of a remark.

"Umm, sorry I thought you were someone else. What are you doing here?" I rasp, panicking.

"I could ask you the same thing." Shane is eyeing me up and down now, licking his lips and I instantly cringe. I feel like he's undressing me with his eyes, and I can't help but feel like I need to run far away. My hands turn to fists and my bladder is now entirely screaming at me. I really got to go. "Well, this was fun," I say sarcastically with a fake high-pitched voice.

"But I got to go to the ladies' room now." I continue before starting to make my way toward the restrooms. I take one step before my hand is being pulled the opposite way and my fight-or-flight senses are now on high alert.

"Dance with me. Just one dance." Shane pleads and I can smell the liquor on his breath, heavily. I look at his brown eyes and shake my head with no remorse and shrug. He tightens his grip on my hands, but I pull away, finally releasing myself from him. His eyes are now darker, and I know that look very well. He never could take rejection well. His facial hair from Chrome Beans is all gone, and it looks like he's gotten a fresh haircut and shaved.

I turn on my heels, not caring about whatever he's feeling right now after I pulled away from him. He never cared about how I was feeling when he would backhand me so hard to the point, I spit out blood, and my cheeks were bruised for days. I would lie about my injuries whenever I was questioned about them by Paul and my mom.

I stumble across the dance floor, and I try to keep my balance straight so I can reach the restroom without twisting an ankle.

What the hell was Shane doing here anyways? He always told me he hated going into bars with me, but he enjoyed going to strip clubs with his friends of course. The way he keeps showing up in my life recently is starting to bother me.

I enter the restroom to find a girl reapplying eyeliner at the sink in front of the mirror, while her mascara is running down her face. After closing the tube of eyeliner, she reaches for paper towels and wets them, probably to clean up the black marks on her face. I wonder what this poor girl's crying about.

After draining my balloon of a bladder, I wash my hands looking at my reflection in the mirror, taking myself in. All of the makeup I chose to wear tonight was very natural, the only thing that stands out is the red lipstick I have on my lips that fits my olive skin tone perfectly.

I force a smile on my lips when all I want to do is curl myself up and scream from grief and frustration. I feel alone. A bar full of more than a hundred people and my closest friends and I feel alone. I'm an only child now and my mother is always hovering, not respecting my boundaries. And my father, well God knows where he's at. He abandoned us when I was still in preschool and haven't heard from him since.

I need to learn how to be a strong independent woman. As cliche, as it sounds, it's true. I don't need to depend on anyone for my happiness. I'm still going to be successful and happy even though the two most important men in my life were no longer here to cheer me on. And then Danny comes into the picture sending me more down a rabbit hole and I don't know how I'm going to forget the way he made me feel that night. I fell for him. I feel hypnotized by his scent, the way he touched me, the way he makes me feel so alive and seen.

I'm so naive, crap, I'm in trouble.

He's older, more experienced, and he's capable of playing me so well.

I shake my head, snapping myself out of these sinful thoughts. He makes me want to indulge in these human desires, but my religion and insecurities keep me from doing so. I scold myself.

I take a deep breath, and I finally decide with myself internally that it's time to go home. My emotions are getting to me. I grab the handle of the restroom door and swing it open and my eyes collide with Danny. His hands and gaze are attentive to securing his belt back into place in his jeans. Then he goes to his zipper and closes it. I can't move. That's what Danny does to me. In this moment, watching him, *I can't move.* My eyes are glued to his hands and deep down inside, I wish those hands were on me instead. We're alone for a good five seconds and he finally locks eyes with me, and he freezes as well. He's exiting the unisex restroom but he's not alone.

Behind him is *the lady* and it looks like she's wiping something off her lips. Danny looks different, his ball cap isn't on anymore and he looks more relaxed.

"God, you taste so good." She says giggling in his ear, tiptoeing to reach his face, while grasping his biceps, she licks her lips, as she eyes me viciously unwelcoming. She doesn't care I just heard her lustful comments. It doesn't take long for me to put two and two together to know what just happened in that restroom and I grimace.

Gross.

I roll my eyes at them before walking away. Danny looks stunned seeing me just a few feet from him.

"Ari," Danny calls out after me but I don't stop walking. I'm disgusted with myself for being so vulnerable around him. I spilled out my emotions. Secrets of my abusive past relationship and the grief I hold for my brother. He's not the same guy I kissed that night. The guy just got sucked off in a restroom.

I start to pick up my pace, walking through the crowd, bumping into body after body, apologizing as I hit them. Seeing the man I fell for at first sight, after he just got sucked off, sobers me up entirely. I'm extremely astonished to witness that and all I can feel is shock and utter disbelief. I really don't know Danny. I don't what I've gotten myself into. I've wrapped myself into a stranger.

I'm doing my best to get to the girls fast so I can tell them I'm ready to go. I want to force the image of Danny and *his lady* out of my mind.

Suddenly, I feel my wrist getting pulled behind me, painfully, stopping me from walking any further. I gasp and let out a cry as I'm being dragged upwards into someone.

Shane.

"Shane what the fuck. Let me go!" I shout at him, pushing his chest with my other arm, wincing in pain. What has gotten into him? He's never hit or hurt me in public, it was always discreetly. We're in the middle of a crowd full of people that are distracted with music, dancing around us and nobody takes notice that I'm being harassed. His touch reminds me of the constant dread I felt during our relationship. *I want to fly. I want to run.*

"Just one dance Ari. I bet you miss my hands on you..." he leans into my ear, as I'm still trying to wiggle my hand out, "My hands on your ass and tits, Ari-cakes. Don't you miss that? I sure do." He whispers into my ear sending shivers down my spine. He grabs my ass with his other hand so tight and squeezes. The pain from my flesh getting pinched so hard, I just know an impending bruise will reflect as evidence in the morning. It hurts and now I'm angry. My free hand turns into a fist, tears stinging my eyes and I feel helpless. I know Paul would want me to be strong and I'm about to punch him in his jaw but someone beats me to it.

Suddenly, the next thing I know, Shane's on the ground. My hand and ass are free.

"What the fuck man?" Shane shouts, rubbing his cheekbone but he's quickly cut off by another punch.

Danny towers over him and his movements are fast. I can't even register what's happening but I'm being forced to. Danny grabs Shane by his collar and repeatedly punches him, pummeling him until I see blood on his knuckles. Commotion beaks out and I don't know what to do. A circle of attention gathers around us and I can't move. I'm paralyzed with fear.

Danny's date starts shouting at Danny to stop and I just watch.

I don't want him to get into trouble, I don't know why but I still care about Danny's reputation. I know if this goes down in Shane's favor and he gets arrested, his career is over. I imagine the military has zero tolerance when it comes to stuff like this. That's why Paul never paid any attention to Shane's antics when he provoked him in the past. He wanted to make sure

Shane threw the first punch so Paul could at least say it was justified with self-defense but Shane being the coward he is, never did.

Finally, I decide to act. My heart beats outside of my chest and the adrenaline starts to kick in. I start pulling on Danny's shoulder, gently trying to get him to stop punching Shane. By the looks of it, Danny's going to kill him in front of hundreds of witnesses. His rage is blinding him and I'm hoping I can stop him before it's too late.

He looks back at me as soon as I squeeze his shoulder, fury in his eyes and they soften as he stares back at me, realizing it's me. A tear falls out of my right eye and I quickly wipe it away. Somehow, it works and Danny lets Shane go.

"What the fuck is going on here?" Gabriel, the bartender, breaks through the crowd pushing them away with his forearms, to get through. He looks frantic and worried but when he spots Danny, he relaxes a little.

Shane's still on the ground now covering his face, frightened. Danny's breathing hard, staring Shane down, probably hoping he would get back up so he can keep beating him. He ignores Gabriel's question and I'm paralyzed by this side of Danny I've never seen. If looks could kill, Shane would be lifeless.

"If you touch her again, I'll crush every fucking bone in your hands *and I'll kill you*. Don't ever come close to her again Mitchell. I know all about you." Danny snarls, threatening him, his tone of voice is laced with ominous wrath, and it scares me yet it sends a wave of butterflies through my chest seeing him so protective over *me*. Gabriel stares at Danny and Shane trying to assess the situation and he comes to a quick judgment.

"Guys, get him out of here," Gabriel orders pointing to Shane.

Two big muscular Bouncers behind Gabriel peer over his shoulder and haul Shane off the dance floor. Shane's covering his face so I can't get a good look at him but I see that his shirt is stained with drops of blood. The fucker finally got what he deserved. Maybe he'll think twice before putting his hands on me or any other woman again without their consent.

I start to wonder how Danny knows Shane's last name. How does he know *all about him?*

Meredith and Emilia appear now and grab a hold of my hands, comforting me on both sides.

"What happened?" Emilia asks me, moving her hands up and down my arms. I shake my head not wanting to talk about it in the moment because I'm too distracted watching Danny. I need to talk to him.

"Oh, baby! Come here!" Danny's date squeals rushing to him, and grabbing his arm but Danny ignores her, and he keeps his gaze on me while flexing his fist open and closed.

"Can we talk?" Danny pleads, his blue eyes softening, and I melt at his question. I quickly nod and swallow. The crowd of people slowly go back to their night of fun and keep dancing, since the music never stopped playing.

"Danny but... what about us?" His date asks annoyed, she looks at me with disgust and jealousy.

"I got to take care of her, Nora. You can either wait for me or get yourself home safe." Danny mutters. Her mouth hangs open, and he's not giving her any attention but instead, walks towards me leaving her standing alone.

"You're choosing *her* over *me?*"

He looks at her and without hesitation, he nods.

"That's not even a question. *It'll never be a question.*" Nora flinches before he finishes, "but the answer is, yes."

"Asshole!" She shouts before stomping off. A part of me feels bad but I could use his protection. I don't know if Shane would be waiting outside for me. He could try attacking me again and I wouldn't put it past him.

"Are you okay?" Danny towers over me, grabbing my hand and leading me toward the bar. I wave off Emilia and Meredith who look extremely worried and I know I'm going to owe them a well-deserved explanation. They both watch me leave and I'm grateful for their understanding and privacy.

"Yeah, I'm fine. I could've handled that myself. Paul has taught me a thing or two about self-defense." I say sitting down on a barstool next to Danny. Normally I have pepper spray tucked into my purse, but I didn't have my purse on me.

I pull out my phone from my pocket sending Meredith a text letting her know that Shane grabbed my ass while I was trying to get back to them after my restroom break.

What is my fucking life right now?

Can't I just have one normal night before starting the job of my dreams?

"I don't doubt it. But I think he deserved to get his fucking shit kicked in for grabbing my cherry like that." Danny says, looking at me with no emotion except pure anger. He still looks extremely pissed off, so I tread my words carefully. Seeing him so infuriated, giving Shane the beating of his life, makes me feel a bit afraid of him. Like I'm watching beast fuming.

Wait, *cherry?*

What does he mean by that?

"Your what?" I ask dumbfounded, I stop texting and look up from my phone screen.

Danny smirks and puts his ball cap back on.

"You're my cherry." He licks his lips. It takes me a while to figure out what he means. I'm squinting while staring at him and it hits me like a ton of bricks.

My virginity.

"Really?" I say sarcastically, a smile tugging at my lips. Danny chuckles and I can't help but feel relief knowing I have someone right here in Paul's place to be protective over my safety even if he just disgusted me not too long ago.

"Plus, I think I overestimated how fucking great it feels."

Danny pauses and I quirk a brow waiting for him to continue.

"To be the person that makes sure he doesn't touch you again.

I know Paul never had the pleasure and I surely wouldn't hesitate to do it again." He smiles.

My heart skips a beat and I feel warmth heating my bones, hearing those words. He's an asshole one minute and the next, he's... Danny. He's being protective over me and I appreciate it. I appreciate the safety net he provides when he's around me. Suddenly our eyes lock, butterflies flying all around again and I feel like we're on his couch in the middle of a hurricane again. The way he looks at me is the same way he looked at me when we were kissing. It's a look of desire. A desire that's almost feral and it sends me into fog. I struggle to remain conscious when he looks at me like this so… I interrupt our intense moment.

"Again… you didn't have to do that. I'm sure you have enough on your plate, Danny. With your job and stuff. You don't have to protect me. I won't be another worry of yours…"

"But you are."

My heart thrashes.

"I'm sorry?"

He clears his throat snapping himself out of whatever thoughts were anchoring him down. It's like he caught himself in a vulnerable moment and quickly changed his demeanor when he realized it.

"What I mean is that you're Paul's little sister. I'll always protect you, whether you like it or not. You're an Alvarez, which means you'll always have me."

I'm weak.

"I'm always going to be here for you, Ari." He says it like it's a promise and I'm hesitant to believe him.

"I appreciate that."

I'm trying so hard to hide my smile. He makes me feel like I'm worthy of more. It feels weird. I haven't felt so respected by a man before. Shane was only nice to me when he wanted something from me… and then he would get abusive when I refused.

"I feel bad for your girlfriend though. You could have taken her home." I try changing the subject hoping it lightens his mood but I don't think it was the right choice of topic with the way his body stiffens.

"He's not pressing charges. You kicked his ass pretty well. I thought you were going to kill the dude. He's not allowed here again anyways." Gabriel huffs out, interrupting, giving Danny another glass of whiskey. Danny is already permanently stained with the smell of whiskey and cigarettes but that doesn't stop him. It's nearing closing time and he still keeps drinking. He takes it gliding it down his throat with ease, his Adam's apple bobbing as he swallows.

"For your hand." Gabriel throws a bag full of ice at him.

"Don't need it. I'm fine." Danny scoffs, dropping down his glass, he gulped down already. I study his right hand, his knuckles are red and swollen. My eyes widen and I can't help but let my nursing education take over.

"Just take it, it's just for the swelling. Don't be stubborn." I order grabbing the bag of ice and forcing it on his knuckles. Grabbing his hand sends a shock in between my thighs, throbbing and I have to internally yell at my body to shut up. I hold his hand for a couple of seconds, not daring to look at the sinful man next to me.

"Your hands are soft." Danny flashes me a soft smile before leaning forward into my ear and I stop breathing. "Just like your lips and I'm not talking about the ones on your face."

My eyes circling, I let go of the bag of ice and gently push him away. "Shut up, you're drunk."

He barely moves before twirling the glass again with his fingers. Looking at how his skin crinkles around his blue eyes as he smiles. It makes me think about how many times I've been around this town, and I've never bumped into him and now I feel like he's everywhere. Maybe before, he was just another guy blending in with a crowd of strangers and I never took notice of him, and I don't know how when he's so sinfully, handsome.

The bar's closing now and my knees start to bounce with anxiety. Emilia is my designated driver, and I'm getting impatient texts
from them, and I know I have to say goodbye. I don't want to
leave but I have to. Nothing is going to escalate further anyways.

"Listen... I've got to go. My friends are waiting on me. I appreciate you taking care of Shane for me... Are you going to be able
to get home safely?" Danny's smile fades as he looks at me.

"Of course, Cherry. But I'm going to stay after closing time
with Gabriel. I'll walk you out. I want to make sure that piece of
shit isn't out there." Danny looks away from me, clenches his jaw,
and then takes another swallow of whiskey and stands up.

He's so tall compared to me, then again everyone is taller than
me. Generally, he is just a mass of a man with all those muscles
but not too much. His muscles are proportionate and match his
height perfectly.

Meredith and Emilia are already waiting in the car for me
with my belongings in a black sedan. The bar is just about empty
leaving Danny and I as the only customers. The employees of the
bar began to clean, and they are locking everything down. The
music has stopped and the only sounds I can hear are small talk
and sounds of cleaning. Danny opens the door and looks around
the parking lot, casually. I follow him and stay behind him as I
wait for him to call me over. He nods for me to come forward,
waving his hand to me.

I spot Emilia's car as soon as I exit, passing Danny. She's
parked her car in front of the bar, with the trunk facing the
entrance to the bar.

Danny lights up a cigarette and blows out the smoke in the
other direction so it doesn't get near me.

"Thanks. I appreciate you walking me out." I wave my hand
awkwardly. Danny studies me for a second then he puts his
cigarette in his mouth again and takes in another hit, blowing
it out.

"She's not my girlfriend."

It takes a second for me to comprehend what he means. Oh... the girl that sucked him off in the restroom, *got it.*

"It doesn't matter. It's none of my business." Shaking my head, I bite my lip nervously.

"I know but it's important to me that you know one thing about me. I'm not a liar, Ari. I won't hesitate to tell anyone the truth even if it's brutal, even if they don't want to hear it." He licks his lips. "I'm leaving for deployment tomorrow night. This was such a fun way to end my short vacation at home."

My eyebrows raise and my heart sinks a little. I'm leaving too anyways, and I can't help but wonder if he will be in the same place as me. I hadn't told him my big news of working for a military hospital in Iraq as a civilian. It wasn't such a casual topic of conversation.

"Where to?" I pry.

"Can't disclose that, Cherry. You know better. I'm sure Paul didn't tell you either where he was being sent." Danny smirks.

"Of course. Anyways... I guess this is goodbye?" I question, feeling heat rise to my face hoping a deep color of red doesn't reflect on my cheeks.

"No."

"What?" I ask confused. My eyebrows furrowed inward. "Why?" I continue.

"Because I know for a fact, it's not a goodbye. It's a see you soon." Danny says and he looks at me expressionless, so serious, it feels like he's staring into my soul with no emotion as usual making it hard for me to read him.

I swallow.

"See you soon then," I say walking backward towards Emilia's car with a smile.

Danny looks at me while holding his cigarette in between his lips, taking another hit as he studies me, hard. He blows the smoke up into the air and it lingers towards the sky.

"See you soon, Cherry."

Three Months Later

CHAPTER 12

DANNY

A full moon is glowing high in the sky giving us all some light to the darkness that swallows my team and me. It's the first mission of the deployment and it has me on edge. I love the thrill of being in a black hawk as it transports us. Every time I get in a helicopter with my team it feels like the first time. Tonight gives me an eerie feeling, I know too well. We are tasked with rescuing two captured soldiers taken hostage by a terrorist group. Rooker, Kane, and I with a new guy named Lopez travel carefully as we near our target area on foot now, the air ominous. The reaper breathing down my neck, as always, trying hard to get into my head.

Tonight is the night.

The words sound condescending and mimicking. I shake my head.

Fuck off.

Our night vision goggles strapped onto my head tight allowing me to see better. We silently get comfortable in a woodsy area near the village that the terrorists have called home for the past few days. Tall trees and bushes offer us concealment to settle in and attain surveillance. We're on a hill that surrounds the village giving us the perfect position on our targets. The middle of the night provides a darkness that gives us an advantage.

"Fuck man, what I would do for some tamales right now and not this MRE shit," Lopez complains while settling underneath a tree. Lopez is our communications guy. He relays any messages or alerts out to higher-up personnel while we work.

"Texas, I swear, if you start talking about food again, I'm shutting off your radio." I snarl.

We all have operator names we use on the mic when addressing each other. We don't want to risk the enemy getting a hold of our real identities. Lopez is Texas. He was born and raised there, and he chose that for himself.

Mine's Grim Reaper. I have the most successful missions on the team, along with the highest kill count in the military so everyone branded me with it. I didn't give it to myself.

Rooker is Cobra since it's his favorite snake species and when he strikes, he's fast.

I look at the stars and I can't help it, but I can feel myself getting distracted. What I would do for whiskey and a cigarette… and a Cherry.

Every time I get stressed, I think about whiskey. Whiskey makes life better. Then my mind saunters to El Devine and how it's been my favorite place to be recently. There isn't a day that goes by I'm not thinking about my cherry... my sweet Ari. Her taste has me addicted but I know this isn't a line I should cross... I can't cross. I can't take her without feeling like a piece of shit. She's already clouding my mind and I can't imagine how I will be if I capture her. Her smell and her touch are already altering my mind. The aftermath of Whiskey can't even compare to the effects she has on me. What she could do to me is ruthless. What I could do to her *is worse.*

"Grim!" Rooker snaps me out of my thoughts, his voice painfully loud in my ear. The earbuds vibrate with his voice. We use these tiny things to communicate with each other.

"Shit, Cobra! What?" I snarl quietly.

"There's movement in that building. You see that open window. Fuckers left it open." Rooker breathes.

"I see it," I confirm as I turn my position underneath a tree that has a brush surrounding the bottom.

"You sure you're okay man?" Rooker doubts me in my ears. He's not concerned about my well-being. He's getting suspicious of my behavior and I don't blame him. He can tell something is different about me and he's right. Rooker is the dad of the team because of his parental behavior around us. He's also a dad to two daughters and husband to his wife, Noel. Even though he's the oldest of the group, I'm still the one in charge of the team.

In a midsize window, there's a room with a light left on, on the second floor of the building. It's our small window to confirm the identities of the hostages. Our intel has led us up to this point so we have to confirm if the hostages were really in this location. Then breach and rescue. If only the process was that simple.

I grab my binoculars and study the room. The room is absolutely plain. Nothing inside of it but concrete walls and floors. Sitting in the middle is a man and a woman sitting strapped to a chair with a cloth over their heads. Their hands are tied behind their back, and they have OCP pants on, and camo shirts with their dog tags hanging over their neck. It looks like they're the hostages we've been looking for, but we need confirmation of their identity.

"It looks like it's them, boys. Intel didn't fail us this time. Bane, can you get a closer look at those dog tags? See if their names match up right." I order Kane while still looking in the room. Bane is Kane's operator name. Bane means cause of great distress. Kane has promising skills and I've taught him a lot since he joined my team. Subsequently, it rhymes with his actual name.

Dog tags are required to wear while deployed. Information like the person's name, blood type, and religion are on it. Our hostages are one female and one male belonging to the army. The female is a medic and the male is an infantryman. Their Humvees were blown up a few days ago and they were kidnapped from the crash site. The other soldiers in the Humvee died on impact when the crash occurred.

"Yup already doing it Grim."

By the looks of it, they've been already interrogated pretty well. Their uniforms are torn in some areas, dirty, and drops of blood on their shirts. Their arms look bruised, and the male has a mark going around his neck as if he had been strangled by a rope.

Fucking vicious psychopaths.

I clench my jaw. This is why I signed up to be in the Navy. I always had an overwhelming urge to protect people from evil. And this... This was just a taste of the pure evil I've seen in my career. I became a Navy SEAL at eighteen. I'm thirty-three now and rest assured, I've seen a lot of sinister shit that war can bring.

"Yup, it's them. Violet Redd and Damon Hawk. And they look beat to shit. We got to get them out of there." Kane says.

We already have a plan to extract them. We're going to wait until they're most vulnerable, hoping they just give us one moment, one minute of vulnerability and we're going to take it. All of us have our snipers ready in case of an emergency but Rooker and I are going to take the lead and physically breach the building along with a team of Green Berets. There are no more than five terrorists in there doing dirty work which we confirmed with research surveillance.

"Alright, you guys know the plan. Texas and Bane, you guys stay put. You're our Overwatch. Cobra and I are going to start making our way down there. Bane, give us the green light to breach. It's gonna be a fun night boys."

"Hooyah sir." The boys whispered into their mics, simultaneously.

Rooker and I begin to descend the hill cautiously and quietly as we can. Rooker's going to breach, and I'll be the first man in the room. We aren't the only ones on this specific mission tonight, conducting the rescue of the hostages. We have green berets surrounding us as well, ready to step in. Of course, we can't see them, but they're there.

"When the fuck are you going to settle down already?" Rooker breathes into the mic, grunting as we both get hit by branches. We're trying so hard not to give away our positions. A simple twist of our ankles on rocks we can't see and we'll be tumbling down, alerting the villagers.

I chuckle.

"Look Grandpa, just be grateful you got to marry the woman of your dreams while the rest of us aren't so lucky." I scoff, quietly.

"So, *there is someone?* And what's stopping you?" Rooker tries me again and I'm getting annoyed. One, I don't like talking about these kinds of things with anyone. Two, I can never reveal what I've already done with Ari.

"Yes, *there is* someone actually," I reply with a smirk.

"I already told you, my mom's taken."

"You should be so lucky. But no. Let's just say she's loyal, mouthwatering and I can never get enough."

We're getting closer now, just a few more steps and we're out in the open, breaching the building, executing.

"Oh? What's the poor girl's name?"

"Jack Daniels. Now shut the fuck up, we're here."

Rooker and I slide out of the bushes, walking fast toward one wall of the building. Rooker starts setting up to breach, creating a bomb. A cloud that was covering the moon, finally moves, shining on his face. It's crazy how different we look with our uniforms on. We have face paint all over and we're covered head to toe with equipment. I don't recognize Rooker. The weight of my rifle is on one side of my body as I hold it close, ready to use.

"Shit, Grim there's movement. They've untied Redd from the chair and it looks like they're taking her downstairs, one of the men is holding a machete to her throat as she walks. Hawk is still strapped to the chair..." Kane shouts in my ear. A few seconds pass by before he continues, "I no longer have visuals on the girl. I can see they've taken her downstairs but that's it. I think they're going to start doing their worst on her." He rasps.

"Almost done here," Rooker mutters as he assembles the breaching device on the wall. My adrenaline courses through my veins and my thoughts are now scrambling. Suddenly, I smell Ari's scent. Her sweet perfume is all I can think about at this moment, and it distracts me from the inevitable intensity that's about to follow. We're about to get into a gunfight. Someone's going to lose. Then I feel the reaper's cold breath return on my neck and I grin wickedly.

I'll be sending a couple of men your way tonight. Don't worry.

A woman screams from inside and we know it's Redd. Rooker and I's bodies stiffen as we look at each other and we both know; it might be too late. The screaming stops and the breach has been set. We back away at a distance yet still close to the wall so we can enter immediately. This is going to sting, to say the least. One of my ears blew out one time a couple of years ago. I was standing too close to the breaching device when it went off, my ears bled, and I couldn't hear anything for a week.

The breaching device goes off and we enter the building at a calculated speed. Rubble flies everywhere, smoke fills the air, and it looks like luck is on our side tonight. We breached into the wall of a living area space that's been turned into some sort of torture room. Two of the terrorists are taken back by the explosion and they're sprawled out on the floor, holding onto their ears in agony.

There's a variety of different blades hanging onto a wall, like decoration, along with guns and glass buckets full with dismembered body parts. My anger is raging inside of me, and I want to burn this whole fucking village down.

Redd is laying down on a table in a fetal position, a cloth still covering her head. She's screaming, crying, and shaking uncontrollably. There's a saw in the corner, making noise and I swallow. They were going to start sawing off her limbs. Rooker and I raise our rifles and swiftly put a bullet in each of the men's heads, neutralizing the threats faster than the speed of light.

Redd is barefoot, still in her OCP pants and camo top. Her hands are tied together by a rope that has dried blood below her wrists. I quickly move towards her, grabbing the cloth off her head and I cringe, internally.

Her whole face is bruised and broken. Her eyes are swollen and black she's only able to open one eye. Her nose appears to be broken as well. Her lips are cut open and she's crying.

"Violet Redd?" I approach her, still holding onto my rifle.

She nods frantically, sobbing.

"You're safe now. Can you walk?" I ask sternly. My voice cut and dry, we have to move fast and get them both to safety.

Again, she nods. Her reddish, cinnamon hair is tied up in a pony and she's wincing in pain.

"Let's go."

I would carry the poor girl, but I can't risk all of our safety by doing that. I have to keep my rifle in my hand and watch Rooker's six and hers, in case more threats catch us off guard.

"Call in the green berets. We've got Redd, she's going to need assistance immediately. We still have to get Damon Hawk. Do you have eyes on him?" I call out to Kane. I'm guiding Redd toward the hole we just blasted through the wall. Rooker watches her get closer and a team of seven green berets enter through the entrance we created. Another special operator carries her off her feet and she's crying into his shoulder. I'm feeling accomplished in this rapid moment looking at her be whisked away to safety but then I feel my adrenaline pulling at me because I know the job is unfinished.

"Fuck! Grim, they've moved Hawk away from the room. They're taking him downstairs. I don't have eyes on him anymore. You might get contact from them." Kane urgently informs me. I turn around immediately and so does Rooker. He also hears Kane's voice in his ear.

Green Berets surround the torture room and we're all pointing our rifles at the only door to the room. Rooker and I are the closest ones to the front of the door and I can feel something is wrong. There's no movement, no sounds of footsteps. I thought Kane said they were coming downstairs.

Suddenly, a grenade is thrown at the entrance of the door. Rooker and I quickly move away, turning our backs toward the impact.

"Grenade!" Rooker shouts and everyone is scrambling to get the fuck out of here. We're able to get to a good distance away but then we feel it. The explosion from the grenade shakes us in our bones. Rooker, the green berets, and I are able to survive the devastating impact, smoke everywhere but my God, it fucking hurts.

One green beret shouts as chaos starts to ensue.

"We're taking fire!" He shouts.

Bullets are coming through the floor, straight at us. *From underneath the ground.* Spraying everywhere.

What the fuck?

We had to abort the rescue mission. The area became too hot and we lost our sights on Damon Hawk. Monsters had hand-built a tunnel underneath the building and we were taking fire from underground as well as our surroundings outside the building. There was no way to finish the mission and it infuriated me to my core. Fire burning inside of me and I was about to boil over. My thoughts swirl around Damon and it stings knowing that he's going to keep getting tortured. We had to leave a soldier behind when we were so close.

I'm breathing heavily as my head rests back to the wall of the cabin. Everyone's quiet and the morale low, knowing the job was left unfinished. Every man in the cabin tense as we sit in the dark cabin of the Chinook going back to base. I run my hands through my beard.

I need a fucking cigarette.

We're all high in the sky and all I want to do is force the pilot to take me back to the village so I can reap more souls to hell.

"Danny... you're hit, man. Don't you feel it?" Kane asks me as he looks at my shoulder, toward my back. His voice is full of worry and I'm trying to feel any pain signaling to my brain where the injury is… but nothing.

"Where?"

"It looks like there's a hole through your shoulder from when the grenade went off. You must have gotten hit with shrapnel. You're bleeding through your uniform bro, all over."

If I'm hit that bad, I know the higher-ups are going to make me stand down until I can fully recover. Meaning I can't finish the mission with my team until I'm healed.

"Fuck."

CHAPTER 13

ARI

"Ari, did you get the I.V. set up in room 3?" Doctor Diaz asks behind one of the nurses' desks in the Emergency Room of the Army Hospital. I'm three months in and I've learned so much. I've saved and helped so many of our military men and women and I feel like I'm destined to do this for the rest of my life.

"Oh, no sorry, I was just finishing giving medications to the patient in room nine. I'll do that right now doctor." Dr. Diaz half smiles at me before looking back down at his clipboard, writing.

Tonight is extremely busy. A training exercise went wrong and we have a lot of military men from all branches coming in with horrible injuries.

I grab the IV supplies before heading into the room. I grab the patient's chart and get information before I step in. The doors in the ER to each room are glass see-through doors. I stand there in front of them reading the doctor's directions. Then I look up to see the patient's last name on the top right of the paper and it looks familiar.

Mitchell, S.

"Ari Cakes? Is that you?"

Shane. His voice makes me freeze.

My heart drops and my legs almost go weak underneath me. My abusive ex-boyfriend is here. *What did I do to be God's least favorite human?* I look up from the chart and I feel like I can't breathe for a second. Hatred pours into my heart, and I take in a deep breath before I walk over next to him.

I try not to make eye contact and keep it professional as I always do with other patients. As if he wasn't someone I deeply cared about once. As if I didn't don't know him personally. Like he's somebody I used to know.

"Mr. Mitchell, I'll be administering your I.V." My voice is monotone.

After I finish doing the IV, I'll be asking one of my co-workers to switch with me. There's no way I'll spend one more minute next to Shane.

I ignore his presence to my right as I set up the IV supplies. Afterward, I grab the room computer and plug in my notes.

"You know I've never stopped loving you. I'm sorry about the night at El Devine. I just can't help myself when I'm around you." I bite down hard on my jaw, my breathing more rapid now.

Just focus on your work, don't let him get to you.

"How the fuck do you know Rider, by the way? Is he your boyfriend now?" My heart flutters when I hear Danny's name.

"My relationship status in general, is of no concern to you." I snap.

Shane laughs.

"God Damn, you look good in scrubs."

He doesn't get a reaction out of me even though I feel his eyes burning into me, in my peripheral vision. I continue typing away.

I sigh and close my notes. I finish up and walk over efficiently and grab his arm gently to clean an area on his arm with alcohol, preparing the needle to pierce. Shane came in with a horrible injury to his left arm. His arm is badly bruised and cut open. He's being evaluated for broken bones. Blood seeps through his bandages and he's going to need them replaced as soon as possible. I make a mental note for my coworker that will be taking over for me.

I set up the IV and then quickly tape it to his arm. All the meanwhile, Shane looks at me, his eyes never leaving my face.

"Sorry to hear about Paul. I never got to tell you... *what a shame.*" Shane says with sarcasm. He hits a nerve inside of me and I'm heated with wrath. I finally give him the attention he wants. My head turns towards him so fast, hair from my ponytail hits my cheek on the other side. I'm glaring at him. This jerk is smiling while saying Paul's name. I quickly feel the rage inside of me. The fact that he mentions my brother's name has me boiling. His smile is wicked. He always hated my brother.

"Don't ever say Paul's name again," I whisper angrily at him. Shane tilts his head to the side forcing a sarcastic frown, mocking me. I scoot the chair I'm sitting on away from him, the chair makes a loud squeak from pushing so hard on it. I grab the leftover empty packaging from the IV supplies and dispose of it.

"Big brother can't protect you now. He can't come between us anymore..." Shane calls over my head.

He's fucking delusional.

Still, I ignore him, with my back turned and I head towards the doors. The asshole is happy my brother died. I feel tears sting my eyes and they start flowing down, hard out of anger. I truly just want to run away and go back home. But my home's just a little room now, in the barracks that the military provided for me.

"Hey, Ari, what's wrong?" I'm in the hallway walking back to the nurses' desk when one of my coworkers stops me. She stops me with her hands on both of my arms, consoling me.

I sniffle and rub my hand on my nose to prevent any snot from coming out caused by ugly crying.

"The patient in room 3 is just giving me a hard time, can you take over for me, please, Lori? He needs new bandages by the way." I beg as the tears keep flowing.

"Of course, anything you need." She sounds concerned. She rubs my arm gently. She's one of the nicer coworkers I have. Any other person I work with would just tell me to suck it up in this kind of situation.

"Just take over for me in Room 5. I was just in there, but I needed to get supplies for him. It's a bad open wound on his back, he's going to need stitches."

"You got it. I'm just going to get myself cleaned up first and then head in." She nods and I head straight for the restroom. It doesn't take me long to find it and I lock the door behind me. I look in the mirror and I'm horrified by my reflection. A bit of my mascara is rubbed off. My eyes and cheeks are red. I grab the tissues in the restroom and clean myself up, trying my best to remove the black mascara smudges under my eyes.

I can't believe Shane's here. He's on deployment which means he might be here for a while.

I grip the sink with both of my hands and look at myself before going back out. I still look like I've been crying but it'll do for now. I look at the ceiling still gripping the sink, leaning on it. I want to cry again as the stress is just too much for me sometimes. I take in a deep breath.

I wonder what Paul would say to me at this moment. He would definitely encourage me and I can hear my brother's voice in my head as if he's right here next to me. I look at my reflection and I picture him behind me talking to me through the mirror. I imagine him in his uniform, and I swear I can see him. His brown hair is carefully brushed to the side as it always used to be and the dimples on his cheeks are vividly present in the mirror.

"Don't let that asshole get to you. My little sister's a badass. Stay strong, you've got this. Make me proud."

I smile and the ghost of him disappears. I take another deep breath in and walk outside after turning the restroom light off. I head straight for the stitching supplies I need to give to the patient in room 9. I grab my chart, in my other hand, and I read the patient's name, before going in as I always do. I always get nervous when I have to do stitches, I shrug my shoulders and sigh but then my heart skips a beat when I see the Devil's name.

Rider, D.

I gasp.

CHAPTER 14

ARI

Rider, D?

As in *Rider, Daniel?*

I look up from my chart to see his beautiful body on the bed, his hands on his phone, typing aggressively. At first, he's hard to recognize. His face is covered in camouflage paint. A skull mask that resembles the Grim Reaper, on his face. Shades of black, green, and brown all over, disguising his features. A mini panic attack unfolds in my chest.

It's him, *I know it's him* because of the the swirl of fire that's in my chest.

Just looking at him right now reminds me of the time I saw him at El Devine.

I quickly look back at my chart, then look down the busy hallway that's full of nurses and doctors walking around, in a panic motion trying to think of *another* co-worker that would take over Danny for me. A mixture of feelings hit me hard. There's no one I know besides Lori that could take over.

I'm excited to see him but scared at the same time. I bite my lip trying to decide what to do. All I want to do is run away. I start to rock on one of the heels of my foot, fidgeting. I don't think

I've fully recovered from Danny's rejection during the hurricane. I just can't take any more embarrassment.

Still looking down the hallway with the supplies and chart in my hand, is when his deep, enticing voice rings in my ears interrupting my panic attack.

"Ari? Is that you?" Danny's voice is full of shock.

Shit.

I turn towards him, putting on an act, as if I didn't just find out he's my new patient.

I look at him and he stares back at me, his eyebrows narrow and his eyes are full of curiosity, burning through me. As if he can't believe he's seeing me through the glass doors. Those beautiful blue eyes look like they're glowing against his face paint.

I half smile, letting out a deep breath.

"Ummm... hi..." I chirp. I try so hard to defy human anatomy and refrain from blushing.

I walk into the room slowly, after sliding the glass doors open. Danny has his shirt off, smudges of dirt, and soot from smoke, all over his body, and his muscular abs on display. His skin has been kissed deeply by the sun and he looks more tan the last time I saw him. He looks tired and beaten. I feel a sting of worry in my chest and I really want to know what just happened to him.

But then I remember, I don't want to be that girl anymore. The girl that wears her heart on her sleeve. The girl that always cares more than the other person. I'm always sweet to undeserving people. I swallow the question that I so desperately want to ask.

What happened to you? How are you feeling? Can I do anything? *Can I kiss you?*

"So you're a nurse for the military? You *work here?*" He asks as I walk over to his back assessing the wound. His question comes off rude and full of anger. He sits up, taking off his skull mask but I don't answer right away. I have to focus on my job. I get closer to him bringing a stool over to the bed. I sit on it as I begin to prepare to clean his wound out.

It's right above his eerie Grim Reaper tattoo.

"Yes," I whisper my voice rigid.

His dark blonde hair's a bit longer and messy. I bite my lip, hard. *Why did he have to be so attractive?*

His wound looks like a deep gash tearing through his back and all I see is ripped skin covered in an open deep crimson pool. It looks like something sliced him open from an explosion. It must have been caused by a grenade. I've seen wounds like this before, a lot in just a short amount of time working here. He has to be in so much pain. Soldiers I've treated in the past like this, usually tremble and beg me for numbing pain medication.

"Did they already give you some medication for the pain?" I ask, professionally.

"No. I don't want it nor need it." He says, his tone bothersome.

"Well you might want it now for when I stitch you up, I have something to numb the area."

"Ari,"

The way he says my name… makes those damn butterflies in my heart and stomach storm around. I hate that this man, whom I barely know, makes me feel this way.

"It's unnecessary, skip the *damn* numbing injections and just stitch me up fast and good so I can get back out there. My team needs me." He says sternly, slightly raising his voice at me.

Well, *excuse me.* Is he really ordering me around right now?

"Mr. Rider, don't argue with me. I will do my best to be fast and precise but if you're not cleared to go back out, you won't be going back to your team. You will not be discharged from this hospital, pending the results of your other tests. Now, I'm going to start with the injections."

Danny stiffens at my threatening choice of words. He grows quiet and his tense shoulders relax. We both sit in awkward silence. I don't want to talk to him. Plus, I just don't know what to say. And I think the feeling's mutual.

I inject him with the numbing solution, the needle pierces through, and to my surprise, he doesn't flinch, doesn't jerk his body, not a grunt from the pain, nothing. Definitely not something I'm used to from my experiences with other soldiers, sailors, airmen, etc.

I begin stitching him up. The numbing injections are strong so he can't feel any pain. I'm focusing really hard to not mess this up. This isn't my first time doing stitches but I'm not fully confident in myself yet and I still feel new to these kinds of procedures. Sweat begins to break out on my forehead and I rub it away with my wrist.

"Ari, what are you doing here?" I'm quickly taken aback by Danny's question. He sounds annoyed and condescending. I stop stitching him when I hear his voice, then I continue.

"What are you talking about?" I ask, trying to keep my composure. Trying to hide the sharpness in my voice, I keep my voice low and unbothered. What did I do to deserve his hostility toward me?

"What are you doing here? It's *dangerous* here. You're not back home in our country. We're in a warzone right now that doesn't get talked about and you're here… getting a front-seat view of the horror that lives hidden. The things you're going to see, the evil that… " He stops, shaking his head, "you shouldn't be here, have them transfer you to another military hospital, stateside," he snaps at the end. Just when I think he's concerned about my safety, he closes his sentence with rage.

Who the heck does he think he is?

I'm quiet as I try my best to focus on stitching and I don't respond right away. I shake my head and scoff. I digest his words. About a minute passes by and I take a break from stitching his wound. I let my hands rest in the air, ensuring everything stays sterile.

"Danny. Stop it. You don't get to order me around like that. You don't have a say so in my life," A sarcastic laugh exits my mouth and I suck in a breath before continuing. I shake my head, "I'm not yours to command." I blush with instant regret.

Danny licks his lips.

"For now." Danny looks to the side so he can get a peripheral view of me. I'm still behind him, on a stool. And I see him grin devilishly, flashing his straight white teeth.

My eyes widen and I feel like they're bulging out of my skull. I instantly blush, in complete utter shock. My mouth hangs open just a little as my heart quickens and tightens with heat. Before I can say something smart back and scold him, the glass doors open.

"Rider, good and bad news." Doctor Diaz walks in. A Navy Hispanic veteran, he's on the shorter side and yet he's fit for someone in his fifties. He looks around his late thirties with short black peppered hair.

My teeth close shut, my lips press together tight against each other and I return to work. I'm already almost done and the wound's closing perfectly.

"Good news is I'm discharging you. The bad news is, you're going to have to take it slow and rest for at least one week. I cannot release you back to your team because of the concussion you sustained and I want to make sure that you're one hundred percent before I send you back out. So one week of bed rest and we'll continue to monitor you over the next couple of weeks. Depending on how your check-ups go then I will re-evaluate your case and clear you when I see fit. You could be here on post for up to a month so prepare for that." Doctor Diaz orders, looking at Danny's reaction, already preparing for an argument to unfold.

"A week of bed rest? Possibly a month out of work? Sir, respectfully, that's too long. I'm fine. Really." Danny's deep voice pleads and at the same time, it feels like he's ordering Doctor Diaz.

"Trust me. I'm being generous. I would like to send you back home with the TBI you sustained. But I want to get you back to your team sooner. It's just one week of bed rest and then we'll see how you're healing." Doctor Diaz studies Danny's face.

"One week is too long. I'm on an important mission right now. My team needs me, *now*. Not later." Danny argues.

"You SEALS really don't like being told no, huh?" Doctor Diaz jokes before continuing but Danny cuts him off.

"Nope. We'll keep fighting until we get what we want..." Danny tells him, his voice lowers, and I swear he looks at me when he finishes his sentence. I can't get a good look to confirm it since I'm on the last stitch and I can't get distracted now.

"Still. One week on post. Rest up. No working out. No training. Just rest." Doctor Diaz says as he crosses his legs while standing, leaning against the wall.

"I truly respect that about you SEALS. Always pushing your bodies until your body has to tell you no, even then y'all will push even farther... anyways, Ari here will discharge you. If there's anything you need, just come back, we're always here." Doctor Diaz says with tired eyes.

The glass doors open and I peak a glance before focusing my attention back on stitching.

"Admiral Ravenmore, to what do I owe the pleasure?" Doctor Diaz says with respect laced in his tone as he stands up straight efficiently fast.

An Admiral? What's an admiral doing here? They're high ranking officers.

"To check up on one the Navy's most important assets. With all due respect Doctor, I need him to be cleared."

He heard all of that?

Doctor Diaz clears his throat nervously.

"I'm sorry, Admiral Ravenmore, I really am, but I have a job to do too. I would be doing Danny a disservice if I cleared him right now, most importantly I'd be doing *his team a disservice.*"

Admiral Ravenmore's eyebrows rise in defeat, the crinkles under his green eyes crease even more with disappointment.

"I'm fine." Danny growls.

"Doctor Diaz with all due respect, Grim needs to be released, can I please talk to you in private?" Admiral Ravenmore orders him and Doctor Diaz nods with a smile.

Doctor Diaz follows Admiral Ravenmore and walks out closing the door behind him, just as I finish cleaning Danny's back. His body was already covered in scars. And he just added another one on top of the tattoos he has on his back.

I get up from my stool and Danny leans back against the hospital bed, rubbing his beard, I can feel him looking at me as I walk in front of him to leave.

He grabs my hand, rough. And it reminds me of the time we were in his house when I wanted to leave the first time. His touch sends sparks all around my body. *This man is trouble.*

I turn around to look at him. I'm confused by the sudden pull, pissed off even. I try to let my hand free but he just holds onto me tighter.

"Let go."

"I meant what I said, you need to transfer. You're not supposed to be here. This isn't your thing, little Angel. Working in this trauma hospital is too much for you to bear. It's too dangerous."

I finally free my hand from his grasp. I can't believe he thinks he has authority over my career choices. He thinks so little of me and I resent it.

"Why not?" I challenge.

"You're naive. Too sheltered."

I can feel the anger inside of me taking over my emotions. How the hell was Paul good friends with this man? It takes everything in me to control myself. I have to stay professional. I can't let him win. I will not lose my shit over him even though it's warranted. Then he really will get what he wants.

He wants me away from him.

"Danny... I'm not as naive as you think I am."

"From what you told me, I think you are. What kind of girl has to have her older brother come to her rescue? What kind of girl falls for a piece of shit like Shane?"

I'm quiet. I'm growing furious. I'm in shock and it shows on my tongue. His words have me in a chokehold.

"A naive one." He finishes.

"Screw. You." I glare at him, harder.

He laughs. *He laughs.*

"Isn't that a sin, Ari? To *screw* me?" He licks his lips, antagonizing me further. "Plus I'm not your type, I don't hit women like your ex."

Wow. He went there.

I hate him so much at this moment, my emotions taking over me and all I want to do is cry. Cry because he's making me regret opening up to him. *I am naive.* He's right but I will never admit that.

A sharpness hits my eyes. My eyes begin to water. I feel so angry but most of all hurt. I don't know why. And I don't know how. But for some reason, I feel like I need to seek his approval. *I crave it.*

Another piece of the old me chips off. I swallow hard and give him a fake small smile, as one tear leaves my eye. Danny looks back at me and he's unapologetic. Right before I turn my head to leave, I can see that he's reading me so easily. He got to me and he knows it.

CHAPTER 15

ARI

A couple of weeks have passed since running into Shane and Danny at the hospital and I have never felt so stressed out in my life. It's Sunday, which means my first day off in two weeks. And I couldn't enjoy it. I'm standing in my bathroom in front of the mirror, and I do finish touches on my makeup. It's around seven at night and I already wanted to crawl into bed and cry myself to sleep. I had a picture of Paul and me as kids sitting on a shelf I installed on the wall behind me, his smile reflecting back at me through the mirror.

It's a picture of us wearing matching outfits, photographed at one of those studios you find at the mall. Paul had his arm over my shoulder, wrapping it around me, protectively. We both looked so happy. I closed my eyeshadow palette, and a loud click follows.

A signature wing on the edge of my eyes as always. My day-to-day makeup look consisted of a light nude pink shade on my lips, a winged liner, and a natural foundation, with pink blush. Paul always teased me about my makeup. He always used to say that girls shouldn't use makeup because they didn't need it. He believed all women were naturally beautiful.

I stand up and grab my picture frame. I lightly trace my finger on the photo. I miss my big brother so much it hurts. It would've been so cool for me to have been here in Iraq while he was here, both of us following our dreams.

A knock on my door disrupts my thoughts. I place the picture frame back on the shelf and walk fast toward the door, prepared to greet my friend.

"You ready?" Lori's cheerful voice asked me after opening the door. We made plans to go to the USO to see a movie. They're showing The Proposal and it's one of my favorite movies. Although I wish they were showing a horror movie. There isn't much to do for fun around here but a movie at the USO sounds like a vacation.

"Are you sure you don't wanna just watch Netflix and just relax in my room?" I plead already second-guessing my choice to be social on my day off. I'm so tired. I'm completely drained mentally and physically. From seeing gruesome injuries on a daily basis in the emergency room to being worried about the words of the two men that plagued my mind. Both in very different ways. Danny's words were harsh but Shane's were laced with evil.

"I'm sure. As much as you don't want to go out right, we need it. For our mental health. Plus, I hear we get to see Ryan Reynolds's abs on a big screen." Lori gives me a wink before dragging me outside of my room. I turn around and lock my door before we leave.

When we get to the USO, there are lots of chairs lined up into five organized, even rows facing a projector that has the movie playing. We're a couple of minutes late into the movie but hadn't missed much of it.

I look around and it's packed with military men and women of all branches, quietly munching on popcorn and snacks.

"Go find us a seat, I'll get us popcorn and drinks," I whisper into Lori's ear. I look around to find the popcorn machine and drinks stand. There's a woman in front of me grabbing popcorn so I wait my turn.

I grab a medium-sized brown paper bag and fill it in with popcorn. As soon as I finish, I grab two water bottles next to the popcorn machine just to turn around into what felt like a wall. A familiar wall. My side bangs fly into my eyes, my entire hair flips with the collision. I've bumped into someone's chest. It causes a shiver down my spine fueled by anger.

Shane. Not again.

What was he doing so close behind me that with a slight turn of my body, my nose landed on his chest? I quickly back away, keeping my balance and I manage to keep the popcorn and water bottles in my hands. I narrow my eyebrows.

"You're still clumsy I see." He belittles me.

I glare at him, my eyes filling with rage and he smirks in return. His left arm is in a cast. So, he did break his arm after all. With his right hand, he pushes my hair out of my face.

"Don't." I hiss.

He quickly drops his hand, and tilts his head to the side mockingly, with a frown.

"Or what?" He's eager to get me more riled up.

Shane drops closer to my level, near my ears so no one else could hear him but me. My chest tightens and I feel like I can't move. I'm having flashbacks of abuse. I flinch, my eyes shut tight. I'm afraid he's going to hit me like he used to do when we were together. Whenever I denied his touch, he would get sent into a rage. I tighten my grip around the popcorn and water bottles. My whole body stiffens. Then I remember, we're not at the park, his favorite place to abuse me… and we aren't *together*.

"It's not like you'll do anything about it, Ari Cakes. I will always own you. I will always want you. Paul ain't here anymore." His breath on my neck.

I clench my jaw. All I want to do is punch him in front of

everybody. Showing him that I'm not that defenseless girl anymore. I've changed. I will defend myself if I have to.

I make the best decision to protect myself from the drama he so badly wants me to get wrapped in. I walk away, tense. As soon as I see Lori waving me over Shane's shoulder, her cheerful face instantly relaxes me.

I didn't expect to see Shane here. I forgot, now that he's injured he'll probably be around this post more often and that makes me nervous. This will probably be the last time I'll be at the USO.

"What's wrong?" Lori asked me as I sat down next to her. She reads me so well, as always. Her green eyes scan my body language. The movie's playing but her attention is on me. She's changed into a concerned friend. She looks back over my shoulder towards the popcorn stand and her mouth makes an o shape. She gasps. I've already told her everything about Shane. I told her every detail I went through with him after meeting him again as his nurse.

"Yeah. He's here. And now I think I just want to leave."

CHAPTER 16

DANNY

I lie in my bed tossing and turning. I hated not being with my team. This gaping wound was just a fucking scratch and now I'm getting benched for a while. Still, the doctor believes I wouldn't be able to keep up with the antibiotics if I went back out there. He says it's to prevent infection and I hate to admit it but he was right. I probably wouldn't take my medication or be on top of cleansing the deep gash on my back. On top of it, the TBI was the cherry on top of my injuries. I hated these protocols. I'm healed already and I can't go against the rules or it would be the end of my career.

It's two in the morning and all I can think about is my team, our next mission, and *Ari*.

This is a first for me. A fucking girl added to my list of worries. I've been a selfish asshole all my life. An unfamiliar feeling slithers through my chest and I hate it. I resent *her* for it. When Paul made us all promise him to watch over his mother and sister if he died, I feel the guilt wash over me like a big ocean wave crashing into my soul.

I hadn't kept my promise and I was always a man of my word. The other guys kept tabs on them but I hadn't. I stayed away, I've never wanted to worry about anyone but myself. Running into her at the bar, taking her to my house, all I wanted to do was fill her up with my cock. As I got to know her, I knew she wasn't going to be easy to forget. She's not going to be like these other girls I fuck and move on, with nothing attached. But then finding out she's Paul's sister, everything changed.

I knew the minute I met her, a pure innocence was attached to her and I couldn't help but feel like I have to taste it. Everything about her intrigues me. The way she smiles, the way she laughs, the way she smells, it's like a sweet perfume. *And her short frame.*

Paul and Ari look nothing alike. Paul was tall. Almost as tall as me. He had brown hair and was fair-skinned, his nose had a strong bridge. Ari is olive-skinned. She has long black hair with honey-brown eyes that almost look hazel. She's short and has beautiful full cheeks I want to bite. Full soft lips that I've pictured grabbing with my teeth. Heat and blood rush to my core at the thought of me, *breaking her.*

I don't know how it happened but I felt like I had to immediately take care of her, watch over her. I never knew how to express my feelings and I'm not about to start now. I had been so cold to her at the hospital but I couldn't help it. I don't want her to be here. I don't want her to see what happens when there's a war going on. I don't want her so close to me when I'm working. My selfishness pushes through and now I have to worry about her.

I was in complete shock to see her that night in the emergency room. I knew she was a nurse but not in a million years would I have imagined that we would reunite on a fucking deployment. In Iraq. In a Warzone.

I run my hand through my beard sitting on the edge of the side of my bed. Rereading the harsh text messages from Kane, one of the men on my team. He was also close friends with Paul. He was filling me in on everything that was going on at the moment and I felt anxious to just try and escape this place.

Against the doctor's orders. But that would land me in a massive amount of trouble and I didn't want to risk losing my job.

I'm in my boxers, sweat on my forehead and chest. Fuck, it's so hot in this place. It's two in the morning and I want to find Ari.

Maybe I can keep convincing her to leave this place. Leave this Warzone and go back home, far away from this type of evil. I was going to be here for a while on post and I feel like I need to see her again before I leave back to my team. Who knows when I would return back to post? My work schedule is always all over the place. I need to fight against this overwhelming attraction toward her. To fight against this drowning need to be watching over her.

I need to protect her though, we're on a battlefield and she needs to open her naive little eyes and go back home. I don't want her to see what I've seen. I want to shield her from it.

Fuck, what the hell is going on with me?

I made a promise to Paul. Maybe it didn't matter to me back then but it wouldn't hurt to start now and keep my promise. Unfortunately, I know somewhere behind the rational parts of my head, it's not just the promise that sucks me in. It's the sinister side of me that wants to indulge in my dark desires and *take her*.

CHAPTER 17

ARI

Working in a military hospital for the past couple of months has taught me many things.

One, my skills in wound care and stitching have improved tremendously.

Two, I'm surprised at the number of men that are afraid of needles and faint just at the sight of one.

It's always so funny to see a grown masculine man grow pale when they see a needle.

And, it's not funny when they fall on you, *crushing all your bones*.

The cold air of the hospital causes me to always wear sleeves. I can't work comfortably without them. I shiver too much. I love the cold but how I hate it when I'm at work.

I haven't seen Shane in a while, and I thank the heavens for that. He keeps popping up in my life and I've noticed his behavior has become more and more erratic. I'm growing more afraid of him.

I'm replacing sheets in one of the empty rooms of the Emergency Room and Lori's helping me. We have grown closer and closer as the time goes by. She's been a nurse far longer than I have and she's been a mentor for me. I'm leaving Iraq before her and returning to North Carolina. I've already started applying to places and I'm hoping to get the job where Lori works when she's stateside.

Shockingly, we both call home, Bloomings. We both come from the same town. We've already made plans to hang out when we're back.

"I can't wait until I get to see my girlfriend again. She's planning to take us on a vacation to Hawaii." Lori says cheerfully.

"Aww, that's so romantic, how long have you guys been together?" I ask, tucking in the freshly dried bed sheets.

"We've been together for two years and never been happier."

I was starting to miss the simplicity of falling in love. The attraction I feel for Danny was immediate. I had never felt so safe and comfortable with a man that intimidated me so much. Yet, he changed his persona so fast on me. One moment he was sweet and the next he was treating me like an inconvenience. I didn't understand him and the degrading treatment when he was ordering me to get transferred away from here… or *away from him.*

Screw him and his dashing blue eyes. And his stupid perfect smile. And dumb muscles that make me forget how to act normal. Screw him… yeah… *screw him.*

Wait, what am I thinking?

I mentally kick myself out of those ideas. I can't *screw him.* Stupid, Ari. Either way, it won't work. He won't order me away from here. No one will ever get a say so in my life decisions.

"Do you have any vacation plans when you return home?"

I shrug.

"I'm supposed to go to this Author's event in Bloomings but I've been on the waitlist. My brother paid for our tickets before he died. I don't think I'll ever get the chance. Everything lately… has been so uncertain. That's amazing you're going to Hawaii, though. My love life is absolute trash." I scoff.

"I'm sorry that you've been getting shitty men thrown at you.

You're such a sweetheart and you should never settle."

"Thanks, girl," I murmur softly.

"Oh no. Who is it? Who is he?" Lori stands up, putting both hands on her hips.

I instantly flush red at the thought of the hot and cold, asshole, Navy SEAL. How every muscle was so well structured and the way he looked like he could just devour me entirely had my lungs drowning in anxiety.

"No one!" I shriek and Lori smirks. I'm blushing hard and I can't hide my smile. I daydream about Danny's tongue every night and I hate myself for it.

"Doctor Diaz?" She wiggles her eyebrows up and down.

"No! I'm pretty sure he could pass for my dad."

"Oh, so you're already thinking of him as your daddy." My mouth drops open and I'm breathless.

"You're something else." I laugh, shaking my head.

"Speak of the devil." Lori mouths to me.

I turn around and Doctor Diaz pokes his head into the room. He eyes us both suspiciously. His brown tired eyes meet us both and he's squinting. His white coat sways as he leans forward.

"How are my favorite nurses doing?" He quirks a brow.

"We're great!" Lori and I both chirp simultaneously. My gaze trails off to the side, trying to remain as calm as possible.

Doctor Diaz steps into the room and walks closer to us. My breath hitches nervously.

Oh gosh. I hope he didn't hear any of that.

"Ari. I've got to say I'm so proud of how far you've come since you first started here. There's no doubt in my mind your brother is smiling ear to ear in heaven proud of his baby sister." He puts his hands behind his back and smiles.

"Thank you, Doctor." My nervousness subsides and is replaced by warmth. When you work so hard it feels so good to be acknowledged by your bosses.

He starts to walk away and before he disappears, he turns

around.

"Oh yeah, there's a patient requesting you."

My heart sinks at the thought of Shane.

"Oh?"

"Yeah. He's in room three, waiting."

Lori looks at me her eyes widening. She's thinking it's Shane too.

I clear my throat.

"What's his name, if you don't mind me asking?"

Doctor Diaz looks at the device he always carries around when he treats his patients. He scrolls for a minute and then looks up at me.

"Daniel Rider."

My eyebrows furrow and I frown in annoyance.

Why the hell was he requesting me? Wasn't he just trying to order me far away as possible from here?

I knew he would be making multiple trips to the hospital for treatment before he would have to back to his team. But what I didn't anticipate was him requesting me for his care. I know the protocol. I have to clear him myself followed by Doctor Diaz, and then he could return to his team.

"Yes. Yes, sir, I'll be right there."

I stand outside the room, trying to recollect myself. I watch Danny through the glass doors and he's in a black sweater with jeans. His hands brush through his beard while sitting on the hospital bed, reading a book. I'm hesitant and upset that he requested me, yet the heat I feel in between my thighs betrays me.

I take a deep breath and open the door, walking inside with new bandages and antibiotics ready to administer.

I clear my throat.

"Mr. Rider, I'll be checking your wounds and evaluating your TBI symptoms. I'll try and make this fast as possible." I try to sound professional to hide my frustration. I refuse to make eye contact with him so I stare at the supplies in my hands.

He looks up at me and I feel the attraction I feel for him, pulling my vision toward his gorgeous face. He bites down, his jaw bending as he meets my gaze. I try to remain as expressionless as I can but once he stands up and towers over me I internally want to scream.

"Umm?" I mumble.

"Just say you want me shirtless, Ari. I thought you pride yourself on your honesty like a good little Angel?" He grabs my cross necklace, holds it in between his fingers, and smirks. Finally, he lets it drop back on my neck.

My eyebrows furrow and my mouth pops open and I want to run away. My heart starts to race, and I feel so hot I feel like I need to fan myself. *He would use my religion against me.*

"Danny." I hiss.

He looks down at me as my eyes are upward, glaring fire at him. I bite my lip and a small hum escapes his throat. His lips curve into satisfaction and I freeze at his gorgeous half-smile. The noise that comes out of him sends me into a daze.

His finger tucks underneath his sweater and he pulls it off over his head smoothly, before sitting back down on the hospital bed. He has his back towards me and a grim reaper is staring back at me. The tattoo artist deserves an award for all the work they've done on Danny's body. It's so realistic it sends spooky vibes through me when I stare at it. Like at any moment, the art will come alive. That's how detailed the tattoo is, it gives me the creeps.

I start applying an anti-septic solution and we sit in silence. It's not that I don't want to talk, it's that I can't. Every time I'm close to him, I'm afraid I'll say the wrong things. I try to stay focused and not let this beautiful God-like man, distract me. He smells so damn good. His cologne fills my nose and I close my thighs tighter.

"I see you're still working here."

I roll my eyes.

"Yup and not going anywhere." I snap.

"Life out here isn't sunshine, rainbows, and butterflies."

I sigh.

"Yeah, I can see that. As long as you're here it'll be anything but that." I murmur. "All done. Now I just got to evaluate your TBI." I back away from him and retreat to the other side of the room as if I had just escaped a shark circling me.

I take off my gloves and turn around to face Danny's chest. He invades my personal space and I suck in a breath, holding it.

"Clear me."

"What?" I rasp.

"Tell Doctor Diaz, I'm ready to get back to my team." He demands.

I scoff.

"It doesn't work like that." I shake my head. I hate the way he thinks he can order me around. I try to move around him but he follows, trapping me with his body.

Suddenly, his finger's below my chin, and tips it upwards so I'm looking at him.

His face is full of seriousness and smugness, just like the time he was antagonizing me at El Devine with Nora.

"The way you act so disoriented around me I think it's you that needs to get evaluated for a TBI." He says, his tone harsh, deep, and cold.

He pulls his hand away from me, watching me.

I can feel my heart pounding so hard against my chest that I'm afraid he can hear it.

I glare at him.

"You *are* my TBI."

He smirks sinfully, his body bends forward and his lips are at my ear.

Why is he teasing me like this? He knows the effects he has on me and he's enjoying every second of getting me flustered.

"Cherry, if I'm your TBI... imagine how harsh of a villain I'd be in your story if things escalated more that night."

I push him away from my ear while sending blades fueled by hatred his way. He pulls away from me and smiles, devilishly, standing tall.

"I think you should get someone else to take over for you. I don't think you have what it takes to work here."

I bite my lip. I know which night he's talking about very well. Something takes over me when I see that his eyes are fixated on my mouth.

"You aren't a villain, Danny. An asshole, maybe. But I know there's more. You think you know me. You think I won't survive you, but I guess we'll never know will we?" He flinches at my response. I'm daring him. I'm surprising myself at this point. His beautiful eyes darken.

I'm taunting him... and he knows it.

He growls and reaches for the curtains behind me. I still as I watch him throw them to the side, giving us privacy from the see-through doors.

Oh, gosh, what did I just do?

Then he pushes me against the wall of the hospital room with his body and I'm instantly feeling like I'm floating with arousal. Anyone can barge in at any moment, and the thought of us getting caught only makes this more dangerously exciting.

I look up at him as his hand reaches my throat, and he gives it a gentle squeeze.

"You're playing games with the Devil, little Angel. Are you sure you want to go to Hell?"

Then, he crashes his lips against mine while leaning against the wall behind me with his hand. We're moving with such desperation I know this is going to be bad.

He's so bad.

I want him. When I'm near him, I feel like I'm going to hell and I'd be okay with that.

When his tongue slips through my mouth, my heart begins to pound and I see golden sparkles. A moan escapes me when I find his other hand pulls me towards his groin and I feel it. I feel *him.* He pushes his hard bulge against the front of my waist and I'm begging for more.

I reach for his pants. I'm eager and flushed. I don't care if I'm a virgin. All my morals and feminism leave my body willingly. If my first time is in a hospital room, so be it.

His lips brush harder, his tongue moves deeper inside of me. *God, I've missed his tongue.* One of his hands sneaks underneath my scrub top, his skin on my skin, reaching for my bra. His familiar calloused palms slither underneath it and he squeezes my breast, hard. I moan into his mouth and he smiles against my lips. I reach for his waistband but then, he pulls away from me, grabbing my hands gently, stopping me. His rough hands grip me tightly, and he places them on my sides. He groans as he stops himself.

He's confusing me and it's driving my insecurities through the roof.

He's still shirtless, an hourglass tattooed on his chest with a skull at the bottom and mysterious words, meet my eyes. His lips leave my mouth and we're breathing heavily.

"I want you," I murmur softly, against his lips.

He looks at me and he looks like he's holding a whole world back from me. Something ruinous in the way his gaze pierces through me. He releases his grip from my neck and instead brushes his fingers against my bottom lip.

"You don't know what you're asking for Ari."

Silence envelopes the room. The thrill of getting lost in Danny anchors to the floor and I'm at a loss for words.

"This is the last time I'll ever touch you." He whispers, walking away from me.

CHAPTER 18

DANNY

Of course, I passed Ari's little evaluation of the TBI with flying colors. It's so satisfying how easily I get under her skin. Her body was begging me to take her in that hospital room. She wanted me to but I held myself back. I won't show her how villainous I truly am and can be. She doesn't get it. I need to protect her. Even if it means, protecting her *from myself*. The fucked up side of me.

I'm just surprised at how stubborn my naive little Cherry can be. I can't force her to go back home, but I'll keep trying. She shouldn't be here. I'll be leaving soon and I can't watch over her and that kills me.

Doctor Diaz cleared me and now I'm waiting for the paperwork to go through. My team carried on without me and everything went wrong on the mission I was benched out of. My phone blew up with notifications and I knew it wasn't good.

They went in without me and shit went haywire. They failed to rescue the other hostage, Damon Hawk. Kane filled me in that Rooker was hurt badly and they were med-evacuating him back to the hospital where I was.

I should have been there.

My hands turn into fists tightly, on my lap, from the anxiety and anger I'm holding onto. I'm in a small waiting room at the hospital, waiting for an update on Rooker. Kane sits beside me and he's just on edge as I am. Lopez took off to get rest.

Rooker is one of the guys I'm closest to on the team, besides Kane. He's the oldest on the team, at the age of thirty-seven and still kicking ass. He's the wise one. When we aren't working, we go drinking, hunting, and fishing together. We all had a brotherly relationship with each other and the respect was unwavering.

Rooker has two twin daughters back at home and a wife. Their faces are in the back of my mind and it hurt me to tell his wife, that something happened to him.

If anything happened to Rooker, he made me promise that I would be the one to make that phone call to his family. Mainly because his wife knows me well. Whenever I was around Noel, it consisted of barbecues at his house or mine. His wife is a sweetheart. A bleeding heart that's always weary for her husband. Rooker made it clear that he'd be more comfortable with it coming from me rather than some random guy that sits at a desk that doesn't know Rooker personally.

She answered on the first two rings. It was around afternoon time for her when I called. We were a couple of hours ahead of her when she received the call.

Noel answered, her voice rushed. I could hear her trembling; she knows a phone call from me while Rooker's on a deployment was never good. I told her that Rooker was in the hospital getting emergency surgery and we wouldn't know if his condition is stable or not.

She screamed and cried, and I winced at the sounds she made over the phone. The sound of someone's heart breaking completely into a million pieces. No one ever wants that phone call. And it almost broke me.

I reassured her his life, but I made sure to tell her everything was touch and go. I turned on my phone not sure of what to do. I wanted to keep myself distracted, something to keep me from barging into that surgery room demanding an update.

It's already the next day for us. It's around four in the morning and I'm wide awake with fury. I'm angry with the protocols that kept me behind. I start to fidget with my phone going through the photo album. I need a distraction. I scroll all the way to the top and I stop on a photo of Kane, Paul, Rooker, and me together.

We're all fishing on Kane's boat in Florida. Paul had caught the biggest Red Drum we'd ever seen. He was holding it up proudly, smiling big. All of us had our Oakley sunglasses on, dressed in shorts and fishing shirts.

I laugh.

I remembered this day like yesterday. I didn't catch shit that day. Paul and Kane were reeling in all the fish and Rooker and I struggled.

"Um... excuse me, Chief Petty Officer Rider?" I was still looking at my phone when that familiar sweet voice interrupts my memory. I smile.

I stand up, looking down at Ari. She's still in a scrub cap and she looks so fucking cute.

"Ari... don't do that." My smile disappears. It comes out sounding like an order. I hadn't meant it to but it's just a habit at this point. I didn't appreciate her calling me by my rank. We know each other and I feel as if she's trying to hide that fact. I didn't expect her to be working but there she is, standing in front of me, cheeks flushed, sweat underneath her surgery cap, and licking her lips.

How I would love to feel that tongue on my lips again.

"Sorry... He's awake now. Bullet through his chest. It didn't hit any major organs and he's very lucky for that. The surgeon was able to dislodge the bullet, taking it out completely from his chest and stopping the bleeding. He's in a lot of pain but he's alive."

A ton of weight lifts from my shoulders. I don't have to make that phone call. Noel can sleep better tonight knowing that.

"Can we see him?" I ask, putting my hands in my all-black sweatpants. I'm in civilian clothing. Wearing a black plain shirt and my favorite pair of vans.

Ari nods and she motions me to follow her. She looks at me then at Kane. Her eyes widen.

"Kane? Mr. Slaughter?" Ari questions, eyes full of familiarity.

"Ari Alvarez, would you look at that, you did become a nurse after all." Kane smiles at her giving her a high five.

"Yes, I did. I've been working here for a while now." She motions her hands around her head, insinuating the hospital.

She returns the smile as she leads the way into the room Rooker is in. I look at Kane with curiosity brewing hard and fast inside of me. We stay back and keep our distance from Ari as we followed her. Kane gives me a shrug. Camo paint all over his face. His black hair is a mess and he's still in uniform.

Asshole never mentioned Ari to me before. A small amount of fire in my heart sparks inside of me. It's a foreign feeling and I'm unsure of how to handle it.

"I kept my promise to Paul, you know that." He says firmly. He's referring to the promise that Paul made us all do, to keep tabs on his girls. His sister and mother. I'm the only selfish asshole that didn't follow through.

"You've been checking in on Ari since Paul died?" I ask, keeping my voice down. A part of me is angry that Kane has a more personal relationship than I thought, with Ari.

Kane nods.

We follow Ari into the ER hallways, towards ICU. The place is packed full of nurses and doctors. It's a busy night. Meanwhile, I'm trying so hard not to make my gaze obvious. I'm watching Ari's ass as she walks and I'm imagining all the things I would do to her ass if she let me. The thoughts swirl into my head and I can feel blood rushing down.

As soon as we enter Rooker's room, my headspace clears, and I feel relief seeing Rooker awake and smiling. It's a forced, *I'm in so much fucking pain*, smile. Nonetheless, a smile.

"Damn, you look like shit," I say with a sarcastic grin. I take a seat next to him in an armchair by his bed. He's hooked up to so many machines. The room's small with a sofa against the other side of the room with a small television in the corner of the room, right under the ceiling.

"Ehh, I've seen him look worse, and this ain't it," Kane adds, chuckling.

Rooker winces, raising his hand up just high enough off the bed, and gives us both the middle finger.

"Nice to see you idiots too." He says looking at me and then at Kane. Ari stands by the door with the biggest smile on her face. I can tell she's proud of herself, looking at us three interact. As she should. She helped save Rooker's life. I'll forever be grateful to her for that. I can feel a slight pull at my darkened heart as she smiles and I grimace at the feeling.

I need some fucking whiskey.

I can't concentrate or keep my thoughts straight around her. Every time I see her, I think about those nights before my deployment and the hospital room.

Now she stands before me *again* and all I want to do is show her what I would have done to her that night before I found out she's Paul's sister. I would have fucked her all night long until she forgot her own name. Make her come over and over again, *painfully*.

Out of respect for Paul, I couldn't go through with it. I couldn't do it. Because my intentions weren't good. Because I want to completely *destroy her*. Break her in ways that she'll learn to love. *And never call again.*

"My shift has ended guys but before I go, do you guys need

anything? Rooker?" Ari tiptoes and rocks on her heel as the question rolls off her tongue. Looking at all of us, eager to help.

"No thanks darling, just please keep the morphine coming." Rooker murmurs.

"We're good," I bite my cheek, trying to ignore her. I clench my jaw, while I keep my eyes focused on Rookers' vitals monitor. It's like the more I try to avoid her the more she appears. I don't know how much more I can take before I give in to the lust inside of me that so badly wants to make her mine. Yet deep down, she already is. She just doesn't know it.

"Actually, Ari, can I ask you a question?" Kane admits, walking closer to her. My eyebrows raise up. Oh, I know that tone of voice. *I know that tone of voice all too well.* We've experienced too many adventures in bars together, for me to recognize what he's about to do. He's going to pull something on her.

Kane leans on the wall with his arm on a whiteboard. Ari seems confused at first and I can't hear them anymore. I keep my vision on Rookers' monitor. Their voices sound muffled and I try to control my seething. I don't like this. I don't like it at all.

Fuck, I need to burn one.

Ari walks away from Kane closing the door shut, softly after her. Their interaction was short but long enough to piss me off. Kane comes back walking towards the other couch, a chip on his shoulder, and he drops his body weight, crossing one of his legs over his knee facing us.

"You did not just hit on a nurse. You know she's Alvarez's sister," Rooker mutters weakly, trying to get himself more comfortable on the hospital bed without pulling on his IV.

"Stay out of it Rooker," Kane orders, getting irritated.

"You know if Paul was here, he would kick your ass for just laying your eyes on her like that." I'm harsh and vindictive. I already feel territorial around Ari and I know this isn't good. I look down at my fingers, popping them one by one before glaring at Kane.

"It's none of your guys' business." Kane snaps. Narrowing his eyes at me, studying my face.

"It actually is. It's all of our business. *We all* made a promise to Paul. To watch over her, not hit on her." I challenge back, through gritted teeth. I'm spitting bullshit when I know damn well, I've already crossed lines to discover Ari's mouthwatering taste.

"Actually, we didn't promise that last part." He argues. "A promise that you didn't own up to. Why start now Danny?" He continues to question me like he already knows his own answer. Wrapping his hands together, intertwining them on his lap.

My heart quickens as I feel the rage building up inside of me. Although I know it's not just rage, it's something more. Kane and I both stare each other down.

"You never worry about anyone else but your damn self. Isn't that why Paul died, huh? Because of a stupid selfish mistake that got Paul killed?"

I feel like someone grabbed a hammer and hit me in the stomach with it. His words cut me deep, the demons from Paul's death come back in full force, howling over my mind, scratching at my sanity, filling me with familiar guilt I had when he died. It's taken me a long time to come to terms with his death. I finally reached acceptance but his sudden cruel words re-open my constant self-blame that I don't think will ever truly close.

The motherfucker went there.

I stand up, throwing the chair I'm sitting on, back. The chair screeches across the floor, hitting the wall, with a loud thud. My anger getting the best of me. I take a slow step, and I'm thinking about storming over to him. I'm just seeing red at this point and who knows what I'll do if I get my hands on him.

"Wha— what did you just say?" Ari's innocent voice, stunned with pain and shock.

Shit.

I feel all my blood drain away from my body in a split second and I turn to face her. My heart drops, and nausea enters my body. She has her backpack swung over her shoulder and it looks like she's about to leave.

"You fucking idiots," Rooker says with a heavy sigh, throwing his head back onto the bed in disappointment. He closes his eyes and shakes his head.

CHAPTER 19

DANNY

Kane's like my brother and his words definitely took me by surprise. He never expressed those true feelings towards me or concerning accusations. And out of all places and times, he decides right now is the best moment to explode. I feel betrayed. Betrayed that he would ever throw something that heavy in my face. *Paul's death.*

I stand there, breathing heavily, my chest moving forward and back. Staring hard at Kane, my eyes narrow and my whole body goes stiff. Kane looks back at me with regret in his eyes and he knows, he fucked up. He couldn't hold my gaze anymore and lets his head fall down, looking at the floor. His elbows now resting on his lap.

"What does he mean?" Ari's voice trembling. I look at her, my blood still boiling, rage filling every single vein in my body, but most of all, pain.

I carry the guilt of Paul's death every single day. Maybe that's why I can't be around Ari. I couldn't kiss her or hold her knowing I felt responsible for her brother not coming back home.

"Hello? Is anybody going to say anything?" She asks again but she's only returned with silence. Tears slowly fall out of her eyes, impatience written all over her face. She starts to walk back towards the door, giving us a defeated nod. She understands no one is going to say anything. She turns on her heels and rushes out of the room.

"For fucks sake, I'm trying to get some rest," Rooker groans, facepalming his forehead.

"I'm not out of the woods yet and I already wanna go at *BOTH* of your throats. Do I have to get out of this bed and chase Ari down myself? The poor girl deserves to know now that Slaughter let it slip and it should come from *you*." Rooker roars but he points his finger at me.

I shake my head, rubbing my hand through my beard. I feel horrible that Kane and I are stressing him out like this.

"Fuck, man I apologize... I'll get outta your hair, let your wife know you're not dead? She almost had a heart attack when she saw that I was calling." I tell him sternly as I start to make my way out of the room.

"Grim," Kane calls out, looking up at me now, instead of the floor. My eyes locked into his, blazing with fury. I could see red again, blocking my vision as I stare Kane down before completely turning around towards the door to our room. I don't have time for his bullshit. I have to find Ari now.

"Rider man, I'm sorry," I hear Kane call out over my shoulder, pleading. But I'm already out the door, moving fast. His tone's full of remorse. He crossed a fucking line and I wasn't sure if I would ever forgive him for that.

I start to get stiff. This isn't a conversation I want to have with Ari. This isn't a conversation I want to have with *anyone*. Yet, here I was running through the halls with Ari nowhere in sight. I run into another nurse, her name tag reads, Lori.

"Hi, uh, Lori?" I startle the poor girl, her eyes widening confused as to why a random man was moving frantically in the ER hallways.

"Yes, can I help you?" Lori frowns, side-eyeing me.

"The nurse Ari, where can I find her?"

Relief in her breath, probably from the realization I'm not going to hurt her or that I'm some crazy patient on the loose.

"She left already, her shift is over. It's five in the morning." Lori says, looking down at her watch, yawning.

"Dammit... where's she staying?"

Lori hesitates, her eyebrows furrow studying me. I was starting to grow impatient.

"I'm not sure if I feel comfortable giving you that information."

"Lori, I've had a very long night. An exhausting one. Long story short, I almost lost one of my men tonight. She helped save him. And all I want to do is show her my gratitude." It was a lie. But not a complete lie. I palm my chest, leaning forward.

"Fine."

Chapter 20

ARI

Paul was everything to me. The only man in my life I could ever depend on. He helped take care of my mother and myself. He helped me get through so much drama in high school and my early years of college. He protected me from Shane when I didn't have the strength to walk away. My brother was my best friend. He was a part of me and ever since he died, *a part of me died*.

I've questioned God over and over again. Why Paul? Why my big brother? And He has yet to deliver an answer to me. All my life I've been living by His commandments but lately, I've only been returned with bad luck. I was trembling with anger and confusion as I ran up the stairs to get to my room. I decided to use the stairs and avoid the elevator, which was jam-packed with soldiers trying to make it on time to PT. They usually do some form of physical training before having to go to work.

What did Kane mean by Paul's death was Danny's fault?

I deserve to know. What were they talking about? My brother died while he was on a mission. He was shot multiple times and died before they could get him to the hospital. Those were all the details that were expressed to my mother and I.

My mind travels back to that day when we found out about my brother's passing.

Two uniformed men knocked on our door. My mother opened the door so routinely as she always does. She was expecting our neighbor to come over that day. They wanted to borrow some of her gardening tools so she didn't think twice about it.

When she saw the men, their eyes full of sorrow, she knew. She knew why they were there and she screamed before they even said a word. My heart dropped and I rushed from my bedroom in the middle of studying, dropping my pencil, thinking she had hurt herself. My heart dropped, my heart already broken and scared just hearing those sounds come from my mother's mouth.

Then I saw my mother crying on the floor clutching her chest. She kept repeating,

"Not my Paul. Not my baby." Over and over again. I stood there at the door, breaking in a million pieces watching the uniformed men try and console my mother on the floor of our entryway.

"You have the wrong house, please leave! Salte! Por favor salte de mi casa! Mi hijo, donde esta mi hijo?" She screamed at them with uncontrollable sobs.

Leave! Please leave my house! My son, where's my son?
And I knew what just happened. My best friend had died.

"For having little legs you sure do walk fast." Danny's deep voice interrupts my horrid memory, suppressing the lump in my throat. I jump not expecting to hear him so close to me. I was a few doors down from my room and we were both standing in the hallway. I turn around to face him. I'm met with a smirk and his blue eyes looking down at me.

"What? How'd you kn—?"

"Lori told me where you live."

Dammit, Lori.

My eyes narrow at him. I deserve an explanation and he

better be ready to tell it. My heart thumps out of my chest. Heat rushes to my core. I hate that every time I look at him I think about his rough textured hands on my body caressing my breasts. He's stunning as hell.

God definitely took his time making him. But the more I get to know him, he isn't a man of God. Scratch that, the devil took his time creating this sinfully handsome man. His black shirt wraps around his muscles, hugging them so well. I feel so tiny around a six-foot-six muscular monster towering over me. Maybe it's a good thing our encounter in the hospital room didn't go any further, this man could destroy me with just his hands.

"Ari." Danny begins but I stop him before he can go on further, my blood boiling.

"We can talk in my room." I snap before turning around, getting closer to my door knob. There are soldiers all around us, rushing to work. I feel Danny's eyes behind me, hearing his footsteps follow me and I swallow, nervously. I hate being around him so close, my head grows fuzzy and I can't think straight.

"Look Ari, this isn't something I want to revisit. It's hard for me because I'm not allowed to say anything." He did not just imply that this is hard for him. I feel like time stops. The old me would have bitten her tongue. And not say what I was truly thinking. I would be too occupied and concerned with how *he's going to feel* once I open my mouth. This time I didn't care. He's going to hear me.

"It's hard for *you?*" I hiss. My eyebrows furrowed and I'm on my tiptoes making damn sure he can hear me clearly up there, in the clouds. He's a mountain and I'm a small hill.

He stares at me hard and emotionless. His blue eyes stare straight into my soul and I can see that he's in pain. His stare intimidates me so much I feel like I'm going to break in half so… I look away at my feet.

Staring at my shoes, I let out a deep breath, trying to calm down. He infuriates me so much. We stand there in silence, without meeting each other's gaze again.

"Ari."

"What?" I snap.

"Did you lock your door when you left because it's open?"

"What are you talking about?" I look at my door and it's cracked open. I stare at it confused.

Why can't I just sleep? Why does tonight have to be one of the most eventful nights of my life? I've worked twelve hours and all I want to do is strip into my pajamas, go underneath my covers, and drift into a deep sleep... with Danny's arms as my pillow.

"I always lock my door before I go anywhere," I mutter softly.

Was someone in my room?

I walk in pushing the door open and I gasp, stopping in my tracks. The lights are on and my room is a wreck. My bed was unmade, clothes everywhere on the floor, and my pillow ripped to shreds causing the feathers to be everywhere. I look to my left to the small kitchen area which was also destroyed. The refrigerator opened and the little bit of food I had in there, spilled on the ground.

"What the hell?"

Terror fills my body, and I begin to shake. I grip my backpack straps tight.

Who would do such a thing?

I head straight into my room, taking it all in. It looks like someone was trying to find something or *someone*. And the other half of the room looks like they just destroyed my stuff for their enjoyment.

"I'm assuming your room wasn't like this before you left. What the hell happened here?" Danny asks, welcoming himself into my bedroom, behind me. Danny's body grows tense and I ignore his question, heading towards my bed, looking for my journal. I don't know why but something inside of me tells me to search for it. I had this journal for the past five years. I've written down very personal thoughts and I can't fathom someone having it. Someone reading my darkest, my highest, my desires, my most memorable moments, in their hands.

I look inside my nightstand, pulling the drawer open, and to my dismay, it's gone. My heart drops and I bite my lip, and my fists clench. High pressure threatening to spill over inside of me and I'm angry. Maybe it's just lost in the chaos of the room. I give myself a pinch of hope but doubt creeps in with each attempt of my search.

I try putting everything back together in its place with Danny silently, helping me. I'm hoping with each object back in its place it will show up, but so far nothing.

"Who would do this?" Danny asks while grabbing his phone. His eyes are searching mine but I'm too lost in my thoughts to meet his.

"I have no idea."

I go to the restroom, still in my scrubs, checking if they went through my restroom too. Sure enough, I'm right. Everything I had on my shelves was now on the floor. My little artificial succulent plants were on the floor, books, and makeup palettes. I shudder when I see the picture of Paul and I ripped apart. The frame is shattered, leaving little pieces of glass everywhere. Seeing my favorite photo of Paul and me as kids shredded to pieces breaks me.

A horrible sting pierces through my heart. My eyes begin to water. The pain is too much. Behind the photograph, is a handwritten message from Paul and now it's gone, torn to shreds. He always gave me one photograph before he would deploy with a message on the back. This was the last one he gave me.

Take care of Ma when I'm away and no, you cannot use my PC to play. Love you, baby sis. I'll see you soon. -Paul

I tried to stay strong these past few months and it all comes crashing down, in this moment. I was like a volcano just waiting to erupt. As each month passed, the more I filled with sorrow and finally, this pushed me over the edge.

I fall to my knees holding a few pieces of the picture in my hands, squeezing them tight, and sob uncontrollably.

"How could someone do this?" I sob.

My tears flow down the sides of my cheek fast, my eyes stinging and glossy. My cheeks are red with pain and I close my eyes tightly shut, hoping this is just another horrible nightmare. The ache in my chest feels like I'm just going to die. *Heartache.* This has to be the shittiest year of my life.

My body makes horrible sobbing noises. I'm breathing heavily as I let my sadness spill over in front of Danny, and I don't care. I'm having an anxiety attack and I can't stop it.

My head sinks down looking at my hands in my lap, still on my knees. I just couldn't stay strong anymore. I've been pretending to be this strong girl for the past few months since my brother died. Since my mother's world was turned upside down and when I met Danny. I just couldn't hold onto this fake person anymore that pretended couldn't hurt. But I'm human.

I feel strong hands grip my shoulders, and I flinch with Danny's touch. Wanting so badly to swat them away but at the same time, I want him to hold me tighter and never let me go.

"Ari... come here." Danny's voice is hard but low in my ear. He holds onto my biceps, bringing me closer to his body, embracing me. I turn around to face him, sobbing into his upper abdomen area.

"I'm calling the military police. You have to file a police report."

I nod against his body, in his arms, trying to control my breathing. I can feel more relief as the seconds go by, my body pressed up against his. His hands are now tangled up in my hair holding me in place.

"Then you're coming to my room. I'll have the lower enlisted clean this up for you."

Confusion sets in. And my deepest desires are running rampant. I shake my head.

"No it's okay I'll be f—"

Danny cuts me off, grabbing my chin, and tilting me upwards to face him with his fingers, rapidly.

"I'm not asking. I'm telling you." His blue eyes are so intoxicating and I feel like I'm in a trance. I don't want to argue. Plus… I think I feel safer in his arms than in my bedroom.

Being in his arms is safer than being alone in my bedroom... *right?*

CHAPTER 21

ARI

Danny walks me to where he's staying after the military police arrived and I filed a report. His room is more private, more spacious, and more secluded than mine. He has government furniture just like the rest of us. Yet his room looks more elegant. The way the room was built, it's more modern and feels more cozy. White walls with dark gray colored doors. Bright ceiling lights illuminate the bedroom. His bed is covered in plain white bed sheets and two black pillows.

He has only three photographs pinned to a bulletin board as decoration. As I walk closer to see them, I see one photo of Danny and his mom. The second one is Danny hiking in tall mountains on a snow-covered trail. The third is a group picture with Kane, Paul, Gabriel, and Rooker all in their Navy uniforms, holding rifles. It's weird seeing Gabriel, in uniform.

I smile looking at the photographs. These photos gave me a little more insight into Danny's personal life. His mother was beautiful and tall, fit, with blonde hair. The photo was from his Navy boot camp graduation day. It looks like the day he officially became a Navy SEAL. And I wondered where his dad was in these pictures. His dad hadn't abandoned him like mine from what I can remember.

I turn around to search for Danny but I bump into a black shirt instead. I look up to meet Danny's eyes and I immediately regret it. I feel like my chest drops to my stomach as if it's anchoring down deep into an ocean. *His* ocean blue eyes. His gaze was as if he was starving and I was his meal, his lips curled up in a small smirk.

I gulped, trying to do anything to relieve my emotions. He had left me in his room when we just got here so he could go smoke a cigarette. *Burn one* as he likes to say.

I break away from our eyes locking and look down instead, letting my side bangs fall into my face.

"Where's your father in these pictures? Wouldn't a day like becoming a Navy SEAL interest him? " I point to the photographs on his bulletin board, turning around.

"He was there that day."

"So why isn't there a picture of him with you and your mom?"

"Why do you like to ask so many questions?" He walks closer to me.

"I'm inquisitive."

He groans frustrated, running his hand through his hair as he stares at the bulletin board.

"We don't talk. I stopped talking to him when I found out he'd been fucking one of his employees while my mom was pregnant with their IVF baby."

My mouth hangs open as I'm digesting the news of a cliche work affair. I can't imagine how his mom felt when she found out her husband's been having an affair while she was carrying their child.

"Oh… I'm, um, sorry." I stutter over my words, stopping myself from asking further questions.

He watches me and I can feel his demeanor completely change

from the protective Danny moments ago to a man hardened with anger.

"Danny, I think... I think we should talk about what Kane insinuated about you and my brothers' death."

Danny stiffens when I say *death.*

"I'd rather revisit this conversation later. I'm tired. I've been up all night dealing with work and you haven't slept either." Danny grumbles, sleepiness laced in his tone.

"No I haven't, but–"

"Another day then... maybe. I'm not allowed to disclose anything about that mission. Kane's an imbecile who can't keep his fucking mouth shut about things he knows nothing about."

I bite my lip thinking of what to say.

"I don't know..." I shake my head. Danny gets closer to my ear.

"Ari. Go. Home. I can't protect you here and on top of that, I'm leaving. I won't be here if that person comes looking for you again. Look what just fucking happened to your room. Why can't you trust me? Listen to me."

"I don't need your protection. *I'm staying.* Why do you even care?" I'm not backing down. He huffs out a breath and gets closer to me.

"Because I made a promise."

I flinch.

"What're you talking about? What promise?" He ignores my question and that just infuriates me even more.

"I hate you."

My heart drops and my eyebrows narrow inwards. I'm confused and thrown off by his words. It came out of nowhere.

"What? Why do you hate me? What have I done to you?"

"Exist."

Ouch.

My mouth goes dry and I'm trying to remain calm.

"Your existence alone brings me to my knees and I hate you

for that. I hate that you've invaded every part of my mind. Before you, I was a *simple man*. Work, train, sleep, eat, repeat. I didn't have to fucking worry about anybody else. I hate that ever since I've got a taste of you, all I want to do is devour the rest of you. I hate that you're Paul's sister because it makes it even more fucked up to want you. " Danny snarls at me, his voice raising louder in my ear. I jump every time he says the word, *hate.*

"Most of all I fucking hate that I *don't hate you.*" His palm collides with the wall behind me, causing me to flinch.

Danny's breathing intensifies.

"Well, I hate you." I snap back. Looking at him ferociously, I push him with my palm away from me but he doesn't move a centimeter.

"You're so fucking confusing! You make me feel things that I never thought were possible. Then you're making me feel horrible… for what? Working at this hospital, as a nurse? I won't apologize for trying to do something to honor Paul. You become this asshole every time I'm near!" I say, walking closer to him, closing the gap between us attempting to intimidate him but failing miserably.

His jaw clenches and I wince. My eyes shuttering closed then opening them again.

"You can't be here and I'm going to make sure of it. Tomorrow I'm going to make some calls to have you transferred back."

My eyes bulge.

"You can't do that to me. You don't get to do that to me Danny! I'm helping people and you need to accept that."

"What you witness at the hospital is only a small fraction of the evil that awaits past this military post. You can't be near me. You're a distraction."

I'm a distraction?

He pauses and licks his lips.

"I know you, Ari. I know deep down you're fucking aching to feel what it's like to indulge in the sins that plague your mind." A smug look on his face and I know he has more intentions than he's leading on. He's trying to distract me from this heavy conversation. I understand it's painful for him but I deserve to get some answers.

"I want to know what Kane was implying." I'm silenced, unable to finish my sentence.

"I. Can't."

"You can't. Funny. Just like you promised you won't touch me again?" I challenge.

He scoffs. The sound was deep and mouth-watering, it sends shivers down my legs and between my thighs. God, even his noises just arouse me. I clench my thighs together trying to relax the throbbing pulsation in between them. I can feel myself getting wet.

Damn him.

"Exactly. I'm a man of my word. I won't touch you. But I know you want me to. I know the way you tremble when I say your name. The way you blush every time you look me in the eyes. Or when you bite your bottom lip when you get so flustered around me. I promise you that if I touch you again, if I give in to all the things I've thought about doing to you… *you won't ever want to leave me alone."* He growls. I stand there taking in his request. Every hair on my body stands up with arousal and curiosity. Danny on the other hand is not moving an inch and I couldn't understand how.

Was I really going to give all of myself to him? The way he looks at me with such desire. His hot and cold behavior towards me that's always so damn infuriating. The way I've always felt safe with him since the day I met him in that bar. It's unfair. It's a sin. *He is the sin.*

For the first time in my life, I don't want to think too hard about this. Every single decision I've made has always been well thought out and calculated. I've been raised to fear sex. To fear being naked around any man that wasn't my husband. To feel insecure about embracing sexuality which I've come to realize is a normal thing to experience at my age now. These kinds of things were engraved into the way I function like a permanent tattoo. For once, I refuse to think. *I act.*

I clear my throat.

"You're wrong Danny. I think if I give all of myself to you, *you're the one* that won't be able to *leave me alone.*"

He huffs out a breath, smirking so wicked, licking his teeth. He lifts his palm over my head, leaning on the wall behind me.

"Ari… This is the first and only chance I'm going to give you to run away from me. I'm growing impatient. My way of fucking isn't sweet. It isn't nice. It isn't soft. If you let me, I will break you but trust me, baby, you'll keep wanting me to, begging me to. I don't care if this is your first time. This is who I am. I like to blend pleasure with pain and fracture boundaries."

My eyes widen.

Oh, fuck.

My heart quickens as I'm trying to understand what he means by his kinks. This is a new leaf I'm turning over so if he thinks he can scare me away, he's wrong.

"Fear me now, little Angel?" He grabs my pink necklace, by the cross.

Instead of talking, I decided to act on my emotions… I grab his other hand and I bring his thumb on my tongue, then I close my mouth on it, hollowing my cheeks, and suck it gently at first then hard. Looking up at Danny now, my eyes rolling upwards, to watch his reaction. Danny stops breathing for a second as he watches me suck his thumb. He lets out a breath and hums.

He's satisfied.

"*Are you scared*, Danny?" I stop sucking and it ends with a smacking noise. I don't know what I just started but I hope to God it doesn't end. My heart's beating fast and I'm wondering if Danny will retreat like last time. Can he hear my heart beating outside of my chest?

He pauses and laughs, a dark laugh that reverberates through his chest it sounds so good.

"Nothing scares me."

One of Danny's hands moves so smoothly around my neck and I flinch, remembering when his tight grip was on me a few days ago. He rips my cross necklace off of my neck faster than I can blink and puts it in his pocket. I gasp as I watch him rip it off my neck so easily. He moves to caress my cheek, gently at first but then he moves to the back of my head pulling my hair tight, making my head whip back as he brings himself crashing to me. Our lips collide with a never-ending passion and another feeling, that treads the definition of hatred and need.

His tongue immediately travels into my mouth exploring the depths of it. I'm immediately taken aback. Unsure and not confident with myself, I do my best to make sure my tongue's dancing and keeping up with his. Something inside me burns as the seconds go by.

Was he really going to do this?

As our kissing heightens more and more, his hands explore my scrubs, untying my pants and throwing them down at my feet. I quickly kick off my shoes and step out of my pants leaving me in my soaked green panties and scrub top.

All I want to do right now is bury my sadness away in his arms. There's no doubt in my mind this is where I want to be right now.

Danny takes off his shirt, throwing it on the floor beside him. His tattoos and scars are on full display. An hourglass on the left side of his chest, in my glossy eyes.

Soon after, Danny grabs my scrub top and yanks it over my head with such force it's frightening. He's eager, impatient, and angry. His huge hands take up almost half of my shirt. I'm way over my head. I don't know what to do to please him. A little voice in my head screams at me to not overthink and follow his lead. To just try and stay in sync with his movements. Danny seems to notice my hesitation.

"I'm going to go easy on your body this time baby, don't worry," Danny reassures me, but I can't help but feel like it's a lie. "Next time you won't be so lucky. I won't hold back like I am right now and you'll know what I really want to do to this perfect cunt of yours."

I swallow. What did he mean by that? How much would he be holding back? And what would he be holding back?

It's six in the morning now and I haven't slept since the day before. I'm going almost twenty-four hours without sleep and I know once this is over I'm probably going to drift into a deep exhausted slumber.

I reach for his sweatpants untying it, I grip the waistband along with the lining of his boxers, about to push his pants down, but Danny stops me, gripping my hands tight with his calloused hands. Both of us panting with lust. I look at him with circled confused eyes. Did I do something wrong?

"Once you pull down those pants, my cock will be the first and only that will ever be inside of you. Do you understand that Ari? If I find out any other man tries to take what's mine, he'll wish he hadn't." He threatens into my ear. Something about his possessive threat has me even more drawn to him.

I freeze.

"Or what?" I challenge. I smirk and I don't understand what's gotten into me. I feel like the lust has taken possession of my body.

"Oh baby, I think you forget that I'm the military's most lethal trained killer…" He smiles wickedly and at this moment I feel like Danny reveals a sadistic part of himself and I'm not so sure I want to unravel it. "I've sent way too many souls to hell, I wouldn't hesitate to send another if they even *look at what's mine.*" I shiver at his threat, yet it sends me craving more.

"Kane asked me out on a date and I said yes," I mutter

through my heavy breathing. *Way to pick a time, to be honest, Ari. Such great timing.*

Danny's smile is gone and he's angry. His blue eyes turn dark and the brightness in them is long gone. He grabs the back of my head palming it, and the next thing I know, he's pushing me up against the wall hard enough that it makes a loud thud when my body collides with it. Before I can react and question Danny, he grabs my legs throwing me upwards so I'm now straddling him against the wall, I cross my legs around his waist securing myself.

"Cancel it. Your Cherry is mine to take."

Chapter 22

ARI

Still straddling Danny's waist, I swallow. Fireworks blow up in my head and I'm seeing stars as he looks at me with his blue eyes staring straight into my soul. He's a beast and there's no taming him now. What am I getting myself into? I'm clutching my hands that I have wrapped around his neck and my clit throbs between my thighs.

"I'm not under your authority, you can't ask this." I breathe into his ear, teasing him. I had no plans on seeing Kane anyways. I look back at him and he smirks.

"*I'm not asking.*"

I bite my lip.

"Why give into me now?" I whisper.

He's invaded every part of me, he's consumed me with just one moment. With one glance that one night at El Devine... I fell for him.

"Maybe it's because I just watched someone try and take what's mine. If anyone is going to take you on a date, it's going to be me."

I look up at him and glare into his eyes. He looks like a bear that just came out of hibernation ready to devour his first meal. At the same time, he looks like he's in pain. As if he's about to pull away from me again like the night he did on his couch.

"I want you so dangerously Ari but I'm no good for you."

He's going to stop himself again but I refuse to let him. He needs to know that I want this just as badly as he does.

I crash my lips to him, moving my lips so feral and needy I lose myself completely. He *lets me command him* this time.

"I want this, Danny. Don't pull away from me now. I won't let you." I say with a shaky breath, my tone breaking so much it almost sounds like a cry. He wants to stop.

He's right, he's no good for me. But I don't care. He thinks I won't be able to handle his kinks and he might be right but I want to decide that for myself.

His body tenses and I can feel how hard he is against my thigh. Internally, I'm shrieking. We're not back in his house on the couch and I don't think anything will be stopping us this time. No interruptions, no cell phone ringing mid-oral, nothing but Danny's extreme need to feel me.

He walks over to the edge of his bed and gently lets me fall on top of it. My breasts bounce as I land and I can feel my nipples harden with the way he's looking at me. I sit up, crossing my legs and cover my breasts with my arms. I take in the view of Danny's build. His back muscles are so defined. He turns around to empty his pockets, throwing his wallet, cigarettes, and lighter on his desk across from the bed. A massive black reaper tattoo erupted in flames is tattooed all over his back. The same tattoo that intrigues me. The detail is surreal.

He finally turns around and he's eyeing me. His eyes start from my feet and he travels all the way up to my pussy, breasts then my face and he hums.

"Don't be ashamed of your naked body, Cherry. You're perfect." His words strike me hard. I hesitate at first. I look down at my arms before I drop them to my sides and relax my legs. Thank God, I kept up with my lady maintenance. Shane never made me feel this exquisite. He made me feel terrible in my own skin. The way Danny touches me sends a current of salacity throughout my body every single time.

Danny grins and he drops his sweatpants with his boxers in one swift movement. And my eyes widen. His cock springs free and I gulp. *He's huge.* His cock is long and thick. How the fuck is that supposed to fit inside of me? There's no way. Nope nope nope.

Danny begins to stroke his dick as he walks closer to the bed and I instantly fear for my life. *Death by huge cock.*

"Danny..."

"Ari?"

"I'm scared."

He chuckles as he positions himself over me. Propping himself up with his hands on each side of my head. He pushes my legs apart and settles in between them. I can feel his cock touching my slit and chills erupt all over my body. My face grows hot and my heart rate is giving me tachycardia. My side bangs cover a part of my face, and Danny brushes them away with his fingers. He's staring at me with such intensity I feel like I could fade away. He's admiring me and I'm slowly dissolving. I love when he looks at me like this.

He leans forward and captures my bottom lip with his teeth, biting down so hard he draws blood. Then he sucks my lip into his mouth, tasting me, sucking the blood, and hums again, licking his lips.

"You should be."

At first, Danny rubs the tip of his cock through my slit smoothly, then he rubs it against my clit gently and a moan slips out of my mouth. He's teasing me with his cock and he begins to kiss me ferociously. Our tongues compete for dominance and of course, he wins. I'm dripping wet now as my hands snake through his dark sandy blonde hair.

He breaks our kiss and he looks at me, waiting for me. I stare into his blue eyes and he stares back into mine. I'm terrified, the thought of the unknown is what scares me. This is a feeling I've never experienced. It's completely foreign. Only in my fantasies that I've experienced these types of moments. I've never had sex before and I'll be forever changed after this moment and I know I'm ready.

I nod and reach for his face with my hand, caressing his cheek. He repositions himself over my entrance and lets out a deep breath.

"I want you." I breathe.

"You shouldn't."

Then he pushes into me, slowly and I let out a gasp. My eyes widen so big at first before I'm shutting them tightly closed as the pain explodes down there snapping me out of the pleasure I was once feeling. *Damn, this hurts.*

"Ari you're so wet for me."

His length stretching me in a way I know I won't recover so easily.

"It's going to hurt at first. But trust me." Danny whispers into my ear and a tear slips out of my eye. I didn't expect it to hurt this much. He kisses my tear away as he pulls out of me and then reenters, keeping a steady pace. Pain is soon replaced by pleasure with each stroke. Although, I can feel my body having difficulty fitting his size inside of me.

"It hurts, you're too big." I whimper. He doesn't stop though and keeps pulling me onto him so greedily and I feel more full as he slams himself inside me. His forehead vein swells as he pounds inside of me.

"You can take it. You're already taking it so well." He thrusts harder. "Fuck, Ari, you're so tight." He groans.

He squeezes my ass so hard with his hand and anchors my waist closer to his body, enabling his cock to go in even deeper than before and I moan so loud, out of the painful pleasure. I'm shocked he was able to fit all of himself inside me. It hurts and I feel like I'm tearing. But it's a euphoric pain I want to feel for eternity. My nipples harden more as he licks my nipple circling it slowly, then he bites down violently and it sends a flock of butterflies in my stomach. Affliction and pleasure just like he promised and I'm loving every single second. Savoring each moment like it's my last on this Earth.

He begins to suck on my nipple then moves to my other breast sucking me into his mouth again, the same way. Then he trails his tongue from my nipple upwards to my neck. I arch my back as his tongue travels on me. He sucks down on the skin of my neck for a couple of seconds before letting go, leaving a purple mark.

His pace is slow at first but that doesn't last long as he's picking up his pace. He starts slamming inside of me, devouring me, pumping hard, our skin repeatedly colliding. Our bodies start making slapping noises and the bed starts to shake beneath us. The headboard hits the wall violently. I moan again loudly and I want to scream but I stop myself from raising my voice louder not wanting to attract any distractions from outside his door.

To help myself keep quiet, I reach for his thumb that rests beside my face, and I start sucking on it as I stare at his beautiful face, still thrusting inside of me.

He furrows his eyebrows as he watches me suck on his finger.

"If you keep doing that, I'll help you keep quiet and make you choke on my cock instead," Danny whispers.

My eyes circle.

The thought of tasting his engorged length has me swooning.

Never did I think that I would be losing my virginity to Danny Rider. A Navy SEAL I met in a bar. Now we're In Iraq while he's on a deployment and I'm a nurse working in a military hospital. I wanted to stay here in this moment forever. Pure ecstasy. And my heart sinks when I remind myself I'd be leaving in less than two months. I quickly shake myself out of that thought, I'm not going to let my thoughts get to me right now. The only feeling I want to cling to is the exhilaration of finally letting go of my innocence.

I let go of his thumb just as he hits a certain spot inside of me. I rapidly try to hold onto him instead, scratching his back hard, so much so, I'm sure I broke through his skin. I feel myself shatter like glass as the orgasm obliterates my existence. I moan into the bed sheets, my eyebrows narrowing, and my mouth gapes open. My lungs expand with bliss.

"Fuck, I love seeing the look on your face as you come."

Danny lets me ride out my orgasm before lifting me up, putting us in a different position. We're off his bed and he's standing. Thrusting inside me. While. Standing.

"I'm not done with you yet." He threatens.

I hold onto the back of his neck, biting his shoulder to lessen the pain but it still doesn't help, my legs wrapped around him, curled into him as he's carrying me. Soon, the pain starts fading away and I'm enjoying every second that goes by. The pleasure has taken over and it feels so good to be full of him inside of me.

I'm bouncing on his cock in the air, his rough callous hands keeping me in place and he's so precise with each thrust I'm amazed.

He's good at this.

It doesn't take long before I'm shattering again with euphoria as an orgasm takes over. I'm straddling his waist, thrusting up and down on his long length, taking every single pound he's giving me. He's not gentle anymore. The sounds we're both making aren't normal. He's holding onto my hair, pulling it as he fucks me hard. We're both panting, my mouth is gaped open, eyebrows furrowed from all the pleasure. I can hear Danny groan with pure satisfaction as his cock goes deeper and deeper inside of me each time I bounce. He grinds his teeth as he takes me.

Then, I hear Danny grunt as he climaxes inside of me, he's clenching my body so tight, it hurts but *it hurts so good*. I can see his jaw tighten and he's burying his face into my neck as his warm come fills me up and I'm shaking.

He really just fucked me while standing.

We both drop onto his bed and he's careful with me. I'm completely exhausted. My breathing's heavy and I feel like I've entered a new world I never wanted to escape from. This is a new era in my life and I was determined to live in it forever with Danny.

He lays on his back and I curl up on top of his chest, trailing my fingers on his scars. We're both trying to make our breathing even again after what felt like a battle. We lay in silence, taking each other in and I'm appreciative of that.

We both hold each other naked and I'm growing clammy from our body heat. But I don't dare move.

The innocence is long gone, now and I'm not repenting. I don't regret what I just shared with Danny. It's a sinful paradise whenever I kiss him.

"What does this say?" I groan, sleepily.

He looks down at me as I trace the sand clock tattoo on his chest, falling into peace, my stress subsides and I'm drifting into a deep slumber. The words aren't in English.

"It's Latin."

My breathing evens out and I'm slowly going out.

"Time waits for no one. Death is a shadow stalking the living. It is a painful inexorable promise while Life is a lovely lie."

CHAPTER 23

DANNY

Ari falls asleep on my chest. This girl makes me feel like I'm not so bad after all. Her breathing has reached an even pace and I don't want to wake her. Poor girl has been awake for so long with work, and the surgery on Rooker, and now I added to her exhaustion. A smile reaches my face as I stroke her soft black hair.

She's finally mine and I think she's right, *I don't think I'll ever leave her alone again.* I had thought about this moment since the day I met her. I admire her naked body on top of me and I know this body was designed just for me. She's a forbidden canvas and I want to interpret every part of her body with my mouth. I went easy on her this time since it was her first but next time, I would really show her just the way I like to fuck.

I need to show her the cruel side of me that I keep hidden and I'm going to confess that to her. Not with my words though and I'll do it when I have her trapped, next time.

I slowly slip out of bed, resting her face on my pillow. Her hair falls over her swollen pink lips and the urge to bite them again fills me. I'm staring at her, frozen, watching her breathe, completely captivated by her and I know I'm in trouble.

She's not the only one that experienced a first time tonight. Because this was the first time I didn't want to leave after sex, I wanted to stay and hold her in my arms. Something I've never done with any one because I *always* leave after.

To make her more comfortable, I grab a folded blanket from my closet. Seeing drops of blood where her waist used to be on the bed sheets, stops me. I'm not surprised she bled during her first time. My cock was too much for her but her sweet cunt took it so well.

I gently cover her with the blanket, dropping it on her beautiful tanned skin body. She lets out a soft groan as she cuddles in closer to the pillow. She's in such a deep sleep.

She's fucking perfect to me. I don't deserve her.

I head towards the shower instead. I haven't slept all night and it was early morning now but how could I? Besides finally exploring the beautiful depths of Ari, my mind is back to focusing on my job. I'm stressed out about the rescue mission that has yet to be successfully completed. I'm losing one of my most trusted men, Rooker. He'll probably be sent home soon to recover with Noel and his daughters. It bothers me knowing he'll be replaced. It's the military, the mission will go on, with or without him. I walk closer to my bathroom, shutting off the bedroom lights.

Ari's mine now. She always has been since the day I met her at El Devine. With one glance at her beautiful face, it was over. The life I had planned for myself… *over*. I've never wanted to commit to any woman before but something about Ari was different. She makes me feel like I'm not a villain, a killer, or a monster. Nothing has ever been able to replace my poisonous addiction. But… she did. She's better than whiskey.

At the same time, she brings back demons from Paul's death. Demons that made me feel guilty for living and not dying the same night as Paul.

I start the shower and the water falls down, steam starts to fill my bathroom. Watching the water fall down puts me in a trance and I go back to the worst day of my career. I clench my jaw, watching the water hit the floor of the tub. I know Ari's going to want to know more about Paul's death since Kane brought it up. Not a day goes by when I don't think about the day my best friend died. Every day since then, I've questioned why he died and I didn't. Not a day goes by that I don't blame myself for it.

CHAPTER 24

ARI

I woke up expecting to feel Danny's body so I snuggle closer only to be met with bed sheets. My eyes flutter open taking in my surroundings. The curtains in Danny's room are black-out curtains, I couldn't see anything if it weren't for a small light coming from a desk lamp. The memories of early morning sex hit me and I smile. I gave Danny all of me a few hours ago and I bite my lip instantly feeling over the moon thinking about it.

I stretch my legs and I feel the soreness between my thighs. I look down at my waist and I can see bruises forming where my hips are. His handprints settle in like a tattoo that will be erased with time. *He said this was him going easy on me.* His monstrous size compared to my short frame, it was to be expected.

I reach over and look for my phone. I found it on his night-stand. I need to get back to my room and go through the disaster that someone caused in my room. And I had a pretty good guess who it was.

Even though Danny had people clean up I wanted to look through the wreckage. I filed a police report so everything was documented.

I want proof before I start accusing Shane. I know he's my

toxic ex-boyfriend but would he take it this far? And on a military post? I had my doubts about Shane but I mean… who else could it have been? Who else would want to target and cause harm to me? What if I was there in my room alone when the intruder came in and not at work? I shuttered at that thought, ice-cold fear radiating inside of me.

Would they have hurt me? *Or worse?*

I catch up on missed text messages from my mother and Lori. I remembered Danny never answered my question about my brother. We got distracted and he ended up inside of me instead. There's no way Kane meant it exactly the way he said it. Kane was probably just all riled up from Rooker almost dying. And it was an intense moment. Still, I need to know what he meant.

I need time alone yet a bigger part of me wants our bodies to be entangled in each other all day and night… round after round. As the memories from this morning wave in, I'm aching from the painful and life-altering sex but at the same time. I'm addicted and I want more.

It's such an unbelievable feeling. I'm changed now. I feel different, and I feel tied to him. And that scares the hell out of me. I feel like every time I show Danny I care about him, he pulls away. And every time I pull away from him, he's right there. I didn't want to push him too far with questions surrounding the title of our relationship now. Were we just losing ourselves in each other with no strings attached? Were we lovers? Were we together, together? He's made it clear to me time and time again, he doesn't tie himself to anyone.

My phone buzzes in my hands as I'm contemplating our relationship. It's from Lori. They're calling me back into work and I need to be there within half an hour.

On my day off. Another shift. Great. I sigh frustrated as I reply.

I'll be there as soon as I can.

I toss my phone on the nightstand. I reach for my scrubs. I

rub my eyes attempting to shake the slumber off my lids. I walk over to where I had left my scrubs and found them in Danny's chair instead, neatly folded. I smile, putting my clothes back on starting with my underwear. That was a kind gesture from him. I ruffle out my pants, sliding them on swiftly. I need to get to the hospital soon. Questions swirling in my head.

Why did Doctor Diaz want me there?

I don't even have time to shower. Great. I'll shower right after work. I usually shower after every shift as soon as I get back to my room but this time it was different. Kane's outburst threw me off and I just felt like I had to get the hell away from everything and everyone.

I managed to put my uniform back on when I hear Danny's front door close shut and a short yelp escapes me. I whip my body around, my long black hair flying across my other shoulder, to find Danny turning on the lights next to his bedroom door, looking at me startled.

My heart pounds in my chest, I let out a deep sigh clutching onto my chest with both hands. I'm so jumpy and on edge since the incident in my room.

"Oh my gosh, I'm sorry, you scared me." I breathe.

Danny stands there smirking. Leaning on the door, eyeing me up and down.

"Leaving so soon Cherry?" He asks, crossing his arms and I'm blushing. His muscles flex through his black shirt. Every time he talks, I fucking melt into nothing but desire. He's dressed differently from earlier. He's wearing dark grey sweatpants and vans. He looks… relaxed. Which is rare.

I grab my hair tie, pulling my hair in a ponytail.

"Yeah, my co-worker just texted me that I need to come in. I'm guessing there's an emergency... Where'd you go by the way?"

He stills.

"I don't sleep well and I don't actually *sleep* with anyone, afterward. I leave when the feeling is done. I don't let it be more than it is." Danny says, looking down at his feet.

My heart sinks. He won't sleep with me but he'll fuck me into oblivion?

"But..." He continues. "This is also a first for me, Ari. You're not sleeping anywhere but in my arms tonight. I won't let you go back to your room where I can't protect you. Someone did that to spite you." I swallow. I can't help but feel blissfully radiant that tonight will be *a first for him.*

"Plus I've been getting phone calls nonstop with work. I went out for a smoke and to meet with the team. Kane and Lopez want to drink before we go." He holds up a bottle of Jack Daniels whiskey in his hand. "I have a lot of shit on my mind. I'm heading back out soon." Danny purses his lips together and I have a strong feeling he wants to tell me more but refrains himself from giving me more information. He takes a swig of the bottle and I watch his Adam's apple bob.

I know better than to ask why or what he was going to be doing, so I didn't try and pry Danny for more. Paul never disclosed any details of his deployments. He couldn't. And I know Danny can't either. I would just have to trust whatever he could say.

"How soon?"

"Tomorrow. Early morning tomorrow."

My heart sinks and I'm immediately devastated.

"Oh okay. How long?" I hope I'm not coming off as needy. At the same time, I just want to be prepared for the answer. Would I even still be here when he returned? I have about less than two months to go before I returned to North Carolina. I don't know how long Danny would be staying in Iraq and that bothers me. I don't want to be home if he isn't there.

"I don't know Cherry. It all depends. I could be back in a few days... or in a few weeks, months even."

I frown.

"Are you even cleared by Doctor Diaz? You have a bad injury that can prevent you from performing your job. If you ask me, you're not ready to go back out. But what do I know? I'm just a nurse that works with him." I say, trying to slip past him but he stops me in his tracks, grabbing my arm.

"Baby, you know damn well this paper cut is not stopping me from anything." Then he leans in my ear and I hold my breath.

"It didn't prevent me from breaking into you and making you scream." He whispers, so greedy.

My jaw drops and I'm narrowing my eyes at him. I'm full of fireflies, buzzing around me in a meadow full of lust. He's smirking and my lips curve into a small smile. I shake my head and walk away from him. He doesn't let go of my arm, he pulls me in closer and plants a kiss on my forehead. I close my eyes, enjoying his lips brushing against me. I stand there for a few seconds, enjoying the short exchange.

"You're out of your mind."

He laughs.

"You have no idea… but *you will.*" His iniquitous words roll out off tongue as he drinks more whiskey and I'm studying him. My heart stops and I'm desperate to know what he means.

"I've never been a whiskey type of girl," I whisper as I watch him drink.

He stills and his blue eyes darken. He holds his breath and drops the whiskey bottle to his side.

Suddenly, he kisses me, pushing himself against me, crashing devastatingly on my lips and I'm instantly lost from the collision. He pries my mouth open and I feel the dark taste of whiskey, burn into my throat. Sweet and hard, he empties his drink inside me as my tastebuds erupt. I swallow it all, as his tongue travels deeper inside. The sensation of what he's doing to me has me arching my back as his hand snakes to my hips, pushing me closer to his chest.

He really is out of his mind. *Or am I?* He spit whiskey in my mouth and I'm howling.

"Are you sure about that, little Angel? *Because you swallowed it all* like you will with my come when I fuck that perfect throat of yours." Danny licks his lips, leaning back against the wall. He finally lets me go and he watches me walk away. I'm completely bashful as I bite my lip. I grab the handle of the door and turn around to face him.

"I'll see you tonight." He tells me.

And I know it's not a question. He's not asking to see me. Every time he says something, he means it.

"I don't know when I'm off work. It could be well into the night."

"It doesn't matter, I'll wait. I've got time." He quirks a brow. Danny's tone shifts and he's being protective, maybe even territorial over me.

"I'll see you soon, then." I nod before exiting his room, closing the door behind me softly. I trust Danny. If Paul trusted him I can too. I never hesitate to listen to him.

Hell, I don't want to be in my room either, alone. I'd rather be in Danny's arms. I start to speed walk my way to the hospital. He's going to be leaving very soon and I won't see him again for a while.

Although, I can't help but feel as if Danny is trying to avoid the conversation that lingers above both of our heads.

Paul.

I try to shake out of those thoughts, I need to clear my mind before I start treating people in the ER. I couldn't be thinking about anything worrisome while doing my job. I start to ponder why Doctor Diaz was calling me into work so promptly. He never does that. There must be something going on at the hospital. Something bad. Then my mind goes to the worst, *Rooker.*

I rush into the hospital, jogging. If something happened to Rooker, I'm not sure how Danny will take it. To lose two good friends within a year. I'm sure it wouldn't be good and I know for a fact, he's a drinker. I can't confirm he's an alcoholic but that alcohol collection at his house was massive. Then seeing him get drunk at the bar was an insight into what I'm dealing with when it comes to Danny.

I push through the doors into the ICU. Running towards Rookers' room. Panting hard as I knock on the door and there's no answer. My heart sinks. Maybe he's sleeping. I gently push the door open to find another nurse, cleaning the bed sheets, and putting in fresh ones. No Rooker in sight.

Oh no. *He didn't make it.* There's no way they would move him from ICU so soon. It could only mean...

"Ari, you okay?" Edward asks me. He's an army nurse that I've worked with on several occasions. I hadn't noticed but my hand was shaking, still holding onto the door knob, a tear slipping out of my eye.

"What happened to Rooker? He was stable when I last saw him? How could? He was stable, dammit! He was okay, his vitals were—" I start to frantically ramble, my voice trembling, tripping over my words.

"Rooker is fine Ari, calm down. They're transferring him to Germany. He's on a plane right now as we speak. Closer to home. That man was persistent about being transferred out of here," Edward cuts me off before I can ramble on further, he begins to walk towards me, putting his hands on my shoulders consoling me. I let out a sigh of relief, wiping my tear away. My heart rate starts to go to an even pace and I feel like a ton of weight is lifted off my shoulder. The downside of being a nurse… you never want to see a patient die on you.

"You know Navy SEALS, stubborn as hell," Edward adds with a reassuring smile. I blink, taking deep breaths in. This job stresses me out so badly. But it's so rewarding.

"Well, that's good. I'm sure his wife's on her way to Germany." I say to Edward. He pats my shoulder and then releases me.

"So why are Doctor Diaz and Lori rushing me to come back to work on my day off? I mean I don't mind, I'm just curious. Are we understaffed?" I ask, my eyebrows raising.

"Ari, when are we not understaffed?" Edward asks me sarcastically. He chuckles before continuing, "But no that's not technically it, it's because of a patient we have. Her name is Violet Redd. She was taken hostage by a terrorist organization and she was rescued and brought from a different hospital. She's a medic for the army, suffered through a Humvee crash, and kidnapping. She was *tortured*."

I gasp, throwing my hand to my mouth. Her story registers in my head and I'm in shambles. This poor woman. *Tortured?* Then my mind goes to the darkest possibilities of what that could entail. Tortured by terrorists... I shiver as I feel the complete devastation of what Violet must have gone through.

"Now, she won't let any male nurse touch her or help with anything, or even get near her. She won't let Doctor Diaz go into the room without becoming violent because he's a male. She only feels comfortable around females. Female nurses or doctors and Lori's shift is up. So... they called you in." Edward explains.

I nod, looking into Edward's deep brown eyes. He looks tired and contemplative. His eyes were studying me, his eyebrows raised with his forehead making little wrinkles. We all look like this after we start our shifts. I'm letting it all soak in and I try my best to remember all the parts of the psychiatric portions of nursing school. How would I approach this situation? I think the best way to approach her was to think of her as the biological sister I never had. Patience, understanding, gentleness, and no sudden movements.

"Wow... I totally understand. I'm more than happy to help... I mean I'll do my best but I can't even fathom what she's feeling right now." I tell Edward.

Edward purses his lips together, nervously. I'm sure nobody knows how to be there for Violet. If she's in the ICU, she must have had almost life-ending injuries. I shiver. I leave Edward with a silent nod and I stop by the main ER desk as I usually do before my shift starts. I drop my backpack underneath the desk, sit down, and quickly log into the system.

"Ahem," Lori pretends to clear her throat before continuing. She's eyeing me suspiciously.

"What's that I see on your neck?" Lori questions me close to my ear. I'm still looking at the computer screen but I can't hide the redness that burns into my cheeks and I know I'm blushing hard. I'm shaking.

Crap I totally forgot that Danny sucked on my neck.

"Nothing..." I lie before turning to her, my pitch high and unconvincing. She looks at me like she doesn't believe me and she's trying to figure me out.

"Mhm..." Lori taps her fingers on the counter, smirking.

"Can I borrow some concealer?" I concede to her mental accusations.

"I knew it." Her smirk turns into a bright smile. She starts reaching into her purse.

"Shut up," I whisper, trying my hardest not to attract any attention from the staff around us. I stand up and she's smiling at me giddy the entire time. I follow her to an empty hallway. She hands me the concealer even though our shades don't match but it would do the job for me.

"Who is it? Oh my God, it's not Shane is it?" She gasps, instantly narrowing her eyes at me disappointed.

"What? No! That ship has sailed and sank to the point of no return." I'm applying the concealer with my fingers to my neck, using my phone screen as a mirror.

"Good. Oh yeah, did you hear? They're sending him home since he can't physically do his job anymore because of his broken hand." Lori shrugs.

"Huh... pity," I say sarcastically. This makes me feel more at ease. If he was the one to destroy my room, it gives me comfort knowing he won't be anywhere near me anymore.

"When?" I ask Lori as she watches me apply the makeup to my neck.

"Tomorrow."

The concealer covered up the love marks Danny gave me. I hand Lori her concealer back.

"So who was it, bitch? You gotta tell me. Oh my gosh, was it Doctor Diaz? I wouldn't blame you, he's a tall drink of sexy." She exclaims, twirling her brown hair.

"Girl no... and I'm not telling. I don't even know what he and I are." I softly say, hiding behind my curtain bangs. I wasn't lying either. I didn't know what Danny and I were now. Not long ago, we were strangers. Then he was distancing himself from me, and now... he was deep inside of me not too long ago.

"Fine. But when you do find out, you gotta tell me all about Mr. Hickey over here."

"I will. Now, I don't mean to change the subject but how's Violet Redd? The patient that was a hostage? How's she doing?"

Lori shakes her head, her smile fading.

"Not good. She's having a hard time, physically and mentally. Her eyes were almost completely shut from bruising. She can barely see in one eye. Her vision hasn't fully come back yet but it will. Her face is finally healing from all the bruising, she was raped, and the fuckers broke her ribs. She had internal bleeding but the other hospital staff were able to stop it with surgery. She's been through a lot. She's stable but her mental state is not good. She's scared all the time and won't really talk. When Doctor Diaz tried to examine her, she started screaming at him and almost got violent so no males enter her room now. She let me into her room with no problem and was cooperative when I administered her medications and IV but other than that she won't talk to me or anyone."

I nod, digesting every single word. Raped? Broken ribs? Internal bleeding? Surgery? This poor woman.

Lori guides me to her room in the ICU. It doesn't take us long to get there. It's about one minute away from where we were standing. The glass door allows me to get a peak and Violet is asleep. I can see her vitals on the monitor and she looks stable. Her face is still a bit red and purple and I just want to cry looking at her. She's in a hospital gown covered in hospital blankets. I look at Lori and I'm nervous to walk in.

I walk away from Violet Redd's room and I need to mentally prepare myself for what's to come. I think this is the hardest patient case I've had since I started working here and Danny's words ring through my head like deja vu.

you're here getting a front-seat view of the horror that lives hidden
The things you're going to see, the evil
you shouldn't be here

CHAPTER 25

ARI

Lori leaves right after helping me conceal my hickeys and bite marks. It's nearing eight at night. Two more hours left on my shift and Violet Redd was still sleeping. I checked on her, walking by her room, glancing at her almost every twenty to thirty minutes.

Danny texted me earlier letting me know he would be waiting in the lobby for me after my shift was over. Another female nurse would be taking over. He said he had a surprise for me and I truly wondered how romantic it could possibly be. We're literally on an military post in a Warzone. There's no way we would be going on a dinner date tonight in a romantic restaurant. But then I thought, maybe romance isn't even in Danny's bones. He doesn't seem the type.

The feelings I have towards Danny are completely different than I've ever felt. The way I felt for Danny... It felt like a dream I didn't want to wake up from. Tangled up in his demons was... world-shattering.

He isn't soft but he's smooth and he burns. Just like whiskey.

The shift was going smoothly. I didn't have to worry about

any other patients but Violet. I was walking the halls again, checking on Violet. Doctor Diaz had me only assigned to her.

I'm staring at my watch when I run into a man in the hallway, bumping into him, our bodies colliding snapping me out of my thoughts. I was passing by Violet's room again, taking a glance at my watch, and wasn't looking ahead of me.

"Oh my gosh I'm so sorry..." I apologize, both of us holding onto each other's shoulders for balance. My eyes circle when I realize it's Kane. His long black hair is slicked back, as always. His eyes are worried but he looks excited to see me.

"Ari Alvarez. My favorite nurse." He chuckles, looking at me, his grip on my shoulders tightening before he lets me go. He loves addressing me by my full name for some reason. Kane's tall and massive like the others on his team. Still, Danny was the tallest.

Were all Navy SEALS this monstrous in size?

"Hey, Mr. Slaughter, what are you doing here?" I ask, politely.

"Come on, Ari. It's Kane. We've been over this. You don't have to keep addressing me by my last name." He smirks.

There's no denying how handsome Kane Slaughter is. His blue eyes are darker than Danny's. A blue shade that reminds me of a deep blue, sea. The darkness in his eyes doesn't match his personality though. Kane was always so sweet in each inter-action we've had. So when he asked me on a date, I was sort of expecting it but definitely not expecting the moment he chose to do it. Every time he would check on my mom and me, I never paid him any mind. I was hurting. I was jealous of all of Paul's friends that got to come home but my brother would never again.

I couldn't help but imagine the possibility of saying yes to Kane. Maybe… it would make everything so much easier for me to be drawn to him, instead of Danny. But it would be based on a lie. My heart wants something else… *someone else.*

The longer I look at Kane I notice there's something more behind his devilish smile. It's a need. And I can't give it to him.

The way he sweet-talks me says it all. But a small part of me...
does want to give in.

"Sorry, "I say softly.

"But yeah, to answer your question I came to check on
Rooker. Fucker didn't tell me that he left for Germany, I could've
been getting some extra rest then. We're heading out again in the
morning."

"Yes... he'll most likely get to Germany then he'll be transferred to the States when he's more stable." I nod, awkwardly.

I still haven't given him an answer to his question. Kane had
asked me if he could take me to the USO to see a movie, on one of
his breaks from work and I didn't know what to say. It was a
maybe at first but now... a definite no. I could not do this to
myself or to them. To see Kane and Danny at the same time would
not sit well with me. Right now, I only had my heart set on one of
these crazy Navy SEALS.

"So, have you thought about what I asked you? I know the
USO isn't much but it's what I've got to work with here." Kane
sighs.

"I have and I just... can't. I'm —"

I'm sleeping with Danny.

But I don't say it, instead, I purse my lips together and rock
myself on my heels, looking down at the floor. I'm so bad at this.

"Seeing someone?" Kane tries finishing off my sentence.

"No!" I cut him off, almost shouting. Kane's taken aback by
my response, studying me.

Am I seeing someone?

I mean technically... yes? But I didn't want to make myself
look like I was taken when I wasn't sure. I needed confirmation of
that. Although, Danny's words were tattooed into my brain. *No
other cock would be entering my body,* so it's safe to assume he doesn't
want me to be with anyone else.

"I mean... maybe? I don't know." I look at him apologetically.
Kane's jaw clenches and his lips curve into a small, forceful half-

smile. It pains me to have this awkward conversation. I couldn't deny the attraction I feel towards Kane but it didn't feel right to chase that feeling.

"I get it. Say no more." Kane releases the clench on his jaw, leaning down towards my face, and placing a soft kiss on my cheek. I close my eyes as his lips brush against me and my whole body grows warm. Kane does that to me. I feel the warmth just being close to him. I look up at him but he's already looking past me.

"Whoever he is… he's a lucky man."

He forces a smile and looks deep into my eyes. Something inside of me twitches with his shocking admission. I open my mouth to respond but I'm stopped.

Suddenly, a woman screaming erupts the entire building. Everyone including the staff around us stops in their tracks and I know where it's coming from. Violet's room. She's awake.

"I've gotta go. Goodnight Kane." I rush out my words before starting to quickly jog towards Violet's room. Kane looks wary but accepts my farewell, turns, and walks away from where we were standing.

I was already close to Violet's room, my sneakers squeaking as I stopped mid-run and it didn't take me long before I'm facing the glass doors. She's thrashing and I hadn't noticed it before but she was restrained to the hospital bed.

Lori mentioned that before but I hadn't seen it with my own eyes yet. My heart is racing, unsure of what to do or say. I'm sure being restrained to the bed is only making her more anxious and scared. We only restrain patients when they're a danger to others or themselves.

Doctor Diaz also rushes next to me. He's by my side and we're both looking at Violet through the glass doors to her room. He whispers into my ear, still looking at Violet.

"Go to her, I'll be outside ready with a sedative but if you can talk to her, comfort her, let her know that we're here to help and that she's in a safe place, that would be better." Doctor Diaz encourages, with a needle in his hand, ready to administer. His tired eyes look at me and await my response.

"Of course. I'll do what I can doctor."

Violet is still screaming and crying. I walk into the room slowly, heading towards a night lamp in her room in the corner. I turn it on giving the room some light. Her IV and vitals monitor are on the right side of her and I'm now on her left, still in the corner across from her. Her beaten face is swollen with fear. I want to cry when all the dark thoughts of what she must have gone through creep into me but I control my emotions and face. We are trained to refrain from showing our concern as it doesn't do the patient any good.

Her long hair is a beautiful shade of brown and red. It's tangled and tussled, around her shoulder. She looks underweight and she has markings around her arms as well.

Every time she thrashes, she's stressing out her vein that has the IV connected to it. She's about to rip it out and I cringe internally.

"Violet, it's okay, *you're okay*. You're safe. You're in a military hospital in Iraq. You can trust me." I plead with my hands, walking closer to her, anxiety fueling my veins and I feel helpless but I try my best to console her. I'm sure she knows where she is but I'm hoping it would help to remind her that she's safe.

She stops screaming when she hears my voice and her vision locks into mine. Tears fall down on each side of her cheeks and I grab tissues from the nightstand that's on her left.

"I'm a nurse. My name is Ari Alvarez." I tread my steps slowly, grabbing the Kleenex tissues out of the box and leaving my hand out for her to take it on her free will. I wanted to make sure she knew that every decision from now on, is of her free will, nobody will ever force her to do anything she's not comfortable with.

Violet is hesitant at first but takes the Kleenex and plays with it in her hands. I watch her silently and frozen. She then puts it to her face, dabbing the tissues to her cheek carefully against her bruising. She still has broken blood vessels surrounding her hazel-green eyes. Probably resulting from her broken nose.

"You're safe. I'm just going to make sure your IV is still on your wrist okay? Is that alright with you?" I smile at her.

Again, she's studying me. She hesitates, looking at her surroundings. She stops looking at me and looks around the room instead. She looks towards the hallway through the glass doors then returns back to me and nods.

I walk over to her right wrist to ensure the IV hasn't been taken out when she woke up screaming. If that were to happen, blood would be spilling out of her wrist everywhere and I would have to re-insert her IV in a different vein which I wanted to avoid poking her again if I could. Inserting IVs was very routine at this point but I didn't want to poke her if it was unnecessary. I silently prayed that it was still connected.

As I reach over to her, Violet flinches and moves away from me on her bed. I stop in my tracks and give her a minute before I would continue. I freeze in my tracks with my hands by my chest. I stop before I can get a close look and touch her wrist. Internally, I brace myself for her to spit on me or thrash again but she doesn't move. Her breathing heightens and she's studying me again.

"It's okay. I'm not going to hurt you. I just want to make sure your IV didn't get pulled out." She's looking at me and I can't tell what's going through her head. She's so scared and frightened.

"Cause that would really suck." I joke, light-heartedly. I let out a soft laugh before I shut my mouth closed, my teeth clicking together.

I look down at the floor before looking back at her. She's stony-faced but then her lips move into a very, very small smile.

"Can I?" I motion towards her wrist that's strapped down to the handles of the bed. Violet nods again.

I walk closer and her whole body relaxes. She gets closer to me, shifting her body to my side, allowing me to treat her. I grab her wrist softly and to my dismay, the IV is still intact. Thank God. My blood pressure can drop now. I want to hug her, I want to help her in more ways than I can, medically wise. I want to tell her everything will be okay but how do you say that to someone who has been through hell?

"Yay, it's still going strong." I cheerfully say as I retreat back into the corner, across from her. Her heart rate was elevated and now it starts to hit an even pace. I let out a sigh of relief knowing I wouldn't need the sedative medication that Doctor Diaz had prepared. At least not yet.

"Is there anything you need? Water? Snacks?" Violet eyes dry up and she's no longer crying and in tachycardia. Violet shakes her head and rests back on the pillow.

After minutes of silence, she grabs the remote to the television that was on her nightstand and turns it on. I just stand there in the corner, watching her, ready to step in if she needs anything.

Sometimes, after something traumatic has happened, all someone needs is just someone there. Their presence alone can make it all the better. So that's what I was trying to do for Violet. I truly didn't want to pressure her into talking if she wasn't ready.

I stood there watching her flip through the channels until she lands on a comedy show, Parks and Recreation. She keeps it there, dropping the remote to her side. Amy Poehler was seriously the best. I turned my head facing the TV, this was one of my favorite episodes.

"I love Parks and Recreation. It's my favorite comedy show." I say, grabbing a chair and sliding it out of the corner. Comedy shows are my safe haven nowadays. Every day has been full of stress and darkness these past few months and the only thing that keeps a constant smile on my face was my favorite TV show.

I sit down next to Violet on her left. Making sure to keep some distance between her and me, unsure of how she's going to react.

Still, she's quiet and I'm understanding. If I had gone through half of what she went through, I'd probably lose the ability to ever talk again. We're watching Leslie Knope in silence when suddenly, Violet speaks.

"Is Damon okay? Has he been rescued?" Her question confuses me and I'm unsure of how to answer. She's frantic and demanding. I change my gaze from the tv to her. Her eyebrows are furrowed and worried. I glance at the monitor and her heart rate is rising again.

Oh, no. What do I do?

Who's Damon?

"I'm sorry Violet. I don't know who that is. Who is he?"

"He was with me! We were together, kidnapped together! Please tell me he's okay, please." She rasps at me, angry. Her fear quickly turns into anger and I'm completely thrown off by her mood change.

"I'm sorry I'll try and get some information about him. Is that okay?" I ask, standing up from my chair.

"Please. He was with me... he... he was with me." Her voice trembles and I know she's about to start crying. She looks down at her hands, fidgeting with her fingers.

I nod and take off towards the ER desk. My steps are fast and heavy. They purposefully placed Violet in an ICU room in front of the nurses' station desk where most of the staff hung around most of the time.

There were two hostages? Where was he? And why wasn't he here?

Doctor Diaz is sitting in a chair, studying his computer monitor, most likely reviewing lab or radiology results. He takes one quick glance at me and he's so deep into his work, I know he doesn't have time to talk. Doctor Diaz is extremely passionate about his job. Once he was in this mode of concentration, there was no interrupting him.

He reaches for the sedative medication that was sitting by his keyboard and hands it to me. I shake my head at him.

"No, it's not that. She's been calm... it's just that she's mentioned a name. Damon. She says he was with her, together. Do you know who that is by any chance? Or where he is?" I ask, tip-toeing over the ER desk.

It seems like my questions snap Doctor Diaz out of his concentration and looks over to me like I said something familiar. He sighs.

"Yes. I do actually. One of the Navy SEALS filled me in on the current situation since Violet was a wreck when she came in. And when I say that, I mean she kept mentioning someone named Damon. We were all confused so Mr. Rider disclosed it with limited staff members. Rider's team saved Violet. The same mission that almost got Mr. Rooker killed. Damon was taken hostage along with her. Unfortunately, he's still out there. She was the only one they were able to rescue. A group of special operations personnel is still working on getting him back. But that's all I know. These missions are super sensitive so... please keep your discretion." Doctor Diaz finishes, rubbing his temples.

I gasp. Holding my hand to my mouth. Doctor Diaz nods to me, frowning, before returning to the computer screen. Pure shock gnawing at my body.

Danny was on that mission? Is that how he got his gruesome injury on his back? Is that where he was going next?

He saved Violet.

The thought of him leaving on the same mission that almost got Rooker killed shakes me to my core. I feel tethered to him knowing he's my first... he's a jerk but *he's my jerk*. Why does he consider himself a villain? Danny saved this woman's life.

But now that he's cleared, he's leaving again.

A thousand questions come flooding into my head and I'm slowly digesting my feelings. The stress I was feeling in that moment, all I could do was close my eyes, tight. If this is the way they had left Violet, I can't imagine how they have Damon. I don't want to imagine.

I have to go back into that room and let Violet know what I was told and I wasn't sure how she was going to take it. I take a deep breath, throw my head back, and look at the ceiling.

I was already falling so hard for Danny. Knowing now… what he was doing, I was painting horrible pictures in my head about what his missions were like. This was his reality. The thought of him leaving tomorrow was making me sick to my stomach.

I tried my best to relax before going back into the room with Violet. Rocking on my heels, taking deep breaths, attempting to think positively about the rest of my shift. Before I went back into the room I thought of the one thing I could probably do at this moment to make her feel better. To try and distract her from her dark thoughts along with mine. It was not much at all but I had to do something. I walk to the supplies closet and get a hair brush. There were always some hygiene tools around. I close the supply closet door that's seconds away from the nurse's station and head back toward Violet's room. It was a slow night in the ICU so I have time. I can't bring back Damon for her. I can't magically heal her trauma and make her forget about the sinister evil she went through, but I can do this. *I can brush her hair.*

I walk back into the room, slowly, and start removing the restraints from Violet. I want her to know that I trust her to not hurt me and she could trust me as well.

"Wh— what are you doing?" Violet asks me. As soon as the first restraint lets loose, she holds her wrist to her chest, massaging it.

I go over to her other side, doing the same. I look at her, my bottom lip twitching out of sorrow.

"Damon is still out there. I know you don't want to hear this, Violet. I wish I had more of a positive update and I'm sorry. I'm sorry that you had to endure such terrible things." I study her, holding the hairbrush to my side, standing. She's looking back at me and her eyes get glossy.

I let her sit with her thoughts silently. She holds her knees to her chest, looking back at the TV. I start gnawing at the inside of my cheek.

"May I?" I plead, lifting the hairbrush in the air next to my chin.

She looks at me, pausing. I could feel her pain with just the look she was giving me. Then, she nods. I walk to her, getting behind her so she could keep watching the TV show. I part her hair in two and start with one side, brushing ever so gently. Her hair was so badly knotted.

"How old are you?" I ask.

"Twenty-five." She whispers.

"Ah. I'm twenty-two. I'll be twenty-three this December."

I keep brushing her hair and I'm able to get almost all of the knots out on one side without pulling her scalp so hard.

Violet doesn't respond. We sit there in silence for a good few minutes. Watching Andy Dwyer and April Ludgate be an iconic couple. They were polar opposites yet they absolutely adored each other and balanced one another out.

"He reminds me of Damon... Andy does."

My heart skips a beat and I realize she's opening up to me. Internally, I was thanking God that she was feeling comfortable enough around me to do so.

"How so?" I ask, untangling another knot. Glancing from the TV and back to her hair.

"He's funny, always saying positive shit in fucked up situations..." She looks down at her hands, I stop brushing when she moves, avoiding pulling any hair.

"Damon... Damon's my lover, I guess. We never put a title to what we were but we acted like we were together. We had been seeing each other for six months and everything was going well. We're in the same unit so we got deployed... together. More time to see each other without getting separated as the military life likes to do... And then this shit happens." I hear her teeth grind together.

"All of our friends died in the Humvee crash. But we didn't. At first, we thought we were the lucky ones... *I was dead wrong.*"

I choke up. I need to figure out a way to stop myself from crying. I keep brushing her hair as she pauses.

Don't cry. Don't cry. *Don't. Cry.*

"He saved my life one night while being tortured." Her voice chokes up. I stand there silently, giving her the space she needs to tell her story.

"One man would hold me down and the other raped me in front of Damon. They wanted him to hear my screams. They wanted to break him and I down, to give them information about our unit and our military posts... so they would rape me. Beat us, starve us, until we were on the brink of death. One day... the creeps demanded information again from him and I but we didn't budge, as always. So..."

She pauses, readjusting herself, holding her knees tight. And I'm internally breaking. I don't want her to go on. I don't want to hear about all the horror she went through. But if I could be that person for her right now, I would listen clearly.

"They stripped me naked in front of Damon making him watch." Violet starts sobbing uncontrollably, gasping for air I stop brushing her hair and I hold her shoulders, gently, trying to comfort her.

"You don't have to continue, Violet. I —" Violet cuts me off.

"No! Let me get this out. I can't keep this in my head. Let me get this out, please! I don't want all of this to be trapped in my head... please!" Violet whips her head towards me, looking up at me, pleading and I want to so badly hug her like she was my sister. A big sister that I never had. A tear falls out of my eye and I nod.

"They stripped me down naked. They lit a fire on a fucking

piece of wood, holding it to my thigh. I start screaming and Damon's shaking in his chair. I'm looking at him while I'm being burned and these fucking evil pieces of shit, laugh at me. They were too busy torturing me, they couldn't see that Damon was breaking his hands to get out of his restraints. I couldn't stand the burning... the pain of my skin getting burnt off... so, I spit on the man's face. The one holding the wood." She scoffs.

"He didn't like that." She smiles, wickedly.

"It got him to stop burning me but it didn't stop him from wanting to kill me for it. It sent him into a full-blown rage. He dropped the wood and grabbed a machete instead. The other creep tried his best to stop his friend, he tried to talk him out of it but the man was charging for my throat. Then Damon gets free and tackles him to the ground, knocking the machete out of his hand."

She starts to sob again uncontrollably.

And I'm crying. I've lost it. I'm balling my eyes silently behind her, my body trembling and I feel like I don't know this world I live in after all. The evil that lives in this world is starting to hit me like a train and I want to flee. The world Danny so badly wants to protect me from. The stories he doesn't want me to hear. I get it now. *I fucking get it.*

"They both tussle but it's two versus one and... and they beat him so bad. He goes unconscious for a day... he saved my life. And... and I was angry. Angry at him for not letting them just kill me. For getting himself beaten so badly."

She's crying, her face in the palm of her hands and her heart rate goes up. Her blood pressure reflects that it's dangerously high. The stress of her telling her story was causing her vitals to jump all over the place and I stood there frozen. Unsure of what to do. I hesitate. I finally make a move. I hug her from behind, softly. I hold her from behind hoping she can feel that she's not alone anymore.

"You're not alone Miss. Redd. You're here, now. You don't

have to heal by yourself. You'll be with family and friends soon and if you want, I'll give you my personal phone number whenever you need to talk. I'm here for you."

Violet sniffles, wiping away her tears.

"They have to get him back," Violet whispers. The tears are falling off my face and I do my best to wipe them away with the back of my hand.

"They have to get him back so I can yell at him. Fight with him. Hug him. So I can tell him that I love him. I never got to fucking tell him that. We've only been seeing each other for a couple of months and I don't care what anyone thinks... but I know. I know that I've loved him since the first day we met. I fucking love him." Her voice is muffled, by her hands but I can still hear her words clearly.

"He knows, Miss Redd, he knows," I say, clearing my throat, as I straighten myself, going back to brushing her hair. I don't know much about Damon but I know for damn sure he must have known that she loved him by the way she talks about him. And I know that he feels the same way about her.

"I'm forever thankful to the men that saved me. Navy SEALS Rider, Rooker, Slaughter will always have a special place in my heart. Even Zeke."

When she mentions the man that infuriates me to my core, I have to force my smile away.

As I brush her hair, her vitals go back to normal and she's resting on her side that doesn't have broken ribs. She continues to tell me more about Damon as the Parks and Recreation marathon continues. She says it makes her feel better. She opens up about how they met, what he looks like, and her time in the military. She manages to laugh when she talks about him and I'm content knowing this is helping her heal.

"Please call me Violet, by the way…" She stares at Andy and April on the TV screen. "Have you ever felt that?" Violet asks.

"Felt what?"

"Love at first sight?"

Her question hits me like a hurricane. I finish braiding her hair and tie it off at the end. The night I first met Danny pops into my head. The mysterious man that read my emotions so easily. The smell of cigarettes and whiskey floods my senses, and butterflies are swirling inside my stomach.

I chuckle.

"I'm only twenty-two." I shrug.

"So?"

CHAPTER 26

ARI

I'm in the bathroom sobbing. I'm sitting on the floor, crying not caring if it's dirty. I feel weak and drained. I could feel Violet's pain and her agony. I felt it through her stories and her cries for Damon. This was her life now. She's getting transferred back to the United States in a few days to continue her recovery and I didn't have the heart to tell her that. I knew she wasn't going to take it well. I don't want to know what she would be feeling, finding out she'd be leaving Damon behind. I don't blame her if she wanted to set the whole world on fire. I would set the whole world on fire if it meant I could bring my brother back.

My shift ended twenty minutes ago and I didn't have the mental strength to leave without letting out what I had just heard. I had totally forgotten about Danny.

It was around ten at night and I felt gross. I still haven't showered and that repulsed me. I couldn't wait any longer so I decided to jump into one of the showers they had at the hospital for on-call staff.

I undressed, wrapping my clothes in my backpack, jumping into the hot water that was running. The hot water felt amazing, the longer I stood under the water, the more stress left my body. Violet's question still lingers in my mind.

Love at first sight?

The feelings I have for Danny are strong but still… I don't know him even though he makes me feel like I could spend the rest of my life with him.

The shower was quick, I finish fast and then I throw my clothes back on before I step out. Violet had fallen back to sleep when my shift ended. She was doing a little better after spilling out the horrid memories in her head. She was begging for me to listen but I was already more than happy to be all ears. This poor girl would never be the same again but maybe with time, she could heal. Maybe when she gets back with Damon, she'll feel whole again.

I grab my backpack, throw it over my back, and head toward the lobby. Danny's nowhere to be found and it confuses me. He said he would be here waiting. I take another glance looking to both sides of the waiting lobby and I only see a few soldiers waiting to be seen but no Danny. Maybe, he racked out and was catching up on rest before he had to leave.

Crap… I really didn't want him to go in the morning.

I exit the doors that lead to the outside of the building and start my way back to my place. I shouldn't be offended. I got out way later than I originally told him. I sigh, dragging my feet out across the pavement. The moon is full, the air chilly, and it was honestly the most clear the sky has looked since I'd been here. It was breathtaking. My head falls back, while I take the whole night in. I could see all the stars twinkling around a full white moon glowing. I take this moment to appreciate the world's beauty despite all the evil crawling among us.

The day before I was saving a life and that meant *everything* to me. I saved my first life with my bare hands.

When Rooker came in, he was bleeding out so profusely. A black hawk just

landed and as soon as we got him on a gurney, I climbed on him. The
bleeding wouldn't stop so I plugged my hands into his wound, pressing it
tight and I wouldn't let go. Rooker was unconscious and I was on top of
him, my hands applying pressure on his wound. His pulse was extremely
weak and I felt like we were going to lose him, for sure.

The entire time, I'm hot and anxious. Multiple nurses and doctors are
wheeling us both into the building, straight to an Operating Room.

"You're doing good, Ari. Keep applying pressure! Don't stop or he'll bleed
out!" Doctor Diaz orders me and I don't hesitate. My hair falls in my face
and I'm looking at Rooker's pale face and all I see is my big brother. Paul's
face replaces Rookers' and I feel like I'm in some bad dream.

"You're not leaving. I won't let you." I whisper, my lips tremble and Lori
looks at me confused at first but then it registers for her.

Tears fall down my nose, I'm sweating, my cheeks red hot and I see blood
seeping through the cracks of my fingers.

I won't let my brother's friend die.

Something catches my attention, interrupting my trance and I'm in awe. I watch a bright shooting star fly by and I smile. I watch it in silence, my eyes following its direction before it burns out leaving me in tranquility.

"So breathtaking," I mutter, looking up at the sky in between two pillars in front of the hospital.

"You are."

Danny's voice almost makes my ass drop to the floor as it startles me. My whole body jerks, my heart skips a beat, and I'm squeezing the straps of my backpack.

I whip over to my right to see a cheeky Danny, holding a cigarette in his mouth taking a hit, leaning on a pillar, smirking so hauntingly handsome. The sight of him almost has my knees shaking. *God, he's so entrapping.*

"Dammit Danny, you scared me!" I shout, stomping my leg, catching my breath. I'm pushing my side bangs out of my face.

"I'm sorry," he blows out smoke in the opposite direction of me, then puts out his cigarette underneath his shoe.

Seeing him in front of me makes my mind go hazy. My body feels like it's getting pulled into him as I remember the last few hours I had with Violet. At this moment I can't help it but *I feel lucky.* Lucky that I even get to see Danny in person. He's alive and breathing. A moment that's so routine sometimes people in relationships don't understand how fast it can be taken away. It's easy to take it for granted but in this second, I decide I won't let it go to waste.

"I went out for a smoke, while I was wa—"

I don't let him finish, I take off, sprinting, and then I crash into him. I hug him so tight and I don't care if I'm coming off as needy. I feel like he's going to disappear if I don't hug him hard enough. At first, Danny goes rigid. He's trying to figure me out but he quickly holds me back, his hands snaking through my hair, gently.

I'm burying my face into his body and I'm sobbing. The air grows thin and my chest is tight. I thought crying in the building before I left work would prevent this exact moment, but seeing Danny only heightens my emotions, making them boil over inside of me. I don't want him to leave. To witness all that I have over the past few months, with my patients, sends fear creeping inside of my mind about the possibility of him not returning. So much death has surrounded me this past year. The sunshine that lives inside of me... I can feel it fading away with so many thunderstorms I've endured. If something happens to Danny... *I don't even want to think about it.*

"Cherry, what's wrong?" Danny's deep voice rumbles through his chest and I go weak.

"You're going out tomorrow to find the other hostage, Damon right? Aren't you?" I peek up at him. Danny stops frozen and he's quiet. He knows I know.

He looks at me so intensely, his blue eyes flicker and I can't tell what he's feeling. It's as if he's upset yet he's holding something else back from me. I'm sure he knows that I've been talking to Violet and Doctor Diaz. It's not going to be long from now that Violet's story would be all over the news.

He licks his lips before changing his vision from me to the sky. And I know my answer. He won't tell me anything and I'm not surprised. My eyes dry up and I bury myself again in his body. His muscles tense over my back. Why does he make falling apart so easy?

"Don't worry, Ari. I'm coming back home to you, I promise you. This is a first for me… but I wouldn't have it any other way." I flinch at his promise. He knows very well I have my doubts about him returning alive after Paul died. Paul promised my mother and me the same thing. But for some odd reason… I trust him. I believe him. Danny is starting to feel like an immortal man to me. As if, nothing can kill him. Nothing can hurt him. The way everyone in the military community talks about Danny… they make him seem like a mythical legend that can't die.

"You have every right to not trust me after everything you've been through," his fingers slide to my chin, lifting it so I can look at him. His eyes are glistening with devotion. Relief washes over me and I'm aching to be in his bed again. A tear escapes and it falls down my cheeks and he wipes them away with his fingers. I close my eyes relishing his touch.

Danny shakes his head.

"Don't cry over me, baby. I won't let you. The only time I want to see you cry is when I'm fucking you." His pressed lips lift into a haunting smirk.

The smell of sweet whiskey burns into my nostrils and it swallows me. The scent is strong like he had been drinking for a while. Instantly, I'm curious as to why he drank so much to the point it stains his clothing. Still, I'm somehow drawn to this scent of his. It arouses me and I feel ashamed. The smell of alcohol and cigarettes mixed together, create a perfect potion of lust that I can't stop longing to taste in him and *only him.*

"Danny… are you drunk?" I look up at him and he licks his lips, followed by a flash of his perfect, white teeth.

"It's my last night here, why would I waste it being sober?" He says nonchalantly.

I frown. I'm starting to realize that drinking is just a part of Danny's identity and it saddens me because I know deep down inside it's because of all the darkness that devours him, daily.

"The sky is so beautiful tonight," I whisper, softly, changing the subject.

"Sometimes, I wish I could fly because I know… I know Paul… he's up there. And I just want to be closer to him. We had plans… *he had plans.*" My voice cracks.

Tonight has just been the most overwhelming, emotional night that I've had since my brother passed. The past forty-eight hours actually. From having my room destroyed, to letting go of my promise to myself and God, to taking care of Violet and her tragic situation, it's all too much.

I notice a change in Danny's body language.

"Let's go. I want to show you something." Danny lifts my chin up to him and rubs his thumb over my bottom lip softly.

"Where?"

"I called in a favor. Funny you mention flying." He smirks.

"Huh? What do you mean?" I ask, wiping away a tear, and laughing.

Danny looks at me with a grin. He grabs my hand and it sends me into a shockwave.

"You'll see."

Danny and I are escorted in a car toward the airfield of the military post. It doesn't take long at all. Everything was built so close together on this post.

The night is dark but the moon gave us enough light to see where we are. There were Apaches, Black Hawks, Chinooks, and airplanes surrounding the airfield, all lined up and organized. But there were a few on the tarmac getting ready to fly. The sounds of helicopter engines and the blades of the aircraft filled the air.

The closer we got, the vibrations and volume grew. Danny opened my car door and I was extremely hesitant about what his plans were. I'm pretty sure I'm not allowed anywhere near this area.

"What are we doing here?" I ask him, as he grabbed my hand leading me out of the car.

"Have you ever been inside a helicopter?" His question catches me off guard. I open my mouth to answer but saliva gets caught in my throat.

Palpitations hit my chest and I cough. I have a huge fear of flying. Airplanes and heights in general. I never rode roller coasters or went hiking in high mountains, it just wasn't for me. Acrophobia is a real thing and a huge red flag.

Danny laughs at my incompetent behavior.

"Are you okay?"

"I'm sorry it's just that... I'm terrified of heights. And no, I've never been in a helicopter before. When would I ever find myself in that situation?"

Danny shakes his head, leaning in my ear.

"Another first I get to take part in then." Danny grins. My mouth falls open and I lightly push him away from me.

"Danny! I am not getting on a helicopter! I'm pretty sure I'm not even allowed to be here." I nudge him in his side as he tries to pull me into his arms.

"No, you're not but again, a good friend of mine is a Black Hawk pilot. I wanted to show you what it's like to ride in one."

He's not giving me the option to say no. His hand finds mine, intertwining our fingers together and he's pulling me against my will. I try my best to run but his grip only tightens on my hand.

"No Danny stop! I'm scared of flying!" I'm trying to pull my hand out of his but it's no use.

We're walking closer to a group of men dressed in their camo uniforms standing next to the helicopters running. I'm literally fighting against his hold like a child throwing a tantrum and the parent has to drag them along.

As we get closer, I stop trying to pry myself out of Danny's hand. My cheeks are heated as I grow uncomfortable the closer we get to them. I'm in my scrubs and the wind begins to pick up leaving my skin in goosebumps. Danny wears a dark green shirt, a particular shade of dark green that's almost brown. Along with all-black Oakley pants and boots.

We're finally a few steps away and all the men turn towards Danny, they all have wide smiles on their faces, excited to see him. He finally drops my hand.

"Oh, would you look who it is? Mr. Grim Reaper joins us on tonight's ride." A tall, handsome man greets us reaching out for Danny to shake his hand. They pull each other into a brotherly hug, a pat on the back and he does the same to the other four men around us. *Does everyone know Danny?*

"You know I never pass up a chance to be in one of these, Reid. If I didn't love the forefront so much I'd be up in the sky with you guys flying these badass machines." Danny says with a wink. His smile flashed his straight white teeth. And I almost faint at the beautiful sight of his thrilling look. I stand there awkwardly behind Danny, hiding behind his massive frame.

"So this is Ari? The nurse that helped save Rookers' life?" Another voice I don't recognize asks and Danny moves to the side, revealing my hiding spot. He must have told them about me.

Shit. I have to socialize now. One of the things I least enjoy doing.

"Hi..." my voice breaks and I clear my throat while waving awkwardly next to Danny.

One of the men, bald and more rugged looking, looks me up and down before drawing his hand outwards for me to shake. The way the man looks at me makes me uncomfortable. Danny senses my uneasiness and placed his hand on my lower back, and I feel like he's sending them a message.

"We can get in a lot of trouble for this but a friend of Grim and Rooker is a friend of ours." I shake their hand, nodding in return.

"Alright, it's just about that time y'all, let's fly." Reid claps his hands together and waves his hand over his head as he retreats towards a Black Hawk Helicopter.

CHAPTER 27

ARI

The helicopter is loud, the sound of the mechanics makes our bodies vibrate as it takes off. Three other black hawks had taken off before us and we were the last to get in the air. I feel like my heart is pounding into my throat and I'm hyperventilating next to Danny the entire time. Danny's incredibly relaxed as I imagine he's been in these types of aircrafts many times. There's a hatch in the middle of the Black Hawk and it's open. We're seated in the back of the helicopter and it gives us cover and privacy from the pilots. I'm holding on to the straps of my seatbelt so tight, my knuckles turn white.

I hate flying. I know I told him I wanted to fly but I meant in a *magical way* like Peter Pan. Or like I had wings. A fantasy.

I hate heights. The most irrational thoughts would enter my head every time I was on an airplane and now I'm on a helicopter. Yet... with Danny, I think this is the most romantic gesture anyone has done for me. I was scared yes, but with him he makes me feel safe in any situation.

He was very limited in what he could do in the middle of a deployment. So this was something, to say the least.

Danny and I were the only ones in the cabin. While the two pilots were in front, flying.

"Relax. I just want to take you to the moon, Ari." He says sarcastically. His killer smile burns into me. "These black hawks usually hold around eleven troops. But it's just us."

"You know, you still haven't answered my questions about my brother. I deserve an answer." I try my best to shout over the heavy winds and roaring blades of the helicopter.

Danny goes stony faced and I immediately feel bad bringing it up. But every time I want to talk about it, he shuts down. He builds up a high wall that I can't climb over. No matter how hard I tried to knock it down, he wouldn't budge.

"I know," he tells me. I feel his hands intertwine with mine.

Still, I would keep pushing him until I got my answers. No matter what Kane had said about him, I believe the full story wouldn't exacerbate Danny. There's a full story with multiple sides and I needed to know Danny's. I needed to know the full truth about what happened.

"You do." Danny squeezes my hand tighter and looks out the hatch.

The helicopter makes a sharp turn and I'm falling into Danny's lap. My head collides with his lower chest and he manages to keep his balance since he braced himself, holding onto the straps off the wall. His bicep flexes hard and it immediately sends my blood thrashing at the sight.

We sit without saying another word and I'm watching the bright stars twinkle against the dark blue sky and I feel complete bliss in this moment. Iraq is a beautiful country. I finally get a glimpse of the country's beauty passed the army post.

My fear of flying starts to fade. Every time I'm next to Danny, he manages to make any dangerous situation, feel okay. I could be in a full-blown panic attack and all it would take was one glance from him to make it all better. He manages to make me feel safe… *always.*

He puts his arm around my shoulder, protectively and I snuggle in close. His scent drives me wild. I lay like that on his shoulder and I'm the most calm I've felt since I got to Iraq. I never knew Danny had a side like this attached to him.

It's cold being a thousand feet up in the air. Chills groom the crisp air and the only thing keeping me warm is Danny's body heat. I'm watching dark clouds move in and his sweet gesture turns into dark lust when suddenly he grips my hair gently, then pulls me down and I'm met with an intense gaze.

I bite my lip and lust begins to swirl in my stomach.

"What is it about the way you look under the moonlight that drives me mad?"

Then he crashes his lips to mine. His other hands travel to the other side of my face and he holds me in place, his tongue tasting every single part of my mouth. Our lips move in sync. Fast, heavy, and full of scandalous need.

"Does flying scare you the most?"

"Yes," I tell him, my lips still moving against his.

Danny unhooks his seat belt, leaving me in a frantic panic. I stop breathing and my eyes widen.

"What are you doing?"

CHAPTER 28

DANNY

"What's it look like I'm doing Little Angel? I'm going to show you that the only thing that should scare you the most, *is me*." I stand over her, my hands planted over her head against the wall of the cabin. My torso facing her, I'm hard and I can feel my cock poking through my pants, it immediately makes her blush and flush red, and she tightens her thighs together. Her body betrays her and that makes her so easy to read.

"Losing your mind that's what it looks like!" Ari squeaks out, quietly panicking. She thinks I'm going to fall out but she underestimates me. She looks so cute when she's afraid but still doesn't cower away from me. Her words mean nothing when I can feel her body heat begging me for more.

"My mind was lost a long time ago." I unzip my pants and I see her swallow her excitement while holding onto the seat cushions. Her brown eyes sparkle with lust and I just know I have this pretty little soul wrapped around my insanity.

"No, I think it's the alcohol that's tainted you" she growls me. "Danny! The pilots will see us."

I look up toward the pilots and they know better. They keep their eyes on the sky just as I expect.

"They're too busy flying. You worry too much. Stop thinking. Stop being so scared."

She bites her lip and I can sense her arousal. She moves her eyes from mine and looks at the zipper of my pants.

"I told you, Cherry. The next time we fuck, I'll show you what it's really like to be with a man like me. You wanted me to show you just *how out of my mind I am*. Well, this is it."

I'm an honest man, I don't hide who I am. I'm fucked up and I'm going to *show her*, not *tell her*. I'm watching Ari and she's frightened by the idea of falling out of the sky… but there's a side of her. A side of her that's enveloped with unhindered curiosity. She wants to be burned in the process of unraveling the sadistic parts of me and I love it. My little Angel isn't entirely angelic, after all.

She bites her lip. Her eyebrows inward, studying me.

"You're different than any other man I've ever met. You don't try to hide who you are and what you want… and neither will I."

I don't blink, I'm watching her with such fascination. No woman has ever been able to get more out of me but here she is… just existing and I'm tempted to give her the whole fucking world. Temptation sinks into me and I begrudge her for it.

She pulls down my pants and my cock is exposed. I fist myself while looking at her beautiful, soft, full lips. The wind brushes her hair away from her face and I watch it shine and glisten against the moonlight. Fuck, how I love that her hair is so long. I can't wait to get a fistful of those soft, long strands, pulling it as I take her from behind, ravenously fucking her. Not yet… but soon.

Her eyes bulge and she fidgets in her seat.

"Danny, I'm not sure what to do." She looks down at my swollen, thick veiny cock. She's already seen me but she's still admiring my cock like it's her first time again. She's taken aback by my size. It didn't fit inside of her. I ended up tearing her. I broke her and fuck do I love doing that. I'm a monster who likes to make my little Ari scream my name as I mix blood and pleasure together.

"I'm going to show you. I've already taken you once, there's no need for me to be so gentle anymore."

She looks up at me, then glances behind her checking if we have our little window of privacy. She's hesitant but when she sees that we're still in the clear, she licks her lips which sends a deep hum in my throat.

"Ari." Her cheeks go a deep shade of pink. I notice what becomes of her whenever I say her name. "Do you want me to stop?"

She looks at me like I just insulted her.

"No, don't ever stop." She's eager to taste me.

I move the head of my cock, colliding with her soft cheek. I start trailing myself toward her lips, slapping her a few times on those lips that I fucking love to cut open with my teeth. Up and down, the head of my cock on her lips, teasing her. A moan escapes her. I can barely hear it as the rest of her moans are being swallowed by the heavy winds and wings of the Black Hawk. The helicopter engine roars over her moans. The loud machinery gives us an advantage from being caught.

"Such a good girl."

She opens her mouth and I don't give in to her impatience just yet.

"What are you doing?"

"Beg for it."

She glares at me and I treasure when I get to watch her hate me.

"Please." She begs.

Something takes over her and she begins to lick me. I'm shocked at her avidity. Her tongue travels across the veins from the end of my cock to the tip that drips with pre-come. She's playing a dangerous game and I'm a master at it. Before she starts to suck, I grab her neck, tipping her head up so she's facing me, forcefully.

"I want to see the look on your face when you're choking on

it." I tighten my grip around her throat, calculated enough to not crush her windpipe.

I push into her mouth and she gladly lets me in. My whole body goes electrocuted, head to toe, when it hits the back of her tight little throat. She gags as she has a hard time fitting me inside but she doesn't stop. Tears start to prick at her eyes and she blinks them away. *I love when my Angel cries.* I pull my cock back out and I thrust once more until it hits the back of her throat again.

I push farther down her throat and she gags harder. She surprises me with each second that goes by, instead of pushing me away or freezing, she sucks down on me harder.

I roar with satisfaction and it turns me on even more with desire. It feels so good to watch her head bob back and forth from the pleasure I'm giving her. She smiles against my length when she hears my roar of devotion.

"My dirty little whore."

I pick up my pace, and the muscles on my ass and balls tighten with each thrust as I fuck her perfect little mouth harder.

Each time I thrust, I hit the back of her throat, filling her with pain and ecstasy. Tears are rolling down her eyes and she grabs my thighs for balance. She's licking me, sucking me with determination. The sound of wet saliva and suctioning leaving her mouth makes me more hungry to make her cry just a little more.

I fuck her mouth hard, and I can feel the buildup coming. My pace is faster, harder but I stop and her sweet eyes look at me with disappointment. I completely pull out of her mouth before I come.

I reach over her seat belt, clicking it open. The darkness fully taking over me. The need to *fracture all of her boundaries* consumes me. Pushing the limits until the reaper knocks *on her door*, intoxicating me.

"Get up baby," I lick my lips and she's confused.

She's panicking when I unfasten her belt and I hold her hand tight, as I sit back down in my seat. The helicopter begins to descend down. Reid is going to land the helicopter soon and I'm determined to finish.

"Danny, what're you doing?"

I pull her over me so her ass is treading my cock. She sits on my lap as I undress her scrub pants down just enough to expose her opening. My fingers hook onto her scrubs and her cold soft ass is on my warm lap and she's soaking wet. I grip the back of her hair and pull. She shrieks from the force and I crash my lips on her mouth, while her face is backward. Her neck is exposed and I snake my other hand around it holding onto her neck, tighter. She stops her hesitation as I pull on her lip, sucking it, kissing her, worshipping her sweet mouth. I'm watching her get lost in me as her eyes are closed.

I'm consuming her soul. We're drinking each other in as if we had spent weeks in a desert with no water.

"Danny! I'm going to fall out." Ari pulls away as she voices her concerns and it turns me on that she understands her situation very well.

"You're going to love it, trust me." I stop kissing her swollen lips and she finally looks at me.

Her brown eyes look intensely at me.

"Don't make me regret it." She palms the back of my head as she looks back at me. Brushing her fingers softly against my hair. She's searching for the vulnerability in me, her eyes watching my expressionless face, and I don't want to give it to her… I'm giving her enough. The innocence of her stings. *She shouldn't trust me.* I clench my jaw when the proposition leaves her mouth.

The sound of the helicopter blades whipping the air fills our ears.

She's scared. Terrified. But the need to pleasure my sick need for Death to be a possible outcome poisons me like a fever and *I don't regret that.*

"You're trusting a fucked up man, Ari." My mouth curves crookedly into a devilish grin.

I yank her by her hair as her dripping wet cunt hugs my cock so perfectly when I push half of my dick into her. Her body jolts at the painful intrusion and she screams. Still... the sounds of the helicopter are unforgiving and no one can hear her.

"Go ahead and scream baby, no one can hear you but me," I whisper into her ear. My tone threatening. I bite on her neck and she moans, seductively.

"Danny?" She says it like she's questioning her decision to trust me and it only satisfies me more. *She's mine to break and only mine.*

My cock fully settles inside her and she's so fucking tight. She gasps as she takes in every inch.

"Don't you feel that? That adrenaline? The vibrations from the helicopter running up your legs so hard it's making your perfect cunt throb even more?"

I reassure her that I'm going to protect her from falling out of the open, unrelenting hatch. I feel a weight lift off her shoulders as she lets out a deep breath.

"So, you get off on *scaring me.*"

She's finally caught on and I pull on her hair harder, congratulating her. She starts bouncing on my cock, and I help her take me in deeper. She's so wet and the lust forces her eyes to go dark with fear.

"You finally get it, my little Angel."

I'm pounding her as the helicopter starts getting closer to the military airfield we ascended from.

She starts to cry out of serenity from the orgasm that's about to explode out of her when my cock drives in and out of her. Rocking her so hard, her nails dig into my legs so deep and I know she's broken through my skin. Fuck, I love it when she does that.

"Welcome to my world." I rasp into her ear, and the heat from in between her thighs intensifies. I'm fucking her with such insatiate, such need, nothing will stop me from taking her so hard. I'm a greedy man when it comes to her.

"Fuck." I growl from behind her. Each time I drive into her, it sends us both into a frenzy, chasing our climax.

"You're insane!" She's not wrong. She yelps as her hips rock down into me and her pussy tightens around my cock.

"I'm going to make this quick." I roar from behind her, anchoring her back from the strong winds that want to pull us both out of the helicopter. But I know damn well, we're going to be just fine.

"Maybe I should pull on your hair more often, your pussy responds well to it."

My pace is fast, rough, and determined to blend the pain with her pleasure.

"Danny, oh God, I'm going to finish. Don't stop!" She calls for me to rail deeper and harder. I push my entirety into her, over and over again, fucking her so mercilessly that every time her body jolts forward from my lap, every time she collides with my cock, I just pull her back by her hair and tighten my grip on her collarbone. She's so wet, soft, and tight.

I help her chase her need for pure satisfaction. I circle her swollen, clit and she shakes.

I'm not shocked at how the pilots haven't heard us or checked on us.

It doesn't take long, the sound of her cries have me on edge. I speed up even faster than before and then, I drop my pace to slower deeper thrusts as I fill her up with my come. I growl behind her. She comes so hard, and I smile against her shoulder, planting a kiss as I let her ride out her orgasm. Our mixed fluids are falling out of her.

I had promised myself I would never let a woman in and Ari is *fracturing my boundaries*. My little Cherry showed me she's not afraid of me. Even when I just showed her how deep the need to break her goes. Now, I'm not so sure of what I want going forward but what I do know is… that this feels so foreign.

I pull her pants up again, guiding her to take her seat next to mine. She sits down trying to catch her breath. I've lost the adrenaline and something else takes over me. An emotion I thought I could never feel, overruns me. I can't quite explain what swirls into my chest and I hate it.

What is she doing to me?

I reach over and drag the seat belt over her curvy waist, securing her. I look at her and she's breathless. Her chest moves forward and down, rapidly, as I pull my pants up, securing my own seat belt.

I give her a short aggressive kiss and she melts, kissing me back desperately. She lets me command her body. But when I pull away from her, she settles into her thoughts. Her eyebrows furrowed as she smoothed out the wrinkles on her uniform. I can feel the hatred boiling inside her. I quirk a brow studying her and she looks pissed… but I'm completely content with that.

CHAPTER 29

ARI

The entire time we make our way back to his room, we're quiet. I refuse to speak to him, I know I'm being stubborn but I'm conflicted. I'm lost in my thoughts the entire time we make our way back.

I was mad at myself. I loved every single second of it and I'm questioning my need to go to therapy.

I didn't like breaking any type of rules. The pilot, Reid, had advised me to keep my seatbelt on at all times since this was my first time and he was well aware of my fear of flying. Yet, with Danny, I had already broken so many of my morals. He was the devil on my shoulder, pulling me to his darkness.

So many rules were instilled into me at a young age, with an overbearing mother and a religion. A lot of them broken to no return.

The adrenaline I experience with Danny is starting to infect every single fiber of my being.

His voice could make me do a million things I was unsure of and at the same time, make me feel like I was the only woman in his world.

This man was questioning every boundary I had thought to set out for myself when it came to the type of relationship I wanted after Shane. Never would I have thought that this would be something that he would leave me begging for.

I keep challenging myself more and more. How much could I take?

The thrill of Danny's demands sent heat coursing through my veins over the edge. I couldn't deny how much our situation turned me on in the helicopter, just as much as it scared me. I can't explain it but I was starting to discover parts of myself I thought didn't exist. I enjoyed the thrill of possibly getting caught. I *enjoyed* the way Danny commanded me but only by him.

I'm loving the adrenaline, the pain, the pleasure, and the fear he gives me all into one.

The blades of the helicopter caused vibrations that made the pleasure more intense. The high winds could be felt against my clit and I could be swept away just from that sensual gratification it gave me.

I had promised myself, my mother, and ultimately God that I would wait to go all the way, until marriage. Now, I wasn't so sure of what was right but I sure knew that this felt so right when I was with Danny. Despite his ways of showing it.

But the more time passed by, the more I realized Danny fucked me while making our whole situation dangerous. We could have been caught or worst, fallen out and died.

We're finally back to his place and I slam the bathroom door in Danny's face. I was seething. Seething at him for holding me like a hostage by my hair, almost falling to my death from a helicopter with each of his thrusts hitting me.

We're back in his room and it's almost two in the morning. It's not like he gave me the option to go back to my room. As long as he's here, he won't let me leave his sight. He feels the need to protect me from whoever's out to get me. I'm insanely drained, physically and mentally. I just want to sleep. I was angry at him but I know deep down that I liked it. Either way, I didn't want him to know that.

Before I enter the shower, I look at myself in the mirror. My lips are puffy and my mouth feels sore.

I was still processing what just happened. Danny was... he's the man that terrifies me yet intrigues me.

The darkness you run away from yet I was walking.

The dark prince I never pictured growing up falling for. Yet I was willing to join him in his shadows.

I stood in Danny's shower letting the warm water run down my long black hair. Letting my mind travel nowhere but focusing on the way the water hits me. There's nothing like a warm shower after a stressful night.

My eyes are closed, my face underneath the shower head and I'm rinsing off all the shampoo holding my hair out, to get it rinsed. I'm using Danny's shampoo and it smells of spice, mint, and wood. It smells like the intoxicating man he is.

Suddenly, I feel arms wrap around my waist and I'm getting pulled towards Danny's bare chest. He turns me around and I'm at a loss for words. I should know better than to try and hide from a Navy SEAL in his own bathroom.

Of course, he knows how to sneak his way past a locked door, he kills bad guys for a living. A six-foot-six trained ninja.

He's under the shower head now and he's rinsing his hair with his hands, while I'm staring at the droplets fall down his chest, all the way down his very well-defined abs, and stopping at his massive cock that's hardening.

I'm instantly aroused, clit throbbing and I'm begging for his touch. Licking my lips remembering I just had his cock deep throating me not long ago and I enjoyed every second of it.

Danny catches me looking at him and grins, seducing me with his smile. I roll my eyes at him, grabbing the shower curtain, ready to get away from him. He stops me, and grabs my wrist, with his giant hand, hard enough to make me flinch but it wasn't painful.

"Danny, I need to relax." I breathe. I'm looking up at him and I'm still angry about the helicopter sex. "You almost killed me!"

"Have you ever thought of relaxing your ass on my cock?"

Immediate heat rises in my cheeks and I can't speak. My eyes widen with temptation.

"Because I want to claim every part of you, baby. I'm going to show you how much you consume me. But I'm not so sure you can handle this side of me, Ari. I've just shown you just how far I'll go and you're mad. You can't take it."

"*I can* take it," I argue.

"Can you? Does your fear of flying still scare you the most or… the fact that you liked how I made you come so hard as I fucked you on it, anger you?"

This man was breaking my body and mind. His kinks were so intense I don't know how I'm going to survive his lust for me. I'm determined because even though he takes it too far, I *like it.*

I swallow.

"You scare me the most."

He smirks as the water falls down on us both.

"Good girl."

I freeze but that doesn't last long before he backs me against the wall rough but not enough to hurt. His hands are around my neck, gripping me, and it's hard to breathe. Yet, he's strategic enough to still let air in and out. Every move he makes on my body is precise and careful.

"I plan on taking you in every single way I've imagined fucking you since we first met. Your mouth choking on me, you're tight pussy tearing on my cock, was just the beginning." His voice is so sinister it's making my head spin, his words were messing with my brain. I look up at him, not fighting his grip and I can feel his massive cock poking at my waist.

He turns me around so I'm now facing the wall of the shower, I feel a bath sponge brush over my shoulders, and he trails it down to my ass. He circles the sponge on my back then back down to my ass and I'm breaking. I'm breaking because I want him to devour me. Every time he fucks me, he makes me enter a world of constant pleasure I never want to escape. The way he blends the pain with the fun is perfectly formulated and he always sends me into a release of bliss.

"Are you still scared, Cherry? Are you still mad?" Danny coos, antagonizing me as he starts to play with my clit. A moan escapes me and he loosens his grip on my throat, he's no longer choking me but instead keeping me in place. His mouth by ear, biting down and I'm falling apart.

His fingers are magical. The way he plays with my clit sends my body trembling, unable to stay still. He starts circling it, crescendoing it into pure pleasure and I'm about to come. My breathing is heavy as I'm about to climax under his fingers, my nails dig into the skin of his hand that's around my neck, and the pleasure begins to build within me, threatening to burst.

Suddenly as my mouth gapes open getting ready to come all over his fingers, he stops.

"I said, are you still mad, Cherry?"

I look at him, my eyes beginning to fill with tears from the devastation that he stopped giving me what I want.

"Because I'll stop. But if you want me to devour every single part of you, just say the words, my sweet Ari."

I bite my lips, panting, angrily.

"Please."

"Please what?" He hisses into my ear.

"Keep devouring."

"Devour what?" He teases and I'm getting impatient. Longing for his cock, uncaring of where it might go. I just want him so badly, the one time I've ever begged for a man to destroy me and I'm internally shaming myself.

"Everything that makes me, me." I bite out.

He smirks, satisfied. He changes my position. He puts me against the wall of the shower head so that the water is hitting his back and not me. I'm facing the wall, palming it as he spreads my legs apart and he licks me from behind, his tongue inside of me, thrusting so delicious. He's on his knees and it feels like he's absolutely worshipping my body. He makes me feel like a Goddess with the way he devours me. I bite my lip and curl my toes with each lick. My eyes bulge open and a breath escapes me when I feel his finger slide into my ass. I look behind to see Danny enjoying every single second as he pleasures my ass with his finger. I'm taking immense pleasure in each stroke his large finger gives me and a moan escapes me. It feels so right.

"Oh, Danny, I'm disappointed."

"Disappointed?"

"I'm disappointed. I want your cock, not your finger."

He laughs so sinfully, it intimidates me.

"Your sass will only get you punished."

He turns off the shower and throws my naked body over his shoulder as he stalks over to his bed. Our bodies are wet, and steam is swallowing us. He drops my body on his bed and my breasts bounce when I collide with the blankets and I'm watching Danny palm himself.

"Touch yourself baby."

I don't hesitate. My fingers play with my clit and I'm throwing my head back in pleasure. Danny climbs on the bed, hovering over me. He brushes his tip with my cunt, using it as lube, stroking his large cock and I look down, eyes widening.

How the hell is that supposed to go in my ass?

The bed sinks underneath his weight as he kneels, he grabs my legs, pulling my entire body towards him in a primal way. He's on his knees, lifting my waist towards him, and I'm laying on my back on top of the bed sheets. I had assumed he would be bending me over, confusion looms in my thoughts.

"Don't you want me bent over?" I ask.

"How can I watch you scream if you're bent over?" His voice was deep and husky.

Danny grabs me with determination, my legs are in the air, my ankles arranged on each side of his face. My feet are relaxed on his shoulders and I grab onto my breasts, bracing myself. I would let this man do anything to me, he made everything seem right. His seasoned experience was intimidating to me but I would continue to trust him. To lose my virginity to someone that knows how to pleasure a woman is both frightening and exhilarating.

He grips my hips, keeping me in the place he wants, and slowly drives into my ass. Instant agony rips through me and I'm clutching my breasts, hard.

I clench down around him and it only makes him grit his teeth with pleasure.

"It hurts, Danny, it hurts." I squeak, softly. Breathing hard, my entire body trembling at only half his length.

"Good." He says pushing more of himself into me and I tense harder.

"Danny… oh, God!" I shriek, closing my eyes.

"God?" He says it like I insulted him. "Don't bother calling out for Him, He can't hear you. There is no God when I'm around baby." Danny says as he drives himself repeatedly into my ass and the pain eases with each thrust. His cock pounds inside of me and my feet bounce in the air, on each side of his shoulders.

Pain and pleasure were something new to me and I never fathomed that both would go together so perfectly. My eyes roll back into my head with each thrust, our moans, and skin slapping filled our ears, and I loved every single moment. Every ab muscle contracts harder and I can see the veins pop out around his torso.

"This is your punishment, Ari. Every time you sass me, it'll lead you here."

I need to sass him more often then. I bite my lip and circle my clit.

I was completely new to sex, and I feel like I just jumped into the deep end, drowning in Danny's lust. My lack of experience led me to drown each time Danny fucked me, yet right when I thought I could die, he was making me come, begging for more.

Danny reaches for my clit as he keeps his other hand holding onto my waist, his fingers sending electricity in my entire body, making my back arch and I'm so close.

Danny continues to ram his cock into my ass, filling me with his entire length, as he fingers me. The feeling was so toxic and I'm ashamed of how much I'm loving it. He makes me come with his fingers and I cry out as I climax into a cloud of tears and paradise.

Danny's watching me as I furrow my brows, mouth gaping open, breasts bouncing, with each pounding stroke, and incoherent sounds coming from my lips.

"I love hearing you scream." Danny's eyes are dark, so sinister, his husky voice groans out and he picks up his speed, a tear falls down my cheeks, as he finishes inside of my ass. His dark sandy blonde hair's messy and it sends me in shambles of attraction. The pain hurts so good and I don't know who I am anymore.

I no longer feel like a mouse caught trapped in his kinks.

As we lay in silence, I'm stuck wondering on how both Danny and Shane keep appearing in my life. Is it fate? Coincidence? The feeling I got from each of them, *very different.*

Another night of no sleep. Danny has to leave in a few hours. The morning was approaching and I dreaded it. I wanted to enjoy every single second with him before he has to leave. These past three days were a whirlwind of craze and I couldn't keep up with it.

We cleaned ourselves up again before we headed to sleep.

I'm laying on my side with my head resting on Danny's arm.

He had pulled my waist close to his so his groin rested on my ass, our feet intertwined with each other.

"How are you feeling?" He hums into my ear.

I scoff.

"Broken." My body was bruised, bleeding, and yet still craving more.

He lets out a short laugh.

"Don't worry. I'm leaving."

He's leaving.

My heart sinks into my stomach, my smile fades, and I'm instantly upset at his reminder.

"I might not be here when you come back. It's a short contract I signed and I should be in North Carolina in about a month or so."

He stays quiet, listening to me talk. Silence swallows us whole. Anything is better than silence. I don't like it when Danny stays silent instead of opening up to me. I never knew where his head's at. What he would be saying or doing next, *he's unpredictable.*

"Danny..."

"Hmm?"

"What are we? Like what is this?" I'm staring out his window. His blinds are open and I'm watching the stars twinkle in the sky awaiting his response. I typically wouldn't confront someone about something I needed to address. I usually held it inside. But this is a new era.

Danny's body stiffens and I feel like I've ruined such a peaceful moment. These moments after sex were always so cozy but I knew if I didn't ask him I would be stuck wondering about our relationship. When Danny leaves, our communication will disappear along with him.

Danny made it clear to me a few months ago, he didn't commit to any woman. Why would I be any different? I gave myself to him knowing the consequences of getting attached.

"I think it's pretty obvious, Cherry. *You're mine.*"

My heart skips a beat.

"One thing you need to understand about me, Ari, is that I'm not a man of words but a man of actions. I won't tell you how I feel, *I will show you.*"

Blood rushes to my cheeks.

"You're not supposed to be here and I'm not supposed to be around you like this, never mind *have you…*" He pauses.

Confusion sets in but I don't pry further. This is the most Danny's opened up to me.

Danny catches me by surprise, grabs my jaw, and climbs on top of me again. He tightens his grip on my jaw, and I'm looking into his beautiful blue eyes, wincing.

"I'm already going to hell, I'll do my best not to take you with me." Then he's crashing his soft lips to mine, moving my lips with his, engraving every second into my brain. He enters me, slowly, and I scratch his back as I take him in deeper.

Danny's life was still a mystery to me, there was so much he wasn't telling me. His life at home. His need for alcohol. I can't help but feel there's more to his estranged relationship with his father… and *my brother*. There's a reason why he's the way he is. A reason for his drinking, *his lust so dark.* Still, I'm determined and I will unravel the secrecy surrounding my brother's death.

CHAPTER 30

ARI

Meredith and Emilia were waiting for me at the airport. A month passed and I finished my contract working for the hospital in Iraq. My false hope of Danny returning before I left, vanished. Leaving Doctor Diaz and Lori was so hard for me. I had made a new family and I was completely devastated when I finished my last shift. Doctor Diaz made every single staff member write comforting goodbye wishes on a card along with a party in the break room. We promised each other we would all reunite on a vacation trip somewhere in the States, one day.

The plane starts to descend and I grip the arm wrests as I feel my stomach float into my chest. Anxiety makes my heart palpitate as I internally plead for the plane to land safely. But I'm immediately reminded of Danny challenging my worst fear. *Flying*. The memories of Danny fucking me while I sat on him, unstrapped, loom in my head. He challenged my fears in ways that made me forget about it. I don't fear flying anymore. I loosen my grip on the armrests.

The plane lands without any of my delusional thoughts coming true. The sound of loud rumbles from the plane vibrates into my ears and I'm celebrating a safe plane ride.

I hadn't heard from him since he left which he told me was going to be normal. We couldn't communicate with each other so I patiently waited for his call or text. He reassured me his safe return but I took it with a grain of salt. My brother always reassured my mom and me, yet we were burying him a few months later after he left.

I fiddle with the new bracelet on my wrist. A red bracelet with a cowgirl boot jewel in the center. A gift from Violet before she was sent home. She thanked me for my kindness, patience, and willingness to listen to her. Bonding with her solidified I was doing more than just being a nurse... I'm a healer and I will forever hold Violet dear to my heart.

Most nights were sleepless, between the constant worries for Danny's safety and even Damon's return. I hoped Danny and his team would successfully bring Damon back home to Violet every day. It had been a month already with no word or updates from him so I knew the mission is still on.

Violet's and Damon's story was all over the news. Her name had occupied the national news at home for weeks and it had just recently died down. It felt wrong to leave Iraq and Danny. Knowing I was farther away from him, worried me. I couldn't imagine how Violet was feeling. It didn't compare. Violet and I exchanged numbers before she left. I made sure she knew that she could reach out to me whenever she felt like it.

I'm off the plane, carrying my backpack. Walking into an American airport felt so good. It felt great to be home. I went overseas fragile and came back an entirely different person. I was changed in such a short amount of time but I felt like it was a good thing.

The airport in my town was small but it was surprisingly packed with people arriving and departing. I had to go to baggage claim before anything else.

I'm walking through the airport, passing by restaurants and

gift shops when something catches my eye. It's Emilia, Harry, and Meredith. They're holding a poster with my name on it,

Welcome Home To Our Favorite Nurse

My eyes widen when I realize what it says. I clear my throat and my chest tightens. I've missed them so much.

I walk faster as Emilia and Meredith head my way, running. Harry is left with the poster in his hands and he's laughing at how excited Emilia is. The girls and I embrace and I'm hugging them as nostalgia hits. I missed my close circle of friends.

"Ari! We've missed you so much," Emilia exclaims, backing up.

"Dude I've missed you too much! You came back just in time, I have this thing growing on my ass and I need you to tell me if I'm dying or not." Meredith jokes and I'm rolling my eyes at her.

"I'm a nurse, not a doctor, go see a dermatologist, you nasty ass." I shove her gently, giggling.

We reach Harry and we exchange greetings. Harry is tall, Filipino, and the sweetest man I've ever met. He's so good to Emilia. The way he treats her is how every woman should be treated. He was so gentle and romantic.

"Ari, it's nice to see you come back in one piece," Harry says, handing me my luggage. I'm not surprised they grabbed my luggage for me. I was lucky to have them as my group of friends.

"So, I already made plans for us tomorrow night, we're going drinking. The same bar we always go to." Meredith claps her hands together, excited.

"All I wanna do right now is see my mom. You guys are more than welcome to join." The girls agree and Harry offers to drop us all off at my house. He had some work to finish up at home. The best thing about his job was being able to work remotely and on his own schedule.

The distance from the airport to my house is about half an hour. Meredith catches me up on her life since I've been gone.

Emilia expressed to me how stressed she's been the past few weeks due to her wedding.

We get to my mother's house and I'm eager to walk in. I rush getting out of the car and I can already smell my mom's delicious cooking from outside. Homemade enchiladas fill my nostrils. My stomach rumbles and my mouth waters. It's one of my favorite recipes.

I walk into my house flinging the door open, with Meredith and Emilia trailing me. The sun is setting and it's around eight at night. I find my mother preparing the utensils for all four of us on the table with a napkin.

Her eyes circle and she's smiling as she sees me. It looked like she had aged a couple more years since I'd been gone and immediate guilt follows. My mother was never the type of person to constantly check on me. She was a woman of faith. Instead of calling and texting me every day when I was gone, she spent her days going to church, praying for me. That's what she did for Paul and now she did it for me.

"Mija! You're home! Finally!" She brings me into a hug and I can feel her radiant with happiness.

I squeeze her.

"I know Ma. I've missed you so much. I'm home! Thank you so much for making me my favorite." I held back tears as my mother greeted my friends. We all sit down at the table. My mother, of course, fought my pleas to help her serve everyone. I wanted to make sure she sat down to eat before I did. My mother always made sure that everyone else was taken care of before herself.

I was telling my mom about Violet and more interesting medical cases I worked on. The surgeries I assisted in such as saving Rooker's life. She listened with open ears, her eyes glistening with pride.

She begins to cry as I finish telling her about Rooker. The last time I checked on him, he was getting ready to go back to his team.

"Paul is so proud of you. As am I. Nunca lo dudes."

Don't ever doubt that.

I nod, swallowing the tightness in my throat. Stopping myself from breaking into a hot mess. I didn't want this to turn into a night of tears.

"So again, you reunite with *the* hot Navy SEAL guy overseas? What a crazy-ass coincidence. I'm convinced it's fate..." Meredith says.

Meredith pauses grabbing her water before continuing, I kick her knee, clearing my throat. My mother doesn't like it when we use curse words in the house. Meredith catches my signal and nods apologetically.

"Or he's your stalker." Emilia shrugs and I shake my head.

"Danny? Paul's friend?" My mother asks, getting up from her chair, and collecting my plate.

"Yes..." I say as I clean my hands with a napkin. I didn't want to talk about Danny around my mother. I was afraid she would catch onto my true feelings for the man and read me so easily. I'm hoping she won't be able to unveil that I had sex. Sex before marriage was a huge sin, according to my mother. If she found out, I would literally die inside. The way she views me was so important to me. The relationship we have is everything to me. I've never wanted to disrespect or disappoint her but for the past few months, I've been doing everything she would disown me for.

My cheeks are flaming hot and I'm sucking on my bottom lip. I was in my fucking twenties for God's sake but she treated me otherwise. My mom's view on raising me is so contradicting. She wanted me to be independent but also wanted me to know that I was going to need her, always.

"He's a very handsome man. I was wondering where these Tulips came from. They were at the front door this morning." My mom says walking away to the kitchen with all of our plates in her hand. She drops them in the sink, grabbing a dozen tulips that were on the kitchen counter. They were hiding behind a fruit basket.

Confusion and bliss excite me. How did Danny manage to pull this off? I hadn't told him my favorite flowers, were tulips. He must have picked someone's brain about me.

My mom hands them to me and Emilia and Meredith start cooing and making kissing noises. I roll my eyes at them blushing, rushing to smell the flowers, and my mind travels to Iraq. This was so nice and unlike him.

"And there's a card. But I didn't open it. Here you go."

There's a single blank small card folded in half. It's white and I'm hesitant to open it. Knowing what I know now about Danny, I'm afraid to open it. This man was dirty and I loved it. I'm afraid of what kind of lustful words await me. My mother hovers around my shoulder, I peek over to her and she holds up her hands, surrendering.

"Okay okay, I'm leaving." She says retreating back to her chair. I chuckle and open it. Meredith and Emilia were across from me rolling over in laughter, anticipating my reaction to the note.

I open it and I immediately frown. My chest tightens, my throat aches, and I'm swallowed with fear.

Here are some flowers for getting deflowered
See You Soon
Ari Cakes

"What in the fucking creepy shit is that?" Meredith shrieks, holding the card in her hand. We're in my bedroom getting ready to sleep. I begged them to stay the night to keep my mom and I company. The more people in my house, the better. Harry brought Emilia pajamas and Meredith was borrowing some of mine.

So many questions erupt one after another. My head throbs from the stress, and nausea starts to get the best of me. My stomach feels like it's burning with acidity. I feel sick. How couldn't I with Shanes' threat? I made a police report right after reading the card.

The policeman that came to investigate was so condescending. He kept downplaying my situation. I told them about the number of incidents starting from my toxic relationship, the bar fight, when my room was vandalized, and now this threatening note.

Either way, he filed my complaint. He mentioned something that set me off. When the cop looked into Shane Mitchell, we found out that he was classified as a deserter in the Marines. Deserting his job was against the Uniformed Code of Military Justice. He stopped showing up to work when he returned home. The military police were looking for him, so this was one useful tip that could lead to his arrest.

That information only made me even more sick. What was going on through Shane's head? He was really losing it. Why hasn't he moved on from me? Why was he more motivated than ever to scare me?

The walls are spinning and I can feel my dinner rising in my throat. I feel the unsafest I've ever been. Paul isn't here anymore and Danny... Danny's halfway across the world, and I feel helpless.

"*See you soon*, like what is that? A threat?" Emilia adds, getting comfortable on my air mattress.

"It's been a long time since we've broken up. I don't get it." I swallow, laying on the left side of the bed.

"Okay but... are we also just going to move past the part where he's accusing you of losing your virginity? Because I'm sure my best friend would have told us something like that. So he must be lying." Meredith raises an eyebrow at me, as she sits at my feet.

"I'm going to be sick."

Instantly, I'm hyperventilating. Questions about my sex life, and now after remembering the horrid abuse I endured at Shane's hands. I had refused to report him to the police before because I believed at one point in our lives, he was good. I cared about him deeply at one point and that always stopped me from running to the police. Our history.

I couldn't handle my upset stomach any more. I take off running towards my restroom. It's attached to the other side of my room making it an easy trip. I lift the toilet seat up and I'm vomiting.

CHAPTER 31

DANNY

Leaving never bothered me before. It excites me. The adrenaline I get from each deployment is my high and I become a different species each time. Grim Reaper is an accurate representation of the way I view life when my uniform's on and my rifle in my hand.

I was leaving no one behind at home, but this time... it's different.

It's going to take me a long while to get used to having someone wait for me. Ari was distracting, captivating, and enraging. I had her pretty little soul wrapped around my demons. Little did she know she also has me sucked into her like a fantasy I didn't deserve.

We're getting ready to raid another village. It's been a couple of weeks of just leads. Our military intelligence would only get us so far. Every time we got intel on Damon's coordinates, my team and I would quickly assemble a plan, act and fail to execute. Our missions were compromised every single time we got closer to him. They would move Damon and the mission would fail.

But each time, *we got closer*. This last time we captured some of them, interrogating the men we got our hands on. Eventually, someone sang lullabies and led us into tonight's mission. At this point, Damon's chances of returning home were slim.

We're in a chinook, it's full of Navy SEALS and Green Berets ready to bring hell. Kane sits next to me even though our friendship is estranged. It hasn't been the same since Kane and I fought. Usually, when shit like this happens, it's not good for the morale.

I refuse to speak to him after such a low blow like bringing up Paul's death in an argument. The fucker went there and he knew he fucked up. To top it all off, witnessing Kane flirt with Ari, had my blood boiling. But I couldn't be mad. It didn't make sense to be mad. *I fucked Ari.*

I've already prepared myself to get so much hate and judgment from everyone that knew Paul in the military, including his team once they found out.

I didn't give a fuck. She was mine, let them fucking talk, let them judge, it won't stop me from consuming her again. The promise to Paul was being fulfilled, just in my own way. I would continue to watch her. Protect her. *Break her.*

"The famous Grim Reaper. Paul's told me a lot about you." A SEAL on my right says. I'm annoyed. I'm well-known in the military community. Not only for my kill count which I despised thinking about but it was *who I had taken out* that made my reputation so widespread. I've killed at least three terrorists on the most wanted list. No other special operator has been able to do that but me.

I glare at him, and his grin fades. Our faces are covered in camouflage paint but I'm wearing my skull mask as usual on top of the face paint. When I enter a chinook, I enter a different state of my mind. The mind of an irrational lethal creature.

He clears his throat, reaching out for my hand to shake but I don't take it. I watch him retract his hand when he realizes I'm not going to take it.

"The name's Zeke." I recognize his voice. He's the SEAL that carried Violet out of the building Rooker and I raided.

"Ah, Aitu. Paul's told me a lot about you." Zeke's operator name means *demon* in Polynesian. Zeke is Samoan. I looked into him when I had to give a full report back to my captain. After every mission, we're required to do a mountain of paperwork. He was a good man from what his reputation says. Same body frame as I, the same height as me, long black hair slicked back, and his arms covered in cultural tattoos.

"We've met before. Just briefly." I couldn't see his face, only his grey eyes. He wanted to talk but I didn't. I never did. My team knew better than to make small talk when we were at work.

I nodded not wanting to continue the conversation. He gets the message and turns back around. I lay my head back resting it, mentally preparing myself for the fucking war we're about to endure. The group of soldiers in the cabin begin to chant the Ballad of the Green Berets. It's a short song and a respectful one.

My hands rub my jaw, my beard poking into the skin of my palm. The air feels ominous. I had a sick feeling something was wrong. Whenever I got this gut feeling I was always right. It was going to be a shit show tonight.

My experience from all the deployments in my career wrecked my way to think positively. I always hoped for the best but expected the worst. Shit, you couldn't even have nightmares of, has happened in my career. And this feeling was screaming at me. *Something is wrong.*

The helicopter begins to descend to our destination and a familiar premonition starts breathing down my neck and I smile wicked, with my eyes closed. It's sending chills throughout my body, making my hair stand up, I flex my back muscles straightening my posture, sighing, making all my knots pop. Death has made his presence known and he would be collecting souls tonight. But I would make damn sure, I wouldn't go down with them.

I've got my little Angel waiting for me at home.

My team is the first to breach the building where Damon is said to be. It's a tall building with lots of rooms about five stories high. There were lots of buildings on this one road. It has been a wild ride up until this point. And finally, we found where they were keeping Damon hostage. The terrorist group didn't know we were coming this time.

The area is surrounded and we made sure to come in with a huge amount of numbers. We would make sure that every single one of these evil sons of bitches would die tonight. Yet, death was looming around me making sure I knew, some of us might not make it back tonight.

You're always here, death. Waiting for me to reap more souls.

I've been around death so much we've become close friends.

The night had just begun, and the villagers were all asleep. We're all on foot with Apache's on standby. Adrenaline is coursing through my veins, as we get closer to the back of the building. Zeke is our new breacher. He's taken Rooker's spot until he recovers and he begins to assemble the bombing device. I give him a nod before he plants it onto the wall.

My mind drifts to Ari. And I swear I can smell her sweet perfume as if she's right next to me. Her scent could bring me to my knees and I wondered why this was starting to become a routine thing.

All the men are crowded around the wall, holding their rifles, strapped with multiple weapons, knives, and grenades.

Ari's sweet floral scent is replaced by something burnt. The smell of wood burning fills the air. My team starts to sniff the aroma, all of us questioning the origin.

This can't be good. Something's burning.

What the fuck are these monsters up to now?

It doesn't take long before the breaching device goes off and it hits all our bodies hard even when we stepped back at a safe distance. All of us flinch, the bomb rattling our bones and ears ringing. Still, I make my way in first and the others all follow.

The first thing I see when I enter is smoke. I clutch my rifle ready to use it. I expected to see men scrambling but nothing yet. I head for the staircase across the end of the hall, quietly, stealthily. It was quiet in the building when we entered but not for long. A man starts to scream with so much terror. The sound erupts in the building and rage starts to blind my vision, seeing red.

Damon Hawk.

Shit. We have to move fast.

Kane is behind me, followed by Lopez, and Zeke. Our boots are quiet as we start to jog toward the stairs. A man appears jumping out in the open into the center of the hallway. He's holding an RPG.

I don't hesitate. I put a bullet right in between his eyebrows. His body immediately goes lifeless, falling to the ground along with his weapon. I didn't even give him a chance to blink. I was fast, accurate, and lethal. My team trusts me to lead them into battles with their lives and I validated their trust every single time.

Death, here's your first soul of the night, do your worst.

The mics in our ears go off, shouting from the teams outside hounding me for questions on where the shots were coming from. Lopez immediately answers them with details. They relay to us that smoke is now seeping into the air from the building. They suspected a fire is about to take the whole place down.

Meanwhile, this is happening, the screaming doesn't stop. It just gets worse and worse and I'm doing my damn best to find Damon before it's too late. My thoughts travel to the worst and I know they're torturing the shit out of him. I didn't want to fail him. I didn't want to fail Damon's family. I want to give Ari good news when I come back from this and I promised myself I would.

The screaming is blood-wrenching, my stomach curls, and I

want to cover my ears from the sounds of pure agony that almost sound demonic.

"Motherfuckers." Kane snarls behind me. I sensed that he was just as disturbed as I was.

We couldn't just rush into any room. Everything had to be calculated and careful or we would pay the price with our lives.

The smoke thickens and it's constricting our breathing. We all begin to cough and smell burnt flesh. I shake my head, coughing into my rifle. The smoke starts to burn my eyes and I'm blinking fast. Trying so hard to keep them open. One blink at the wrong time meant my life or my teams.

I reach the top of the stairs and do a quick scan for threats.

Nothing.

"Clear!" I roar. Kane, Lopez, and Zeke are a couple of feet away from me, on the stairs waiting for my orders. The smoke has gotten so bad and something catches my eye. There's a black fog of smoke pouring out from under a door and I'm positive that it's Damon. His screaming is starting to fade, his voice hoarse. Still, I'm hopeful that it isn't him.

Suddenly, a shiny machete encapsulates my attention, I'm on high alert, and I manage to dodge the attack but I'm getting tackled to the ground, deeper into the hallway away from my team. My rifle flings out of my arms and a massive amount of weight is on top of me, snarling.

A man just about the same size as me is attacking me, with no remorse, spit flying into my face, as animalistic noises spill out of him. He punches me in the face, busting my lips open. The asshole raises his machete over my head but I react so fast, I return with a punch, and we're both exchanging hits. This son of a bitch is fighting back and we're wrestling on the ground.

"I can't get a fucking shot Grim!" Kane calls out to me, panicked. His laser pointing straight at us. If he misses his shot, he risks shooting and killing me. If he takes a shot killing the threat, the bullet could penetrate us both. It's a lose, lose situation.

"Don't worry, I've got this." I laugh, as the darkness takes over my body.

I'm not panicked. *I'm fucking excited*. I've trained hard for moments like this. In fact, I'm relishing every single second. I start laughing harder, sinisterly, grinding my teeth. Blood and spit fall from my lips and I love it.

I hold him back with one of my forearms supporting the man's entire weight with one of my arms. It gives me enough time to reach for my six-inch knife that's tucked into my kit. It's amazing what adrenaline could do in a fight-or-flight situation. His eyes are burning holes in me, holding so much darkness and hatred.

The man wiggles out of my hold, yelling, cursing at me in a different language. He's fast but I'm faster.

I plunge the knife towards his neck, slicing the blade across his throat. Blood sprays across my face and chest and I throw his body off of me, he's scratching at my arms desperately, my uniform protects me from the impending cuts.

Life is slowly fading from his grasp and I'm having too much fun like a kid in a candy store. I don't waste any more time before I'm stabbing him in his chest, eliminating the threat, giving Death another soul. My blade is so sharp, it pierces straight to his heart without a problem. The man's eyes widen with pain.

I stand up breathing hard watching the man on his back, choking, blood squirting out onto his long beard. I'm searching for my rifle while Kane and the rest follow, searching the halls for more threats.

We're all breathing hard due to the lack of oxygen. Sweating and eager to find Damon. He's no longer screaming. And that's never a good sign.

Kane towers over the man I just killed making sure he's really dead. He checks his pulse, clenching his jaw, sweat dripping from his brow. He looks at me and nods. The entire time Lopez and Zeke are working on getting the door open.

I re-adjust my rifle.

"That was fun." I cough.

Aitu breaches the door and he's engulfed in black smoke.

"Fuck, I can't see shit!" He rasps.

We wait until the smoke subsides a bit to see the source of the fire. I'm squinting and I already know what awaits. Finally, it's clear and I assess the situation. The anger I'm feeling enrages me until I'm shaking, dropping my rifle to the ground, disappointed.

It doesn't take a rocket scientist to know that Damon has been burnt alive. Once the building and area get secured, a team would pull out a DNA kit to confirm.

The smell of burnt flesh is so potent it wreaks, making us all sick. I had one straw of hope that we would be bringing him home alive. That was long gone now. My heart drops. I didn't want to fail another family. *Another mother, another sister.* We were too late. Damon's dead. Another son, another brother to be buried. A soul I couldn't save. The flames have completely consumed him and we had to get out of the building so we could let in another team to extract Damon's body and prevent the building from completely burning down. There's nothing my team or Zeke's could do at this point.

Something breaks inside of me and I'm unsure what it was. All I feel is straight disappointment in myself. My sanity chipped once again, shaking my head in distress. I let my head fall down as I rub my beard. I walk out of the building, to get a break from the suffocation. The cool night air hits me and it's relieving. My thoughts scramble for the taste of whiskey. I've felt like I've been spiraling out of control ever since I met Ari. I had fully grieved Paul and was just about healed. But… she reopened the trauma when I met her. The shadows of demons in my head now clouding over me like a meal to devour, my soul for theirs to take.

A mission failed. *Fuck.*

My blood is boiling. My teeth are grinding so hard. My temper rises to unnatural limits replaying the burnt body of Damon in my head. Bright red, orange, and yellow shades blinded me. And now I'm replaying Paul dying in my arms. At this moment, I'm no longer Grim Reaper. I'm weak. I do something I've never done before and I walk away from my team, aggressive with each step, tearing off my skull mask. My boots are heavy on the ground as I head for the chinook. I pull out my cigarettes, and smack the box, packing them against my thighs as I walk.

"Grim! What the fuck man? Where are you going?" Lopez calls after me, confused but I ignore him. My monstrous height passing by Lopez. Military operators of all kinds surround the building, finishing the investigation. We had expected more terrorists but knowing that tonight was the execution of Damon, it made sense there were hardly any of them to fight.

"Let him go, man." Kane grabs Lopez by the shoulder, pulling him back. "Let him be. I've never seen him like this before."

CHAPTER 32

ARI

Before I left Iraq, my application got approved to work in a military hospital at the same post, Danny is stationed on. I started in a week and I was so excited. I feel more confident than when I first started. I wanted to keep working and keep my mind busy.

Meredith and Emilia left early in the morning but they were meeting me at Target later today, I needed to buy clothes and new hygiene products for myself now that I was back home. It still feels so unnatural to be back. And of course, my homecoming had to involve police showing up at my house.

This morning I woke up and had breakfast with my mother. I managed to keep the details of the note away from her. I brought up the idea of getting an apartment on my own now that I was making enough money to support myself. She was of course against it. She didn't want to be alone in the house. Paul never moved out of the house since he was always gone. So instead he saved money by staying home. I felt bad leaving her alone in the house but I also wanted my independence.

I spent most of the day in bed nauseous, constantly snacking, and watching comedy shows. This nausea is coming out of nowhere and I'm starting to think I've picked up a stomach virus from the airplane.

I kept looking at my phone hoping Danny would send me a text, telling me he was back. Every time my phone lit up I rushed for it but only to be disappointed. My sex injuries were long gone by now and I was craving Danny's touch every single day and night. I've fallen so hard for this man. He intimidates me in a way that keeps me hungry for more. He has tested every single boundary and moral of mine with no remorse and I don't hate him for it.

Sitting in my room alone, I want to binge watch horror movies all day but now I feel like my real life was turning into one because of Shane.

The thought of being alone in the house was unsettling. I'm laying down in my bed, under the covers and I keep looking out my window to see if he's watching me. But, nothing. The thoughts were running rampant. Shane's threatening note had me scared in my own home. I kept looking over my shoulder, jumping at any little sound my mom or house would make.

I refused to stay in any longer. I've rested enough. It was time to get out. It was almost time to meet up with Meredith and Emilia anyways followed by a night at El Devine. So I decided to head for the bookstore first then Target. I grab my leggings and running shoes and head out the door.

I get inside my brothers' car, Paul's scent still occupying it. Paul had an old green and brown Bronco. He was so in love with his car. He fixed it up the best he could and was so proud of it. I didn't want anyone else to have it when he passed. I refused to sell it, so I kept it.

As I pulled over my seat belt, securing myself in, I look at my rearview mirror. My thoughts go the worst and I'm scared that Shane's already in here... *waiting for me.* It's quiet. My eyes search around violently through the mirror but the back seat is empty. My heart continues to pound hard in my chest. *God, I'm losing it.* I continue to look around my surroundings inside of my car looking for any sign of intrusion but nothing.

I drive out of the parking lot and head toward the bookstore. The bookstore was by a massive park. It's very popular for walks, dates, and picnics. For me, it was Shane's favorite spot to hit me. It was my favorite spot until it wasn't. Every time I go to the bookstore I have to pass by this park and it brings back the abusive memories.

"How does it feel to be back home from boot camp?" I ask. It was a cold November night. Thanksgiving was right around the corner and Shane was able to come back home after his graduation before he had to go to his tech school.

"Great." He says sarcastically. He takes a swig of his beer before setting it down in the grass. He has his forearms resting on his knees and I'm leaning on his shoulder, sitting. We're in a secluded area in the park underneath a tree. Bushes circling us in. The park's almost empty as it nears midnight.

He's upset and I don't know why. This is our favorite place to talk, hang out, and do over the clothes stuff. I've missed him so much and I was so excited to see him. But this wasn't the Shane I knew. He had an unfamiliar attitude and he was more aggressive than usual. He was acting like an overconfident entitled prick.

"What's wrong?"

"I don't know Ari. Maybe it's because we've been together for a while and you still have this ridiculous underwear rule." He spits, shrugging me off his shoulders.

There he goes again pressuring me to have sex with him. Making me feel guilty about my choices and morals. I wanted to wait until marriage. And I wasn't ready to settle down with anyone, especially Shane.

"Shane. Please let's not fight tonight, please." I sigh. I was annoyed that this had become such a constant fight in our relationship. My phone keeps buzzing so I reached into my pocket. Paul keeps texting me, asking where I'm at. He's complaining that it's late and wants me home but really, he

was worried I was with Shane. I text him back, sharing my location, and reassured him that I'm fine.

"Then suck my dick." Shane orders. He stands up, positioning his groin towards my face. I'm taken back by his words. I'm in complete shock and I don't know what to say or do, I freeze, looking up at him.

Was he serious?

I'm still trying to comprehend the situation.

He unzips his pants, finishes his beer, then throws it to the ground. It shatters in pieces and I jump. My whole body flinches and goosebumps erupt on my skin.

"I can't fuck you. So." He pulls out his hard length and strokes it. My eyes widen and I look away.

"Put me in your mouth Ari Cakes. You said you missed me. Show me how much you miss me." His voice is unrecognizable.

"Stop it, Shane. I mean it. Or I'm leaving." I threaten, looking at the bushes to my side.

"Ari. Stop acting like you don't want it." Shane grins and I'm getting on my feet. I shake my head angry and I'm anxious. This was the first time he was forceful with me.

"Where the fuck do you think you're going?" He stops stroking himself and I'm trying to get passed him. I don't know where I'm going but anywhere is better than here. He grabs me by the hair and pulls me so hard I fall.

My eyes circle and I start shaking.

"Shane! What the hell!" I yell, soothing my scalp. Then he's on top of me, pinning me down with his body weight. Pushing his waist into me and I cry out. I'm attempting to push him off me but he's bigger than me.

He slaps me so hard, he makes my head whip to the other side and I stop screaming. I'm crying now, silently sobbing, holding my cheek. I'm afraid if I scream again, he would hit me.

"Shit, I'm sorry babe. I'm so sorry. I don't know what's gotten into me." He starts to kiss my cheek and I'm studying him, afraid.

He pushes himself off of me, lifting me off the ground.

He just hit me. The first time he put his hands on me and I'm frozen.

He hit me.

"I'm sorry babe. I am. I just miss you. I want you. I want more from you and I'm sorry... it won't happen again." Shane starts pleading with me to stay longer with him. And I can't talk. I can't move. Instead, I feel guilty that I couldn't give him what he needs.

"This is what you do to me. I love you so much and I just get overly excited to know what it's like to make love to you." He's crying into my shoulder, tears seeping through my thin shirt, holding me so tight against his chest and I'm rubbing his back, confused.

"I just want to make love to you. This is what you do to me." He repeats. He finally said it. He loves me.

Little did I know, this was just the beginning of the rest of our relationship.

"I love that there's a coffee shop in here." I smile, before downing my iced coffee and walking behind Meredith and Emilia. Emilia had to tackle her wedding list and Meredith was helping her.

"If I didn't have the shits every time I drank it, I would love it. So I'll just stick to the refreshers." Meredith scoffs and Emilia laughs.

"You guys have to get fitted for the wedding! It's next month. I'm taking you guys sometime this week to the dress shop. I gotta get this out of the way. One less thing to stress about." Emilia tells us as we walk through the aisles of the store.

"Of course, I can't wait. This is going to be my first time as a bridesmaid! I'm so happy for you and Harry. This was a long time coming and I'm so excited for your happy ending." I say, hugging her with one arm.

"Me too. I can't imagine myself with anyone but Harry I know I'm still young but I don't care what anyone thinks. Harry's twenty-five and I'm twenty-two. I feel like I'll get criticized for getting married too young or too late. It doesn't matter. *He's the one."* Emilia rants and I can hear the frustration in her voice. She's been dealing with criticism from everyone about her marriage to Harry. From her family to her friends. She was frustrated but I was so proud of her. She hasn't let that stop her from marrying the man of her dreams.

"What about you, Ari?" Meredith asks, opening up her panini sandwich.

"What about me?" I ask confused, raising a brow.

"Do you think Danny's the one for you?" Meredith teases and I stop in my tracks, shrugging. I don't know if Danny is the one, but it *feels like he is*. We had just met and it was a whirlwind of emotions, craziness, and lust. The chemistry was undeniable in such a short amount of time. Whenever we were together, I couldn't think straight. Just the sight of him made me weak. His voice, something in the way he moves, the way he walks, his ambition, his passion for his career, his scent, his smile. The way he was so protective of me. I was completely enchanted by Danny.

Meredith takes a bite of her panini and it sends my stomach upside down watching her eat it. The smell of the chicken and bacon getting to me and it was disgusting.

"What's wrong?" Meredith asks, talking with her mouth full and I throw my hand to my mouth to stop myself from hurling.

"It's the smell of your sandwich," I say scrunching my nose.

"You have a stomach bug don't you?" Emilia asks, rubbing my back comforting.

"Or she's pregnant." Meredith's voice muffled with food, chewing.

My heart drops and my eyes widen. I can feel myself growing pale and my mind starts racing.

No, I can't be. Shit. I can't be. There's no way. *But there is…*

"Oh, my God. Are you pregnant?" Meredith swallows and I'm trembling.

I wasn't ovulating when I had sex with him. I was always irregular in my periods so I used an app to keep track of them when I did get them. I remember this because I checked right after we had sex and I was in the safe zone. I checked...

Fuck, fuck, *fuck.*

"Shit," I murmur, hyperventilating. Emilia and Meredith both look at each other worried.

"Look, this poor girl looks like she's about to faint. We'll buy a test right now. We're at a Target for Godsakes. They also have restrooms. Let's not worry unless we have to." Emilia starts to jog towards the family planning section and I'm freaking out. Anxiety's getting the best of me and my skin grows clammy.

If I'm pregnant... *no I won't start this rabbit hole.* I'm not pregnant.

Danny and I just met this year. I know situations like this happen all the time but still. This can't be happening to me. It's too fast. It's too soon. I don't know what I would do. I'm too young to be a mom.

I have a stable job, thank God, but what about my mother? Oh God, my mother. She still thinks I'm a virgin for crying out loud. I shouldn't be thinking about what she thinks, though. It doesn't matter. I needed to set boundaries with her already. It was long overdue. I'm in my fucking twenties. A successful nurse. A good daughter.

We hurry out of the self-checkout and I run into the restrooms. I enter an empty stall and take off my pants and start urinating on the pregnancy test.

Emilia and Meredith burst through the restroom doors, setting their belongings on the sink counters.

"So are we going to be aunts or what?" Meredith claps her hands eagerly. Emilia smacks her shoulder, hushing her. I clean myself up and flush the toilet. My heart's racing, unsure of how to calm my nerves.

I open the stall, dropping the test on the counter, upside down so I can't see the results. I need to wait a couple of minutes which drives me even more crazy with anticipation.

"I need some words of encouragement right about now." I rasp, looking at myself in the mirror. I've always wanted to be a mother. Just after marriage. I wanted a husband first, that was always the plan. Yet lately, everything in my life *wasn't* going as I had planned.

"You're not pregnant. Meredith is crazy. You're fine. You just have a stomach virus." Emilia chirps, her voice high.

"Or you're pregnant," Meredith says nonchalantly.

"I swear Meredith. If you don't shut up!" Emilia exclaims, glaring at her.

"What? If she's pregnant, I will be so happy, I will spoil the baby! I'll babysit all the time."

Emilia and I stop breathing and look at her, dumbfounded. "You're not babysitting." We say synchronized.

If I'm pregnant, I'll stay positive no matter what. I truly believe that everything will be okay. I don't know how Danny feels but I'm sure he would be okay... right? If I'm not pregnant, then I can relax and go back to my normal daily life and get my ass on birth control as soon as possible. I didn't expect to become sexually active in Iraq so I didn't think I needed to be on it.

It's about that time to see the results so I flip it over, backing myself up on a wall so Meredith and Emilia couldn't see. My hands are shaking, my body sweating and the nausea hits me like a tsunami.

My eyes lock onto the results and I drop the test.

CHAPTER 33

ARI

I walk into the doctor's office, numb. Photos of pregnant women and newborn babies hang on the neutral-colored, yellow walls. A mother of three who looks well into her third trimester sits, flipping through a magazine. I check in with the receptionist which led to new patient paperwork.

After filling out a mountain of papers, it wasn't long before I was called in by a medical assistant.

After finding out I was pregnant, I shut everyone out of my life. My friends and my mother. This was such a big moment and I wanted to digest it on my own. My life had been changed forever in such a short amount of time and I was doing my best to stay the "positive, sweet Ari" I've always been.

There was still no word from Danny. I didn't know anything. I didn't know how he was doing, when he was coming back, or if his team had saved Damon. It was driving me crazy. Now that I know I'm having his baby, I worry even more than before.

I want him to be okay. *I need him to be okay.* I don't want uniformed men to show up at my door, ever again. I'm pregnant and I couldn't even tell the father. This military world was frustrating. I couldn't call him and he couldn't call me. I didn't want to tell Danny over a text or phone call either way. I'm going to wait until he returns. Depending on the length of his deployment.

I had a good idea of how far along I was. I was just about to turn four months pregnant. I still couldn't believe it had been four months since I first had sex with Danny.

Emilia's wedding is just a few days away and I've been pushing them all away. I took care of the bridesmaid dress fitting before I completely ghosted everyone. I promised her I would show up for her wedding.

I was still hiding the pregnancy from my mother. I didn't want to face her with this. The less stress I put on my body, the better. Stress affects the baby. Anything I feel, the baby feels. I don't think a screaming match with my mother would do any good to anybody.

I wasn't showing. If anything, after I ate was when I showed the most. Everything was moving so fast. I had no idea where my life was going but I knew I had to focus on this pregnancy and my transition to motherhood.

Situations like this happen all the time. One-night stands turning into pregnancies but Danny wasn't a one-night stand. We're together but I can only imagine that this isn't what he had planned. It definitely wasn't what I planned.

My sickness had died down quite a bit as the days go by. My nausea has gotten better and the vomiting has stopped. This was my first doctor's appointment and it was already going unlike I had imagined. *I was alone and scared.* The father has no clue and neither does my mother.

I can't believe this entire time I didn't know I was pregnant. I had no symptoms besides the nausea. My periods were always irregular. My app completely failed to track my fertile windows.

My doctor goes over paperwork with me before she conducts the ultrasound. I'm nervous, biting my lip, and sweating. The cold jelly around my naked stomach makes me flinch at first and my eyes are glued onto the monitor.

"Would you look at that? The little one looks healthy." Doctor Moore cheerfully says.

I'm looking at the monitor and I see a fully formed fetus with a strong heartbeat. My heart grows warm, my worries go away and I'm mesmerized by this little blip on the screen moving around.

"It looks like it's dancing in there." I laugh, breathing hard, trying to hold back the storm of tears that threatens my throat. My eyes narrow, fully encapsulated, and my smile grows stronger. My life was about to change and it was because of a little baby dancing inside of me.

"Yes, baby looks healthy and happy. Is your husband wanting a boy or girl?" Doctor says pulling away from me and turning off the ultrasound machine. I grimace at her words and she quickly catches on.

"Sorry, we don't have to talk about that." She clears her throat, standing. I clean off the jelly that's left over on my stomach with napkins and my small window of happiness disappears at the mention of the father. I pull down my shirt and sit up on the table.

I had never felt so happy like that before. It was a different kind of experience seeing your baby for the first time on a monitor. This baby was my number one priority and I wouldn't let anyone take the joy out of it with their opinions. Things don't always go as planned but I was going to roll with it.

"You're far along enough to do the genetic testing. It checks for abnormalities the baby could have or does not have. Are you interested in the test? Your insurance covers it." Doctor Moore says taking off her gloves.

"Of course," I say standing up, gathering my things.

"And it checks for the gender. Would you like for us to check that?" She asks, raising a brow.

I hadn't given much thought to finding out the baby's gender. I wanted to wait for Danny. I'm just assuming he would want to be here for that.

"Umm, no. I can wait until the anatomy scan to find out if that's alright?"

"Of course it is. Some mamas don't want to find out until the baby is born. Everyone is different."

Doctor Moore hands me black and white pictures of the baby's ultrasound. I slowly take them into my hands, trailing fingers on my baby's face, picturing the baby in my hands when he or she is born. My mind travels to the future and I can't help my hormones. Daydreaming about what my future days would look like as a working mother. I couldn't help but get excited even though there was a lot of uncertainty. Still, the disappointment in myself lingers. I don't know who I am anymore.

Right after my appointment, I went to work. I continued working as a trauma nurse at the military hospital on post. Keeping the pregnancy under wraps was getting harder. I've managed to avoid anything dealing with radiology to maintain a healthy pregnancy. I didn't tell anyone at work just yet until I tell Danny. Then, I can celebrate freely without this secret weighing me down. I was afraid someone would get a hold of him and ruin the announcement for me. Just about everyone I worked with knew Danny Rider.

Operator, Grim Reaper.

A lot of my coworkers were active-duty military members and I couldn't risk it getting back to him. I hadn't realized how big of an impact he had on the military community until I started working.

Everyone around work also knew Paul. I was known as Paul's little sister and everyone welcomed me into the work environment with open arms.

I've been communicating with Violet over text messages and

phone calls. I've stayed in touch with her to keep up with her new life at home and if she's heard any updates on Damon. She's been going to therapy and has recovered pretty well from her injuries. Still, there's no Damon updates.

My shift ended around seven at night and I went straight home, completely exhausted. Lately, all I want to do is sleep.

I arrive at my house and I find my mother watching her routine novellas in the living room. She left a dinner plate for me in the microwave.

"How was work mija?" She yawns and repositions herself on the couch.

I stop walking and sigh.

"It was fine, I'm just tired. I'm going to eat in my room." I shrug.

"Okay. Oh, Emilia is in your room. I told her you were still at work but she said she would wait for you." She says, her eyes never leaving the television.

"Great," I mutter. It's not that I wasn't happy to hear that she was in my room I just didn't have the energy to socialize. I've been on my feet constantly for hours and I just wanted to eat and sleep.

I drag my feet to my bedroom. Wondering why Emilia couldn't have texted me to give me a heads-up. I open the door to my bedroom finding Emilia scrolling through Netflix, in her pajamas.

"Ari! Before you try and kick me out, don't bother. I'm not going anywhere." Emilia rushes out. She crosses her legs and pats down my bed next to her. Her large engagement ring glimmers with her swift movements.

I give her a small tired smile.

"I'm not going to kick you out silly." I throw off my shoes and sit down at my desk in the corner of my room.

"Good."

"You didn't say anything to my mother about the pregnancy, right?"

"Of course not. You still haven't told her? Ari, what is wrong with you?" Her tone was baffled.

Her questions sting and I feel like I'm about to explode. I needed time to process the unexpected pregnancy without my friends or my family's input. I sit down, setting the plate of chicken down.

"Nothing is wrong with me. I'm just going through a phase. Pregnant by my dead brother's, best friend. A Navy SEAL who I just met this year. Yup, just one of those phases. I'm four months pregnant and the father doesn't even know." I shrug, sarcastically.

"I'm sorry Ari. I need to choose my words better. I'm just concerned for you. You're my best friend and I want to help. Will you let me help?"

"How? How are you supposed to help? I'm a fucking mess! How could I be so irresponsible with my body? I had a plan, Emilia. I wanted a husband and career first. Now look at me. *I had a plan.*" My eyes are watering, breathing heavily, and watching Emilia.

"Ari! Stop it! Stop being so fucking negative. This baby is a blessing. Who the hell cares if you didn't do it the way you had planned? Nothing ever goes as planned." Emilia stands up, walking towards me. She's rubbing my shoulder, soothingly.

"That's easy for you to say. Mrs. Harry Santos." I scoff.

"I know you think I don't understand... and I can't imagine what you're going through." Emilia pauses and sits down at the edge of my bed.

"My mom had me when she was a teenager. Now look at her. I know you're not in your teens but still. She's still with my dad and they both have a successful marriage and careers. Shit like this happens and it's not the end of the world. You're a boss ass, hot, nurse with cheekbones and long black hair to kill for. You're going to be one hot young mom. You have your career set in stone. And I'm sure Danny will be right by your side through it all."

My frown turns into a smile. Emilia was always the friend that comforted me in dark situations. Meredith was the one friend that threw you in the fire and laughed. Then get an extinguisher.

"Would you like to see the ultrasound picture I got today? My baby already has all their fingers and toes, it's insane." I pull out the pictures from my pocket.

"Oh my gosh, that's crazy." Emilia yanks the pictures out of my hands and I watch as a smile pulls at her lips and her eyes light up with happiness.

I'm finally starting to enjoy my pregnancy journey. It feels good to share this experience *with somebody.*

Emilia and I could talk about everything and anything. She was ranting about the stress of her wedding yet she was excited about the date getting closer so she could enjoy her honeymoon afterward, with Harry. It was in a couple of days, just around the corner and I was so happy for her.

I vented to her about my pregnancy app and my current symptoms. Telling her all the names I've picked out for a boy and a girl. The baby was due sometime in the spring of next year.

Rain starts to pour down outside and I'm getting more and more sleepy as the night goes on. I encourage Emilia to go home. I reassured her that I would be fine and she could leave. I truly appreciated how much effort she puts into our friendship.

She leaves and I wave at her through my window. The rain starts pouring down harder and thunder erupts, making me flinch. The trees outside are swaying back and forth with lots of force from the winds. My window starts to scream like a ghost weeping. I'm startled by the sound of the wind trying to force my window open.

I decided to check on my mother before I fall asleep. I changed into my pajamas beforehand. I slip on a silky pajama set. It's a leopard pink pattern with shorts and a long sleeve.

My mother and I have started to keep the house cold even more now that I was pregnant. I was always hot.

I walk into the hallway barefoot, my bones cracking as I walk. Her bedroom isn't too far from mine and I slowly open it. She's sprawled out on her bed with her bible in her hands and rosary in the other, asleep.

I'm not surprised to find her with her bible and a picture of Paul in his uniform on her nightstand with the lamp on. I couldn't fathom the pain of a parent losing their child. I think I would die. Paul's death was getting closer to hitting one year.

I shut off her lamp and took her belongings from her hand. I exit her bedroom door after covering her lower half in blankets.

I do my nightly routine as usual. I make sure the doors are locked and all the lights are off. As I'm darkening the house, thunder strikes hard and I swear I can hear footsteps down the hallway. I stop in my tracks as soon as I hear the eerie noise. *Shane? Shit.*

I walk slowly toward the hallway, grabbing my brother's baseball bat that had been put away in a storage closet. The wooden floors creak as I walk closer to the hallway. I switch the light back on quickly, bracing the baseball bat, ready to strike.

The light reveals an empty hallway.

I really am going crazy.

I take in a deep breath, releasing the built-up tension that took over me. I put the baseball bat back into the closet and rush into my bedroom down the hall.

I climb into my bed and I tuck myself under the blankets. I toss and turn until I find a comfortable spot, listening to the rain and wind hit my window.

The weather outside brings back memories of Danny and me at his home during the hurricane. My heart warms at the thought of him and I'm tempted to start touching the fire crackling in between my thighs.

I touch my lower stomach and brushed my fingers slowly across my skin, wishing they were Danny's instead. My belly was not yet showing but I was carrying his child and it burned.

It burned knowing I couldn't tell him and the constant worrying about his safety. Violet's story gave me an insight into what kind of danger they put themselves in and I start to tear up.

It doesn't take long to lose myself in my thoughts and I'm drifting into a heavy slumber.

CHAPTER 34

ARI

I wake up to the sound of thunder. It jolted my body awake. There's no sunlight as my eyes struggle to open since the skies are still gray outside and I'm in love. I love the rain. It's still here, keeping me company and there's something about waking up to rain that relaxes me. I check the time on my phone and it's eight in the morning.

Placing it back down on my all-white nightstand, I turn and stretch my body out. I lift my arms and curly my feet. The smell of my mom's cooking fills the room and my stomach is rumbling.

Gotta feed the baby.

I'm reaching toward the inside of my drawer searching for my ultrasound photos and I can't find them. I start to panic. I jolt forward, ripping the bedsheets off my bed and I'm internally screaming.

I whisk the drawer open and I frantically start throwing stuff out everywhere.

Did my mother come inside my room when I was sleeping? Does she know?

Oh no. This can't be happening.

I stand up, trying to get a deeper look at my nightstand and I stop. Suddenly, something catches my eye.

A massive chunk of my hair falls to the ground.

What is happening?

And then another chunk falls out. Watching huge amounts of my black hair fall to the ground, hitting my feet, sends horror ripping through my chest. I grab my hair, running to my vanity mirror in my bedroom, breathing hard.

I grab my hair and start pulling on my hair and more hair keeps falling out. It looks like I had gotten a botched haircut. Jagged crooked edges run across my hair at my shoulders and I'm freaking out. I'm hyperventilating, tears falling down my cheeks rapidly, my chest heaving up and down, my fingers trembling amongst the strands of my hair as it falls onto my desk. I'm panicking as I brush my hands through my hair, frantic.

This can't be real.

Red letters catch my eye. There's a message written on my desk with my lipstick along with my ultrasound photos, ripped to shreds.

You're going to die just like Paul

I scream at the top of my lungs.

Someone was in my room.

Someone was in my fucking room!

Someone came into my room while I slept and wrote this message and cut my hair.

I can't take this anymore.

Someone broke into my house, into my room, and did this to me. He want to kill me.

Shane wants to kill me.

Why didn't he do it last night? Why is he slowly terrorizing me?

I collapse on the floor holding my hair, watching it fall out, crying uncontrollably. It just keeps falling out...

"Mija! What's wrong?" My mom swings my door open, with a

loud, thud. She's scared to death and rushes towards me. I'm still on the ground sobbing. Not caring if she catches me with pieces of the ultrasound in my hand. She bends down and puts her hands on my shoulders.

"Someone broke into our house while we were sleeping. They cut off my hair! They said they're going to kill me!" I shriek, pointing to my desk.

I must have slept through the break-in. The thunderstorm must have drowned out their sounds as they broke in.

"We need to call the police." My mother's voice in distress.

She stands up and she catches the message written on my desk and I'm hugging my knees. Still gripping onto the hair that's no longer attached to my scalp.

"What's this?"

I look up and she has a piece of the ultrasound in her hand.

"Is this yours?" She asks. My heart drops and I'm still sobbing.

"Y— yes. Ma... I'm pregnant." My aching voice rasps and I'm shaking. She stumbles back still holding a piece of the ultrasound. Her breathing quickens and she looks at me, disappointed. She's frozen and it looks like her eyes are searching for something.

Every single second that I'm waiting for her reaction, it feels like forever. I'm going through so many emotions at once, I clutch my stomach trying my hardest to calm down. I didn't want the stress of this to drive me into a miscarriage.

"Ma?" I ask, looking up at her. It's like she's frozen. My questions snap her out of her trance. She readjusts her cardigan across her chest. She's avoiding my gaze and turns on her heels.

"We'll talk about this after the police get here. *Another* police report we need to file." She seethes. She's cold-hearted and angry. She pulls out her phone just before she leaves my room and dials 911.

I'm sobbing uncontrollably. My failed attempts to keep myself calm are failing.

Screw this, from now on, I'm sleeping with my brother's Glock and knife. Let's see how tough Shane feels then.

"Ma'am, I would invest in security cameras. The next time, and hopefully there's no next time, you and your mother will be able to collect solid evidence on who's breaking and entering your home." The same cop that came to my house a few weeks ago answered the call.

He's back here with the same condescending tone, leaning on the doorway. His hand rests on his belt, yawning. He took down our statements and photos of the break-in, filing another report.

"Yup. I'll look into it, sir. Thank you for *all your help* and safety that you provide." I sarcastically nod, crossing my arms. He glares at me before he goes back to chewing on his tobacco. He closes our front door and I instantly lunge to lock it.

Shane cut most of my hair off and left me with short hair. My long hair is no more. I called my hairdresser, Sadie, and pleaded with her to take me in on such short notice, sometime today. Sadie was always booked with clients. She only took appointments but she said I could go in at anytime today.

I turn around from the front door to face my mother. She's sitting on the dining room table, at the end. She has one of her hands tucked into the sleeve of her cardigan. She's fiddling with her cross necklace with the other, as she motions for me to sit down at the table, nodding.

I swallow and walk towards her, dreading every step. I changed into jeans and a white sweater after my quick shower. My head feels lighter with half of my hair gone. I purse my lips and sit down, tucking my hands under my thighs, nervously.

"Quien es el papa, Danny?" My mom breaks the silence with a straightforward question.

Who is the father?

She was diving straight into my situation with no remorse. I didn't expect anything less.

"Yes," I answer softly.

She takes a deep breath and cringes at my answer. Her eyes shut tight and she releases her cross necklace. Her hands fall down to the table and she intertwines them together.

"I just don't know where I went wrong. You were supposed to wait until you were married, Ari Natalia." She stares at my collarbone. "Where's your cross necklace?"

She calls me by full name and I start biting my lip. It's been a while since I heard my middle name fall from her mouth. The last time she said my middle name, I was in high school. I almost failed my math class and she was so angry when I told her I might not graduate with straight A's.

I don't know how to explain to her that my necklace stayed in Iraq when Danny ripped it off right before I had sex for the first time.

"I…" She doesn't let me finish.

"I don't understand... *you know this*. I've raised you in a Catholic household. One, you're supposed to wait until marriage to have sex. Let alone, get pregnant with a baby out of wedlock." She rushes out, her voice rising.

Her words sting and my hormones are getting the best of me. I won't let her talk to me like this. I was done letting her control every single thing about my life. It was time for me to set boundaries with her. I need to ignore my need to please her with every single decision in my life.

"Ma, stop it."

"How far along are you? I imagine a couple of months." She shrugs her shoulders, her eyes widening with anger and impatience.

"And Danny? Where's he at? He just knocked you up and disappeared? Hasn't called? *He probably wants nothing to do with this.*

How could you be so irresponsible?" Her questions are bursting out of her one after another not giving me a chance to answer them. The way she assumes she knows Danny irritates me. Ever since my brother died, I hadn't recognized myself. The day I met Danny was the day I started to change and grow into a different kind of woman. Danny isn't the only reason for the change in me. He brought out the pieces of me I was ashamed of. He pushes me to my limits. Makes me face my fears with no remorse. I admire him for that.

This was a side of my mother I wasn't aware of. I'm betting she could say the same thing about me. I brush my hands through my hair tucking the short strands behind one of my ears, my anger elevating.

Still, I'm listening to my mother without interrupting her, out of respect.

"You just started your career. You've done such amazing things to make me proud and now this?" She seethes, throwing her hand out in front of her, referencing my surprising pregnancy. Her tone is icy and cold. It's extremely unfamiliar and unpleasant.

"I should have never pushed you to go to his house that day. I thought you were smarter than this, Ari Natalia. What would Paul think that you've slept with his best friend? You should be ashamed of yourself."

Something erupts inside of me and I've decided I've had enough. I've had enough of her ignorant, hurtful comments. I stand up from the chair, my hands turning into fists at my sides. I'm breathing quickly through my nose, hot air releasing.

"Ma, that's enough! I don't have to be here. I don't have to stay here with you in this house but *I do it for you. For Paul.* I have my own life and career set, I can do this on my own. I don't need anyone that's not supportive of my life choices. I don't need you. I don't even need Danny."

Her eyes circle and she's taken aback by my defensive tone.

She sits back in her chair, her hands resting on the arms of the chair, looking up at me.

"My faith in God hasn't been the same since Paul's death. I'm sorry, I know you don't want to hear this. I don't know what I believe anymore but what I do believe is that I don't think anyone should have to wait until they are married to have sex if they don't want to. That's such a big part of someone's life. It's not taboo to want to discover that part of being human before getting married! I will not be afraid anymore. I will not let this trauma from our religion hinder my life choices ever again."

My mother scoffs and crosses her arm. She shakes her head and looks away from me. She's offended by my outrage but I don't care. I love my mother but she needs to understand that I'm not the same Ari anymore. I couldn't keep this inside any longer.

"Yes, Danny and I just met. My pregnancy was an absolute accident but you know what?"

I choke up. My throat hurts and I swallow the lump beginning to form.

"I will be the best mom I can be despite any obstacles life throws at me. Even if I do it alone, I know I'll be okay." My voice cracks. My mom is in silence and I see that her face has softened. She releases a harsh breath, looking at her surroundings. She's trying to gather her thoughts, her lips trembling.

"I'm sorry. Mija, come here. I'm sorry." She apologizes and I'm stunned. My knees are weak but I mentally remember to stay strong. This was a new era in my life and I'm glad that instead of crying and cowering from confrontation, I stood my ground.

"It's just ever since you got back it's already changing my life. I'm worried about you. This ex-boyfriend of yours has me fearing for your life and mine." She starts to tremble. "All of this is stressing me out. Shane wants to kill you. He wants to take the only child I have left?" Her voice breaks and she's crying. Tears fall out from both eyes as she struggles to look at me.

I walk fast to her and hold her shoulder. I hate seeing my mother cry.

"You have to look at this from my point of view. I was raised my entire life, by my parents to wait until marriage, until you have met a man of God. A man who worships Him." She points to the ceiling. "To live your life by His commandments..." she pauses.

"But your happiness means more to me. I know you're changing. And I'm proud of the woman that you're becoming."

I'm shocked. This was not the reaction I was expecting.

I walk over to my mother and she turns around in her chair, looking at my stomach. Her eyes lock onto my sweater and she places her hand on top of it.

"I'm going to be a grandma..." she laughs and tears up.

"I'm too young!" She jokes, wiping at her eyes, preventing tears from falling. She brushes her black peppered bangs out of her eyebrows.

"I'm going to be a grandma." She repeats, holding her cheeks with both of her palms, happiness sparks from her body and weight falls off of my shoulders. The initial shock of my pregnancy finally settles in.

"Yes, you are. And Paul is going to be an uncle."

She stands up and embraces me. I hug her back tightly and refrain from crying. She steps back and grabs my hands with hers. Her touch is cold and soft. Her veiny hands are underneath my palms.

"I have questions I need answered though." She arched her brows, studying me.

"Yes, Ma?"

"Does Danny know you're pregnant? How old is he anyways?"

"No, he doesn't... His job is just like Paul's, mom. I can't talk to him when he's doing special operations. And I believe he's thirty-three."

"When in the world is he coming back? Hopefully, it's before the baby is here!" My mom exclaims dramatically.

"I've been wondering the same thing." My chest tightens at the thought of him.

I'm starting to worry about his safety. Something pulls my attention to the front windows and the flashback of two uniformed men at my front door, comes back sickeningly. I shake my head out of that delusion. He's going to come back. *Danny promised me* he would be back.

CHAPTER 35

ARI

"You're fucking kidding me?" Meredith's amber eyes look at me, full of fear. She brushes her curly hair out of her face, tucking it behind her ear.

We're all at Meredith's apartment the night before Emilia's wedding and I fill them in on why my hair is cut unexpectedly short. Shane still hasn't been found by the police and it was driving me crazy.

I was scared for myself, for my mother, and for my baby. I was having trouble sleeping the past couple of nights afraid Shane would be standing over me with the same scissors he used to cut off my hair.

My under eyes have become dark and my face lifeless. I was so jumpy even at work. This incident has made everything I do an obstacle and I get scared every time I turn around or fall asleep.

Shane had an awful childhood. Both of his parents abandoned him and he was left to be raised by his grandparents. Even then, they were absent. When I fell in love with him, I fell in love with his humor and the way he persevered through his life without his parents. But now, it looks like it's biting me in the ass.

We were friends in high school and then became more after

we both graduated. Shane was handsome and at one point, *good to me*. I stupidly looked over all the red flags when we were together because of his story but now? After he joined the military, every single flaw he had just multiplied. He's become one of the biggest regrets of my life.

"No, I'm not kidding you. I'm scared Meredith. I'm sleeping with my brother's gun and we set up security cameras. Hopefully, he doesn't come back and the police catch him. I just don't know what to do. I can't sleep." I groan. "I worry not only for my life but I worry for my baby and my mothers. She is at an age where I fear for her health when she gets stressed out."

"Oh, honey..." Emilia rubs my shoulder comforting me, frowning concerned.

"So, your mother knows now?" Emilia asks. We're all sitting in the middle of her living room, eating pizza. The sounds of a romantic comedy movie playing in the background on her widescreen TV. Meredith's apartment was almost empty. She had just moved in and she only had limited furniture and decorations. A thick brown blanket was a barrier between our butts and the floor.

"Yes, she knows... At first, she was mad. *Shocked*. But we talked it out and now she's getting excited. She's called all of her sisters and they're already planning a baby shower for me. They should be flying in sometime before the baby is born."

"This honestly makes me feel so relieved. I thought you were going to have to move in with me, thank the heavens!" Meredith jokes while her eyes bulge. I laugh and nudge her away.

"Harry already told me he wants five kids." Emilia exposes, looking at the ground.

Emilia's confession sends Meredith choking on her soda. We both start patting her back laughing.

"Yeah, no thank you... good luck with that. I don't want kids..." Meredith says before snapping her eyes at me, full of guilt. "No offense."

Emilia rolls her eyes at her before we all laugh.

"So… I have a confession to make, Ari." Meredith puts down her cup of soda and gets comfortable, repositioning herself.

"Oh, gosh. What?" When Meredith confesses things, it's never good. I was already mentally preparing for the worst.

Meredith stays quiet, and her breathing pace changes. She studies me and Emilia while both of us look back at her waiting for a disaster to pour out of her mouth.

"I always had the biggest crush on your older brother," Meredith says with a tone of sadness. I frown at her admission. I always knew she did.

"I know you did. I'm shocked you thought I never knew."

"It was that obvious huh?" Meredith arches a brow.

I nod, rubbing her biceps.

"How do you think Danny will react to all of this with Shane?" Meredith asks, taking a bite of her pizza.

The question makes me freeze. The thought of Danny still has me feeling empty on the inside. The amount of information I have to spill to him when I see him has me overwhelmed. At this point, I just wanted him to come home safely. Alive. From Paul's death to Violet's story, I'm traumatized.

"I don't know… but I'm more scared of what *Danny will do to Shane*, than Shane himself."

The man almost killed him for assaulting me at El Devine. If Danny finds Shane before the cops do, it will be Shane's karma.

I park my car in the driveway of my house. I left Meredith's place at around midnight.

I twist the keys out from the ignition and look at my house. Every single light is turned off inside except the front porch light. My mom always leaves it on for me when she knows I'm coming back home. It's her way of saying that she's waiting for me.

I grab my backpack and throw it over my shoulders.

The sound of a helicopter rumbles through the air and I immediately snap my attention to the dark sky.

It's a Black Hawk.

I smile. It sends me back to the night I overcame my fear of flying. And the night I found out just how dark Danny's sadistic desires go. My smile relaxes as I watch it fly further and further away from the area. We live near the military post so it doesn't surprise me to see military aircraft. Never did I think twice about watching them fly by but recently, it has me thinking of the man that has me wrapped around his finger.

I'm about to unlock my house when I feel someone grab me by the wrist and push their body up against me. My cheek is glued to the door and I can feel both of my hands trapped tight in someone's grasp.

I scream.

"Oh Ari Cakes, we wouldn't want to wake the neighbors, would we?" Shane covers my mouth against his palm, my sounds now muted and I'm sobbing.

This can't be happening. *This can't be happening!*

Shane is behind me and the terror I feel has me sweating. I feel like I'm going to faint with the massive scare he's giving me.

"You fucking slut. I can't believe you fucked him. I can't believe you're going to have *his baby*. You should be *having mine!*" He seethes into my ear, careful not to attract any attention from the neighbors or from my mother inside.

I look up at the security camera we have installed at the front door. It's hidden in the top corner and Shane watches my eyes move from the door to the cameras.

My common sense starts to kick in and I bite down on his fingers, the hardest I can.

"Ahh! You fucking bitch, you bit me!" He shouts. He lets me

go, stepping away from me and I take this as an opportunity to threaten him.

He's holding onto his fingers, comforting himself as he looks at the security camera.

My front door swings open and my mother pulls me in.

"Mija!" She shouts.

"You better leave now, Shane! The security system alerted the cops and they're on their way, your face is all over our cameras." I shut the door on him, locking it and sure enough, sirens can be heard from a distance. I look through the peephole and Shane is red, full of wrath, and has a psychotic craze expression all over his face.

He takes off running and I no longer have sights on him. I'm breathing hard, crying into my mother's shoulder.

Why can't he leave me alone? And when the hell is Danny coming back?

CHAPTER 36

ARI

Emilia is walking to the altar. The song she walks out to is an orchestral version of *Thinking Out Loud* by *Ed Sheeran*. It's playing loud and I have the biggest smile on my face while I watch Emilia walk. We're all standing on a podium that sits on the sand. Emilia is dressed in a long white gown that trails behind her feet. Her hair is curled and her makeup is professionally done.

My short hair was cut into layers all over. Sadie managed to salvage my side bangs and turn the chaos of a mess into something stylish. For Emilia's wedding, we decided to go with beach waves. I haven't told anyone about the latest encounter with Shane. I didn't want anyone to be worked up or worried about me when it was Emilia's day. The cops didn't find him and I'm not surprised.

Emilia looks completely enchanted with her future husband. She was becoming his wife. Entering a new chapter in her life. Her gaze kept switching from Harry and the bottom of her dress as she walked.

Emilia and Harry got their fall wedding on the beach as they planned. The air was fresh, the weather sitting around seventy degrees for a late October wedding. Pumpkins and orange lights were decorated everywhere. Emilia steps on artificial autumn leaves as she walks up to the altar.

A fall wedding beach isn't the most common thing to see but that's exactly what Emilia wanted.

Harry's watching Emilia and he brings his palm to his mouth, mesmerized by his love for her. He starts to tear up as she gets closer to him. His best man stands next to him and grips his shoulder, comforting him.

Her father holds her hand the entire time as he escorts her. Something I would never experience. My father was permanently absent from my life. I didn't need my father for my wedding day. I had my mother.

I thought to myself,

If my man doesn't cry for me when on our wedding day, I'm running away.

The love Harry has for Emilia was evident.

Emilia grabs a hold of Harry's hands and everyone claps as the music dies down. The waves of the ocean crashing against the shore are music to my ears. I glance towards the water and the beautiful blue shade reminds me of Danny's eyes.

My chest tightens at the thought of him.

It's been a while since I've heard his voice. Touched his lips.

Danny was starting to feel like a ghost. Like a figment of my imagination, I conjured up. His absence was starting to affect me. Whenever he started to feel unreal, I just looked at my lower abdomen and that was my only verification of his existence in this world.

I was so nervous waiting for his calls or texts. I kept busy between work, friends, family, reading, and the gym. It made the time go by faster. Right after the latest incident of Shane's threats, I would get regular alerts to my phone from the front and back-yard cameras.

"You may now kiss the bride!" The minister exclaims into the mic. His voice disrupts my thoughts. Meredith nudges me gently on my arm, making sure I'm okay. It's obvious I was lost in thought. I nod with a smile.

Harry grabs Emilia's face with both of his hands, kissing her so deeply, everyone in the venue feels it. The crowd of families and friends erupts in cheers and claps. I whistle, putting my fingers to my mouth, jumping up and down with Meredith. Too bad I couldn't pop a champagne bottle and drown my sorrows tonight.

Everyone heads towards the built-in tents in the secluded area on the beach. I sit down next to Meredith brushing my long blue dress down. We were at our assigned seating in the venue. It was very crowded inside the tent. Music was blasting loud, I could feel it in my chest.

Our bridesmaid dresses were one-shoulder dresses that were loose around my waist. They had a long v-cut across the chest that revealed a good amount of cleavage. I didn't mind. My pregnancy gave me more to work. One perk of growing a tiny human.

Meredith is on her fourth glass of wine. The alcohol percentage was higher than usual and it showed. She was already slurring her words and the after-party was just beginning.

"I just love wine. Alcohol is the best." Meredith sighs twirling her wine in the glass. She leans her chin on the palm of her hand, placing her elbow on the table supporting her head. The wine swirls fast and it look like it's about to pour out of the glass.

"Woah there Meredith, slow down." I cringe, backing away from her. I'm trying my best to avoid getting wine spilled on my dress.

"Why? I'm not the one that's pregnant. I don't have to slow down if I don't want to." Meredith's tone is sharp and I'm taken aback by her candor. She burps and rolls her eyes.

"Thank you Meredith that's so kind of you to point out." I bite the inside of my cheek gently, taking a sip of my water. Sometimes Meredith has a stick up her ass for no reason and she rambles with no filter.

We sit in an awkward silence as the music changes to a slow song. Our food comes to our table. Salmon, baked potatoes with broccoli. My mouth waters and I start nibbling on my food.

Meredith and I both look up from our food to see a short, red-haired man approaching. He stops in front of me, holding out his hand.

"Hello there beautiful. I was wondering if you'd like to dance with me. My name's Larry I'm a friend of the groom." He asks, his tone overconfident and flirtatious. I grow uncomfortable.

"Oh, that's very kind of you, really. But I'm fine, I'm eating right now." I point toward my plate with my fork, hoping I'm letting him down easily. I give him a comforting smile trying to hide my unease. Larry frowns and pulls back his hand.

"Really, Ari? Come on, go with the nice guy, *your baby daddy* isn't here to dance with you anyways." Meredith cuts in, taking another swallow of her wine. Her tone is emotionless and I'm hurt. Her words pierce through me like a knife. She's clearly unaware of her actions and I freeze with embarrassment. She doesn't realize she's outed my pregnancy to a complete stranger and I'm exasperated with her ruthless character.

Larry puckers his lips awkwardly, chewing on the side of his mouth, reading the room.

I glare at her and stand up from my seat.

"Excuse me. I'm just going to get some fresh air. I've lost my appetite." I mumble, throwing my napkin down on my seat.

Meredith freezes and she stops herself from drinking more of her wine. She fidgets in her seat and comes to self-realization.

"Ari, I'm sorry." Meredith groans putting down her wine glass. She stands up walking behind me. I'm boiling over on the inside with fury.

"*Don't.*" I whip my head towards her, ordering her away from me.

Meredith stops following me, frowning, leaning on one side of her body. Larry has walked away from the table, disappearing into the dancing crowd.

I continue walking out of the tent and head towards the ocean. I take off my heels as I jog slowly, one by one. The sun has completely gone down leaving only a full moon to light up the sky. Carrying my heels in one hand together, the waves call out for me.

There's something about a beach that soothes my soul. It's so peaceful and it stops me from balling into a complete mess. I stare at the waves crashing, listening to them, doing my best to drown out the music from the tent. The moonlight reflecting off the dark blue water calms my nerves.

I reach the shore and my feet touch the damp sand. The waves reach my feet and I'm enjoying the sensation of cold water.

Meredith's words hurt me and I make a mental note to stay away from her for the rest of the night. It felt like she was throwing my pregnancy in my face as if it was such an inconvenience *to her life.*

I hadn't announced my pregnancy yet and I can already picture all of the harsh judgments and opinions when friends and family find out I'm pregnant. I'm not even sure I have a boyfriend. Never mind, a husband. My best friend revealed her true attitude towards my unplanned pregnancy and it hurt. I can't imagine what others will say.

A strong wind brushes against my skin, and the cold air makes me grab onto my biceps to keep warm. I crave my warm bed and thick blankets. I rub my arms fast trying to get myself warm from the friction.

My mind drifts and I palm my lower belly. I'm trying to picture a boy or girl but I can't. I don't have a preference. I just want a healthy baby.

I wonder if Paul's happy for me. If he was here, he'd probably be upset. *Especially if the baby was Shane's.* Thank God, I never fully gave myself to him. But knowing it's Danny's, I have a feeling he would be embracing his role of a new uncle with open arms.

Maybe he'd be hesitant at first but I'm sure he would have come around.

I could already picture him teaching his nephew or niece how to play the guitar before they can walk. I laugh softly to myself at the thought of him trying to change poop diapers. I wonder what kind of parent he could've been if he was still here.

Someone clears their throat behind me, sending me into shock.

"You're gonna catch a cold out here, little Angel."

I turn around so fast and my heart flutters into fire. My whole body is electrocuted with euphoria. This is a dream. It has to be.

"*Danny?*" My eyes narrow and I find his beautiful massive frame in front of me. He's dressed in a black tuxedo and the sight of him sends my head spinning. He's so magnetic it feels like he's pulling me toward him just by the way he's looking at me.

His dark sandy blonde hair's gelled back and his beard is a little shorter than when I last saw him. I'm blinking fast, ensuring that he really is in front of me. I take off running towards him and he smirks, his sexy expression turning into a wide smile, flashing his perfect white teeth.

I drop my heels on the sand right before I crash my body into his, wrapping my legs around his waist, and straddling him. He instantly wraps me up in his big arms, carrying me, his monstrous calloused hands holding me tight. Sparks fly all around me, and a familiar storm of fire ignites, and the attraction I have for him, throbs in between my thighs. I'm panting fast and hard as I watch his blue eyes intimidate me as they always did before.

It feels like the world has stopped and I'm inside my bubble of passionate seclusion once again.

"It's really you." I breathe into his shoulder low and soft, tears falling down my eyes.

"I'm home, baby, *I'm home.*"

He kisses my cheek, gripping my short hair. His fingers snake through it. His other hand grips my ass and he squeezes it so hard, a moan slips out of my mouth.

He smells so delicious. Spice, wood, and a hint of cigarettes.

"I've missed you so much." I back away from his shoulder, looking at him.

"You have no idea. I've been thinking of this moment every day since I left." He cups my cheek, rubbing his thumb across my lips. A low growl rumbles through his chest and I can feel his hardened length against my thigh.

He crashes his lips against mine and I'm weak. The kiss is aggressive, hot, and desperate. Both of us moving in such a way, I don't think I'll ever recover from this moment. It sends me into another world of ecstasy, and I press my body closer to his. His beard softly prickles my skin and I love it. His tongue pries my mouth open and I let him. Our tongues dance in sync, tasting each other's longing absence.

He bites my lip before he releases me and when he breaks away from me, I'm at a loss for words. I already miss the way his lips feel against mine and I'm devastated he pulled away.

"You are so beautiful." He tells me as he stares at me so intensely.

I smile.

"How'd you know I was here?" I ask, dropping down back to my feet and he grabs my hand, pulling me towards him. I grab my heels still holding onto his fingers.

"I have my ways, Ari. There's nowhere you could go where I couldn't find you." Blood rushes to my cheeks.

"Are you home for a while?" I ask, arching a brow, dreading the answer.

He looks at me clenching his jaw. His smile fades and in return, he looks like he's hiding something.

"Yes, baby."

There was something behind his changed expression though, that had my mind swirling with curiosity.

Questions about his missions swarmed me. The status of Damon and Violet gnawing at me. I had to tell him about the pregnancy, and the horrifying incidents involving Shane. But I didn't want to ruin tonight. So I bit my tongue, locking the information somewhere in the back of my mind, saving it for another day. I would tell him soon, just not right now.

I refused to indulge in these heavy conversations. I wanted to be selfish just in this one moment and savor having Danny back home.

"When did you get back?" I ask.

"This morning. I wanted to surprise you." Danny reaches into his pocket. "I think this belongs to you."

My pink cross necklace shines in the moonlight as he pulls it out, slowly. I watch it glimmer and sway in the wind and I'm stunned. He ripped it off of my neck the first time we gave in to each other.

"I kept you close even though you were half a world apart from me."

He kept it this entire time... He fixed it somehow.

"Turn around."

I stare back out at the ocean as he hooks my necklace over my collarbones. I'm fighting so hard against the tears that are desperately trying to crack me open. *He kept my necklace.*

"Let's go inside. I have friends that I'd like you to formally meet." I chirp.

He sighs rubbing his hand through his beard, looking down at the sand.

"Come on, don't be shy." I pull him towards the tent, teasing him.

"Okay. I'll play nice guy for a while and then," Danny lowers his mouth to my ear. His cool breath sent shivers down my spine. "When we get to my place, you'll be screaming my name all fucking night from all the ways I'll break into you again."

CHAPTER 37

ARI

Danny's eyes never leave my body. He's undressing me with his eyes and I can feel it. His presence alone has me intimidated. I'm eager for him to whisk me away to his house and drown in each other's lust. But I also want to formally introduce him to Emilia and Harry with the exception of Meredith. I thought it was best to avoid her for the rest of the night.

Holding Danny's hand, I plunge through the dancing crowd to get toward the bride and groom.

"You cut your hair." Danny's words send my heart sinking. The dreadful reminder of my long hair cut by a maniac while I was sleeping sends me into a pool of sadness. I wouldn't tell him anything just yet. I purse my lips, thinking.

I saw what he did to Shane when he grabbed me at the bar. *Who knows how Danny would react to this?* I just wanted one night without anything tainting our reunion. Just one night of no worries and to start where we left off.

One night. And then I would explain everything to him.

"Yeah, I did. I wanted to try something different." I lie. The words sting as they leave my tongue. I pride myself on my honesty and it hurts to hide the truth from Danny. It's a small lie. But still, a lie.

"I love it." He replies and it sends me into a ball of nerves. "Ari, some of my teammates are here. Kane, Lopez, Rooker, and Aitu. I hope that's okay with your friend."

"Oh wow really? I'm sure it's alright. There's an open bar area, I'm not too sure if they'll get to eat anything..."

"They'll be just fine with the open bar. I'm sure they're already there getting hammered."

We get to Emilia and Harry. They're engaged in a conversation with Harry's cousins. Emilia spots me getting closer, her expression shocked. Her mouth gapes open as she stares at Danny beside me. She taps on Harry's shoulder signaling for him to join her gaze. He stops mid-conversation with his cousin and they're all laughing at something Harry said.

He turns to me and sizes up Danny with his eyes.

"Danny, meet the bride and groom. This is Emilia my best friend and this is Harry, her husband."

"Thank you for your service," Harry turns towards Danny, lifting his glass of champagne.

"Nice to meet you guys. Congratulations on tying the knot." Danny reaches his hand out for Harry and Emilia to take. Harry shakes his hand first then Emilia. Emilia looks star-struck, her mouth still open, with a huge smile, and takes Danny's hand into hers slowly.

She's blushing and I can't help but laugh.

"It's nice to see you somewhere other than a bar. I've heard a lot about you two." She jokes and we all smile.

"I wouldn't be so sure. I hear there's an open bar somewhere around here." Danny says unashamed, he winks at me and pulls me into his body. Danny can pull off any look. I've seen him in his uniform, naked, sweats, and now an all-black tuxedo that has me questioning if he's even real or not.

"I see your friends have already made themselves at home."

She points to the open bar that's outside by a bonfire on the beach. The tent is spread open and we spot all of Danny's friends right away. They're standing by an open tiki stand. It's hard to miss four tall massive special operators. They don't blend in too well. They each have drinks in their hands, dressed in tuxedos berating each other about something, lost in conversation.

"Help yourself, except Ari of course." Emilia continues and I swear I can feel time stop.

My eyes widen and I shake my head at her frantically, biting my lip. I mouth to her,

He doesn't know.

She reads my mouth and purses her lips together in shock, immediately apologetic.

"Why can't Ari drink?" Danny asks full of confusion, looking down at me, his eyebrows arched. He's always been able to read me so well and I'm hoping just this one time, he won't. *He can't find out like this.*

I immediately start acting like I have my foot in my mouth. I look at Danny, with a forceful smile then at Emilia, letting out a deep breath. I'm begging for her help through my eyes.

"I... uh—" I stutter not knowing how to continue my sentence. I'm panicking and Harry looks at me concerned.

"Because she's Meredith's designated driver!" Emilia explains nervously, throwing her hands up in the air and I feel safe hoping Danny will buy it.

Yup, that's believable.

"Yeah. I'm supposed to drive her home." I shrug, placing my hand on my waist leaning on it and something flashes in Danny's eyes. I can't tell what he's feeling but then he gives me a reassuring smile, eyebrows furrowed.

Kane's familiar voice roars through the crowd interrupting the dreadful awkward silence between us four.

"Rider! Get the fuck over here man, we're about to take some shots!" Kane shouts over to us. We both turn towards him, and

Danny's team all have shot glasses in their hands. He waves his hands over and Kane locks eyes with me for a split second before returning his gaze to Danny. Something about Kane's gaze has me questioning his intentions. His gaze was unwelcoming. Danny gives him a nod and grins.

"I want to introduce you to some friends of mine. I know you met Kane and Rooker but I want you to meet Lopez and Aitu." Danny says in my ear.

"Congrats Mr. And Mrs. Santos but I'll be stealing Ari for the rest of the night and for the foreseeable future. Is there any way Meredith can get a ride with another sober guest?" He asks and Danny tightens his grip on my waist. I'm addicted to his touch. It feels like forever since I've seen him. Not too long ago, I had thought he was a figment of my imagination. His absence was so long it did something to me. Now, he was standing right beside me holding me. If this was a dream, I didn't want to wake up.

"Of course, we have tons of sober cousins that don't drink, Meredith will be just fine." She lifts her drink, still looking at me with an apologetic frantic expression.

I return her expression with a smile, exchanging glances from her to Danny.

"Nice meeting you and congratulations again. I'm going to make sure these guys don't give the bartender too much of a hard time." Danny jokes and I'm waving goodbye to Harry and Emilia.

Danny's quiet but his hold on me doesn't sway. I've missed the feelings his touch would do to me. My inner thighs haven't stopped throbbing since I saw his beautiful silhouette on the sand.

As we meet with his team, Kane's handing a shot to Danny.

"Men, this is Ari." Danny pulls me in front of him, showing me off like a diamond.

This is a big moment for Danny and me. He knows the amount of backlash he's going to receive and it's inevitable with the pregnancy. He didn't know about it and yet he's still exposing our relationship to his team.

"Wait... aren't you? She's—" a tall, warrior-like man questions. He has black hair that reaches his shoulder, and the same body frame as Danny. He has grey eyes, and I can't help but notice how mysteriously handsome he is.

"Paul's sister." Kane's curt voice finishes, through gritted teeth. Danny ignores his tone and looks at me like I'm rare jewelry on his arm.

Rooker gives me a comforting smile and he looks better than ever. The last time I saw him, his chest had a bullet inside of it and he carried a pale reflection due to blood loss.

"Nice to meet you, darling. I'm Zeke, also known as Aitu. I worked with your brother. We were on the same team." He reaches his large hand out and I shake it. At the same time, another man gives me a welcoming smile and a handshake as well. I'm assuming he's Lopez.

"That's awesome. Rooker, how are you recovering?" I asked cheerfully.

Rooker smacks his teeth and holds his hand to his chest, palming it.

"You and Doctor Diaz saved my life. I'm forever grateful to you the medical team that worked on me. I'm recovering well though, I already got cleared to get back to work." Rooker flashes me a grateful smile and I choke up. It feels good to know I was a part of his survival. Moments like this make me feel like all the hardship that came with my career was well worth it.

"Your brother was a good man. My condolences." Zeke says.

"Yes. Yes, he was." I turn towards him.

"We never thought we'd see the day when Grim finally settled down. Apparently, Ari knows how to make miracles happen, guys, starting with saving my life." Rooker jokes and everyone laughs except Kane. He looks extremely tense and unsure of himself as he downs more of his drink, his eyes never leaving me.

"Alright let's get this fucking night started the right way." Danny interrupts us and holds his shot of alcohol in the air. "You too Grandpa, let's go," Danny orders Rooker. Rooker rolls his eyes, shaking his head. They all synchronize holding their shots up.

"Hooyah!" All the Navy men roar and they down their drinks. I'm standing by awkwardly watching. Lopez orders them all more drinks and gets Danny his favorite.

Jack Daniels.

Rooker begins telling them about his wife and how she's going to kill him if he gets back home too drunk. Lopez starts gloating about the state of Texas and Zeke argues that Hawaii is better. They engage in a brotherly argument about the pros and cons of both states.

Everyone from inside the tent starts surrounding the bonfire. The toasts to the bride and groom were just about to begin. Family and friends fill the beach with chatter and slow music begins to play outside. I'm watching all the women hold up their dresses to avoid getting sandy.

I decided this is my window to leave Danny alone so he can let loose with his close friends.

"Danny, I'm going to head towards the bonfire. I have to make a toast to Emilia." I motion towards the bonfire, breaking Danny from his circle of friends. They all look at us and then turn around to give us privacy, but Kane doesn't. His eyes linger on me a little longer before they change to Rooker.

Kane probably realizes I've been seeing Danny since Iraq.

I can already smell the whiskey and I can't help but subtly enjoy it. The scent of whiskey reminds me that he's alive. He's right here with me and not halfway across the world.

Danny smiles in agreement. He gives me a kiss on my lips, and I melt from the soft clash, kissing him back. His light blue eyes trail toward the bonfire behind me. I'm watching his movements like a cinema movie.

When I catch the reflection of the bonfire flames in his eyes, his body stiffens, and his gorgeous smile slowly fades.

Danny clenches his jaw and he looks lost in thought. He freezes and I can't help but feel confused by his demeanor. It feels like minutes pass by as I watch his blue eyes reflect fire. He doesn't blink and continues to stare.

His actions send me in a looming weary. I touch his shoulder and it breaks him out of his trance.

"Danny? Everything okay?" I ask, my eyebrows furrow and the need to pry is gnawing.

Danny clears his throat. Still not looking away from the fire that illuminates the beach but he finally blinks, downing the rest of his whiskey glass.

"I'm fine." He's cold and emotionless and the side of Danny I don't like comes back to me full circle. He's closed off and mysterious. The stone-cold facial expression is familiar and I don't like it. I let go of his shoulder and my hand falls to my side.

Biting down, his jaw twitching, he finally looks away from the fire and turns his back towards me.

"More whiskey. And keep them coming, please." He requests from the bartender like he's forcing himself to sound normal. The bartender nods, filling up his glass.

What just happened?

"Fuck yeah!" Lopez pushes his shoulder, laughing, encouraging Danny but he doesn't react. He doesn't even flinch.

I bite my lip debating with myself as I turn around making my way to the bonfire. I thought giving him space would be the best thing. My feet sink onto the sand, and I'm swallowed with each step.

Questions swirl into my head and I grow nervous. I keep reminding myself that tomorrow would be the day of questions and answers but not tonight. *Tomorrow.*

Nothing will ruin tonight's homecoming.

The toasts of the wedding were emotional. People that love both Emilia and Harry gave their good wishes to the couple along with advice for a happy long marriage. I was one of the first to speak.

I sat down next to Meredith after she apologized for her crude behavior. We both sat and listened as the toasts went on, but my concentration was elsewhere. I was worried about Danny's drinking.

The whole time I sat at the bonfire, he didn't stop drinking with his team. All of them were a hot mess of intoxication. They probably can't help it after months of being in Iraq.

"What are you going to do about Shane? I'm terrified for you and your mom. *This guy's scaring me.* I can't imagine how you're feeling." Meredith says.

"I know," I murmur, stressed out.

"Does your mom know Danny's back yet? How does she feel about being alone in the house tonight?"

"Yes, she knows. I sent her a text. She wants to talk to Danny about the pregnancy. She's ready to go full mama bear on him but yeah. She's fine. We set up a security system now, so she feels more comfortable when I'm not home with her."

Meredith nods. "Who's that guy with slicked black hair? He's yummy." Meredith whispers into my ear looking behind me. I turn around squinting in their direction and my eyes land on Kane. He's in mid-conversation with Danny. Danny takes a hit of his cigarette before blowing it into the air.

"His name is Kane. Kane Slaughter. He works with Danny." I reply nonchalantly, fixing the bottom of my dress.

"Well hot damn. They're all so tall. Is that a requirement or something?"

I shrug, giggling. "You make a fair point."

"I need a big boy in my life." She jiggles her brows and I laugh. "Look, I'm sorry again for being so rude. It's my own insecurities coming through. Between Emilia's marriage and your pregnancy, I guess I'm just low-key jealous that your love lives are exploding and mine is non-existent. It's drier than the Sahara's desert down here." Meredith sighs, crossing her arms.

I shake my head, rolling my eyes.

"Just watch, when you least expe—"

I'm cut off by a hard grip on my shoulder, but the touch sends a sensation in between my thighs with familiarity.

"Sorry to interrupt, but I think we should go." Danny's voice is deep and husky.

I look behind me, my eyes upwards to see Danny's hand. My vision trails from his hand to his face. His expression sends me into a whirlwind. He looks different from earlier. His eyes are glossy, and I just know he's drunk.

The way he watches for my obedience has me thrilled. He looks emotionless but his blue eyes say otherwise. When I investigate them, they seem impatient, lustrous with need, like a beast ready to devour. It sends a fire down my body and my nipples harden through the blue dress. I swallow as he reaches for my hand. I smile and take it. He pulls my body up so easily off the sand and I'm internally trembling with excitement. We're finally going to be alone.

We get to the parking lot, and Danny holds my hand, guiding me toward his all-black F250 truck.

"Keys?" I ask.

"Let me drive us home. I'm okay."

"No, you are not, Danny. I saw you drink shot after shot, whiskey after whiskey."

He stills and I know he's upset but I don't think it's at me. Something changed when I caught him staring at the fire.

"Danny… what happened to you when I left? You're different. Something changed when…"

He doesn't let me finish.

"When, what?" He argues.

"*Talk to me.*"

"Ari." He groans, frustrated.

"Danny."

"I can't talk about it. You know this. This is a part of my job. I can't say shit. I'm fine." He shoots me down with the iciest coldest expression, I'd ever seen. He didn't need to say any more words, his face says it all and it's terrifying.

In this moment, I hate his job.

The entire drive back to his house is complete silence. It took him a while for him to give in to driving us home. His stubbornness gets the best of him sometimes as I've come to realize. I made sure he knew this wasn't an argument he wasn't going to win.

The air was full of tension, and I didn't know where it was coming from. He was so happy when he found me on the beach and now... I couldn't recognize him. I was afraid to speak, that one word would set him off.

Cody Jinks plays softly as we travel back to his place in darkness. There are hardly any towns on the way back to his ranch home. I'm following the GPS and it says we're less than an hour away.

The whole time I kept thinking... maybe, I don't know Danny at all.

CHAPTER 38

DANNY

I fucking hate being home. The need to go back on missions always haunts me right when I step on American soil. The need to continue to work always consumes me. I can't help it. I don't have control over it. It's my first day home and I already want to go back to Iraq or start the next mission. My job will always be my number one priority. *Always.*

Being a Navy SEAL is my whole identity. My parents branded that ambition into my head like I was cattle. Nothing else matters but taking out the evil in this world, one deployment at a time.

She was right though... Ari is so compassionate and empathetic, she's quickly caught onto my demons. That's what I love most about her. When the flames from the Bonfire caught my attention, it took me back to Damon's dead body absolutely, catastrophically burning in an unforgiving fire. A soul I couldn't save. A man I've failed.

Watching Ari stare at the crashing waves when I found her... she's the only reason why I haven't completely dreaded being home. I've looked forward to having her back in my arms since the day I left her sleeping in my barracks room.

She makes being home so worth it. Just being close to her, she makes everything in my fucked up world, better.

She truly is the best thing that could have ever happened to me.

I love her sweet, innocent, soul. Her heart is so pure. I've known that about her since the day I first met her. I knew she was different.

She's my little Angel that I like to break and please the way I want... the way she begs me to.

I love when my Angel cries for me when I fuck her.

She was very naive in the beginning but as time goes by, she's starting to see who the true monsters are in this world. *The kind of monsters that are in this world.*

I'm one of them... but not in the way she thinks and she needs to know that.

Alcohol and Ari are the only light that distracts me from the evil that tries to plague my head. The stress of constant death, it's too much sometimes but I can handle it.

"I need honesty from you. It's unfair how you shut down. It's not fair to me... it hurts me." Ari says as her little hands grip the steering wheel.

"I'm not Shane. *I won't hurt you.* At least in the ways you think." My kinks are an exception to that. The way I like to fuck, the way I like to scare her to the point that death lurks while I do it. That won't ever change. Of course, I'm careful to not ever actually harm her. She's mine and I won't ever do things she's not begging me to.

"But you will hurt me, Danny. Can't you see that I've fallen for you? You'll hurt me because it's inevitable. It's inevitable now that I'm in lo—" She stops herself and I swear my heart sinks. She was about to say it.

"Now that I'm totally wrapped up in you."

Don't say those three words, Ari.

"I am honest with you but there's things you don't need to know. I'm not a very good person."

I look out the window, stuck in my thoughts. *I like to kill people.* Bad people. I enjoy it. I'm a bad person who sometimes does good things.

"I'm going to Hell one day and I'm okay with that. What I'm not okay with is dragging you down with me, I won't let myself." I manage to get my words out and I'm already regretting opening up to her. She does this to me. She doesn't know what she's gotten herself into.

She's quiet and looks lost in thought.

"Just… don't lie to me, Danny. I want honesty. That's it. All I've known are lies and constant betrayals with Shane. Don't. Lie."

I look at her and even through my blurry vision, even through the night, I can see her. She's so fragile and I'm breaking her but this time it's not in the way she wants me to.

"My job will always come first. That won't ever change. I told you that from the beginning."

Ari sighs.

"I know."

CHAPTER 39

ARI

Danny closes his car door with such force I flinch at the impact. His demeanor hasn't changed since the wedding. He walks over to my side and opens it for me, helping me out of his truck. I hit the gravel with my heels.

His grip on my hand makes me question the night I'm about to endure. I'm slowly getting disappointed at the sudden change in his behavior. Tonight was supposed to be pure bliss. His return was something we both dreamed about, but something changed in him when I caught him staring at the fire. The hot and cold Danny was back, and I didn't know how to handle it.

I stand there fixing my dress, next to his truck. The sound of crickets is the only thing that fills the silent tension. Danny's porch lights are on, and the moon is still glowing bright with no clouds in the sky. It's a beautiful night, stars twinkling in the sky and it reminds me of the helicopter ride.

I peek at Danny through my short hair tucking it behind my ear. He has his hands in his pockets, looking at his ranch home that's behind me. His nostrils flared and eyes mysterious. We stand there in silence, and I so badly want to throw questions at him even though he's shutting me down.

What happened during the rest of his deployment? How'd he get the new scar on his bottom lip? It wasn't there when he left.

"Go inside. I'll meet you there in a bit, I'm going to burn one." Danny's still as the words roll out. His eyes never meet mine.

"Danny," I call out for him, leaning on one side of my body, hand on my hip.

He doesn't respond. He doesn't move. The anxiety cripples me.

"Yes, Cherry?"

My heart flutters and my Danny is back.

"Is something wrong?"

He finally looks towards me. He gives me a smile that disguises what he's truly feeling. It's forceful but I'll take it. Just by the way he looks at me, I'm sent to a different realm of intense emotion. He takes his hands out of his pocket, walking to me with purpose. I hold my breath, while I watch him get closer. Every step has me stunned.

When he gets to me, he cups my face into his hands and kisses my lips, hard. Our lips move together perfectly and so passionately they fit so well together and never miss a beat.

"Go inside." He breaks our kiss, leaving me breathless and wanting more. It takes a minute for me to open them, and I manage to whisper.

"Okay."

He drops his house keys in my hand, and I walk away, leaving him reaching into his pocket for smokes.

His house looks the same as when I left it. Rustic wooden floors and there's a cozy scent filling my nose. I walk towards the living room, letting myself get comfortable. I take off my heels and sit down on the couch.

I experience deja vu as the memories of our first date come back to me. I'm rubbing my feet with my hands as I sit, massaging the soreness from wearing heels. When my hands touch the fabric of his cushions, I remember the first time he obliterated me with his mouth.

So much has changed since then.

I sit in front of his fireplace staring at it contemplating my next move. Something inside of me clicks and my heart takes over. I turn off all of the lights on the first floor. The kitchen. The living room. The hallway to get inside the house. The back porch. Everything is dark like the way I want it to be.

I turn on his fireplace, starting a small fire. Staring at the wood burning I start unzipping the back of my dress. I wanted him to walk in on me.

The fear of him taking notice of my pregnancy sends my nerves flaring. Still, I'm hoping he won't notice. I wasn't showing yet. My baby bump was just that. A small bump.

My zipper goes all the way down and I reach for my shoulder strap.

Suddenly, I feel Danny's breath on my neck.

Whiskey and smoke.

The smell sends my heart pounding. The fact that I didn't hear him enter his home isn't surprising.

I would have jumped out of fear, but his presence sends me back into comfort. No worries about Shane creeping in knowing I was right beside Danny. No worries about anything when I'm around him. I'm in my own world when he's nearby.

"Don't let me stop you. *I want to watch.* I can get off just by watching you undress."

I continue to undress myself. Still facing the fireplace, I can feel his eyes burning into my back, loving the attention I'm receiving.

I pull over the thin spaghetti strap off my shoulder. The entire dress falls to the floor, and I'm left in my strapless bra and lace thong. I close my eyes tight basking in this moment of vulnerability. I'm not sure I'll ever get used to being naked around him. I felt like my insecurities were always going to seek his approval. But not because of Danny. Because of Shane. Shane abused me whereas Danny worships my body.

"Fuck, I've missed this, your perfect body. I've missed the way your ass hugged my cock and how much I enjoyed watching you take it." His hand smacks my ass so hard; my skin flares and it hinders my balance. I reach out for the brick wall that's above the fireplace to catch myself. My dignity completely gets thrown out the window every single time and I just love the way he possesses my body. The more I let him take from me the more I'm unashamed.

The memories of the shower sex come back and I close my eyes when I remember that night so clearly. He was so hesitant to give in to me… thinking I couldn't handle him and now look at us.

A high-pitched noise escapes my mouth.

Danny squeezes my ass hard and the pain sends my clit throbbing. I'm addicted to the pain he inflicts. Still wondering how he does this to me. Making pain and pleasure coexist. When he lets go, it sends my ass rippling.

"Turn around, Ari." He orders.

My breathing begins to rise. I've thought about this moment for what felt like forever. These past four months had me questioning his existence. It made me question our whirlwind of a relationship. Was he real? Or was he a figment of my imagination with the way he had me wrapped around his finger so fucking fast? I was longing for his touch. Aching for his attention. Now it was here, and I was in complete euphoria. I'm so in love with this man, it scares me. I'd let him do anything to me. I'd do anything to please him. Even if it meant going back on everything I once believed.

I turn around facing him. My eyes meet his all-black tie and I trail my eyes upwards watching his Adam's apple bob up and down as he swallows me in.

He licks his lips, and he lets out a cool breath. I'm mesmerized by his cologne. Just his scent alone has me wanting to smother myself on top of him. The sight of his tongue has me howling internally. His tongue on my slit is all I can think about.

Danny takes off his jacket throwing it on top of his couch. He takes off his shoes, followed by his belt. He's left in his long black sleeve button-up, pants, and tie.

I reach for the waistband of his pants, eager to rip them off. His big hands grip mine, stopping me from going any further. The sound of his skin clashing against mine sends me into a cloud of confusion. I look at Danny and he clenches his jaw.

"Has anyone touched what's mine since I've been gone?" He growls.

"No."

Technically another lie and I loathe myself for it. Shane managed to put his hands on me while I was sleeping, cutting my hair off. Touching me without my consent. Terrorizing me. Before my mind wanders, I snap myself out of my worries.

"Good girl." He praises. He takes off his tie and holds it in his hand. "Open wide baby." He brushes my lips with his thumb before prying my mouth open.

I hesitate to look at him and then at his tie. I give in to his request. I trust him.

He embraces me closer to his body with his arms behind me, unclamping my bra. It falls to the ground, and I kick it away from the fire that's behind my feet. The warmth of the fireplace causes sweat to coat every single particle of my body.

He begins to plant kisses, starting from my collarbone down to my breasts. Taking one nipple in his mouth and he bites down hard. My nipples are extremely sensitive to his touch, and I moan.

"What I admire most about you Ari…" he continues to trail kisses after sucking on my breast. His lips softly meet my stomach and I internally freak out. Fear scowls at my insides, scared he's going to notice the small bloat appearing on my lower belly.

But he doesn't.

He takes off my underwear as he bends down on his knees, placing his face in front of my dripping wet pussy. My hands snake through his dark blonde hair, gripping it to stop my body from visibly trembling.

"Is how fucking sweet you taste." He snarls.

He takes me into his mouth and sucks my clit. I moan against his black tie. No warning. I'm in shock he went straight for the spot that has my body shaking.

"Oh, God!" My mouth muffles against the fabric of his tie, the words incomprehensible.

He ignores me. Danny keeps sucking on my clit and I feel my nipples harden. Every single hair follicle stands up across my skin. My stomach is tightening inwards, fighting the urge to scream. My liquids keep flowing outside of me and I feel like I could pass out at this moment, go completely unconscious from the pleasure.

He stops sucking and instead, his tongue flicks across my clit up and down causing my climax to heighten and close to rupturing. He keeps working his tongue on me, electrocuting my clit with destructive sensations. My head falls back against the brick wall, and I moan, soaking in every millisecond of his detrimental movements. I'm about to orgasm and he moves his tongue away from me leaving me in desperation.

His tongue starts trailing down the inside of my slit. My heart begins to pound harder. My feet curl on the ground. He stops consuming me and stands. I look up at him as he wipes my juices off his lips with his tongue.

"Your taste is so fucking divine. No one has ever come close to what you do to me." He growls in my ear. He grabs the tie out of my mouth and throws it to the floor.

He kisses my lips, and I can taste myself in his mouth. His

tongue pries my mouth open, and he devours me, commanding me with his kiss. I follow his aggressive movements trying to keep up. He still manages to completely intimidate me, and I've come to accept I will be bowing down to his dark shadows.

With every single swift movement, he tries to deepen his mouth more inside of me and I'm getting lost with no intention to be found. The more aggressive he gets with me the more worried I get for the second heart that beats inside of me.

Our baby he knows nothing about. My maternal instincts go on high alert, and I have to do something before we keep going like this. I can't afford him to bruise me all over again like the first few times he fucked me into his submissive lover.

"Danny." I let out a shaky breath, begging him to listen.

His hand goes to my throat and he tightens his grip on the right side of my neck rubbing his thumb across my collarbone.

"Hmm?" Danny hums through gritted teeth, arching his brow.

"I'm in the mood for something more…" I grabbed his thumb, pulling it into my mouth and sucking hard. It sends a deep low growl rumbling through Danny's chest.

"Vanilla."

Danny pulls his thumb out of my mouth, forcefully. He looks disappointed and I'm starting to panic.

"I'm not a vanilla man, Cherry. When I fuck you, it's to break you." He pauses and looks straight into my soul through my brown eyes.

"Then, I mold you back into place when I'm making you come." He growls, grabbing my hair, and pulling it into his palm. I wince.

"When I'm fucking you, I send you into a place you don't ever want to come back from, and then when I'm ready," he pulls my hair again and I gasp.

"When I'm done imprinting myself on your body, is when I allow you to finish." He argues.

I bite my lip and I so badly want to let him devour me like he truly wants in his own sadistic ways…

But I can't.

"Just tonight?" I beg, stalling.

He bites down on his gritted teeth, off and on.

"Is that what you want?" He asks, letting me go, and instead, he begins to caress my cheek, as he starts to back away giving me space and I'm craving for him to come close again.

I nod. My eyes squint at his beautiful ocean eyes.

"Then that's what you'll get." He picks me up in one swift movement. I hook one of my arms as he takes up the upstairs, he's ravenous against my mouth. Our kisses are full of passion as he holds me close to his chest. His arms are under my thighs as we breathe each other's oxygen. He carries my body so easily up to his bedroom as I lose myself completely as we kiss.

This was probably his version of vanilla.

It doesn't take long before we're in his bedroom. The same bed I fell asleep in by myself when he pulled away from me on our first date. He leans down slowly so I'm on my feet again.

He turns on his lamp when we get to one side of the bed. The light from the lamp illuminated his bed, revealing different shades of black and dark grey sheets.

Danny's silent as he begins to undress himself. His eyes never leave my body. I sit on the edge of his bed, letting my ass collide with it. My breasts bounce with gravity and the sight makes Danny stiffen.

Danny grabs the opening of his shirt where the tie used to be and rips it open with ease, causing the buttons to dislodge from his shirt and it hits the ground fast, as he watches my breasts the entire time. I suck in a breath, watching his ripped shirt get thrown to the floor. He tore his shirt so easily, as if it was made out of thin paper.

I watch his muscular chest move up and down as he breathes, desperate to have his cock inside of me. The sand clock tattoo written with words in Latin, intrigued me once again and I can't remember what they mean or say. He did tell me but I don't recall, I had fallen asleep before I got a chance to hear it.

I can see the beautifully detailed Angels and Demons sleeve tattoo on his arm, veins from his forearm coming out. The lighting from the lamp was just enough to see them. He turns around, his back toward me and I bite my lip watching him. He sways his shoulders back and I can hear the bones in his spine crack. He throws his phone and pack of smokes onto his nightstand.

His massive ghostly, Grim Reaper tattoo stares back at me as always. Tt's terrifyingly detailed. It looks so real. The longer I stare at it, the more anxious I get. Every time I look at it, it sends shivers down my spine. This is getting ridiculous, how can I be so afraid of a tattoo? *It's silly.*

The gaping wound I helped stitch up when I was in Iraq is just another scar. It healed so well I can barely see it now and my heart flutters knowing I helped him recover.

I lean on my elbow, half of my body laying down. He turns back around facing me and he smirks. He pulls down his pants, kicking off his socks.

His large cock springs free. My eyes widen and fear bellows inside of me. This is a sight of him I will never get used to. His Long. Thick. Mouthwatering cock is rock hard and ready to destroy me.

The veins on his dick send me licking my lips. I miss the way he tastes. I miss the way he had me choking on his dick with no remorse on the helicopter.

He pulls his blankets over the bed. The sheets land on the side of my elbow. He lays himself down on his bed pulling me with him. He yanks me on top of him and I'm panting hard.

I love the way his rough textured hands feel against my soft skin.

"You're going to sit on my cock." He's breathing hard, his cool delicious breath blowing against my hair, making it sway. He smells so good.

"You're going to take every inch of me inside you and you're going to ride me until you're screaming my name." I sit up and he forces me to position myself over his waist, his cock standing up against my clit.

"This is as vanilla as it's going to get."

I bite my lip, trailing my palm against his rock, hard concrete abs. I grab his massive cock into my small hand, stroking it. I lift myself up just enough to get myself ready to take him inside of me.

Danny groans and grinds his teeth as I stroke him. He's so massive in my hand. Pre-come glistens at his opening and I bend, my mouth closes the distance but I stop myself before I give in. I peek up at him and he looks like a beast, eyeing my every moment, eager.

I lick his pre-come clean off his tip and swallow.

"Fuck." He rasps.

Then I rub his monstrous tip against my pussy. I start at my clit, circling it. Danny flexes his thick thighs underneath me, making my whole body jerk forward but I control my balance. He's growing impatient and I smile with satisfaction.

Then I trail the tip of his cock down my slit and leave him at my entrance, holding him there.

"Tell me." I breathe out, demanding his attention.

"What?"

"How does it feel knowing I'm yours?" I surprised myself with my own question. The lust I have for Danny takes possession of my body and I lose myself every single time I'm around him. He does this to me.

I want to know what he feels when he's around me. I don't ever get much out of him when I pry about his emotions so I'm taking this moment to hold him hostage.

He smirks so sinisterly; I immediately regret my curiosity.

"Fucking heavenly baby."

Then he pushes his cock inside of me slowly, making me cry out as I take the first inches of him. My attempt to take control of his need completely backfires.

My breathing halts, my chest tightens, and I feel like I can't breathe from the painful yet remarkable intrusion. His cock slows as he forces his entire length inside of me.

"Damnit baby, I hardly fit inside of you. You're so tight." Danny snarls as he watches his dick go in and out of me.

I close my eyes, throwing my head back, holding onto his waist. I begin to bounce on his wet hard cock and he groans with each thrust.

I'm watching him as my short hair falls in front of my face. I'm riding him and I'm enjoying every second as I watch him, *watch me* with irrational eyes. Our bodies begin to sweat from the heat of our sensuality. The sounds of our indescribable moans fill his room, and I don't ever want this moment to end.

I'm scared that if I close my eyes too long, he'll be back in Iraq and I'd be alone in my room again. Fearing for Shane's return to take my life.

But that was a delusion. Because we're here together, right now.

Danny's hand trails to my ass and squeezes it as I rock up and down on his cock. I feel it stretch me once again but ignore the pain and keep going until I'm close to finishing. Each time I move, it's full of passion. We're both hot and desperate for each other and our pace changes faster with each needy movement. The way he fucks me, the way he worships me, the way he talks *to me*... I know he's holding back his true feelings for me.

Danny's impatience gets the best of him and he sticks a finger into my ass as I ride him. A loud moan escapes me as he puts it in further.

"Fuck I want to break you so bad, I want to make you cry but I'll take what I can get."

His voice sends me into a world of serenity. I can't stop my rhythm, I pick up the pace, bouncing harder and faster on his cock. Danny's finger slides out of my ass, and he grips my waist, lifting himself off the bed and now he's in control.

I stop riding him and I fall forward as he begins to fuck me on his own terms. Every single inch of him slams inside of me. At the same time, I make sure he doesn't lose control and I keep his strength at bay with my hands, preventing him from giving me pain and protecting my abdominal area.

He's forcing all of his cock inside me, his hands on my waist and then he hits a spot that sends my head back, and my eyes shut tight.

"Danny!" I scream his name as my orgasm bursts inside of me, shattering my entire existence on top of him. My eyebrows furrow and my teeth shut against each other, as a sharp moan cries out of me.

He hums devilishly, right before he picks up his pace and then he's grunting hard. He's filling me up with his come and my body falls on top of him, exhaustion overtaking me.

He slows down his pace making sure I get the full amount of his come inside of me. I'm about to crawl off his gorgeous unreal body but he stops me.

"This is the way I want you for the rest of my days and nights, *full of my come.*"

He grabs my chin and brings my lips toward him. My entire body shakes from all the emotions and sore muscles.

He takes in my bottom lip. At first, he sucks on it but then he switches to his teeth, biting down so hard, he draws blood, just like the first time we had sex. He licks the blood off my lips with his tongue and I freeze in complete shock.

"Mm, the color Red, just like a Cherry."

CHAPTER 40

ARI

I t was painful getting out of Danny's bed this morning. The alarm I set on my phone wakes me from the most peaceful slumber I have had in the past few months.

I dreaded going to work today, I simply didn't want to go.

Danny was already awake when my alarms went off because I woke up alone. I'm staring at his ceiling, watching the fan move in a blur. My phone lights up with a text from Lori.

My screensaver reflects a happy wide-eyed Paul. He's in his PT uniform. He has me in a playful chokehold while his hand is knuckled into my scalp. My hair was a mess, and my annoyed expression says it all. I'm rolling my eyes at my big brother with a smirk.

The sight of Paul causes curiosity surrounding his death, to bloom again. I'm so wrapped up in Danny again that I almost forget the one question that I'm determined to get answers about.

The smell of eggs and bacon sucked into my nose and my mouth waters. I force myself out of bed, somehow finding the energy to do so. I rub my tiny bump before I do anything else. It's my way of saying good morning to our baby. The thought of

Danny holding our unborn child makes me giddy with excitement. First I have to tell him, of course.

I start my search for clothes. The air hitting my naked skin caused me to shiver. I rub my hands up and down against my arms trying to keep warm.

I walk towards Danny's dresser, the bottom of my feet feeling icy as they touch the wooden floor. I go through Danny's drawers and find an oversized sweater that reads *NAVY* titled in the middle, then I grab a pair of his black boxers.

I send a text to my mom as I head down the stairs to check in on her. It makes me nervous knowing she slept alone last night while Shane is still on the loose, hiding from the military police. I would never feel comfortable again in my own home until Shane's locked up and can't terrorize me anymore.

But I got no notifications from the security camera so I can hold off from completely freaking out.

The smell of breakfast gets more intense as I get closer to the kitchen. My vision locks onto Danny, rubbing jelly on his toast with a butter knife. He's wearing a dark blue shirt and shorts. His hair slightly wet and messy, falling over his forehead that's coated with sweat.

He hasn't taken notice of me, yet. Or so I think. The sunlight from the open windows illuminates the entire kitchen and living room. The only thing I see are open fields of green grass and tall evergreen trees. His land was breathtaking.

My heart begins to pound at the sight of him making breakfast. Something about a man that cooks has me swooning.

"Good morning." Danny meets my gaze, placing his toast on a plate.

"I'm pretty sure I'm the one that's supposed to be making you breakfast," I announce sitting on his kitchen island bar stool. He looks up at me and smiles.

"I disagree." Danny places a plate of food in front of me.

Eggs, bacon, and toast.

"I'm completely capable of making my girl breakfast before she wakes up."

My heart skips a beat. I will never get used to being his.

"What time did you wake up?" I take a bite of the eggs, first.

"Around five. I usually wake up early. I got a workout in and then went on a five-mile run outside. I have a home gym in the basement. You're more than welcome to use it." He grabs an iced glass, with amber liquid inside of it and my heart drops like an anchor.

He's drinking.

It's still early in the morning and he's already modifying his mind.

Did he always drink this much? Or was this something new?

Today was supposed to be the day of answers. I had to tell him about the pregnancy. I had to tell him about Shane.

How could I if he's already yearning to be drunk?

I wanted to confront him about his drinking instead. I wanted to bombard him with questions about his deployment. Were they able to rescue Damon? The most important question that lingers is, *what exactly happened to my brother?*

Something's seriously off about Danny, and I was hesitant to pry. He continues to deprive me of the information that I need.

The need to announce my pregnancy to him is faltering and I'm growing disappointed. I wanted him to be sober when I changed his life with my words.

You're going to be a dad.

"What's wrong Ari?" He holds his glass to his lips, studying me.

"Nothing." I rush out, biting off the crispy end of the bacon.

"I'm just thinking about work. I've gotta go in today. I work at the ER on the Navy base now. I have to leave in about an hour."

"Really? That's fucking amazing. I'll take you to work then." He offers, swallowing.

"Thanks. The staff accepted me with open arms when I

returned from Iraq. It's been an amazing journey." Danny drops his glass of whiskey and smirks. I just know the memories of him taking me into his room flow into his mind because that's what's happening to me. The sound of the glass colliding with the counter, rings, and he leans on the counter with both of his hands causing his biceps to flex and veins to pop out of his skin.

The sight devastatingly encapsulates me.

"I'm proud of you, baby." Butterflies begin to flutter in my stomach as the word baby rolls off his tongue. He turns around to the stove and starts to serve himself eggs on a plate from the pan.

My phone buzzes and my phone lights up with my mom's reply. I pull myself away from getting lost in the sight of him.

Ma:

Everything is good here mija. How did Danny react to the news of the baby?

I quickly snatch the phone from the counter preventing Danny from seeing her text. The pace of my breathing becomes erratic. I'm on edge. I can't keep this secret to myself any longer.

Danny deserves to know that I'm carrying our baby. There was no good time to do it though but I couldn't risk him reading this text from my mom. This was not the way I wanted him to find out. I can only imagine how he would feel finding out about everything through someone other than me. It should come from me.

"I need to go home. I've gotta grab my scrubs and shower before I'm late."

Danny turns around and sits on the barstool across from me. He sets his plate down, grabbing a piece of egg with his fork.

"You can shower here and then I'll take you to pick up your scrubs. I can drop you off at work too. I plan on picking up your Bronco later today." He clears his throat as the food passes down before continuing. "I've gotta stop by the office at work for an hour then I should be back home before five in the afternoon."

"Okay." I smile.

He looks up at me before taking another sip of his glass. I'm in so much trouble with this man.

"Okay." He winks at me and I freeze at his actions. God, just with him closing one eye, I'm blushing hard. I look down at the food on my plate as my appetite disappears.

Before I get to my house, I inform my mother that Danny's still in the dark about my pregnancy. I ask him to wait for me in his truck while I run into my house and grab my necessities for work. My black scrubs, headband, and tennis shoes.

I rush into my house. The door was unlocked, and I find my mom on the phone with one of her sisters from Mexico, in the kitchen. She's deep in her conversation and she only manages to wave when she spots me. She points towards the couch with her finger, and I find my black scrubs freshly ironed and ready for me to put on.

The way my mother loved us unconditionally was what I envisioned myself striving to be with my own children. I'm in my twenties now and she still loves me the same way when I was just a child. She was even more overbearing with my brother when he was alive. Always doing everything she could to support him and make his life easier when he was home.

I run to my room and grab a positive digital pregnancy test I took at Target when I initially found out. I had it tucked away in one of my cardigans that hung in my closet. An idea popped into my head of how I wanted to tell him when we were driving over.

I threw off Danny's clothes and replaced them with my scrubs. I hide the test in one of my pockets, securing it from falling out. I'm running late to work and I'm pressuring myself to hurry.

I do a quick scan of my room to ensure it hasn't been broken into while I was gone. So far, everything looks the same as when I left it before Emilia's wedding. Even though I have a security system now, I wanted to double-check. I search for my Glock that I placed underneath my bed and it's still there. I push my body up from the floor and steadily head out of my room, rushing.

"I'll see you later Ma, love you!" I call out before I'm closing the door. I held it open, with one foot out onto the porch outside waiting for her to acknowledge me.

"Love you too, que Dios te bendiga!" She palms her cell phone with her hands to bid me farewell.

God bless you.

I close the door and jog towards Danny's truck, tennis shoes in my hand. His phone captures his full attention so much he doesn't flinch when I jump into the passenger seat. I start to push my feet into the soles of my shoes and my mind runs rampant.

Who is he texting?

For some reason, my mind travels to the blonde woman that I saw him with at the bar, the night he almost beat Shane to death.

He wouldn't.

I bite my lip and ignore my curiosity. I trust him.

He turns off his phone, throwing it in the center console. Cody Jinks begins to play through the speakers of the truck as he puts the vehicle in reverse, backing us out of my driveway.

The engine roars as he puts it into drive and presses on the gas. His truck smells like leather and cologne and I want to cling onto it. The plastic edges of the positive pregnancy test pokes into my hip bone and it sends my head swirling. My palms grow clammy, and I don't know how I'm going to announce my pregnancy without hurling.

I'm hopeful that he'll be just as excited as I am but Danny's extremely unpredictable. One minute he's the man I fell hard for. Next, he's someone else.

I put one hand on my lower belly, running my thumb on top of my belly button over my shirt, wondering what my little one is up to in there. Are they sleeping? Are they dancing? Are they sucking on their thumb? I read in a pregnancy book they do those kinds of things. Thinking of what the unborn baby is up to is a good distraction from my impending future. Will he be mad that I've been keeping it from him?

I look at Danny and the sun shines across his face, his shadows outlining me. He squints at the road in front of him. He reaches towards the center console of the truck and grabs his aviator sunglasses and places them on. The lenses reflect obsidian black.

"It's almost been a year since Paul died." Danny manages to say through gritted teeth. I watch his hands tighten against the steering wheel. His knuckles turn white.

I start to chew on the insides of my cheeks, anxiously.

"I know. It's almost December." I intertwine my fingers, resting them on my lap. I look out the window as we get into the line to enter base. Every military post is guarded by security forces and the only way to get in is to show identification that you're affiliated with the government in some way. Whether you're a spouse, veteran, dependent, or contracted worker.

The line isn't too long, and my heart begins to pound in my chest. I can't hold onto this news any longer.

A marine takes our IDs, his scanner hovering over the barcode of my ID. He scans it and a loud beep follows. He grabs Danny's and his eyes circle as he reads it. He looks up at Danny and finishes scanning his ID.

"Well, I'll be damned. It's Grim Reaper in the flesh. You're a fucking legend, sir." The marine hands him back his ID and then salutes Danny. Danny grows uncomfortable and clenches his jaw, looking down at his wallet, and tucking his ID away, and doesn't say anything in return.

"You're good to go, have a good day sir." The light in front of us turns green, signaling us to drive forward. Danny finally acknowledges him with a nod.

He rolls his window back up and I take my ID back from Danny's hand. He looks tense and I feel like any good that was in the air has been sucked out dry.

I wait until he parks his truck in the parking lot of the hospital before I open my mouth. He spins the dial of the volume down, and the music crescendos with his actions.

Nausea enters my head, clouding my ability to stay focused. I grab my backpack that I always take to work with me. I squeeze the straps, bouncing my knee anxiously. The uncertainty of his reaction is driving me insane. But again, the old me has a voice and it's shouting at me.

Trust him. He's a good man. Tell him.

The *new me* is hesitant and worried.

"Danny. There's something I need to talk to you about." I whisper. My voice comes out so low I'm surprised he heard me. I peek at him, and he turns towards me. I can see my reflection in his sunglasses. I look nervous and I hate how easily I can be read.

His stone-cold expression has me on edge and I feel like I can't breathe.

"I'm not talking about the deployment. I'm not talking about Paul." He snarls, perfectly displeased by my statement. His voice is so deep and angry, it sends fear throughout my nerves.

"Danny... I'm not... I wasn—"

He cuts me off.

"You're going to be late, Ari." He turns away from me, licking his lips. He keeps one hand on the steering wheel ignoring my presence.

I'm hurt at his change of behavior. I start to wonder, what set him off this time? It had to be my house. It probably reminded him of Paul and triggered something he wants to keep buried. I sigh, my patience is unwavering.

There's no way to say this perfectly. Not too long ago we were strangers and now it's a swarm of chaos. I can't hold this in any longer.

I grab the pregnancy test in my hand and place it in the center console.

"I'm pregnant."

Danny snaps his head towards me then at the pregnancy test. I hold my breath. He takes it into his hand, studying the small screen that reads *pregnant*. His nostrils flare and I'm in shock. My disappointment grows when I realize he's not happy but breathing fury through slow steady breaths. He's quiet and I'm paralyzed. I had a few minutes to spare before my shift started and, at the moment, I didn't care about being a few minutes late. I needed to know what he was thinking.

What's going through his head?

"This is the part where you say something... anything." I plead.

He drops the test back down in the console.

"You're going to be late."

Danny shatters my heart into a million pieces. It's a different feeling this time. Usually, I'm breaking from the intensity we share together but now it's just pain. I purse my lips, staring at him watch the medical staff members walk out of the emergency department. This is the side of Danny that he talks about. The bad side of him and I don't like it.

I shake my head as the realization hits me like a train. These are my consequences coming full circle, falling for a man I didn't know. The brutal reality settles in as I accept my faults. I let this man drown me in his dark world that holds a broken system.

I'm shaking. I take the test back into my hands, wanting to get as far away as possible from him. I grabbed the door handle, and I jump out. He doesn't try and stop me or say another word regarding my announcement.

Instead, he's reversing his truck out of the parking spot. Meanwhile, I'm trying my hardest to not fall apart in public, but my hormones get the best of me and a thick hard lump forms in my throat.

A sharp sting forced me to blink, fluttering my lashes as the tears begin to fall out, running down my cheeks. The status of Danny and I's relationship surrounds me and I'm questioning everything. Every single kiss, touch, and exchanged conversation.

I think I've just become my own mother.

A single mother.

CHAPTER 41

ARI

I'm going through the motions at work, unable to concentrate on anything I'm doing. I feel lost and the sweet reunion of Danny and I is ruined by the reality of responsibility. I feel like I'm dragging my feet as I walk the hallways.

He looked infuriated when I told him I was pregnant. Still, he stayed silent and I hated it. This was a moment I had dreamed about growing up and I felt like he had ruined it. I don't know what I expected. I was hoping for at least a smile but instead, I got disdain.

I can't be totally hurt that he didn't react the way I wanted him to. Maybe he's in shock. Maybe he just needs time to let it sink in… I know I did. I pushed everyone away when I found out I was pregnant. Still… All I want to do is cry. Cry until I have no tears left. My coworkers notice a change in me and immediately ask me what's wrong. I refuse to let them in on my personal life. Instead, I message Meredith looking for some support. My first thought was to reach out to Emilia but I didn't want to disturb her honeymoon.

I'm halfway through my shift when I get a text from Danny.

Danny:

Your Bronco is parked outside.

He returned my car from the beach and still, no reaction about him being a father. No questions. No yelling. No happiness. Nothing. So, I don't reply.

I walk to the waiting area and the lobby's full of patients. Flu cases have spiked leaving us bombarded with sick families. I open the doors and announce the next patient's name.

"Mrs. Johansson!" I shout.

Everyone looks my way, hopeful for their turn. An older woman who looks to be in her fifties walks towards me. I give her a warm smile while opening the doors to the emergency department, welcoming her in. I walk toward her, offering her my arm. She limps as she walks and she takes my help for balance.

Suddenly, something catches my eye and I look towards the rotating doors of the Emergency Room. I see a familiar stature, walking out of the building and I'm frozen. I know who it is and I refuse to accept it. His back is turned to me and I start to hyperventilate. My chest rises up and down, panting with horror.

Shane.

I hitch a breath as I try to get a closer look to verify my paranoia. I take one step forward to get a glimpse of his side profile view but it's too late. He disappears outside, passing a wall, leaving me horrified.

CHAPTER 42

DANNY

The entire ride to the beach I'm thinking of how my life's going to change. Kane sits beside me in the passenger seat and I'm smoking a cigarette with the windows rolled down. The smoke lingers in and out of my truck and it sends a painful reminder of my responsibility to quit.

Ari's pregnant.

I would no longer be able to smoke around her and I'm completely okay with it but the shock from her announcement has me lost. *There was a point in my life when I did want kids.*

When I did crave the sight of my woman swollen with my child. The perfect family picture. That was before I started my career as a SEAL. Before I witnessed with my own eyes the fuckery of evil that creeps on this Earth.

My little Angel is pregnant and that means another soul for me to protect.

The addiction of my career is the only thing that matters. It started when I got my first kill on my first deployment. My lethal skills and mental capacity of knowledge I had influenced the military to brand me as The Grim Reaper. From then on, I've been a lethal killer for the Navy and after witnessing the evil that lives in the world, lurking in the shadows, I knew I would never bring my own children into this world.

I didn't want to ever experience the pain of losing a child to something so evil. Or vice versa. My son or daughter worried for their father as he fights the hands of Satan's variants when he's on deployments or missions.

The amount of sick twisted people that I've killed helps me balance out the demons in my mind. But it doesn't deter the scars that get tattooed on my brain and physical body. I have scars all over constantly reminding me of the battles I've faced when I look at them.

The most recent twisted picture that will forever be engraved inside of my mind, was Damon getting burnt alive. I can still hear his screaming, haunting me every day since then.

It's going to be a while before it stops.

I got a scar on my lip from that mission when I got ambushed. When I was forced to engage a terrorist in hand-to-hand combat. Soon after, we discover Damon Hawk's body, burnt to a crisp, his body engulfed in flames.

He was long gone when we got to him and that drives me insane. A brother we couldn't save. Everyone that was assigned to that mission was surprised it hadn't leaked yet. They usually do. The government can remain happier knowing this story was still buried.

It didn't sit well with us at all. But it bought me more time to ignore it and not talk to Ari about it. Damon's family has been notified but I wasn't sure if his girl knew yet but that isn't my business.

We're nearing the parking lot where Ari left her Bronco. About twenty minutes away, I put out my cigarette.

"I'm not drinking ever again. How the fuck are you not suffering right now? This hangover is wrecking me." Kane says, rubbing his eyes, and placing his sunglasses on the bridge of his nose.

"Unlike you, I have a high tolerance you fucking lightweight."

Kane was going to take my truck and I would drive Ari's Bronco to the hospital so she could have her vehicle back and not have to worry about it anymore. I was definitely not happy about her pregnancy. I know that makes me a terrible man but in my own head, it's justified.

She's the only girl I've ever filled up with my come without a condom. I assumed she was on birth control but I guess I was wrong. Still, I didn't dare place blame or fault her for getting pregnant.

I couldn't fathom a future with a child. I was just starting to get accustomed to having someone wait for me to return home from deployments... And now? A baby?

I can't help but assume I'll be a horrible father because my father was.

He's a shitty man, raising me to be just as cold-hearted as he is but my mother made sure I had some sense of humanity.

There's a reason we don't speak anymore.

My mother was pregnant with my sister. I was a teenager at the time and her pregnancy was high risk due to her age. She went through years of infertility and with the help of doctors, hormones, and medications, thousands of dollars later, she finally carried out a pregnancy that passed two months.

Of course, money's no problem to my father, a successful businessman worth millions.

But deep down inside his fucked up world, he was worth nothing.

My mom caught him having an affair with one of his employees. The stress and heartache of his betrayal caused her to miscarry at around four months of gestation. She was able to move on from his infidelity but I never have and never will.

Holding my mother's hand during the years she was depressed and couldn't do anything for herself after losing my baby sister, made me resent my father. All the respect I had for him disappeared the day I found out he cheated on my mother. My distant cold behavior towards him doesn't sit well with him which causes us to be estranged.

It wasn't because of his harsh parenting that made us estranged. It wasn't because of all the times he physically beat me, punched me, or kicked me as a kid. It wasn't because he abandoned me as a child, for weeks, on his ranch properties in the middle of nowhere, that needed work when his employees wouldn't come into work.

No it wasn't because of that.

It was because he hurt my mother. And that's a line I've made him constantly regret crossing every day.

I can see the beach in the distance and the memory of Ari in her blue bridesmaid dress makes me flinch. She's so fucking beautiful. But not just beautiful in appearance, it's in her ambition. Her need to help people makes her beautiful. The way she trusts people and the way she wears her heart on her sleeve is what makes her so beautiful to me.

Ari is like my ocean. I was caught in her waves of beauty, struggling to get back to shore. *Back to my old ways, back to the old me.* I'm afraid I'm stuck in her ocean now and I'll gladly drown in her waters if it means she'll always be mine.

Kane has always had the ability to read me very well. After failing to rescue Damon, I separated myself from the team and I didn't want to be near anyone. I didn't want to talk or even breathe. The smell of burnt flesh made me sick. It hit me hard, changed me, and something about seeing a human burnt alive, took a piece of my sanity with it.

Kane and I talked about our differences while we were transported back to a safe haven created in a secret location amongst enemy lines. Paul was the closest to me but after he passed, Kane, Rooker, and I grew closer. His death scarred us.

Kane regretted placing blame on me that day in front of Ari.

He apologized, explaining that he was upset we almost lost Rooker and it brought up emotions surrounding Paul.

"I've known you long enough to know you haven't been okay since the failed mission. I thought you would be happier being home *with Ari.*" I grind my teeth when I catch his tone as he says my girl's name.

Something possessive takes hold of me and I want to cut out his tongue just for saying her name. I can't help but feel territorial around what's mine. It's an unfamiliar feeling and I don't recognize myself when it comes to Ari. He thinks I don't notice the way he looks at her. *But I do.*

My body stiffens and I take in a deep breath before letting it out.

We sit in silence and I'm biting my tongue. I hated opening up about anything personal, especially now with all the recent changes. The mother of my child is a new boundary for me but Kane's the only one I could really talk to about this kind of stuff.

I'm not close to my parents and I couldn't go to them in this situation, at least not right now. I want to avoid having their opinions thrown at me left and right. I want to keep Ari safe from their intrusion of opinions and comments about our relationship. She's sacred to me, our relationship is sacred and even if that means I need to protect her from my overly opinionated parents, I'll do just that.

The way I feel about her is something I've never quite felt before with any girl. She inhabits every single part of my mind changing me to be a more vulnerable man. I don't like it but for her, I'll be the man she deserves. It just would take some time.

Clenching my jaw, I decide to give in and show Kane a glimpse of what's been on my mind.

"Ari's pregnant."

Kane's body freezes and he's visibly in shock. I take a quick glance at him before returning my eyes to the road.

"Con—, congratulations man. Happy for you both." Kane stutters. He looks out the window in the opposite direction. He takes a few moments to gather his thoughts. "So, when did you guys, uh, I'm just a bit confused on the timeline... when did this happen — "

I cut him off.

"None of your business. That's all you get." My voice vibrates through my chest.

He nods and rubs his lips together.

"I'm going to be a dad. Me? A dad." I scoff, still in disbelief.

"Why don't you sound happy? This is great news Rider." Kane replies, dumbfounded.

I shake my head.

"I didn't think this would ever happen. I purposely avoid situations like this for a reason. We're always gone. At any moment, any of us can lose our lives. I don't want her to break into pieces when I leave after what she's been through. She lost her brother and yet she still somehow wants to be with me knowing how hard this life is. It's hard on the family. Noel gives Rooker shit all the time. She's always begging him to get out of the Navy. The toll it takes on kids isn't something they need." I pull into the parking lot, and I spot Ari's Bronco.

"I get it. I do. But Ari seems like a great girl that knows what she wants. You're a good man, Danny and you'll be an even better father. Who cares about the rest? Ari and you will make great parents." I park into the lot and grab Ari's keys into my hand.

I'm about to exit the driver's side when Kane's voice interrupts.

A quirk a brow.

"Look man all I'm going to say is... I better be the Godfather to that little girl or boy!" He grins.

I smirk, shaking my head.

"It's a boy, I don't know the gender yet but I know for a fact it's a boy. My swimmers are all men."

"Hah. We'll see. Anyway, are we still headed for the bar? Lopez wants to go drinking again tonight at your favorite place."

I'm hesitant to answer. A small part of me knows I should go home and be there when Ari returns home from work but a bigger part of me can't say no to a night of liquor and fun with the team. The addiction to drowning out the noise was too high.

"Hell yeah."

CHAPTER 43

ARI

I end up getting out of work later than usual. It's nearing midnight and I'm completely drained emotionally and physically. I kept thinking about how I was going to live my life as a single mother. My negative thoughts just always go to the worst possibility, I can't help it. I'm dramatic but that's where I just go nowadays with the year I've had.

There were no more sightings of Shane for the rest of my shift, at least to my knowledge. The possibility of Shane attacking me again is valid. His threat still lingers in the back of my head.

One crisis at a time...

The drive from the hospital to my mothers' house is short.

I so badly want to crawl into bed with Danny but instead, I'm driving home, wanting to cry my eyes out. My mind's running wild already.

I expected to have missed calls or text messages from him but to my surprise, nothing. My heart ached knowing I had pushed him away with the announcement of my pregnancy. I dropped my phone out of my hands letting it fall back into my backpack.

I hadn't expected this either. This was a milestone in my life I thought would come at least five years from now. I was just as surprised as he was, but I resented the way he reacted. I'm still in my car, parked outside of my mom's house not wanting to go in just yet listening to music hoping it would take some stress off.

Suddenly my phone buzzes with a text message.

DANNY:

Where are you, Cherry?

Did he really expect I would drive to his house after the way he reacted?

What do you mean? I'm out of work, just got to my mom's. What do you expect?

I stare at my phone waiting for a reply and sure enough he doesn't take long. I don't understand why he thinks I'd be at his house right now. After the way he reacted to finding out I was pregnant... he left me disappointed.

Danny:

You better be naked in my bed by the time I arrive at my house.

I swallow. My cheeks flushed.

Where are you?

Where could he be at this time of night?

DANNY:

Don't worry about that. Just worry about what I'll do to you if you're not at my house in the next thirty minutes.

CHAPTER 44

DANNY

The world's buzzing and nothing matters anymore but the simplicity feeling I get when I'm drunk off whiskey. The guys wanted to go to a gentleman's club after the bar but I refused.

I have a sweet tooth for my Cherry.

Rejecting Lopez's invite to see naked women dance all over us, was new to me. Ari was already changing me. The only naked woman I'll ever admire from now on will be *her*. I was still trying to let the news of her pregnancy sink in without distancing myself from her.

I'm really trying… in my own way.

I hadn't eaten anything all day besides breakfast which made the alcohol hit harder. I didn't want to talk when I got home, instead, I want to fill Ari with my cock and hear her scream. Her screams are like music to my ears and I want her to play me a fucking symphony.

I told Ari thirty minutes but every time I tried to leave Lopez and Kane would order us more shots. It's now two in the morning and I feel like an ass for not getting back sooner.

An Uber takes me home as I'm too impaired to risk my career.

I know for a fact I could make it home safely even though I was gone.

But I wouldn't do anything that would risk losing my job. My career was still the number one priority in my life. Yet, Ari and the baby that she carries inside of her are changing that.

I should have known that she was pregnant when I first saw her. Her breasts have grown since the last time, and her friends slip up at the wedding. Still, I didn't put two and two together. Now that it's crossing my mind, her curvy body has widened hips.

I was too distracted to notice any minor details. I was thinking about breaking into her like I enjoy doing the entire time I was away from her. Her swollen breasts send me into a craze. I could take them into my mouth all day and night and it still wouldn't be enough for me.

I pay the Uber driver at the gate to my ranch. He reverses off my property and I watch him leave. I turn back around and plug in the passcode, granting myself access.

It's a ten-minute walk to my porch and it's the perfect time to smoke before I walk into my house. My body buzzing, extremely inebriated. I went a little too far drowning myself in alcohol tonight. I keep pushing my limits farther and farther and my tolerance is too high. Nothing changes. No matter how much I drink.

A year since Paul's passing is coming up and it's triggering. The guilt came back in full force when I met Ari and there's a part of me that hates her for it.

Another overwhelming fraction of myself that I hate, is the fact that I wasn't able to resist her and it drives me insane. Everything would have stayed the same if I could have just stayed away from corrupting her innocence. Everything would have stayed simple.

Still, I'm sure I'm ready for the impending changes to happen but it doesn't matter.

I was falling hard for Ari and our baby was on the way.

I watch the stars in the sky as I blow out smoke from my lungs.

How was I going to be a father to this child? I'm a fucked up person. My father was a horrible dad and I've already convinced myself, I'll be the same… *or worse.*

I spot Ari's Bronco parked in my driveway and my cock hardens. *Such a good fucking girl.*

I walk inside my house and it's quiet. I kick off my shoes and head towards the stairs. My cock hardening for her sweet pussy.

I lighten my steps as I open the door to my bedroom, trying my hardest to keep quiet. I doubt she's awake. She worked over ten hours today and I'm sure she's exhausted.

In the morning, I'm going to ask her to take it easy on the number of hours she's been working. I want to give her the option to stay home, stress-free as possible while she grows our baby.

She's tucked underneath the sheets, the lamp illuminates her innocent cute face and my chest tightens from the feral need to rail into her.

Her short hair sprawls over hiding one side of her beautiful face. I take off my shirt throwing it into the corner of my room where my dirty laundry lays in the hamper. I shrug my shoulders back, making all the knots pop and my spine crack. I'm still in my pants as I walk towards her.

Just seeing her makes me go crazy. The drunken haze I'm in transforms me into a thirsty beast that needs to devour every part of her.

I'm going to wake her up with my cock.

I throw the blankets off of her aggressively, exposing her perfect body. She's naked just like I asked her to be and I'm pleased. I hum with satisfaction when I see her captivating body. She's laying on her side and I get closer.

She's just too fucking perfect, I don't deserve my little Angel but she's mine. No matter what happens, she's always going to be mine.

I lean forward placing one hand on each side of her, the bed sinking under my weight. She muffles something in her sleep before she comes into consciousness.

Her eyes slowly blink open and she smiles when she realizes I'm home.

"Where were you? You smell like you just walked out of a bar." She groans.

I move her shoulder down gently, forcing her to lie on her back. She's surprised by my touch, her eyes bulge and something takes possession of my body and I can't help it.

CHAPTER 45

ARI

Danny's aggression shocks me when he pins me down to his bed by hovering over me, caging me in with his strong arms. The bed is cold without him here. His eyes spark with something I've never seen before. Pure darkness and hatred.

"Danny, stop it. Let me sleep." I cry out. Fear bellowing inside of me. I'm still trying to escape the deep slumber I was in. His unfamiliar touch breaks me out of my tired mind and I'm determined to confront him.

"You know what you were getting yourself into Ari. You know this is the way I am. I fucking warned you and you didn't listen." He snarls. He lets me go and stands up towering his massive, muscular frame over me.

He begins to unbuckle his belt and I'm forcing myself up on my elbows. I'm completely naked like he asked me to be, vulnerable. My eyes squint as I try and adjust my vision to study his face.

He looks like he's feral, impulsive, and impatient. He's angry and drunk. The Danny I've fallen for is replaced by something else.

"We're not doing this right now. We need to talk. I won't let you distract me anymore with sex." I demand, pulling the blankets back over me.

When I cover up my body, it seems to piss him off.

He rips the blankets off of me and I back away from him. I flinch as the air blows into my face. He grabs my jaw firmly but not hard enough to cause me pain.

"Oh Cherry, but *we are* doing this right now." He demands harshly.

My pussy throbs even though his harsh treatment internally hurts me. I want to let him fuck me. I want to let him drown his sadness in me like I always do, but I can't anymore.

It sends me into a rage and I'm determined to finally get my answers about Paul's death. His drunken state snaps me out of the trance he usually puts me in.

I crawl underneath his grasp and I stomp over to my clothes. I throw one of Danny's oversized white shirts on my body. It's so big on me that it goes all the way down, covering my ass and front. My nipples are hardened with arousal, poking through his shirt, the cold temperature in his house doesn't help.

Danny hasn't faced me yet. He still stares at the bed where my body used to be. Every single muscle in him stiffens. I can see all the muscles in his back and it sends my clit throbbing. A grim reaper looks back at me sending shivers down my spine and I'm tempted to look away but I stand my ground.

"Tell me how Paul died," I shout. My voice is cold and hard.

He turns his head towards me and his eyebrows are furrowed. I get a good look at his side profile view and I swallow.

"Now." I demand.

He sucks in a deep angry breath.

He finally faces me. His blue eyes darken and his breathing quickens. His abs flex with each breath he takes. The muscles contract on his abdomen as his lungs expand. The v-cut that goes down his torso almost makes me want to give into his drunken lust but I stay strong.

He storms over to me and I back up, getting closer to the wall. His hand collides with the wall behind me and I flinch. It takes me back to my first time in Iraq.

"You wanna know what happened Ari?" He shouts into my ear and I jump at how loud his voice is. I turn my head to the side and I scrunch my face, afraid.

"I. Killed. Him." He hisses. His voice is so dark, it scares me.

I snapped my head towards him confused. I purse my lips, glaring at him. He looks so terrifyingly out of control. He grinds his teeth causing his jaw to clench and his nostrils are flaring.

"Keep going."

He backs away from me and brushes his hand through his beard. Instead of anger, his face carries a painful expression.

"Fuck, Ari! Why? It doesn't fucking matter anymore he's gone! He's not coming back. And it's my fucking fault." He roars.

"Tell me damn it! Talk to me! Nothing is ever that simple Danny." I plead.

He lets out a deep frustrated breath. My heart pounds inside my chest and I'm scared to know the answer but not enough to cower away. Not this time.

"No!" His voice sends shivers down my entire body. His wrath gets to me and I want to run.

"You're right nothing's fucking simple. Nothing is fucking simple about you getting knocked up. Everything is moving so fucking fast. Why did you have to make this so complicated?" He shouts, his teeth grinding, flashing his sharp incisors. He's loud and indignant.

"I made it complicated? I did?"

"I never wanted to be a father, Ari. And yes, I drink! Do you know why I drink? Huh? Do you? I drink because it's the only time anything and everything makes sense."

"Enough is enough! I will not put up with this. I will not let you bury your guilt inside of me anymore. I will not be this woman that waits for her partner to come home drunk." I yell.

"Talk to me. Or I'm gone. I will raise this baby by myself. I will not watch you drown yourself in whiskey." My words spit out of me like fire. This was a different side of me that I wasn't familiar with. I was never confrontational but that side of me has changed. Danny was bringing this new brave era out of me, *forcing it.*

I look at him and he's breathing heavily. He softens as my threat jolts him, sobering him up. Moments of dreadful silence pass by before he finally opens his mouth.

"We were on a mission. A joint mission with his team and mine. Paul and I were both leaders of our own teams. We were supposed to pull security on an area. A safe area, where we were tasked to eliminate a terrorist leader. We had our snipers ready to engage with them from a distance. This leader was number one on the most wanted list. This fucker was hard to find and finally, we were able to track him down."

My eyebrows are furrowed and I never move my eyes from Danny. His body begins to tremble.

"Paul... he's my brother. I trust him with my life and he trusts me with his. Some of the guys he was in charge of, *didn't trust him.*" He sighs. "The only problem was, nobody could agree on a safe area. He thought we could get the perfect shot from some other place in the woods. And he was right. It would have made the most precise shot. But, it wasn't a good idea. Deep down inside me, I knew it was a bad idea. The area was too good to be true but he really believed in his own plan." Danny sits down on his bed, resting his elbows on his lap, staring at the floor.

"An argument erupts between both teams. The vote was pretty much split down the middle of what to do and everyone was at each other's throats... except me. I stayed quiet the entire time everyone was arguing, trying to figure everything out in my head. Trying to make a calculated decision without having anyone interrupting. I was trying my best to *see both sides.* Paul got frustrated and everyone looked towards me for answers. Rooker has the most experience but I have the most polished record out of everyone there which leads them all to *demand me* to take charge."

Danny lets out a shaky breath and he moves his neck to the side, popping it. I'm starting to grow fearful. I know I said I wanted the answers to his death but now I want to scream. I don't want to picture my brother dying now that I'm getting the details.

I want to just tell him to forget about it and cover my ears with my hand. I don't think I'm strong enough to hear about the details of my brother's death. *Shit, this was a mistake.*

"And I can't bring myself to disagree with Paul. My instincts were telling me otherwise but I just couldn't do it. I had faith that Paul was making the right choice, so... " He swallows. "I order everyone to follow Paul's lead. I warned Paul that this could be bad but he was sure of himself."

He looks up at me. Guilt in his demeanor. His eyes are blood-shot and I hold my arms into place.

"Sure enough, on our way towards the safe area, Paul gets hit in the fucking neck. Then the chest and then his leg that makes him take a spin and he hits the ground hard." Danny points to his own neck, chest, and leg as he explains everything to me. He's here with me but I can tell his mind is trapped in the dreadful memory. I've never seen Danny like this before. He's full of remorse.

"We all take cover and hit the ground. We don't leave our men behind and for sure as hell, I wasn't going to leave my best friend. I run towards him, God only knows how but I dodge every single bullet that sprays in my direction." He lets out a breath and I'm biting my lip, wanting him to stop recounting the memories.

"He's in my fucking arms Ari, choking on his own blood. I'm trying my hardest to stop the bleeding but it's too much. It's too much blood. And he dies in seconds." He stands up infuriated, his hands curling into fists and he storms towards me again.

"If I would have just followed my instincts he would still be here. I'm the reason you don't have a brother, Ari. I made the call.

I did. I made the final decision that ended Paul's life." His deep husky, voice starts to shake and my breathing hitches.

Survivors' guilt.

"Stop it!" I don't want to hear the details anymore I can't take it. I thought I could take it but I can't.

"You fucked your brother's murderer. How do you feel about that?" He keeps going and I can't take it.

"When the hurricane hit, you wanted to know how I got all my scars. Do you still want to know little Angel? Do you still want to know all the little details of how I almost died every single time? Or how other men had to die each time for others to live?"

"*Please...* stop." I beg. "Stop blaming yourself. You're not a monster. You're not *Grim Reaper.* Just be Danny. *Be My Danny.*"

I grab his face and I pull his lips towards mine. I crash my lips against him and he doesn't respond. I need him to feel something. Something, good. Anything.

After a few seconds of pressing myself hard against him, I let him go.

"This was a horrible accident Danny, it's not your fault. It's not. You need to let that go, you hear me? Despite what you think, you have to let him go. He made his choice. I know that for a fact."

"I could have stopped him. It's my fault your mother had to bury her own son. And now?" He pauses, hatred spewing off his tongue. "Another mother that gets to mourn her son. Death claimed another soul because we were too late." Then he finally makes eye contact with me and I'm bracing myself for what comes next. "I don't want ever to want to see you in a Warzone again. Seeing all this shit will catch up to you Ari and I don't want that for you."

Tears start to fall down my cheeks as I blink them away. Danny doesn't move, he looks completely broken and I'm in shock at how he still manages not to let himself fall apart. Even in his lowest, darkest moments, he's still trying to figure out ways to protect me.

It doesn't take me long to realize he's talking about the other hostage. Violet's lover. *Damon.* My heart breaks and I'm at a loss. I don't know what to do. It all makes sense. Violet stopped returning my calls and texts, *she's grieving.*

All this stress and trauma is taking a toll on Danny and I need to figure out a way to help him. Help him realize that things just happen and it's out of his control, despite what he believes. It breaks me knowing he puts so much blame and death *on himself.*

He's been trying to kill himself slowly since his addiction started with alcohol. His career defines him. His need to always win and save people that need saving… it's drowning him.

"You have to let this go. Stop drinking yourself to death." I grab his hand and hold his palm onto my stomach.

"This baby needs you. They need all of you. I need you."

He looks away from me, his hand retreating.

"I loved my brother but he died because it was his fate!" I cry out. "I know my brother and he wouldn't want this to be yours. To drink yourself to the point there's nothing left." I murmur.

I don't want to lose Danny. I'm praying to God that my words are getting through to him because I don't know what else will… if our baby and I aren't enough for him to change, I will let him go. I will let him go and never look back.

Danny looks around the room and he's lost in thought. He's fighting with himself. The horrible temptations. I reach out toward his face wanting to brush my hands against his cheek, but he stops me.

He picks me up, forcing me to straddle him and a sharp, harsh breath leaves my lips.

He lays me down gently onto his bed and he hovers over me, ensuring he doesn't push any of his weight on top of me.

"Ari, you should be running far away from me." He pauses

and brushes my hair from my face. His expression is emotionless and rigid.

"But even if you choose to leave, you will always be mine. Even if you decide to run, your soul is trapped within me and I'm never giving it back." His eyes are glazing with demons.

I've never seen this side of him. He's gentle with my body and finally opening up to me... something I wasn't accustomed to. Tears are still falling out of my eyes, desperately trying to help him while I'm processing everything.

CHAPTER 46

ARI

I can't move and I feel like I can't breathe. The details of the weight Danny holds on his shoulders are too much for me to bear. I can't imagine spending one day in his shoes, *in his mind*.

"I choose you, I don't care about anything else." I respond, looking into the eyes I love so much.

Danny has so many scars that carry beyond his physical ones and I wasn't going to let that curse me from loving him. Whatever is left of his sanity, I want it.

He looks at me and a low growl thunders inside of him. The sound drenches my inner thighs from the longing lust calling for him.

"My naïve little Cherry. My world will tear you apart. You're choosing wrong but I'm the selfish asshole who won't ever stop you from doing so."

His eyes move from mine and trail down to my mouth. His eyes are red and burning with desire. His lips fall onto mine with so much need I'm seeing twinkling golden sparkles while my eyes are closed and I'm just focused on feeling him.

Our kisses are hard. He's searching for any type of release

from my lips, and I am too. Our kisses are not enough. His tongue is claiming mine I gladly let him dominate my mouth.

The way we kiss each other transports me into a haunted dream-like fairytale. We're waves from different oceans crashing into each other and the paradise is so dark I can't walk away from it. I don't want to.

"From now on, everything I do isn't for myself anymore." Danny backs away from me, holding my knee.

The realization that Danny and I aren't so different hits me. We're the same in some ways. I feel so stupid for not understanding this sooner. Both of us want to help people that need it. We're both trying to save people when we're having trouble liberating ourselves.

I sit up on the bed following him. This wasn't the type of love I had ever imagined myself having and I don't think I would be getting a typical happy ending. Diving into a journey with Danny scares me because his career holds so much uncertainty. At any moment, I could lose him like my brother.

I reach out and touch his chest, my hands trailing the sand clock tattoo. I'll let him take me the way he wants, the way he needs. I reach for his cheek but he stops me. He looks relieved and the most relaxed I've ever seen him... so when he stops me from going any further, I'm stunned.

"Not tonight." He leans in and kisses my cheek.

He looks tired, drained, *and vulnerable*. He wants to just... sleep instead. Something, he's still getting used to doing. Letting himself drift into a deep slumber... with me *after sex*. Every morning I wake up alone and I wonder when that would end... would it ever end? Will he ever comprehend that I accept him and every single fucked thing about him?

It doesn't take long until he's turning me around and we're lying down. We're both quiet and we both have said enough. I didn't want to talk anymore. I just wanted to enjoy his visible presence alongside me.

Danny falls to the bed, grabs my hand, pulling me down with him. He kicks off his pants and gets comfortable.

"I need to pee." I crawl out of his grasp until my feet hit the floor.

I can't help but feel like I need a moment to fall apart... alone.

As I walk through the hallway to Danny's bathroom, I notice how it's completely covered in all of his military achievements, awards, and graduations. They're all framed and neatly organized on each wall representing a successful and accomplished Navy career. Medals, and photographs with high-ranking admirals, glimmer in my eyes. This man truly was incredible.

I brush my teeth as quickly as I can. But once I look in the mirror, I fall apart. I start sobbing, breathing heavily and I grip the edge of the sink. I break away from my own reflection and look up at the ceiling.

I'm questioning my faith once again. I hate that Paul had to die like that. One wrong decision and it was lights out for my big brother.

I make sure to sob quietly. I didn't want Danny to worry. I was worried for him.

"Paul, why did you always have to be so dang stubborn?" I whisper to the ceiling.

My brother made his choice but I know for a fact he wouldn't want anyone feeling sorry for him. Hearing these words come from Danny's mouth felt like dark poison being spilled into the air. The story was so hard to hear... and I would never be able to open my mouth about it. I can't help but think of my mother and how I'll never be able to tell her the gruesome truth.

Would she hate Danny? Or would she be able to accept it without placing blame? The thought of her blaming Danny makes me cringe.

I have to take this to the grave with me. She wouldn't want to picture the horrid night of his death either way. It could very well kill her to picture such gruesome details about her son.

Danny put his whole career on the line for me. I demanded to know classified information and he gave it to me. He revealed information that was buried alongside Paul very much risking everything, possibly breaking laws. Being a Navy SEAL is who he is and I've accepted that since the day I met him. I'm no stranger to the military lifestyle and I understand how it works. Paul was just as passionate about *his job*.

His career is everything and if he truly wanted to he could've just stopped pursuing me. Or he could have been the monster that he thinks he is, and fucked me without ever calling again. He could've kept his secrets. But he's crossing lines and breaking his own plans... *for me.*

This whole time Danny feels responsible for Paul dying and if that doesn't show me how strong this man is, I don't know what does. I don't know how he stays strong but he does.

I calm myself down before I head back into his room. When I open the door, the lamp's turned off and Danny lays with his arms crossed behind his head.

I walk towards him, relaxed. He's staring at the ceiling, waiting for me. A part of me feels relieved from his confession.

Everything in our relationship feels like it's going at warp speed with no slowing down in sight. I envision it's only going to get faster when our baby is here. Only five more months and I'm giving birth to a baby whose gender's still a mystery to both of us.

Danny lifts the blankets upwards for me and I blush when I realize he's naked underneath the covers. All the muscles on his abs, contracting. I take off the shirt I'm wearing and it hits the floor. Instead, I reach for the baby doll lingerie I had packed earlier. I slip it on slowly as he watches me the entire time.

"Are you trying to torture me?"

I laugh.

It's a light, thin, velvet material that barely covers anything.

"How am I torturing you?"

"Because I want to tear that off and break you the way I've been wanting to since I've been back."

I want that to.

I crawl into bed. I lay on my side and Danny pulls me in closer to him gently. His fingers circle my nipple on my breast. When I get closer to him, his scent fills my nose. Spice, wood, and his mouth-watering cologne but I can still smell a bar. Curiosity gnaws at me.

"Where were you tonight?" I ask.

"El Devine."

I quirk a brow. The last time I was there I was with Emilia and Meredith having the time of my life. Not pregnant and drunk. *The last time he was there*, a beautiful perky blonde woman was savoring the taste of him on her lips.

"With another blonde on your arm?" I tease.

He groans and his muscles go rigid.

"Don't question my loyalty to you. No one has ever come close to the woman that you are. I'm not a liar. I've always been honest with you. I've been brutally blunt with them every single girl before you, with what I want and who I am. I never promised them anything but Ari… *I promise you,* you won't ever have to worry about me being faithful to you."

A fire ignites inside my chest. When we first met that's all I've been getting. Raw honesty. He means what he says.

"I was with Lopez and Kane." His fingers trail from my breasts to my small bump and he palms it. "How's my boy cooking in there?" He whispers.

I smile with sparkles in my eyes.

"It could be a girl, you know?"

He chuckles.

"All my swimmers are future Navy SEAL men like me."

I shake my head, rolling my eyes.

"Or princesses. I have some pictures of the ultrasou—" I cut myself off as the realization creeps into me and my heart sinks.

The problem of Shane, still here. *Shit.* The past few days have been absolute insanity and I almost forgot that I have a psychotic ex-boyfriend who wants me dead.

My body stiffens and Danny notices.

"What's wrong Ari? Where are the pictures?"

Shit. I shouldn't hide this any longer from him.

I breathe deeply, sighing.

"It's Shane." I can't face Danny so I stay on my side staring at his nightstand in the darkness.

"He's been terrorizing me non-stop since he saw me with you at the coffee shop... when I came back home, he's been breaking into my house and leaving me threatening messages..."

Danny freezes and my heart pounds in my chest.

"What kind of messages?" Danny growls enraged, his voice deeper than I've ever heard it before. I close my eyes shut.

"Well one, and I don't know how he knows this, but he knows you and I had sex. And he knows I'm pregnant. He found the pictures of my ultrasound from one of my doctors' appointments and tore them. He also..." I breathe unable to finish.

"He what?" He spits.

"My hair's short because he cut it off in my sleep. I woke up to locks of my hair falling out." I tremble.

Danny vanishes away from me so fast I can't even blink. I turn on the light.

The lamp reveals Danny throwing on clothes. He starts with his boxers and then his jeans.

"What are you doing? Where are you going?"

"I'm going to fucking kill him."

I shake my head, my eyes bulging.

"No, Danny! The cops are already on it. I've reported it. The military police are already looking for him. He deserted the Marines and he's been missing for some time now."

"He's fucking with you." Danny snarls and it takes me back.

I'm in shock, seeing him transform into a full-blown rage has my skin crawling.

"I won't let it happen again. The piece of shit took advantage of you knowing I wouldn't be here to stop him."

"Big fucking mistake and this will be the last he'll ever make."

I shake my head. I have to stop him.

"Danny no! You're drunk! Stop it. Let the police take care of it, you're not thinking straight."

He turns around and starts walking towards the door ignoring me. It's almost three in the morning and I don't want Danny doing anything irrational.

"Please..." I beg.

"Danny, stop, please." I grab his arm pulling him towards me. He's infuriated, his light blue eyes are darkened and full of wrath. His blonde hair is shaggy and he's lightly flushed with madness.

"Don't be like him." I try my hardest to convince him to not commit homicide tonight.

His face softens and his whole body relaxes. Danny clenches his jaw and the fire inside of him dies down, but not entirely. He finally gives in and starts stripping off his clothes. Holding my hand and leading me back to his bed.

CHAPTER 47

ARI

I feel warm breath on my neck as rough hands snake over my slightly, swollen stomach and it awakens me from a deep, peaceful slumber.

"Danny…" I groan, restless. A smile pulls at my lips as I grab his hands that lay on my belly. I keep my eyes closed not wanting to interact with any type of light that peaks through his curtains.

"Hmm?" He hums, pulling my loose baby doll sleepwear upwards. His fingers slither in between my underwear and he pulls it aside.

"You're not going to let me sleep, are you?" I rasp, sleepiness laced in my tone.

A low, deep, sexy laugh reverberates in his chest. I grip my pillow with my hands as he pulls my ass to his groin.

"You deserve to be worshipped every second of the day little Angel and I'm going to do just that for the rest of my life." Danny trails kisses in my hair down to my shoulder.

Heat breaks through my cheeks and I smile.

Danny's adapting to vanilla sex very well, in such a short amount of time.

"What time is it?" I groan.

"Five in the morning."

"Why are you awake?" I feel the tip of his hard, thick length at my entrance and a breath escapes my lungs that are burning with passion.

"I'm always awake at this time." He palms my ass, squeezing it gently, gripping me and he slowly pushes into me. I'm on my side and I moan, a breath escapes me and I bite my lip from the pleasure. I think Good Morning sex is my new favorite thing...

His thrusts are slow and deep and he keeps a steady pace while he buries himself inside of me. His grunt's reverberating in my ear as he's glued his face onto my cheek, as he moves inside me. His facial hair collides with my skin and it pricks my skin softly. I lick my lips.

He moves his hand to my breasts, giving them a gentle squeeze and a squeak of pleasure escapes me. Danny licks my cheek with his tongue, starting from my jawline up to my cheekbone, as his thrusts speed up.

"You're mine and I am yours, forever."

My brows bend inward, amused at his confession, does he truly mean that? Did I hear him right? The man that promised me he would never commit to any woman?

My heart palpitates as I imagine myself wearing a diamond ring on my finger and I'm breathing heavily. I can feel my orgasm about to obliterate me and Danny senses it. He starts toying with my clit and my feet curl from the intense, dark euphoric paradise that is my life when I'm around him.

I'm moaning uncontrollably, gripping his hand tighter and my sounds come out breathy and high-pitched.

"Say it." He repeats into my ear, his tone threatening me. He stops circling my clit and I'm breaking, already aching from his touch.

"I'm yours forever. I will always be yours." I rasp, I reach over to his face and brush my fingers through his hair behind me.

His teeth sink into my shoulder gently, enough for it to send shocks all over my body and I love it. He's continues to thrust inside of me, gently, slowly, going deeper and deeper.

He palms my pussy and I'm riding out my orgasm. He picks up his pace faster and then he holds onto my neck, as he finishes inside of me.

We're both catching our breaths as he kisses my shoulder.

Yup. *Good Morning sex is my new favorite way to wake up.*

In the morning, I awake to birds chirping outside of Danny's window. I shift in my sleep expecting to be embraced in his arms and yet again, I'm met with an empty side of the bed. I flutter my eyes open and they feel absolutely heavy and swollen from crying last night. I fell back to sleep after morning sex.

After a few blinks, I find a small amount of sunlight peeking through the curtains. My phone vibrates signaling a text message.

MA:

Ari. Come home this morning. I have a surprise for you. A gift for the baby.

Right above her text, is a missed notification from Danny.

DANNY:

I'm sorry for leaving this morning. I'm on base. I got called into work unexpectedly. The team just got the heads up we might be leaving again. I'll let you know more details when I get home, shouldn't be long.

I'm taken aback by his work schedule. Another deployment? I know he said that he's always gone but I thought he would at least have a few months at home before he would leave again.

I'm halfway through my pregnancy, would he really miss the birth?

Or would he get back in time?

It's eight in the morning and my hormones get the best of me.

All I want to do is cuddle into the bed sheets and fall back to sleep. After last night's confessions, I have high hopes that Danny will start to rise above the alcohol addiction and let go of the horrible guilt that consumes him.

I stretch my legs, a yawn escaping my mouth. I start to get myself dressed in the maternity clothes I recently got. A pink blouse that hugs my small bump and jeans that are loose around the waist. I'm excited to see what she gifted the baby. A crochet gift is the first thing that pops into my head. My mother's really into crocheting so I imagine it's a blanket or beanie.

I text my mom back that I'm on my way. Then I respond to Danny.

Good morning baby, I'm going to be at my moms' for the day.

It's the first time I'm calling him baby.

CHAPTER 48

ARI

On the way to my house, a phone call rings throughout my car, stopping the music. It's Emilia.

I don't hesitate to answer it through the car.

"Emilia, you're supposed to be enjoying your vacation!"

"I know, I know. Well, hello to you too. I'm offended by your hostility." She exclaims.

I can't help but smile.

"I have a few minutes before we have to go to dinner and I wanted to check on you. How's baby doing? Does your man know finally?" She asks.

"It's going. And yes. Yes, he knows."

"Well? Is he excited?"

I frown. We hadn't talked much about it. Danny finally opened up about my brother's death and I couldn't bring myself to pry further into his emotions. I always take what I can get from that man.

"Yeah, he's very excited. Shocked, of course since it's so soon but nonetheless happy." *Not a total lie.*

"Oh, that's good! I'm so happy everything worked out. I was so stressed out when I let it slip, please forgive my stupidity."

I chuckle.

"You're forgiven."

"Anyways, I gotta go. Harry's rushing me off the phone, we've gotta go but I should be back from Europe soon and I'll call you."

"Sounds good, talk to you later."

"Talk to you later, love you baby girl."

Click.

I drive my car into the driveway in front of the garage. I get out of my Bronco, locking my car. My mother's garden looks well-kept even with the cold dry weather approaching. The skies are dark grey almost black. Another thunderstorm was approaching, I hadn't checked the weather app on my phone, I would have packed an umbrella before leaving.

Lightning illuminates the sky followed by heavy thunder piercing through. The air smells different, like nature and soil. I open the door to my mothers' house, and I'm met with darkness.

I frown when I don't see my mother in the kitchen or living room watching tv. She's usually in those two places when she's home. I take off my jacket throwing it on the couch in the living room as I turn on the living room light.

Something isn't right. An eerie feeling shutters through me and I'm confused.

"Ma!" I call out. "I'm home! Where are you?"

Silence.

My heart begins to pound and I quickly whip my phone out of my jeans. I plug in my passcode, swiping fast to my security cameras app.

My eyes widen when I realize my mother and I forgot to charge them. The battery on them is dead and has been since last night. My heart drops and fear begins to swallow me whole. My mind travels to the worst and I'm frozen with my phone in my hands, staring at the screen.

Something catches my eye when I see black peppered hair

peaking out behind the couch, on the floor. I feel like I can't breathe. My chest tightens when I realize it's my mother's hair.

I run fast towards her, she's on the floor sprawled out unconscious in the middle of the dining room. She has clotted blood on the top of her forehead. It looks like she took a fall or worst. Someone attacked her.

"Ma! Oh my God, mom!" I fall to my knees carrying her head into my palms. She doesn't respond to me and it only heightens my frantic actions.

I check for a pulse on the side of her neck. Seconds pass by like years and my throat begins to pulse from the horror. My mother is my world, she can't be dead, she can't.

And then I feel it. It's faint but it's there.

"Ma, wake up!" I shout. I lay her head back down on the floor gently as possible before I shake her shoulders. She's not responding and I quickly grab my phone out and start to dial 911.

Suddenly, I'm being pulled back by my hair, I drop my phone before I can press the green dial button. I immediately go to defend myself. A loud shriek escapes me. I scream from the pain and I'm clawing at the hands that hold my short hair. My legs fight to gain balance and my attempts to turn around fail, my shoes make loud squeaking noises as I'm being dragged away.

I'm thrown to the side with so much force my waist hits the ground and my maternal instincts kick in and my palms stop my stomach from colliding with the floor. I protect my baby bump and I whip my head around to face my attacker.

My eyes bulge in confusion and I'm in shock.

It's Nora.

The same beautiful blonde woman that Danny was with when I saw him at El Devine.

"You fucking bitch just had to take what's mine." Nora has a shiny thick knife in her hand, twirling it like it's a game.

Suddenly another shadow appears behind her, sweat beginning to coat my skin as I realize there are two attackers and I'm outnumbered. I balance myself up with my palms still on the ground afraid to move.

Shane.

They both hover over me and Shane walks towards me, kneeling down and getting in my face.

"You spread your legs wide open for Danny Rider. You've whored yourself out to a man who won't ever commit to you but for your high school sweetheart who loves you so deeply?" I look up at him, tears start to sting my eyes. He slaps me hard and it burns. I feel weak and hopeless. My gaze starts to search for my phone and I find it next to my mother's arm.

Shane grabs my jaw forcing me to look up at him.

"Don't even fucking try it." He spits.

"Why? Why are you sick fucks doing this to me?"

Shane and Nora look at each other, evil expressions across their faces as they grin.

"Heartache bonds people together, you see. After the bar fight, we met and started talking, and looks like we both have something in common. We share the same particular interests. *We both want you dead.*" Nora explains.

"You used your religion to get out of having sex with me but for him? You tossed it out like it's nothing and now you have his bastard seed inside you?" I cringe as Shane shakes my head by my jaw. "You're going to hell, sinful Ari Cakes." He laughs wickedly.

"You're a predictable little whore." Nora walks closer to me as her hands tighten around the handle of the knife. My eyes widen and I start to crawl away from her but Shane prevents me from escaping.

"You think trapping Danny by getting pregnant will make him love you?" She slaps me hard. My cheek is hot and I grimace. She kneels before me waving the knife back and forth in front of my face. "He's not capable of love."

I raise my hand to punch her but Shane stops me and holds

me down by both of my arms, retracting them behind my back. I begin to thrash.

"Please stop this! This is insane." I beg. They both ignore me.

"He's not capable of loving anyone. He's not capable of commitment. He told me that the first night he fucked me. And holy shit, he fucked me hard, and good. He choked me as he pounded me. I can still feel his handprints all around my neck and I love the way he did that to me. He's a fucking God." She claps her hands and squeals as she remembers her nights with Danny. She says these things with the intention to make me jealous but I'm far from that emotion, I'm just trying to survive.

"It was painfully delicious the way he fucked me so hard. It made me beg for him. And sure enough, *I did beg him for more* but he denied me. He denied me because he met you!"

She slaps me again.

"Please stop it! I'm pregnant, you wouldn't kill a pregnant woman!" I beg.

"You think this baby will make you special?" She threatens. "You don't even know how to please him the way he likes. You're fucking useless when it comes to his world! When I'm finally rid of you, he'll come back to me, I know it."

She's smiling so crazy, flashing her snarling teeth and then I feel it. The knife pierces through the side of my stomach and I let out a blood-curdling scream as the pain rips through me and I'm pushing her away. Shane lets my arms go and when he does, I manage to throw her down to the floor, pushing her with all the strength I have. I reach for my wound, but Shane stops me from trying to stop my bleeding.

Then I feel another sharp pain and I lose my breath. Shane drives a knife inside of me, this time from my back. He pulls it out and I scream as loud as my lungs allow me to.

He pushes me back down, my back hitting the floor and the back of my head collides with the ground, pain shoots through me and I feel like I black out for a couple of seconds from the collision.

This isn't happening. I'm going to die, pregnant.

Shane spreads my legs open with his knees. He's on top of me unbuckling his belt. I'm too dazed to move from how hard my head hit the floor, I'm weak but something else is draining from me causing me to grow even weaker.

My blood.

The realization of the real possibility that Nora and Shane may have drove through a major artery settles in and I'm spiraling down a black hole. Everything feels so heavy and it's hard to move a muscle. I'm gasping for air, attempting to scream but nothing comes out. My chest is heavy and it feels like an elephant is sitting on my chest.

"I've always wanted to fuck a pregnant chick." Shane hisses into my ear. I manage to glance at his face and it looks like a demon has possessed his body. His brown eyes aren't the same and he's grinding his teeth.

"This wasn't a part of the plan, we have to get out of here." Nora tries to pull Shane off but he pushes her off to the side.

"This won't take long."

My head falls back and my hands fall to the side of my waist. I'm defenseless. I manage to still hold onto my lower belly where it swells with my baby underneath my palm.

My baby. I'll gladly die but please God, let my baby live.

I can't think. I can't move. All I see is my vision starting to blur and my hearing starts to fade. My eyes close and I feel like I'm falling into a horrible sleep.

Suddenly, Shane's off of me and I manage to pry my eyes open. But it takes too much energy to do so. The darkness tries to anchor me down but I see familiar faces hovering over me before I close my eyes again.

Danny and Kane.

I try to call out for Danny but I'm completely drained and my conscience reality is pulled away sending me into a black hole. My eyes are being forced shut and I swear I can hear Paul's voice in my ear. His voice makes me smile. Everything goes black and the last thing I see is Paul. He's in his Navy uniform and he's playing the guitar to a song we both love so much. He looks up from his guitar, his brown eyes meeting mine and he looks like he's glowing. He smiles and says,

"Don't fall asleep. Don't fall asleep."

CHAPTER 49

DANNY

Last night was a complete shit show. After sharing the details of her brother's death I couldn't sleep. This was something I thought would stay buried forever. I never in a million years thought that I would be having this conversation with anyone. Let alone, *Paul's sister.*

After finding out that Shane was fucking with my girl, it sent me into a murderous rage and I wanted to kill him last night. I have a lot of connections and no one would hesitate to help me if I had to look for him.

But Ari stopped me. Her cute little eyes bleeding for me to stay with her instead. The sight weakened me and I changed my mind. But it wouldn't stop me from searching for him. I made plans with Zeke, to find out if we could track him down in any way possible. He has connections with people in military intelligence and if I wasn't mistaken, he was trained to do that job as well. His level of expertise didn't stop just at being a special operator. If he wanted, he could track down anyone he wanted to.

I got called into work this morning. The higher-ups just got word of other missions that need my team. My short vacation would be short-lived. I didn't want to tell Ari this. I didn't want her to feel disappointed when I gave her the news. After last night's confessions from both of us, I felt like this was going to be a fresh start to our relationship. No more secrets. Just our bright future with our little one.

I don't know if I'll ever truly let go of drinking. They call it an addiction for a reason. Ari came into my life at the worst time. She only heightened all of my demons and yet, her love was starting to become my *newest addiction*. The only thing I was beginning to care about was making sure she was always safe. If anyone was going to come after her or cause her any harm it would be me.

I decide to surprise Ari with gifts after work. Some flowers for her and her mother.

Tulips and tickets to the Bloomings Author's event.

When I got home, I made some calls to some friends that had connections with the authors that were to be in attendance. I got us both tickets and I wanted to go with her before I had to leave.

I never did stuff like this for anyone. This was extremely new to me. A different side of me that Ari has unlocked and she held the key.

I ran to a baby store after that... a baby store. I still can't believe this will be my new life. My mother will finally get what she wants. *To be a grandmother.* I can't help but feel excited that she's going to be around a small baby again after her infertility struggles.

Still, I can't help but feel protective around Ari even if it's from my parents. I don't know how my parents would take the news. I needed to protect her from their judgments so I would make sure to have a conversation with them before I even introduce the mother of my child.

Kane decided to tag along and get a baby a gift as well. I bought a newborn-sized onesie for a boy and Kane bought some newborn shoes.

We're getting closer to Ari's house and I'm already mentally preparing for her mother to bombard us with questions.

"Thanks for letting me tag along. I wanted to check on Paul's mother. See how she's doing. The last time I was here she wanted me to help her fix the garbage disposal. I want to see if there's anything else I can help her with."

"Of course, man."

I turn onto Ari's street, and I notice Kane leans forward, removing his sunglasses from his face and squinting ahead.

"What is it?"

"Nothing it's just, uh, isn't that the chick's car you used to hang with? What's her name again? Nora?" He points to a white sedan with a pink teddy bear sticker on the side of it. It does look just like Nora's. It's parked a few houses down from Ari's house.

I grow suspicious. My eyebrows furrow as I park my truck and I'm on high alert. An eerie feeling slithers through my chest and I know something's wrong. Kane looks at me confused.

I rush out of the driver's seat, opening the door. I walk towards Ari's door and I hear someone screaming and it sounds like Ari.

My heart begins to pound in my chest and I'm panting hard like a bull through my nostrils. I swing open the door to Ari's place and Kane follows behind.

The sight sends me into a different version of myself I'm extremely familiar with. Death, itself. This version of myself stays trapped inside and only comes out when I'm behind enemy lines *but this*. This is another level of darkness that comes over me and I don't recognize myself anymore.

I drop the flowers, tickets, and baby gifts from my hand as the terrifying sight makes my blackened heart bleed into nothing.

Seeing Shane over Ari I know I'm going to send his soul to the fucking ground. He's dead. The piece of shit thinks he can touch her, *rape her?*

I charge towards him and I pull him off so easily not giving him a chance to unclothe my girl. I throw him to the side and start giving him the excruciating suffering he deserves, my bones collide with his nose first and it breaks underneath my knuckles.

He cries out from the pain and he tries to defend himself but it's too late. He tries to pull out a thick knife but I don't let him, I'm burning with rage. This evil motherfucker hurt my little Angel with this?

"Danny! Baby! We had to do it. She's come in between us. I did this for us!" Nora's in the corner squealing while Kane checks on Ari. He hovers over her body and dials 911. He relays what's happening to the 911 operator, gives them our address, and hangs up.

I don't stop myself from trying to kill Shane with my bare hands. He will feel the wrath that's seething in my blood along with Paul's. I'm torturing him with my hands. Each blow sends his bones shattering.

'Don't you fucking move!" Kane growls in Nora's direction, his voice is so loud it makes the whole house shake from his anger.

Nora freezes throwing her hands up.

The distraction from Nora and Kane gives Shane his last window to reclaim himself. He plunges the knife inside my chest. The pain is dull and my adrenaline doesn't let me feel the extent of it. I laugh at his weak attempt to stop me. Nothing in this fucking world could ever stop me from reaping Shane out of this world, straight to the pits of hell. As I laugh, Shane's whole demeanor drops. He doesn't understand how I'm not dead and neither am I. I grab his wrist and twist it until I feel all of his bones break and he cries out in pain. His wrist is completely useless. I promised him this would happen if he ever touched her again. I take out the knife from my chest. Motherfucker managed to hit straight through my hourglass tattoo.

I grip the knife by the blade, tight in my hand. It pierces through my skin, causing me to bleed as I jab it straight down on Miss Alvarez's wooden floors, hard causing it to stick out.

"You don't get to die a quick death. I won't grant you that luxury." I tell Shane as I continue to torment him with my bare hands.

"What the fuck are you?" Shane's last words weakly come out through his broken jaw.

"Danny, she's dying. She's losing too much blood. Her pulse is weak!" Kane panics as he puts his hand on her belly. His words make my heart sink all the way down to hell and it stops me from moving. Shane's unconscious from all the blows and I know he's dead. My anger screams at me. I don't want to stop torturing him even though his soul is long gone and his heart has stopped.

I freeze, my breathing heavy and chest tight. My lungs feel like they're constricted and I'm breaking. Shane and Nora just might have killed her. I feel sick as I feel warm bile rise in my throat.

I grip Shane by the collar of his shirt tight, then I let go.

I rush over to Ari and I see blood spewing out of her side and back. They fucking stabbed her way deep. Ari's eyes look empty like she's no longer there in her body. Her brown eyes have lost the sparkle I love so much. They're vacant. I've seen the most disgusting evil horror that lives in this world but nothing could ever prepare me for seeing this. Nothing comes close to the way I'm feeling. Kane has his hand pushed into her wound and I look down to discover there's a puddle of blood that has surrounded us three.

Her mother lies a few feet away and she's starting to come back into consciousness.

"What, what happened?" Miss Alvarez groans, rubbing her head, and sitting up.

My knees are drenched with blood. The dark crimson blood starts to seep through my jeans and I'm losing my mind. I grab her petite body and hold her close to my chest, her head falls back, and she's lifeless. I start to shake. I'm broken. I'm angry. I'm in denial. If only Shane could revive so I can kill him all over again.

Ari, my perfect little Angel, taken away from me.

She's the one person in my entire life that has made me feel like I have the capability to love and be loved. I've fallen so madly for her and because of that, I can't accept this. *I won't accept it.*

"Fuck!" I growl loud and my throat constricts. Kane watches me and Miss Alvarez is screaming incoherently. I hear sirens from the ambulance approaching the house and I'm internally grateful.

This pain is unbearable. This pain is unforgiving. This pain is unknown to me. I've never felt anything like this. I feel as though my soul has been taken from me and it's because Ari has it. And if she leaves me, I refuse to live without her. I refuse to *live in this world* without her. I won't breathe if she doesn't. My heart won't beat if hers doesn't.

I won't let her go. I know what I have to do. I have to unravel who I truly am, the monster that I am. I meant it when I told her that her soul was mine, *forever.*

"Ari, baby, don't fall asleep. Don't fall asleep." I whisper. I kiss her forehead and cheeks over and over again, aggressively. I don't stop kissing her as my hands caress her black hair repeatedly.

Kane backs away from me, consoling Miss Alvarez.

I lay Ari back down on the floor gently, and get to work. I'm performing harsh compressions on her chest, my hands pushing down hard, determined to get her heart beating again.

"Don't fall asleep."

CHAPTER 50

ARI

I try to call out for Danny but I'm completely drained and my conscience reality is pulled away sending me into a black hole. My eyes are being forced shut and I swear I can hear Paul's voice in my ear. His voice makes me smile. Everything goes black and the last thing I see is Paul. He's playing the guitar to a song we would listen to growing up. *Rayando El Sol by Mana.* When we were kids, it was a common song that we both loved to listen to. It reminded us of our trips to Mexico when we would visit our Tia's house. He looks up from his guitar, his brown eyes meeting mine and he looks like he's glowing. He looks happy. He smiles and says,

"Don't fall asleep. Don't fall asleep."

I muster all the energy I can to open my eyes, but I can't. I'm weak. I'm completely drained.

Oh no, my baby.

"Ari, baby, don't fall asleep," Paul says to me but it doesn't make sense.

He's repeating the same words over and over again but instead, it's Danny's voice coming out of Paul's mouth.

Then I'm starting to get some feeling back. I can feel harsh pressure on my chest. It's tight and it hurts so much. Somehow, I regain just a blip of strength and the image of Paul disappears and I manage to open my eyes. To my surprise, *it's Danny.*

Everything around him is so blurry and I can't make anything out. His face fades in and out as I'm trying to move but nothing does. I'm looking at Danny and I want to beg him to help me, *to save me* but nothing comes out. I need to warn him about Shane and Nora before they try and attack him or Kane. That's when I realize his hands are on my chest. He's the reason why I feel intense pain and pressure.

I can't breathe, I'm trying to suck in a breath but nothing happens. I feel like I'm drowning but there's no water swallowing me whole.

Come on lungs, don't fail me. Expand.

Why can't I breathe?

Danny looks completely distraught, and worried, while his hands are on my chest. I can feel the darkness pulling at me again but before it pulls me back entirely, I see something. Something in Danny shocks me and if I weren't so damn weak, I would be crying. I'd be thrashing against him.

Danny blinks and the white that surrounds his blue eyes flash to obsidian black. I'm trying to gasp for air when I see how his eyes transform.

This has to be a nightmare, I'm in a nightmare.

His eyes turn black leaving only his light blue iris. He doesn't look human. Humans can't do this. Am I hallucinating? As I stare at Danny, his face is slowly replaced by a familiar figure. Everything's lonely again, I'm losing consciousness when all I can see is his tattoo. His back tattoo that always frightens me. *Danny's tattoo.*

The familiar Grim Reaper engulfed in flames, comes alive, whispering hauntingly into my ears, and I feel a freezing, cold breath on my neck. It's a dark, monstrous whisper, and it doesn't sound normal, nor human. It's deep and demonic.

"Time waits for no one. Death is a shadow stalking the living. It is a painful inexorable promise while *Life is a lovely lie.*"

To Be Continued

See You Soon, Little Angels...

Acknowledgments

To my husband, best friend, my biggest supporter, thank you for always pushing me to follow my dreams, I love you.

A special thank you to my grandparents, Jesse and Kena. They're everything to me.

To my friends and family that showed up and showed their love for the book, thank you so much, I really appreciate each and every one of you.

ABOUT THE AUTHOR

A genuine thank you to everyone who read my debut novel. It means more to me than you think. I wrote this crazy love story of Ari and Danny a few years ago and one day I thought I'd share it with the world. I hope you enjoyed it, I really do! I never thought I'd publish it but here I am.

I'm a foodie who loves to travel and play video games. I'm from South Texas, I'm hispanic and I love horror movies. If I'm not at the bookstore browsing, I'm nose deep reading a book.

Visit lexieaxelson.com for more information on all of my works.

Join the Facebook group for updates and teasers!
https://www.facebook.com/groups/1718058931953720/

instagram.com/lexieaxelson
tiktok.com/@lexieaxelson

Printed in Great Britain
by Amazon

27334876R00215